Also by Tom Cain

The Accident Man
The Survivor
Assassin
Dictator

Carver

TOM CAIN

BANTAM PRESS

LONDON • TORONTO • SYDNEY • AUCKLAND • JOHANNESBURG

TRANSWORLD PUBLISHERS
61–63 Uxbridge Road, London W5 5SA
A Random House Group Company
www.transworldbooks.co.uk

First published in Great Britain
in 2011 by Bantam Press
an imprint of Transworld Publishers

A CIP catalogue record for this book
is available from the British Library.

ISBNs 9780593067659 (cased)
9780593067666 (tpb)

Addresses for Random House Group Ltd companies outside the UK
can be found at: www.randomhouse.co.uk
The Random House Group Ltd Reg. No. 954009

The Random House Group Ltd supports the Forest Stewardship
Council® (FSC®), the leading international forest certification organization. All our
titles that are printed on Greenpeace-approved FSC® certified paper carry the FSC® logo.
Our paper procurement policy can be found at
www.randomhouse.co.uk/environment

Typeset in 11/14pt Caslon 540 by
Falcon Oast Graphic Art Ltd.
Printed and bound in Great Britain by
Clays Limited, Bungay, Suffolk

2 4 6 8 10 9 7 5 3 1

To Clare, Holly, Lucy and Fred

Prelude

East Hampton, New York: 5 June 2007

Malachi Zorn walked out of his house on Lily Pond Road and strolled across the grass to the path that led down to the beach. He was a man of medium height and slim build with tousled, dirty-blond hair, the year-round tan of a lifelong sportsman and a three-day growth of stubble that glowed golden in the bright early-summer sunshine. He wore an old Brooks Brothers button-down shirt whose pale-blue fabric had faded almost to white in places, and was frayed around the top of the collar. It hung loosely over a pair of khaki cargo shorts. His feet were bare.

He stopped for a moment and looked with disgust at the edifice rising on the plot next to his own. A hedge-fund manager had torn down the elegant, eighty-year-old house that had once stood there, and was now building a vast, white temple to tastelessness and excess. The new building dwarfed Zorn's own traditional beach cottage, built in 1896 by a pupil of Stanford White, with its gabled roof, shingled walls and cosy veranda looking out towards the sea. His neighbour's monstrosity summed up everything Zorn most despised about the amoral, self-enriching vulgarians who had turned Wall Street into a gigantic machine for extracting money from everyday Americans and pocketing the profit for themselves.

Fighting hard to contain the simmering rage that now threatened to ruin his day and, more importantly, distort his thinking, Zorn got moving again, relishing the warmth of the sand beneath his feet as he strolled to the water's edge and let the incoming waves ripple and eddy around his ankles. He stood for a while, looking out to sea, hardly taking in the view but using it as a backdrop to the inner workings of his mind. Finally, he gave a single decisive nod of his head, turned on his heels and walked back up to his property.

Five minutes later, having made a cup of strong, black coffee and picked a couple of home-baked cookies from a large glass jar, Zorn was back at his personal workstation. Racked in front of him were eight flat-panel screens, arranged in two rows of four. They showed a constant stream of real-time market data and global TV and internet news coverage. A yellow legal pad lay on his desk, next to an old Harvard University coffee cup filled with freshly sharpened HH pencils. Zorn picked up a Bluetooth telephone earpiece and put it on. He looked at the only other item on his desk: a twenty-year-old picture of his parents. 'This one's for you,' he murmured, and punched a speed-dial number.

When the call was answered there were no hellos or small talk, just a simple instruction. 'I want to make a short call on Lehman's,' Zorn said. 'Start with a hundred in three-month options. Be ready to write a lot more.'

'You sure, Mal?' asked the voice on the other end of the line, with the carefully modulated tone of surprise that a broker reserves for a client about to embark on an insane course of action. 'Lehman's is trading at almost eighty, and it's only moving up. You've got a hundred million dollars says it's gonna go the other way?'

'Yes.'

'OK. Well, it's your money and you've always been right before, but . . .'

'But nothing. Write the calls. And something else: what's the premium on Lehman's credit default swaps at the moment?'

'Less than a basis point, couple tenths, maybe . . . but why do you want to know? You wanna bet that a one-hundred-and-fifty-year-old bank . . .'

'Hundred-and-fifty-seven-year-old, to be precise.'

'Whatever . . . you're saying that this great institution, the fourth biggest bank on the Street, is about to collapse?'

'That's right. At some point over the next year or two, that's exactly what I'm saying. Buy ten billion bucks of Lehman's CDSs. If people want to sell you more, buy it. Don't stop.'

'You're risking millions, you know that?'

'I'm risking a couple of tenths of one per cent of ten billion. That's two mill a year downside, against ten billion up. That's not a bad deal. So make it.'

'You got it . . .'

'And my name is nowhere near this. Nowhere near it at all.'

The Penthouse Executive Club, 45th St, New York City: 18 September 2008

'How did you do it, Mal? I mean, you told me Lehman's would crash and burn. I thought you were totally fuckin' nuts. And then it goes and does exactly what you said it would. So how come you were right and every other son of a bitch in this business was wrong?'

Three days had passed since Lehman Brothers Bank filed for Chapter 11 bankruptcy, its share price evaporating – from a high of eighty-two dollars – to just three cents in a little over a year. After a weekend of desperate negotiations involving the heads of all the major Wall Street banks, US Treasury Secretary Hank Paulson, UK Chancellor Alistair Darling and senior executives from Bank of America (BoA) and Barclays, both of which had shown interest in buying the stricken bank, the Chief Executive Officer of Lehman's, Richard Fuld, and his board had been forced to admit defeat. Fuld's reputation as one of the masters of the financial universe now lay in tatters, just like the institution for which he had been responsible. He was pleading poverty, too, but his critics weren't convinced. They pointed to the estimated half a billion dollars Fuld had received from Lehman's between 2000 and 2007, none of which he was asked to return.

But by betting against Lehman Brothers Malachi Zorn had done even better. He had walked away with a little over $10.7 billion.

Now he looked around the table at the Penthouse Executive Club, which he was currently sharing with his broker, Donny Trimble, two of Trimble's hottest dealers, and the three strippers they had showered with fifty-dollar bills and the promise of unlimited Cristal.

'Because Wall Street is filled with guys like you,' Zorn thought to himself, in answer to Trimble's question. He was not in any way a prude, but he neither liked nor needed the business of paying for female company. Still, the club's steaks were among the best in the city, and he did not want to deny his brokers the chance to celebrate a coup that had made them all millions, too. So he had come along for the ride and done his best to be civil.

'You know, Don, what I find unbelievable isn't the fact that I could see the whole damn system was bust,' Zorn said. 'It's that so many other people couldn't. I mean, three years ago the FBI was reporting that mortgage-related frauds had gone up by a factor of five. Record numbers of people were falling behind on their mortgage payments or flat-out defaulting, and there were just two things keeping the whole thing going. The first was all the suckers who thought that their house price could only go up. And the second was all the lenders who gave money to anyone, absolutely anyone, who asked for it. And even if you didn't ask, they shoved it down your throat anyway. I mean, did you ever hear of an interest-only negative-amortizing adjustable-rate subprime mortgage?'

'Uh, no, can't say I did,' said Trimble, who was evidently less interested in obscure forms of mortgage than in his companion's fine young breasts.

'Well, I'll tell you then, Don. It was a mortgage that didn't require the borrower to repay any of the capital, and if they fell behind with their payments, that was OK because the value of any missed payments just got added on to the mortgage debt. So some poor dumb bastard who probably didn't have a job, let alone enough income to buy a home, just kept getting deeper and deeper in the hole till he said, "The hell with this," and walked right away from the property, the mortgage, the whole damn shebang. And all he left behind was a pile of debt secured on a worthless property.'

One of the strippers, who called herself Misti, was paying her way through Columbia University Business School by giving private dances at a hundred and twenty-five bucks a time. She could make more money in one night than her more conventional waitressing girlfriends would see in a month. Now she looked at Zorn thoughtfully. If she could just keep the drunken sleazebag who had bought her company for the evening quiet for a few minutes, she might actually learn something here.

'But what about the management of Lehman's?' she asked. 'I mean, couldn't they have done something about the situation earlier, like, before it got totally critical? And if they'd done that, wouldn't you have lost all your premium?'

Zorn smiled, appreciating the sharp intelligence that the girl had until now kept hidden beneath her professional bimbo mask. 'Good questions, Misti,' he said, saying the name in a way that let her know he was well aware that both it and her persona were fake.

'If those guys had ever been honest about their situation – starting with being honest to themselves – maybe they could have saved the business. They could have resigned their positions, allowing more responsible individuals to take over. They could have drastically controlled the risks their people were taking, and reformed their accounting practices. They could have looked for smart deals based on genuinely undervalued assets – and by the way, they'd have made and kept a lot more money that way. They could have looked for a buyer when they were still in a position to negotiate from strength. They could have done a whole lot of things, and, sure, it would have cost me a heap of dough. But you know what? They were never, ever going to do that, because they were a bunch of arrogant assholes – just like most of the guys in all the other boardrooms on the Street – and they would never, and will never, admit that they were responsible for creating this disaster.'

'But what about BoA and Barclays? How could you have known they weren't going to close their deals and buy Lehman's?'

Zorn reached into his jacket, pulled out his wallet and extracted a thousand dollars. He pushed them across the table to Misti's companion, a brash young dealer by the name of Luis Ferrone, and said, 'Buy yourself another friend.' Then he looked at Misti and gestured at the empty space on the banquette next to him. She was round there in a flash.

'So,' Zorn said, 'you want to know about those other banks? Well, that's a no-brainer. Those deals were never going to happen. The moment the purchasers looked at Lehman's books it was obvious that their true assets were nowhere near as big as they claimed. Officially, Lehman Brothers had around forty billion in assets. My understanding is the true figure was closer to twenty-five. That was when Bank of America decided to buy Merrill Lynch instead. Which left Barclays. But they had a problem. Lehman's was bust. It couldn't keep trading or even running as a business without fresh cash, and Barclays couldn't hand over any till the deal was signed and sealed. So come Monday morning, someone was going to have to step in with a bridging loan to cover a deal that could still fall apart. So who could do that?'

'Uncle Sam?' Misti suggested.

'Funny you should say that. Dick Fuld had the same idea, till Paulson told him no way was Washington going to hand over a single taxpayer dollar to bail out his bank. Now they got personal. There was a guy at Lehman's, George Herbert Walker, who's a cousin of the President. Word is, they asked him to put in a call to the Oval Office. Well, if he did, Dubya didn't take it. So then people said, "Well, gee, Barclays is a Brit bank, maybe their government'll give us the money." That was when the Brits pointed out that hell would freeze over before their taxpayers were going to risk billions of bucks to support a US bank. Believe me, I didn't lose a second of sleep over that. And you know what? Nor did Barclays. Yesterday they went picking through the wreckage at Lehman's and acquired most of its US divisions for less than two billion. I reckon they paid about ten cents on the dollar. Wish I'd seen Fuld's face when that news came through.'

Misti gave him a warm, genuine smile: one that came from the real woman, not the stripper.

'You sound so passionate, like this isn't just about business. It feels much more personal.'

'Yeah, right again. This was very, very personal.'

'Well, you put on quite a show.'

Malachi Zorn shook his head with a wry grin. 'No,' he replied. 'That wasn't the show.' Then he laughed again so that Misti laughed too, assuming Zorn was just kidding as he said, 'That was just a rehearsal.'

Washington DC: 17 March 2011

Three years in, and still the repercussions of the banking crash had not even begun to be resolved. At a congressional hearing into the practice and regulation of short-selling, Malachi Zorn effortlessly ran rings around the members of the House Committee on Financial Services, who attempted to portray him as an unscrupulous profiteer. Dressed with uncharacteristic formality, Zorn made his point not with any firecracker display of wit or mockery, but by speaking with a seriousness which suggested that the politicians questioning him were guilty of an improperly frivolous, exploitative attitude to the subject, whereas he was genuinely acting in the public interest.

Zorn was asked whether there was any truth to recent rumours within the financial community that he had taken a number of very significant short positions in leading energy and oil corporations. Zorn replied that, 'It's my practice never to disclose any of the positions that I've taken while they are still active. There are many reasons for this, commercial confidentiality being the most obvious. But I'm also wary of creating self-fulfilling prophecies. I have, as you have suggested, a certain reputation in my field. I don't want to sound unduly arrogant, but if my trades became public knowledge, it's very possible that other traders might wish to copy them, hoping to ride my professional coat-tails, so to speak. This would have two effects. Firstly, it would create exactly the kind of downward pressure on the corporation in question that you, sir, seem so keen to avoid. And second, it would actually destroy the market. After all, someone has to buy my trade. So I can't go short on a stock unless someone else wants to go long. I depend upon genuine and healthy differences of opinion within the market – a kind of commercial democracy, if you will – to create the margins from which I profit.

'But I'll say this about the general subject of the energy industry in all its forms. My personal view is that there are many members of extremist special-interest groups who'll look at the impact of Islamist terrorism and be tempted to apply it to their own causes. In business terms, terror is a product that works. I therefore anticipate that environmental activists will seek to emulate the activities of groups like al-Qaeda by attacking specific targets related to oil, nuclear generation and power transmission – to take three examples. If by my investments I highlight the current vulnerabilities of a particular sector, I believe I'm not only doing good business, I'm doing my patriotic duty, too.'

More than one reporter present at the hearings picked up on the phrase, 'Terror is a product that works,' and contacted their newspaper or TV network, alerting editors to its headline potential. Sadly for them, however, one of Hollywood's leading action heroes, a tough yet sensitive Australian much loved for his clean-living, family-loving lifestyle, crashed his Ferrari 458 Italia that afternoon in the parking lot of the Hideaway Inn, Malibu while severely intoxicated. With him in the car were a young Asian woman and a small, zip-up leather holdall in which were a number of plastic bags containing cocaine, marijuana and various illegal and prescription pills. On arrival at the Malibu/Lost Hills police station, his 'female' companion was discovered to be a nineteen-year-old Thai ladyboy. A recording of the star's heated but barely coherent insistence that he had no idea of his companion's true gender was online within the hour. The line, 'I thought she was a Sheila!' was a talkshow punchline around the world that night.

No one, anywhere, wanted to hear about terrorists in the subsequent news cycle.

Zorn repeated his warnings about the vulnerability of energy and oil installations in remarks made to a specialist blog aimed at hedge-fund managers and investors, and also in private conversations with a number of extremely wealthy individuals. None of his warnings, however, penetrated the public consciousness or had any immediate political or economic effect. So it seemed that for once in his life, Malachi Zorn had failed to make the impact he desired.

Friday, 24 June

1

The Greek island of Mykonos

Pelicans honked. That was something Samuel Carver had never known before. But there was the pelican, its feathers a pale baby-pink, like an anaemic flamingo, and it was clearly honking.

'I'm going to take its photograph. Want to come?'

Her name was Magda, but everyone called her Ginger, for reasons made obvious by one glance at her freckled skin and fiery hair. She had wide-spaced grey-blue eyes, soft, slightly pouty lips, and a little groove at the very tip of her nose. She admitted to being 'about forty', but looked no more than twenty-eight, and worked, she said, in corporate finance. Carver was driving a small, hired Japanese Jeep. He'd pitched up next to Ginger's Porsche Boxster in the line of cars at the port of Piraeus, outside Athens, waiting for the ferry to Mykonos. Both cars had their tops down. Carver and Ginger had exchanged looks, started talking, and discovered they were two un-attached adults who'd both chosen to spend a couple of weeks exploring the islands of the Aegean. It made sense to join forces and see how that worked out. So far it seemed to be going pretty well.

'Thanks,' said Carver, 'but I think I'll stay here and enjoy the view.'

'Ah, yes,' said Ginger with a knowing smile, 'the famous wind-mills.'

'Exactly,' said Carver, and kept his cool, green eyes fixed on Ginger as she picked her way between the open-air restaurant tables in tiny Daisy Duke shorts that a woman her age had no business wearing so well. He smiled to himself as he realized he wasn't the only man looking. A waiter was standing by the open door that led to the kitchen, leaning against a glass aquarium filled with live fish and lobsters, and nodding in appreciation as Ginger went by.

They were lunching at a waterfront joint called Little Venice, their table pressed right up against the waist-high sea wall, so close that they could feel occasional sprinkles of sea-spray against their faces. Ginger was about fifteen metres away now. She had reached the pelican and was crouching down on her haunches in front of it, with her camera to her face. The pelican seemed entirely un-troubled by her presence, posing like a seasoned professional for a few seconds before opening its beak wide, its leathery throat pouch sagging beneath it like a fat man's chins in expectation of a reward.

The first bullet blasted through the pelican's neck, blowing the head right off its body. The second, third and fourth hit Ginger, the vivid scarlet eruptions on her chest lifting her off her feet and throwing her to the ground, where she lay quite still, sprawled on her back. The last echoes of the gunfire mingled with panic-stricken shouts and screams, and the clattering of chairs and tables as people made desperate attempts to get away. Carver remained still, committing the two shooters to memory. The first male was tall and blond, in a loose blue shirt and jeans; the second one shorter, darker colouring, all in black. Both were using handguns. Carver's instinct was to go to Ginger's side, but the two men were within a couple of metres of her now, and it would be a suicide run. They'd shoot him long before he ever got to her.

The men were scanning the restaurant, looking for someone,

and Carver didn't wait around to find out whether it was him. Keeping his movements as slow and unobtrusive as possible, he slipped below the surface of his table and scuttled away beneath the one directly behind him. All around him other crawling, scrambling people were fighting their way to the exit, men pushing women and even children aside without a second thought as the instinct for self-preservation overruled any patina of civilized manners.

There was a khaki baseball cap lying discarded on the floor, and Carver jammed it on his head to cover his short, dark hair and break up his silhouette. It was hardly much of a disguise, but anything that made identification even marginally tougher amidst the bustle of the town's crowded streets might help.

He didn't know for sure, of course, that they were looking for him. Ginger might have been the primary target, or simply the one person unlucky enough to be in plain sight and close range when they hit the restaurant. But life had taught Carver always to act on the basis of the worst-case scenario. That way any surprises would be pleasant ones.

Two more shots were fired. The stampede became even more desperate. From the sounds of the gunfire, Carver judged that the men had advanced further into the restaurant – under the awning that stretched over the tables between the building where the kitchen was housed and the sea wall. They were, he realized, driving the crowd of people ahead of them, shepherding them in one direction. That suggested they had a destination in mind, a point where the flock would be divided and the object of their attack singled out. Carver had other plans. He got to his feet, swivelled to his right and, keeping his head down, started forcing his way across the line of escaping customers towards the kitchen door.

Then the crowd suddenly cleared, leaving Carver exposed for a second or two. That was long enough. He heard a voice shout, 'Over there!' Then he was up and running full-tilt for the door, followed by the sound of rushing footsteps.

That answered one question. The men were after him. Now he just needed to know why.

Carver reached the fish tank, crouched down behind it, then shoved with the full force of his body against the weight of glass and water. It lifted a few centimetres, then a little more, until finally it toppled over and shattered against the floor. A slippery, slithering mass of fish and crustaceans poured out, blocking the pursuers' path with flapping, claw-waving bodies.

In the second that diversion bought him, Carver darted through the door and down a short corridor towards the kitchen. There were more shots behind him. He felt the fizz of the rounds going by and saw the glass front of a wine cooler disintegrate up ahead.

Leaping over the shards of shattered glass, he careered into the kitchen itself. Two women were standing by the stove: one elderly and clad in black, the other barely out of her teens. They shouted unintelligibly at Carver as he looked around, searching for an escape route.

The men were only seconds behind him. The women were shrieking. The stress seemed to dull and confuse his vision, making it impossible to see clearly. Carver tried to stay calm, to concentrate on the immediate task in hand and ignore the voice in his head telling him he was soft and out of practice, reminding him of the days when he had never gone anywhere unarmed or unprepared.

Surely the kitchen would have a rear exit? If it didn't, he was a dead man.

2

Yes, there it was: a door half-hidden behind a pile of empty boxes. Carver sprinted across the room, kicked the boxes out of the way, barged through the door, and found himself at one end of an alley that ran between two other buildings. It opened up on to one of the narrow, twisting streets, lined with shops, that wind through the town of Mykonos like tangled strands of spaghetti.

Island custom mandated that you could paint your house any colour you liked so long as it was white. But no one said what colour the doors, the windows, the verandas and the staircases that ran up the front of almost every building had to be. Vivid splashes of deep-blue, turquoise and scarlet paint clashed with the shocking magenta of the bougainvillea that grew from every tiny open scrap of bare earth.

The street was packed with tourists, oblivious to the chaos down by the waterfront: couples; groups of women out shopping together; men walking arm in arm in testament to Mykonos's reputation as a place where anything went so long as no one got hurt. Carver plunged into the crowd, making his way as quickly but unobtrusively as he could, a lean, fit figure in olive-green cargo shorts and a pale-blue cotton shirt, slipping purposefully between the ambling sightseers; a natural predator among a crowd of herbivores.

As he moved Carver was constantly scanning the faces around him, his senses alert for any sign of danger, his subconscious constantly analysing what he saw. Two young women shrieking with laughter at something one of them had said: safe. A young couple nestling together as they walked, his arm across her back, oblivious to everything except their own love: safe. Two men together, both shaven-headed, looking around ... one of them glancing at Carver ... catching his eye ... reaching beneath his jacket ... not safe! Not safe!

Carver ran, barging the lovers out of the way; crashing between the two young women, who reacted with shrieks of indignation; charging up a pale-blue staircase. He looked round as he ran, and saw the two shaven-headed men, now joined by the shooters from the restaurant, pointing in his direction. Carver reached the out-door landing at the top of the stairs. Immediately to his right a pair of shuttered French windows led into the house. He looked left, across the street. Another staircase ran up the building opposite. Its landing was barely a couple of metres away. Beyond it the doors into the interior of the building were open. Carver scrambled up on to the wooden balustrade that surrounded the staircase and land-ing, perched there for a second on the balls of his feet, and then, as the first shots rang out from down below, sprang across the gap to the far building. He cleared the far balustrade, landed on the planking, then curled straight into a roll that took him through the open doorway into a room beyond.

A grey-haired man was lying there, on a large brass bed, taking his midday rest. He grunted an indignant but sleepy protest, then slumped back on to the pillow as Carver dashed out of the room into a corridor. A staircase at the far end led down to the ground floor, or up to the roof. Carver went up and out on to a flat expanse of dazzling white. A clothes line was tied between two chimneys at either end of the roof. Carver undid one end and ran to the other, still holding the line.

He was about to abseil over the side when he looked down and saw a black-clad figure turning into the far end of the narrow alley to the rear of the house, holding a gun in his hand. Carver gave the clothes line a sharp, hard tug to make sure it would take the strain, then tied a honda knot to creat a lasso loop on the end of the line.

He peered over the edge of the roof.

The gunman was not far away now, walking slightly hunched forward, his pace tentative, his head extended as he peered from side to side, eyes set at ground level, looking out for his prey but nervous in case he himself was ambushed.

The angle of the man's neck was ideal, but Carver would only have one chance to get this right. He played out the line, trying to calculate the amount he would need for what he had to do. Then, as the gunman walked by, Carver began lowering the looped clothes line, gently swinging it back and forth above the man's head, not so fast that it would generate any wind noise, praying that he would not look up. The gunman was two paces past Carver now . . . three . . .

Carver swung the line to its fullest extent, past his target, then brought it back the other way, dropping it lower until the centre of the loop slipped over the man's head and snagged against his neck.

That was the first the gunman knew of it.

He raised his free hand to tear at the line around his neck, then looked up, bringing his gun to bear on Carver, who was now standing, clearly visible, at the edge of the roof.

Before the man could fire, Carver pulled the line hard, tightening it like a hangman's noose around the gunman's neck. Now the gun was forgotten, dropped to the ground as both the man's hands fought for purchase on the line. Carver pulled again and then a third time, increasing the pressure on the exposed neck, crushing the larynx and forcing his victim to stagger backwards towards him in the hope of creating some slack. But Carver kept pulling the line tighter and tighter, his jaw set in unrelenting determination as the man's efforts to resist became more feeble and then ceased entirely. The body on the end of the line slumped into immobility. For now, Carver knew, the man was only unconscious. It would take a few minutes yet for death to follow, but follow it certainly would.

Now he used the line for the purpose he had originally intended, letting it out again and abseiling down the wall to the alley below. He looked at the man's purple face and the grossly distended tongue that flopped out of his open mouth.

'That was for Ginger,' Carver said. He picked up the discarded gun and frisked the body for the spare clip. Then he looked around. About ten metres further down the alley, at the back of a restaurant, stood a large, wheeled dump-bin. Carver dragged the body across to it, heaved it in and covered it with a foul-smelling mix of half-eaten food, kitchen waste, empty bottles and containers. He wiped his hands on an old, discarded dishcloth, then closed up the bin and walked away down the alley.

At four to one, without a weapon, he'd not liked his chances. But now the enemy were a man down and he was armed. The odds were swinging in Sam Carver's favour.

3

MI6 headquarters, Vauxhall, London

'All right, then, tell me the worst,' said Jack Grantham as he strode into the meeting room. 'What's that grinning money-grubber been up to now?'

He slapped a file down on the table top, pulled out his chair with an energy that suggested limitless depths of pent-up irritability, and sat down.

Half a dozen staff were already in place. They looked at one another with raised eyebrows and quizzical expressions. After a decade of MI6 heads who were essentially political placemen – their every word calculated to avoid accountability; their only desire to tell Number 10 exactly what it wanted to hear regardless of the actual facts – Grantham's cantankerous frankness took some getting used to.

'Are you referring to our former Prime Minister?' asked the amused, languid voice of the second most senior officer in the room, Piers Nainby-Martin, a thirty-year veteran of the Service, educated at Eton and New College, Oxford.

'No, Piers, I'm referring to Simon bloody Cowell ... Yes, of course I mean the Right Honourable Nicholas Orwell, one-time member for the constituency of Blabey and Trimingham, now fully occupied feathering his nest. What's this I hear about his new business venture? Some kind of investment fund for the stinking rich ... Come on, let's be having it.'

Another officer, Elaine McAndrew, a bespectacled, mousy, blue-stocking type in her thirties, stood up and pointed a remote control at a large plasma screen: 'This is footage from last night ...'

The screen came to life with grainy shots of a lavish outdoor party. A large circular dinner table, decorated with a splendid floral centrepiece, had been set beside a spotlit swimming pool. At the far end of the pool stood two silk-draped pavilions. Within one of them, two uniformed chefs stood behind a spread of whole lobsters, spectacular king prawns, a perfectly pink joint of roast beef, golden glazed chickens, silver bowls of pasta, rice and salads of every description, and a pair of chafing dishes whose fragrant, spicy contents would have graced a three-star restaurant. In the adjacent pavilion, a barman was ready with premier cru wines and vintage champagnes, European, Asian and American beers, and a selection of single malt whiskies for those who preferred spirits.

'This is the Castello di Santo Spirito. It's an estate in Tuscany, about ten kilometres from Siena, owned by an American called Malachi Zorn,' the woman continued.

'The American speculator?' Grantham asked.

'That's right, sir, yes.'

Grantham harrumphed. 'His speculations appear to have been successful, then.'

'Yes sir, he's believed to be worth in excess of fifteen billion dollars.'

There was a shuffling of papers from down the table and a voice piped up: 'Fifteen point three, to be precise, according to the latest *Forbes* magazine list of the world's richest individuals.'

A grimace of indifference tinged with disgust crossed Grantham's face. 'So what was the occasion?'

'A dinner party, sir,' said the female officer. 'For guests of similar wealth.'

The camera turned to look back up a flight of stone steps towards a country house. From the champagne glasses whose rims were occasionally visible at the bottom of the picture it appeared to be attached to one of the wine-waiters. The camera came to rest on a man. His black suit was perfectly cut, but artfully crumpled, and his white dress shirt was tieless, its top three buttons undone to reveal a tanned, hairless chest. A group of guests – Grantham counted nine men and women – were following him down the stairs, like children trailing the Pied Piper.

'Mr Zorn, I presume,' said Grantham.

'Yes, sir.'

'What's the story with him, then?'

Nainby-Martin took over: 'Could you pause the video a moment, please, Elaine?' As the image froze, he glanced down at a file in front of him. 'Malachi Vernon Zorn. Born in Westchester, New York, in 1970. His father was a banker, his mother a full-time housewife. Malachi was the only child. Educated privately at Phillips Exeter Academy, then went up to Harvard to study mathematics, for which he had a phenomenal aptitude. As a boy he was also an accomplished horseman, played a lot of tennis and was a competent yachtsman. So far, so conventionally privileged. But then came an unexpected twist. Both his parents died: mother first, then the heartbroken father.

'Zorn was in his final year at Harvard, but walked out without graduating. He proceeded to hit the New York party circuit, apparently set on throwing away every penny of his inheritance as fast as possible. Aside from occasional mentions in the gossip columns, no more was heard of him until 1995, when he set up a small company called Zorn Financials. It was a one-man band. Just Zorn, alone in an office, surrounded by screens, essentially placing bets on a variety of financial markets.'

'Any market in particular?' Grantham asked. 'I thought most of these people were highly specialized: particular commodities, currencies and so forth.'

'Absolutely,' Nainby-Martin agreed. 'And what's more, they tend to use other people's money. Young Zorn, however, took positions without any apparent regard for the type of market, or its location, or the nature of the play. And he did it by risking every penny he had, all the time.'

'Sounds like a typical death wish to me,' said Grantham. 'His parents had left him alone, nothing to live for. He was just tempting fate to get him, too.'

'That's certainly a theory,' said Nainby-Martin. 'And the rest of his behaviour seems to give it a certain credence. Once Zorn started making big money, he spent it seeking thrills: seriously fast cars, speedboats, skydiving, mountaineering expeditions to the Himalayas, all that sort of thing. An adrenalin junkie, you might say.'

'So how did Nicholas Orwell enter the picture?'

'Ah well, a year ago, Zorn let it be known that he was thinking of going into business in a more conventional way, setting up a hedge fund called Zorn Global that would accept investments from exceptionally high-net-worth individuals. He was contemplating a minimum stake of one billion dollars. And the man he had in mind to act as his personal ambassador to the world's super-rich was Nicholas Orwell.'

Grantham laughed to himself. 'Orwell must have loved that idea.'

'He's not shown any sign of objecting,' Nainby-Martin replied drily. 'Our information is that Zorn offered him a fee of five million dollars, plus the same again for his charitable foundation.'

'So he's doing this for charity? How very noble.'

There were stifled sniggers round the table at Grantham's acid sarcasm.

'Quite so,' said Nainby-Martin, maintaining an impressively straight face. 'But in any case, rumours of Zorn's new fund went round the smart set in an instant. In no time people were practically begging to be allowed to give him their cash.'

'In this financial climate? Aren't they all hanging on to their money for dear life?'

'Apparently not. The problem for the rich appears to be that there's nowhere to put their money. Stocks and commodities are all over the place, property values are going nowhere and interest rates on savings have been rock-bottom for years. They're looking for a magician who can buck the markets.'

'And Zorn is happy to oblige.'

'Precisely.'

'So this event in Italy – I assume it was aimed at possible investors? Orwell does the schmoozing, Zorn takes all the money?'

'Something like that.'

Grantham nodded thoughtfully. 'I see. Let's carry on with the show.'

Zorn and his guests started moving down the stairs again. The men of the party were dressed in more formal variations on Zorn's dinner suit. The women, by contrast, wore dazzling couture gowns in silk and lace, decorated with jewels worthy of a pirate's treasure trove; a description that in some cases was disturbingly close to the truth, given the dubious means by which their men had come by their fortunes. Through this select little group flitted a man known the whole world over for the bright, shiny charm of his smile and the deceptive plausibility of his words. He strode jauntily to the front as they all descended the steps and exchanged a few words with Malachi Zorn.

'Aha!' said Grantham. 'Nicholas Orwell himself, the very man I was . . .'

Grantham fell silent as he peered, frowning more closely at the video. He waved at McAndrew. 'Pause it!' Then he got up and walked towards the screen, stopping just a few feet away. He stared intently for a few more seconds, and then tapped his forefinger against the screen, directly over the motionless image of a blonde, whose slender elegance stood out from the other women there, despite all the time and money they had put into perfecting their appearance.

'I'll be damned,' murmured Grantham to himself.

Behind him there was another shuffling of papers and a voice said, 'If you give me a second, sir, I think I should be able to identify her.'

'No need,' said Grantham. 'Her name's Alexandra Vermulen. Born Alexandra Petrova. She's Russian, age around forty. Also known as Alix. Fascinating woman.'

'You sound as though you know her well,' Nainby-Martin remarked.

Grantham said nothing. He was thinking back to the only time he had ever met her: at a funeral in Norway, saying farewell to a good man who had made one bad mistake. And then he thought of a time before that, and the events that had linked him to Alix through the man who had loved her, Samuel Carver.

'No,' Grantham finally replied. 'I can't say we're particularly close.' For a moment he sounded uncharacteristically wistful. But then, to his staff's relief, he snapped back to his usual, acerbic style: 'But one thing I do know, from my experience, is that whenever that woman enters the picture, trouble's never far behind.'

4

Mykonos

Over the years, Carver had made a lot more enemies than friends. That was the nature of his business. When you spent your adult life getting rid of criminals, terrorists and malevolent psychopaths of every description, you were bound to provoke a grudge or two.

Carver wasn't his real name. When his mother had abandoned him as a baby he'd been adopted by a couple who called him Paul and gave him their own surname, Jackson. He began his career as a second lieutenant in the Royal Marines before being selected for the Marines' own elite-within-an-elite, the Special Boat Service. He quit after a dozen years in uniform, and dreamed of a peaceful, normal life on Civvy Street, until a hit-and-run driver killed the woman he planned to marry. Carver had gone off the rails and been sleeping off a drunken brawl in a police cell when his former commanding officer, Quentin Trench, offered him a job perfectly suited to his particular talents and training.

He became a freelance assassin, his major client a group that called itself the Consortium. It consisted of men whose wealth and

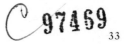

influence enabled them to commission work that could not be attributed to any elected government, removing individuals whose guilt had long since been proven beyond any doubt, without recourse to judges or juries. Carver provided them with deniability: calculated hits that either appeared to be random accidents, or could be attributed to another, false perpetrator.

He was very good at his job and paid accordingly, but as long as he possessed a shred of humanity he could not help but be affected by the taking of another man's life, however evil that life might be. He tried to justify his work mathematically: every guilty life he took saved many more innocent ones, but that rationalization could not stop the steady erosion of his soul, or ease his emotional isolation.

And then, one August night in Paris, in an underpass beside the Seine, Carver committed an act for which there was no justification. He had been set up, and he took fearsome revenge on the men who had deceived and betrayed him. Still, the stain on his conscience had never quite washed away, and his need for atonement had never been satisfied.

This was not, however, a subject on which Carver liked to dwell. He saw no point in trying to repair an unchangeable past or speculate about an unknowable future. He dealt in the here and now, and saved his mental energy for problems he could solve, like the two now confronting him. First he had to deal with the three remaining gunmen pursuing him through the streets of Mykonos. And then he had to get the hell away from the island.

He had not had anything to do with Ginger's murder, and a decent lawyer might be able to argue successfully that the dead man in the alley had been killed in self-defence. But there was no telling what pressure would be put on the local police and prosecuting magistrate to come up with a guilty man whose arrest and conviction would put tourist minds at ease. Carver had no intention of being that man.

He stepped out of the alley, back on to another crowded shopping street, indistinguishable from the last. The crowds looked no different. The only thing missing was the presence of any threat. Carver scanned his surroundings, searching for any trace of his pursuers, but could see none. He walked out into the middle of the street, clearly visible to anyone who was watching. Nothing happened.

He frowned, made more uneasy by the absence of danger – the dogs that did not bark – than he had been when running for his life, pursued by men with guns. Where had they gone? And why, come to think of it, had they not killed him when they had the chance? These were men who had gunned down a completely innocent victim without a second thought. Yet when he had been running through to the restaurant kitchen they had somehow managed to miss his exposed, defenceless back at virtually point-blank range. And now they were nowhere to be seen.

Carver's phone rang.

He took it from his pocket, wondering whether to answer.

He looked at the number that had appeared on the screen, recognizing it at once.

Carver pressed the green button, put the phone to his ear, and heard a voice that had recently become very familiar.

'Hi, baby,' it said. 'This is Ginger. If you want to get off the island in one piece, do exactly what I say . . .'

5

MI6 headquarters

Jack Grantham gave a sigh that seemed to hint at disappointment. 'Hmm ... I don't suppose there's too much to worry about. Nicholas Orwell appears to be making a few more bob by helping this Malachi Zorn – and sundry other equally plutocratic types – to become even wealthier than they already are. They're all consenting adults. If anything goes wrong they have no one to blame but themselves. Who are we to object?'

Piers Nainby-Martin cleared his throat. 'Well, there's just one more thing.'

'Really?' Grantham became instantly alert, like a hound that has just caught the scent of a distant fox. 'What would that be?'

'There's a freelance reporter in New York called Camilla DaCosta, who helps us out from time to time. I asked her to look into Zorn, tell people she was writing a newspaper profile of him. Well, she managed to get quite a bit of material, including an interview with an old girlfriend of his ...' Nainby-Martin glanced down at his notes. 'Name of Domenica Cruz, an ex-stripper.'

'You mean he's kinky? If he's vulnerable to blackmail, that could be a problem.'

'No, that's not it. The woman was only working at a club to pay her way through college. She sells insurance now . . .'

'A rather less honourable profession than stripping.'

'Quite possibly. Anyway, her views on Zorn's personal demons caught my attention. And there's something at the end that might interest you, too.'

'What do you mean?'

'Just a remark she makes. It's nothing concrete, but it's been niggling at me. See what you think. I must apologize, by the way, if Miss DaCosta's interrogation technique is a little, ah, fluffy for your taste.'

There was a suppressed chuckle around the table. Grantham was one of nature's bad cops, known for the speed and toughness with which he liked to extract information. He took a deep breath, as if preparing himself for the worst, and then said, 'Let's see it, then.'

Once again a grainy video image appeared on screen, this time shot at a sidewalk café on a busy Manhattan street, two cups of coffee on the table. An attractive brunette in a formal business suit was looking into the lens with a worried look on her face.

'You promise me that you're not going to write nasty things about Mal? I mean, I don't want to end up in some supermarket tabloid,' she said.

The voice that answered her was that of a young, upper-middle-class Englishwoman. 'Oh no, I quite understand. That would be terrible. But don't worry. You're quite safe with *The Times*. We were founded more than two hundred years ago and we're terribly respectable. The paper of record, and all that sort of thing.'

'For heaven's sake,' Grantham groaned.

'She knows what she's doing,' Nainby-Martin assured him.

On screen, Domenica Cruz relaxed a little, though there was still a trace of hesitancy as she said, 'Well, in that case, I guess it's OK if I help you.'

'So tell me about Mr Zorn. You met at the Penthouse Club, isn't that right?'

A fresh look of alarm crossed Cruz's face, and she held a hand to her mouth. 'Oh my God! I was just trying to pay my way through college and . . .'

'I think pole-dancing's terribly sexy,' said Camilla DaCosta, encouragingly. 'I went to classes for a while. My boyfriend absolutely loved it!'

'Huh! I hope he was nicer than some of the assholes I had to dance for!'

'Was Mr Zorn an asshole?'

'God no, Mal was great!' Cruz said, smiling for the first time. 'Really smart, you know. He just, I don't know . . . got it. And people, too. It was like he knew what they were gonna do or say next. Got a little spooky actually, sometimes.'

'How do you mean?'

Cruz frowned, trying to find the right words. 'I guess he could just take in an incredible amount of information, analyse every-thing, and then figure out what to do faster than anyone I ever met. And, believe me, he had a LOT of information. He has people all over the world working for him.'

'Like spies?'

'Kinda, I guess. He's always one step ahead, that's for sure.'

A little laugh from DaCosta, then: 'I'm not sure I'd like a man who knew what I was going to do next!'

Cruz laughed, too. 'Totally!'

'It sounds like you had a real connection. I mean, I can see why any man would be drooling over you. You're so gorgeous!'

'Oh, for God's sake, someone get me a sick-bag!' Grantham interjected.

'Wait!' Nainby-Martin implored his boss. 'She's getting good material here.'

On the screen, Cruz was making the obligatory self-deprecating woman-to-woman remarks about how much she hated her own body – her upper arms and ankles seemed to give particular grounds for concern. 'But, yeah, I know, most guys don't seem to care. They just want to bang a dancer.'

'Zorn doesn't sound like that kind of man, though.'

'No, that was what I liked about him. He saw beyond that. He was interested in me, you know, as a real person. I think we kind of bonded over our parents, too, you know?'

'How do you mean?'

'Well, I was raised by my grandmomma, 'cause both my parents died in an auto smash.'

'Oh, I'm so sorry . . .'

'Thanks, but it's OK. I mean, it was a long time ago.'

'Didn't Mr Zorn's parents die, too, when he was a boy?'

'Exactly. We really connected over that. And for Mal, losing his people was just a huge, huge issue.'

'You mean he hadn't got over it?'

Cruz sighed: 'You have no idea . . . What happened was, Mal's mom got sick in the head. She was stuck at home all day. Her husband was away in the city working totally crazy hours, and she just got lonely and bored and miserable. You know what it's like for a guy who works for one of those big banks. They own him. If it's a choice between doing something for the bank or doing something for his family, the bank wins. And the little woman back at home still has to be the pretty, smiley wifey. It's like *Mad Men* or something. If Mal's mom started drinking or popping pills, God, who can blame her?'

'Is that what happened?' Camilla DaCosta's hand could be seen coming into shot and lifting a coffee cup.

'Uh-huh, pretty much. And Mal's dad tried to help. I think he really loved her. But he couldn't ever take the time to really be there for her, because Lehman's always came first, and it really tore him apart. From what I heard—'

The cup was almost slammed back on to the table. 'Sorry, did you say Mal's father worked at Lehman Brothers?'

'Oh yes, didn't you know? Mal hated Lehman's . . . The way he saw it, the bank had killed his parents. What happened was, his dad had to put his mom in rehab because he couldn't look after her at home. She'd been there a coupla months or something when they let her come home for a weekend. But while she was in the house, Mal's dad was called back to the city for a meeting, and had to leave her. You know, just for an afternoon, or whatever. Anyway, when he came back, she was dead. Took an overdose. Mal found the body.'

'God, how terrible.'

'I know ... Mal's dad lived for a few more years, but he was totally heartbroken and guilty about not caring for his wife. He passed away from a heart attack while Mal was at college.'

'Poor boy, he must have been totally devastated.'

Cruz nodded: 'Oh yeah ... but totally motivated, too.'

'How do you mean?'

'Well, that was what drove him to be successful. He wanted to get his revenge on all the people who had wrecked his family. And I guess he did.'

'You mean when Lehman's collapsed?'

'For sure. But I don't know ... It sounds crazy, but I don't think he's gonna stop there. I mean, I really like him, but he does have a whole other side that's so intense it's scary.'

'You mean he's violent?'

'God no! He was always a total gentleman ... It's just, well, the night we met, he told me that bringing the bank down was just a rehearsal.'

'A rehearsal for what?'

'He never said. I don't know, maybe he was just kidding around. It definitely got to be that way after a while, like a private joke between us. You know, if one of us did something cool, or out-rageous, we'd be, like, "That was just a rehearsal, baby!" '

'So how come you broke up? It sounds like you were great together—'

Cruz sighed. 'We were ... I really loved that guy, and I think he loved me. But it just got to the point where he wanted to be by himself. It was like he was on a mission, and he just didn't want the distraction of a relationship.'

The screen went dead.

'And your point is?' Grantham asked.

'My point is that there's more to Malachi Zorn than meets the eye,' Nainby-Martin replied. 'I agree with DaCosta. I want to know why he's rehearsing, and what for.'

'I should have thought that was obvious. He made a lot of money betting against Lehman's. But he wants to make even more. Hence, presumably, this fund of his.'

'That's a perfectly reasonable interpretation,' Nainby-Martin agreed. 'But I can't help feeling there's something more to it than that. Something bigger.'

'Bigger than, say, the threat of Iranian nuclear weapons?' Grantham asked. 'Or Chinese industrial espionage? Or al-Qaeda? I'm sorry, Piers, but unless we have some concrete evidence of a threat, I can't divert resources from our major priorities to investigate the vague possibility that Malachi Zorn might be any-thing other than another greedy financier.'

Nainby-Martin began gathering his papers with the frustrated air of a man who has just lost an office battle.

'But,' Grantham continued, 'I will concede that the Orwell connection bothers me. So keep an eye on this fund of Zorn's. And if there's any firmer information, I'll be willing to take another look at it. Fair enough?'

'Completely,' Nainby-Martin said, his normal self-possession restored.

'Good, then I think we're done.'

6

Mykonos

Carver wasn't inclined to trust Ginger any further than he could throw her, but he needed to get off Mykonos as fast and inconspicuously as possible. If she was offering him a way out, he was at least prepared to listen.

He followed her directions through winding, crowded streets to a small hotel. Passing under a grey and white striped awning, and through a marble-framed front door, he came to a small lobby. To one side stood an antique reception desk, topped with red leather, on which sat a brass bell. The padded leather seat behind the desk was empty. The only other person in the lobby was Ginger. She walked up to Carver, took his right hand in both of hers, squeezed it, and looked him in the eyes as she mouthed the words, 'I'm so sorry.' Then, in a brisk, clear voice she instructed him: 'Please follow me.'

She led him through to a garden at the back of the hotel. There was a man standing by the entrance. Carver recognized him at once from his straw hair and blue shirt: one of the two shooters from the restaurant.

They didn't bother with introductions. The man just said, 'Legs apart, arms out,' and Carver obeyed. He was frisked. The gun was found. The blond man clearly recognized it, and glared at Carver.

'The original owner didn't need it any more,' Carver said. Then he walked with Ginger into the garden, towards a marble-topped table set beneath a sunshade. Three chairs had been arranged around it. One of them was already occupied by an Asian man, somewhere in his mid- to late-fifties. He had a swept-back bouffant haircut, streaked with grey like his moustache. His pale-blue denim shirt was open to reveal a hairy chest. He would have looked like an ageing, slightly overweight nightclub playboy, were it not for the muscle that was evident beneath all the signs of good living, and the direct, unflinching way he looked Carver in the eye.

'My name is Shafik,' the man said. He waved at one of the chairs opposite him. 'Please, take a seat.'

'You interrupted my lunch,' said Carver, sitting down while Ginger took the third chair. 'Any chance of a beer, something to eat?'

'Of course.' Shafik gestured at the blond man as if he were a waiter, then told him to fetch drinks, bread, olives, tomatoes and cheese. He turned back to Carver. 'My background is in the Pakistani Army and security services . . .'

Carver knew what that meant. Shafik had been an officer in Pakistan's legendary, but also notorious, Directorate for Inter-Services Intelligence, or ISI. It had worked hand in glove with the CIA for decades, while maintaining links to the Taliban and even al-Qaeda. So Shafik was a spook, and probably a tough, un-scrupulous one at that.

'. . . but now I am a private security consultant to various financial institutions,' Shafik continued. 'You know my associate Magda Sternberg, of course.'

'Only too well.'

Ginger had the decency to look embarrassed.

'I am about to make you an offer of employment,' Shafik went on. 'It is worth two point five million dollars, payable in any currency, commodity or financial instrument you specify. Nevertheless, I confidently expect you to turn it down, despite this considerable financial inducement. I know that you have no interest in pursuing your old line of work any more, and no financial need to do so. You have an interest in a mining operation in southern Africa, I gather?'

'I've a shareholding in the Kamativi Mining Corporation, yes.'

Carver wondered if Shafik knew who he'd had to kill to get the shares.

'Remind me what your mine produces?' the Pakistani asked.

'Coltan.'

'And that is . . . ?'

A year earlier, Carver would not have had the first idea how to answer that question. Now his response was automatic. 'A mix of two minerals: columbite and tantalite. They're refined to produce niobium and tantalum respectively. Very useful metals: got a lot of industrial applications.'

'You sound very knowledgeable.'

'Getting there.'

'And it is doing well for you, I imagine.'

'Shares up fifty per cent in the past six months.'

'So the dividends will be generous this year?'

'Very.'

'And yet,' Shafik repeated, 'you will still accept the job that I am about to offer you.'

The blond man reappeared, followed by a hotel employee carrying a tray laden with bottles, cutlery and plates of food. Carver took his beer and had a sip before he replied, 'I doubt that very much. And you don't need me, anyway. You've obviously got people who can handle wet work.'

Shafik gave a dismissive shrug. 'At a low level, yes, but they have their limits. You, on the other hand, have quite a reputation in certain circles.'

'What circles would those be?' said Carver, cutting himself a slice of bread.

'Ones in which men of great wealth and power continue to seek ways to exercise their influence at the highest level.'

'Ah, those men,' Carver said. He placed some goat's cheese on the bread, took a large bite, and in-between chews said, 'Yeah, they used to like what I did.'

'Quite so. And of course, I knew Quentin Trench quite well: we had a shared professional interest in special forces operations.' Shafik sighed. 'I wonder what happened to him . . .'

Carver thought about the storm-whipped night in the English Channel when he had last seen Trench. 'Yes, I wonder,' he said, swallowing the last of his bread. He looked Shafik in the eye. 'But this reputation I have, and your friendship with dear old Trench, didn't stop you jerking me around. What was that crap at the restaurant all about?'

'I wanted to see how you responded under pressure. You did very well. You reacted immediately to what was happening. You were resourceful, efficient, ruthless, even merciless . . . And that is why you will say yes to my offer. For whereas my people evidently did not kill Miss Sternberg, you did, in fact, leave a dead body lying in a rubbish bin barely two hundred metres from here. The local police are at present unaware of its presence. My men can ensure that they never will be. The moment I give them the signal, they will do what is required to make all trace of your crime disappear . . .'

The longer this conversation went on, the less Carver liked it. 'Crime?' he said.

'Of course . . . how else would you describe an unprovoked attack on a man who had not harmed you in any way – who did not even know you were there?'

Carver did not respond.

'Your silence speaks volumes. You committed a murder, and you will be found guilty of the charge if it ever comes to court. Your victim's name was Eriksen, by the way; he has, or rather had, a wife and a young daughter. I am sure that when they appear in court, they will touch the hearts of everyone who sets eyes on them.'

For a second, Carver was ashamed at what he had done. He was also unnerved by the ease with which Shafik had played him . . . was still playing him.

'You have every reason to want Eriksen's body to disappear, and none at all to encourage me to do my civic duty and report both the dead man and you to the police. The clothes line is still there. There will be small fragments of your skin on the cord. You will be found guilty, count on it. And you will spend many years in prison. Do I make myself clear?'

'Yes.'

'Then I will assume that you will accept my offer . . .'

7

Shafik pressed a speed-dial number and spoke: 'Remove Eriksen. But do not dispose of him. Not yet.'

Carver had no intention of taking Shafik's job, whatever it was. On the other hand, leaving now would entail either killing or at the very least disabling the other three people in the garden. It was doable, but it would only complicate the situation still further, and he didn't need the aggravation. 'So who's the target?' he said.

Shafik relaxed, sitting back in his chair, confident that, for now at any rate, he had got what he wanted. 'His name is Malachi Zorn. He is an American, based on Long Island, New York.'

'And what's his problem?'

'He costs other people a great deal of money. My clients are usually competitors, but they are united in the conviction that their businesses—'

'Their banks?'

'Yes.'

Carver gave an exasperated sigh. 'Unbelievable. You want me to stop bankers losing money. I never thought I'd stoop that low.'

Ginger laughed. Shafik looked at her sharply, then allowed himself a smile. 'Very good, Mr Carver, but this is not just about bankers. Malachi Zorn makes a great deal of his money placing very large bets against corporations. He takes short positions or uses derivative instruments that capitalize on falling asset prices and even total collapse. The very act of taking these positions taints his targets. Perfectly good, well-run, solvent companies can be destroyed. And all these companies have shareholders, the majority of whom are funds run for the benefit of ordinary citizens: investing for their future, for their pensions. They are the ones who get hurt by a man like Zorn.'

Carver had been eating olives while Shafik made his speech in defence of shareholder capitalism. 'And there was I thinking this had something to do with senior executives getting nervous that their bonuses might be a zero or two short this year,' he said when it was over.

Ginger laughed. 'I hadn't realized that you were such a cynic, Sam.'

'Huh ... no matter how hard I try to be cynical, the truth is almost always far worse.'

Shafik gave a contemptuous snort. 'Grow up, Carver. The only way all the little guys make a small amount of money is if the big guys make lots of it. That is how the system works. Anything else is just ... communism.'

'But why do you want Zorn removed now?' Carver asked. 'It sounds like he's been operating for quite a while. Why the sudden desire to stop him?'

'Because ...' Ginger began. Then she stopped herself and looked at Shafik. 'I'm sorry. I didn't mean to interrupt.'

'Not at all ... go ahead.'

'Up until now Zorn has always worked alone,' Ginger continued. 'That's been the source of his mystique: one man, betting his own money against the system.'

'Or a spoilt playboy playing his selfish games at other people's expense,' Shafik snapped.

Ginger flicked her eyes up at the heavens in mock exasperation. 'You'll have to excuse my boss, Sam. He takes our work very personally sometimes.'

'I don't give a damn about your boss,' Carver replied. 'Tell me about Zorn. What's changed?'

'He's getting partners for the first time in his career: serious investors. He's using their money to start a fund: Zorn Global. Very private, very exclusive, but also very well-financed. He'll have tens of billions of dollars behind him, all provided by ultra-high-net-worth individuals. No institutions at all.'

'So he'll have more leverage, and be able to do more damage, as they would see it, to your clients?'

'You have got it in one, Mr Carver,' said Shafik.

'Well, you're right about one thing. I'd certainly have turned down the job.'

'But . . . ?'

'But now I'm considering my options. And I want to know the details. When does this have to be done? Where? How? That kind of thing.'

Ginger spoke again, 'It has to be done quickly. Zorn is launching his fund at the end of next week in London.'

'How come he's not doing it on Wall Street?'

Shafik answered the question, 'His new fund has investors from around the world. It will operate globally. Wall Street serves the world's biggest domestic economy, but London is the centre of international finance.'

'And it's also where many of his investors like to be at this time of year,' Ginger went on. 'They go to parties, Royal Ascot, Wimbledon. You know the kind of things. Zorn's crazy about tennis. He's going to be at Wimbledon for a few days next week. He's going Monday, Wednesday, Friday and Sunday.'

Carver couldn't stop himself from asking, 'What about the days in-between?'

'Ladies' quarter-finals, semis and final,' said Ginger. 'Zorn ignores them – he's a sexist when it comes to tennis.'

'Or a realist,' Shafik observed.

'But for the men's days,' Ginger went on, refusing to rise to the bait, 'he has tickets for himself and his guests: debenture seats, the best for Centre, Number One and Number Two Courts, six at a time. He likes to know that he has his choice of all the most important matches. He's spending tens of thousands of dollars a day, but what does he care?'

'He even enquired about hiring a box at Lord's,' Shafik said, with a shake of his head. 'As if he could possibly appreciate cricket.'

'Well, who cares about cricket, anyway?' Ginger laughed, getting her own back. She smiled again at Carver, trying to make him complicit in her gentle mockery of Shafik, doing what she could to draw him again into some kind of relationship. 'The crucial day is this coming Friday, 1 July. That's when Zorn will formally launch his fund with a reception at the Goldsmiths' Hall, in the heart of the City of London, for a very exclusive selection of guests – his investors, senior politicians and bankers.'

'Including the men who want him dead?'

'Possibly,' she admitted.

'And you wonder why I'm cynical?'

'There will also be a number of figures from the media and entertainment industries,' said Shafik. 'Zorn is not foolish. He knows they will attract more attention than any number of middle-aged, unattractive male billionaires.'

'But you do want Zorn to make it to his own party?'

'Indeed not.'

Carver drank some more beer. He put the glass down and said, 'So you're looking for an unfortunate accident?'

'Precisely – the tragic end to a brilliant career. And it must be visible: Zorn must be seen to die.'

'To send a message?'

'I'd prefer to say: to encourage any other independent operators not to be so greedy,' Shafik suggested. 'In any case, you can be sure that my clients will attend the funeral and send many magnificent wreaths.'

'Well, then they'd better hope I don't decide to pay my respects as well. I don't have any views about this Malachi Zorn one way or another. But I'm taking a serious dislike to your clients.'

8

Brick Lane, London E1

The package was addressed to Brynmor Gryffud at the office of his graphic design agency, Sharpeville Images. The company specialized in branding and website design for charities and pressure groups involved in controversial fields, such as minority and animal rights, environmental activism and anti-war campaigning. Gryffud was a tall, thickset, heavily bearded Welshman who looked and sounded as though he should be farming sheep, playing rugby and drinking a dozen pints a night – all of which he had done in his time. As he liked to tell clients in a rich, musical voice made for lyrical speeches, 'Whatever the *Daily Mail* is against, *that* is what we are for.'

In addition to his design work, Gryffud ran a small, but vociferous, group of his own, the Forces of Gaia. It specialized in stunts that drew attention to what Gryffud and his supporters viewed as unacceptable assaults on the environment. Inspired by the fathers' rights campaigners, who had attracted global coverage simply by appearing at high-visibility, high-security locations such as Tower

Bridge and Buckingham Palace dressed up as superheroes, Gryffud had relied on wit and imagination to make his point. His actions had given him a high profile, and even brought in new clients for his business, but he'd long since accepted that they hadn't made a damn bit of difference to the environment.

The screensavers on his office computer were pictures he had taken of the Welsh hills where he had been raised, and to which he still returned whenever possible. Gryffud's connection to that landscape and, through it, to the planet as a whole was part of his very soul. His certainty that man's abuse of all the bounty that nature had bestowed on him was leading to the inevitable desecration, even destruction, of the planet caused him intense pain. Now his patience had run out. Recently, Gryffud had been listening to angrier, more radical voices. He had been persuaded that it was time for a total change of tactics.

He was looking at a standard white postal packing box, 180 mm long by 100 mm wide and 50 mm deep. Inside it were four clear plastic packets, each containing ten fat marker pens, along with a delivery notice stating that each packet cost £4.99, plus £7.75 post and packaging, making a total of £27.71, paid through PayPal. Two of the packets contained blue pens, the other two red ones.

It was an everyday transaction for a company like Sharpeville Images, one that had attracted no official attention whatsoever on its way through the postal system. In the choking atmosphere of state-sanctioned paranoia that pervaded early twenty-first-century life, any phone call or email was liable to interception. But old-fashioned snail mail was a much more secure means of sending covert messages and goods: provided, of course, that the postal service was up to delivering them.

When he had opened the box and seen the pens lying within it, Gryffud had got up from behind his desk and walked across his office. He had closed the door and lowered the blinds that covered the window, through which he could normally keep an eye on his staff and they on him. No one had thought anything of it. The lowering of 'Bryn's blinds' was the accepted sign that Gryffud was deep in creative thought: that mysterious process through which he came up with the unexpected, innovative concepts that had made the company's name and kept them all in work.

But it wasn't a desire to tap into his creativity that had prompted Brynmor Gryffud to cut himself off from the world.

He went back to his desk and took one of the blue pens out of its packet. Using a scalpel, he cut open one end of the pen and held it at an angle, the open end above the palm of his other hand. Under normal circumstances, the reservoir that contained the pen's ink would have slid out. Instead, an innocuous white plastic tube, about 70 mm long and 8 mm in diameter, landed on Gryffud's hand. The burly Welshman's beard was spit by a piratical grin. The tube was a detonator. Fitted with a fuse and inserted into a mass of explosive material, it would turn an inert collection of chemicals into a highly destructive bomb.

Gryffud repeated the process for a randomly chosen red pen, from which a bright yellow tube, similar to the white one, appeared. This was an igniter, virtually identical to the detonator, except that its purpose was to start an instant, short-lived, but highly intensive blaze.

The two devices were replaced in their respective pens and returned to the appropriate packets. Gryffud picked up his phone and made a call.

'The pens have arrived,' he said. 'They're exactly what we asked for. How about you?'

'No worries, mate,' replied Dave Smethurst, 'Smethers' to his mates, a former army staff sergeant who now worked as a private contractor. Like Gryffud, Smethurst had a specialized clientele. He went on, his voice imbued with the adenoidal flatness of the East Midlands – as dreary an accent as Gryffud's was mellifluous – 'The lads have grabbed all the containers we need. And the gardening supplies are piled up in the barn.'

'I hope you shopped around, Smethers.'

'Oh yeah, we went to at least ten different garden centres,

looking for the best value. And meanwhile the ladies, God bless 'em, are hard at work making the cakes.'

'Good, sounds as though we have everything we need for the party. I'll see you at the farm, then.'

'Oh yeah, this is going to be fookin' great. It's really going to go with—'

'Don't say it,' Gryffud interrupted.

There was a laugh at the other end of the line. 'Take it easy, Taff. I was just winding you up.'

Gryffud ended the call.

'. . . a bang,' he murmured to himself, finishing the other man's sentence.

Then he pulled up the blinds and opened his office door to the world once again.

9

The Old Town, Geneva, Switzerland

Shafik had a helicopter waiting to take Carver the eighty-five miles across the Aegean Sea from Mykonos to Athens. 'Don't worry,' Ginger had said. 'I'll get the hotel to send you your luggage.'

'Will you, now?' thought Carver, wondering how many bugs and tracking devices would have been tucked away among his possessions by the time he saw them again. Thinking also, 'Funny, I haven't told you where to send them . . .'

Thanks to the mid-afternoon Swissair flight, Carver reached Geneva within three hours, but it was long enough to consider a number of different options for extricating himself from the Malachi Zorn hit. Forty minutes later his cab was pulling up on a narrow cobbled street in the Old Town district, beside the four-hundred-year-old building where he had a top-floor apartment.

There was a café next door, with a few plastic tables and chairs on the street, and steps down to a tiny, low-ceilinged basement room within. Years before, it had belonged to a friend of Carver's called Freddy. Two nights after Carver's fateful assignment in

Paris, a Russian psychopath, Grigori Kursk, had forced Freddy to lie face down on the floor, then shot him through the back of the skull at point-blank range. Now the café was run by Freddy's widow, Marianne, and her nineteen-year-old son, Jean-Louis.

Marianne had insisted on staying on, despite the terrible memories. To leave, she said, would be an act of desertion. At first she had struggled to keep the café going and pay the rent. Then, about nine months after Freddy's death, her lawyer had called to inform her that a life insurance policy of which he had not previously been aware had just paid out, enabling her to buy the lease outright.

Marianne was certain that there was no such policy. It seemed clear to her that Carver was the source of the money. Kursk would never have walked into the café that night had he not been looking for Carver and Alix; this was a private act of atonement, and it was accepted, graciously, without a word on either side. Had Marianne asked, Carver would of course have denied having anything to do with it. But in his own mind, this was just one of a number of debts of honour he chose to pay: no different, for example, from the two teenagers in southern Africa – the son and daughter of a man who had saved his life – whose education he was funding.

Carver had more money than he needed for himself. There was no point hiding it away in a bank if it could be useful. And it made it easier to sleep at night knowing that something he did, however tiny in the great scheme of things, was unequivocally good.

'Sam!' Jean-Louis said, seeing him come through the café door. 'I thought you were going to be away for a month?'

'Me too.'

'So the vacation, it was not fun?'

'It started well.'

'But turned to shit?'

'Something like that.'

'You want a coffee, a cup of your English tea, a glass of wine, maybe?'

Carver was still a Royal Marine at heart. He rarely said no to a brew. 'Tea would be good. Thanks.'

Silence descended as Carver drank and Jean-Louis busied himself with other customers. When the cup was empty, the boy came over to take it away. Carver reached for his wallet.

'*Non!* Don't be crazy . . . I will put it on your account,' Jean-Louis loudly insisted. Then, as he bent forward to take the mug, he added, much more quietly, 'There is a man at the front, by the window.'

'Dark-blue business suit, playing with his phone, yeah, I spotted him,' Carver murmured back.

'I think he has not just played with his phone. I am certain he has taken a photograph of you.'

Carver nodded fractionally, then got up from his seat. 'See you tomorrow. Give my regards to your mum,' he said, clearly enough to be heard.

Yes, the man with the phone had looked up. And it hadn't just been idle curiosity.

Carver gave the man a good long look on the way out, letting him know he'd been made.

The man with the phone looked right back, letting Carver know that he didn't give a damn.

Carver walked out, feeling the man's eyes on his back, listening for the slightest sound of movement behind him. None came.

Outside, on the street, he turned into a cobbled yard. On all four sides stood centuries-old buildings whose floors were linked by a complex web of external staircases and covered passages that wound around their walls like the endless, logic-defying stairs in a Maurits Escher drawing. Carver made the way to the top of his building and let himself in. Within seconds, his landline started ringing.

He picked it up. 'Carver.'

'Check your email.'

The voice was Shafik's. Carver got out his iPhone and touched the mail icon. He had a new message with two jpeg files attached to it.

'Open the files,' Shafik said.

Grinding his teeth in silent irritation, Carver did as he was told. The first photo showed the body of the man he had killed on Mykonos, lying in the restaurant dumpster. The second had been taken in the café within the past five minutes. So Jean-Louis had been right.

'And your point is?' Carver asked.

'I was concerned that you might have had a change of heart about our agreement. As you flew away from our meeting, you might have imagined that you were escaping my sphere of influence. I wanted to impress upon you that this was not the case. I know where to find you, Carver, and my intention remains the same as before. If you fulfil our agreement, I will reward you very handsomely. If you do not . . . well, I don't like making threats. I'm sure I don't have to.'

'I don't do threats, Shafik. I don't pay any attention to the ones people throw at me, and I don't bother making any of my own. But since you're on the line, I remembered something while I was flying home—'

'And what was that?'

'I remembered what happened to Quentin Trench. He double-crossed me: set me up on a job and then tried to have me killed. Clearly he didn't succeed. In fact, the last time I saw him, he was bobbing up and down in the middle of the English Channel, dead as a doornail, with a distress flare blazing away where the middle of his face used to be . . . Do you see what I'm getting at here?'

'Absolutely.'

Carver frowned. He could swear there was a smirk in Shafik's voice. 'Glad we've got that sorted,' he said, ignoring it.

He hung up and walked through his apartment to the kitchen. The fittings along two of the walls had been updated a couple of years ago, but the granite-topped island unit in the middle of the room was the same as when he first moved in.

One side of the island was given over to a wine-rack. Carver got down on to his haunches, reached in, and removed a bottle of St Emilion premier cru claret from the second row down, three bottles along. He put the bottle down on the floor beside him, then reached into the space where it had been. At the very back was a small, round, rubber-topped button. Carver pressed it.

There was no other noise in the flat. So it was just possible to hear the soft hum of an electric motor as the centre of the granite top slowly rose from the island, eventually revealing a chromed steel frame within which were fitted six plastic drawers of varying depths.

A thick pad of charcoal-grey plastic foam filled each drawer, with specifically shaped openings cut to fit the different contents: precision tools in the top drawer; specialist power tools in the second; circuit boards, timers, detonators, remote controls, auto-motive brake and accelerator overrides and explosive tyre valves in the third and fourth; then blocks of explosives, arranged by cate-gory, in the fifth. The final and deepest drawer contained the two brands of firearm to which Carver had been loyal since his days in the SBS: the Heckler and Koch MP5K short-barrelled sub-machine gun and the Sig Sauer P226 pistol, along with accessories and ammunition.

Tucked in next to the firearms was a bundle of yellow plastic handcuffs that looked like oversized cable-ties. Sometimes it came in handy, being able to immobilize a man without having to stop him permanently. Carver never left home without them.

These were the basic tools of his trade. In his wardrobe he kept a safe containing a variety of passports and credit cards in different identities, plus cash, diamonds and bearer-bonds. These were intended to fund any mission he was likely to undertake and, in the event that he had to disappear fast, get him anywhere in the world and fund a modest lifestyle for the next year or two. If he needed specialist equipment or materials – drugs and poisons, for example – he went to one of a small and very discreet group of expert suppliers. If security measures and customs barriers made it impossible to carry weapons across borders, he specified what he would need from his clients as one of the conditions of his employment.

Still, he found that it helped him to look at his gear when he was contemplating the practicalities of a job. The contents of those foam-lined drawers spoke to him, giving him ideas about the how, what, where and when of what he had to do.

Although, in this case, there was something else for Samuel Carver to consider. Because he hadn't yet decided who his target would be.

10

London N1

Jack Grantham was having a hard time relaxing. On the surface, everything appeared to be going well. He was sitting in the living room of his Islington flat. He had a glass of Scotch on the table by his side. The TV was on in the background, and he was reading a hardback spy thriller, set in the early eighties, about a KGB sleeper who had penetrated British intelligence. Grantham wasn't a big fan of spy novels. He spent too many hours dealing with the realities of secret intelligence to bother with the fiction. This, however, was the debut effort by Dame Agatha Bewley, the one-time Head of the Security Service, known as 'SS' to Whitehall insiders, and MI5 to the rest of the world. He'd always admired Dame Agatha, despite their regular inter-service disputes, and was now smiling to himself as he enjoyed the characteristically canny ways in which she'd managed to convey a sense of absolute authenticity, while leaving out any unduly revealing insights into how the job was actually done.

It was very nearly an enjoyable experience, spoiled only by the thought that niggled and itched at the back of his mind. The Malachi Zorn investigation was bothering him. By any logical analysis of the threats facing the United Kingdom, Grantham had been right to make it a low priority. Still, that throwaway remark about Zorn bringing down Lehman Brothers Bank as a rehearsal for a far bigger stunt wormed away at him, making it impossible to relax.

Grantham tried to distract himself by looking at the news. A TV production company, working on some kind of *Candid Camera*-style reality show, had caused a riot at a restaurant on the Greek island of Mykonos by staging a fake attack by a couple of gunmen. By pure chance – in no way connected with the TV people's desire for global publicity – a passing tourist just happened to have been filming the scene using a high-definition video-camera.

Grantham glanced up at the sound of gunfire and watched as two men appeared, blew the head off a live pelican (the bird's death, the newsreader solemnly intoned, had caused outrage and controversy around the world), and then appeared to kill a woman in cold blood. Grantham watched the panic that ensued, while the voiceover described how a British tourist had been injured in the melée and was now threatening to sue both the restaurant owner and the TV company. Grantham was just about to switch channels when something caught his eye.

He rewound the scene, then watched it again twice more. On the second time through, he froze the image at a particular point. Several hours earlier he had done exactly the same thing with the feed from Malachi Zorn's Italian party and spotted Alix. Now here was another face with which Grantham was all-too familiar: her ex-boyfriend Samuel Carver. And however much trouble she brought into Grantham's life, Carver brought infinitely more.

'That's all we need,' Grantham muttered to himself. He ran through the scene a couple more times, just to make sure that his instinctive reaction to it had been correct. Yes, there was no doubt: Carver had tried to make his escape and been pursued by the gunmen. Grantham couldn't believe Carver would ever have consented to clown around for the benefit of a TV camera. He was genuinely running for his life.

'Well, so what?' Grantham told himself. Carver was no more a concern of his than Malachi Zorn. And yet, like Zorn's 'rehearsal', Carver's image on that TV screen kept gnawing away at him.

He spent a moment or two wondering what, if anything, he should do, then called the office. A junior officer, assigned to night-duty, picked up the call.

'This is Grantham,' his boss informed him. 'Get me passenger manifests for all flights in and out of Mykonos, Greece, in the past, oh . . . seventy-two hours. Ferry traffic, too, if you can get it. And CCTV footage. Then cross-ref it with our databases: names and faces. I want to see if anyone we're interested in has paid a visit there recently.'

'Yes, sir.'

'And if you find anything, call me. I don't care what time it is. Call anyway.'

Grantham put down the phone. He gazed at the frozen image on his TV screen, then turned off the set. He put the book down on the side-table next to the now-empty whisky glass. Then he hauled himself off up to bed.

11

Kensington Palace Gardens, London

As she stood at her bathroom mirror wiping the make-up from her face, Alix knew that she had just lost the argument that would almost certainly end her relationship. But at least no one could say that the subject-matter had been trivial. She and her current partner, Dmytryk Azarov, had not fought over some insignificant domestic quibble. They'd been debating what to do with a billion dollars.

Azarov intended to borrow the money against the value of his massive agricultural, food-processing and supermarket holdings in Eastern Europe. The exact figure he had in mind was $1.35 billion, all of it intended for Malachi Zorn's new investment fund. The contracts had been drafted and awaited his signature. His bankers were arranging the transfer of funds. The entire deal would go through within twenty-four hours.

And Alix had done everything she possibly could to stop it.

Two weeks earlier, Azarov had been ecstatic when the invitation to join the fund had been presented to him in person by Zorn's right-hand man, Nicholas Orwell, the former British Prime Minister. They had met over dinner at the Sommelier's Table, which sits in a private underground dining room in Mayfair, next to the wine cellars of the Connaught Hotel. Azarov had insisted that Alix should accompany him to the meal; whether to show her off to Orwell or him off to her, she had not been entirely sure.

Either way, it was the sort of occasion to which she had become accustomed since she had first arrived in Moscow almost a quarter of a century earlier, a gawky, unsophisticated, acutely shy teenager from the distant city of Perm. In those days she'd been anything but a beauty. She wore shapeless clothes and thick spectacles that failed to disguise the squint for which she had been mocked throughout her childhood and adolescence. Yet one woman, a KGB officer called Olga Zhukovskaya, had spotted Alix's potential. Thanks to her, she had been transformed by a combination of surgery, diet and arduous training into a professional seductress. By the age of twenty-two she'd been able to converse in English as easily as in Russian; to charm a man into bed; to give him the erotic experience of a lifetime once he was there – and to extract whatever information her masters required from her pathetically grateful target.

Orwell, Alix concluded, was little different from the diplomats, politicians, military attachés and businessmen who had been the victims of the honeytrap operations on which she'd once been sent. For all his stellar political reputation, all his familiarity with the most elevated corridors of global power politics, he was now essentially a salesman. Over dinner he had come out with slick, persuasive patter about the genius of Malachi Zorn and the huge returns to be had from his fund, being careful never actually to say that profits were guaranteed, but making sure that vast returns were clearly implied. He had been well-briefed for the meeting, and displayed his knowledge well. He showed a keen, flattering interest in Azarov's commercial prowess and took care to compliment Alix not just on her beauty, but also on the success of the Washington DC military and political consulting business she had inherited from her late husband, General Kurt Vermulen, and subsequently run herself.

'This Nicholas Orwell is a fine man,' Azarov had reflected, as the chauffeur-driven Rolls Royce took them back to his red-brick Queen-Anne-style mansion in Kensington Palace Gardens, or, as London estate agents liked to call it, 'Billionaires' Row'. 'He understands how the world works. For a socialist, he appreciates the value and power of money.'

'His was not the kind of socialism that you and I learned when we were growing up,' Alix remarked.

'No, but it was the kind our masters practised. Make all the money you can, and let the masses fend for themselves. In any case, he is right about Zorn. That man is a magician. You know they say he cleared over ten billion in a single play against Lehman Brothers?'

Alix had placed her hand on Azarov's forearm in a gentle gesture of restraint. 'Are you sure that Zorn will work his magic on your behalf?'

'Why would he not? The more money I make, the more he makes. Of course, there is bound to be some risk. We are playing for the highest possible stakes and a man should not pick up the dice if he has not got the balls to lose everything on a single roll. But I am confident that Zorn's scheme will make us all big, big profits. I can feel it in my guts.'

Alix was not so sure about that. So far as she was concerned, Azarov's guts were filled to the brim with the Connaught's legendarily fine food and wine. If he was feeling anything, it was mostly likely to be indigestion. As for his brains, Azarov had a Russian's head for alcohol, but even so, his judgement seemed less piercing than usual. In fact, the more she thought about it, the more Alix concluded that Orwell had not resembled her former targets so much as herself. He had been engaged on a mission of seduction. And it appeared to have been a success.

The following morning she called the Connaught and discovered that the hotel charged one thousand two hundred pounds

for the Sommelier's Table, exclusive of the wines, which must surely have cost far more than usual. Of course, such expenses were minuscule next to the sums Orwell was hoping to secure on Zorn's behalf. But Alix had never known a rich man who did not keep a very close eye indeed on his spending. Malachi Zorn was not known for being unduly extravagant in his own lifestyle. If he was willing to fund such extravagance for others, then he must have a reason for doing so. And Alix was by no means certain that the reason was as straightforward as Azarov assumed.

Her feelings had only intensified when she and Azarov had met Zorn himself at his Italian villa. All the guests owned their own private planes, yet jets had been laid on to spare them the cost of flying on their own account. The champagne had been served from magnums of 1982 Krug Collection, which retailed for around two thousand dollars each. The quantity of food provided had been far in excess of what could ever have been needed. Zorn's reputation was surely enough to guarantee his fund all the money it could possibly need. So why was he going to such unnecessary lengths to impress?

When she had got back to London, where Azarov was spending the early summer before departing for the Mediterranean, Alix called her office and put two of her best researchers on to the task of compiling a dossier on Malachi Zorn's new fund. The results were skimpy. There had been some coverage of Zorn's plans in the media, especially from publications and websites aimed at financial professionals and wealthy individuals. Yet amidst all the promotional puffery and awestruck descriptions of both Zorn's financial prowess and his investors' vast wealth there was very little hard detail about precisely what he planned. She emailed back a terse message. 'I need more. Want to know about his set-up: offices, staff, overheads, etc. What's he paying Orwell? Where's the investors' money going? More! AV'

Again, the response was disappointing. For all the hype, there was little to be seen of the fund itself. Perhaps that was no surprise. Zorn had spent his entire working life as a one-man band, working his magic from a single desk. Why would it be so different, just because the money he was risking came from a new source? And then one detail caught her eye. Zorn had leased office-space in London and Manhattan. In both cases he had chosen prime properties in exclusive locations. But when Alix looked closely, the offices had something else in common: Zorn had only signed three-month leases, of which more than two months had already expired. She had produced this fact as a trump card earlier in the evening, as she had pleaded with Azarov to reconsider his decision.

'If this is intended to be such a great new business, why will the leases run out so soon?' she asked. 'That does not sound to me like a man who is planning for the long term.'

'Maybe it is a man who thinks he will need more space by then,' Azarov had countered. 'Maybe he looks at the way the real estate market is going, and knows that he will soon be able to get a better deal. Or maybe he is just smarter than you, my darling, and is making decisions that you cannot understand.'

'Maybe he is being too smart for you too, Dmytryk. Have you considered that? Have you asked yourself why this man who already makes billions without a single penny of anyone else's money suddenly runs to men like you for help?'

'Because he wants to make even more billions for himself.'

'Why? How much more does he need?'

Azarov laughed. 'How much does anyone need? It is not about need. It is about winning. It is about being the best. It's that way for all of us. The money is just the way we keep score.'

'Well, I hope you know what you are doing. I think you are making a terrible mistake, and you will live to regret it.'

'Oh, really?' sneered Azarov. 'And how would you prefer that I spend it? On more jewels and pretty dresses for you, my pampered darling? I suppose that's what you expect, after all. Your services have always come at a price.'

Her slap hit his face like a full stop at the end of the sentence.

'How dare you?' Alix hissed. 'I have never asked you for a penny. I earn my own money and pay my own bills. And what right have you, a petty thief from the gutters of Kiev, to look down on what I have had to do to survive?'

Azarov stepped towards her, raising his fist. The red mark left by her hand was clearly visible on his cheek.

Alix stood her ground. 'Go on, then,' she said raising her chin defiantly, presenting it as a target. 'Hit me. Show me what kind of a man you really are.'

Azarov stood for a moment with his arm raised, then took a step back, his breathing heavy and his lips white with a fury it was taking all his self-control to contain. They seemed to stare at one another for an age before he turned on his heel and strode to a console table on which was a telephone. He picked it up.

'Tell Connors to pack me an overnight bag. Now,' he commanded. 'I want my Ferrari brought to the front door immediately. And book me a suite at the Ritz . . . Yes, for tonight. Mrs Vermulen will be staying here.'

Azarov slammed the phone down, then turned to face Alix again.

'Satisfied?' he said.

Burlington, Ontario, Canada: six months earlier

The shoes were a statement of defiance. Classic black brogues by Luca del Forte, reduced from three hundred and fifty bucks to one-eighty at the Browns store in Mapleview Mall, right off the Queen Elizabeth Way. These were investment shoes, the kind that would never go out of style; shoes a man could treasure for years, feeling the leather mould itself around his foot, getting ever more comfortable as time went by. Kev Lundkvist was forty years old. He should have had decades to get those brogues just the way he liked them.

Kev didn't want to come home with nothing but presents for himself. He went along to the Swarovski crystal outlet and got his girlfriend, Alyson, a couple of little beagle figurines. They were cheesy as hell, but Kev knew that she would think they were cute. She'd stick them on her special shelf, right by her dressing table, and they'd make her think of him, every time she saw them.

He stopped off for coffee and a double-chocolate muffin. So by the time he left the mall it was dark. When he got outside, the wind off Lake Ontario whipped up the thin snowfall so that it almost stung when it hit his face. Ken had to stop and wipe his glasses clear just to see where he'd left his car, and it was while he was standing there, right in the middle of the parking lot but well off the main driveway, that he was hit by a speeding Nissan Frontier truck.

Kev was knocked right off his feet, and sent crashing into a parked SUV. His body ended up motionless on the ground, with his broken limbs splayed in unnatural angles around him. He was dead on arrival at Joseph Brant Hospital.

As for the Frontier, it slewed after impact and skidded on the slushy tarmac, but the driver managed to regain control and was racing for the exit before any of the other shoppers making their way to or from the mall had worked out what had just happened.

When it was found a couple of hours later on a residential street close to the Tyandaga Municipal Golf Course, the Frontier stank of whisky from the discarded bottle of Crown Royal, whose dregs had seeped into the carpet of the passenger-side footwell. A forensic search yielded no significant fingerprints. Detectives were disappointed, but not surprised, by the negative results. They'd already opened the glove compartment and found a crumpled receipt that indicated the truck had just been cleaned inside and out by a local company. The people there couldn't remember much about the guy who'd picked up the truck, but they did recall that he was wearing mitts. It was midwinter. Who wasn't?

The truck belonged to a contractor more than seven hundred kilometres away in Sault Sainte Marie. He'd reported it stolen four days earlier, and was in a bar with four of his men when the hit-and-run occurred. One of the guys had even posted a picture of them all on his Facebook site that same evening.

Someone had got drunk in a stolen truck and committed an act of homicide. But who that person might have been remained a total mystery.

'Don't feel too bad about it,' the pathologist reassured the detective in charge of the investigation when he handed over the post-mortem report. 'Lundkvist had Stage 3B liver cancer. There were a bunch of tumours in the liver itself, and it had spread into the lymph nodes around the organ as well. He didn't have too long to live: somewhere between six to nine months would be my guess. Twelve if he was very lucky. A quick end like this, well, I guess you could call it a small mercy.'

Saturday, 25 June

12

London N1

Grantham was woken at quarter to five in the morning by the ringing of his phone. The duty officer was on the line.

'You said I should call, no matter what time it was,' he said.

'I did, yes, but there's no need to sound so damn smug about it,' Grantham grunted, propping himself up on his elbows.

'Sorry, sir.'

'Well?'

'We found something, sir . . . a chap called Ahmad Razzaq. He's ex-ISI. Nothing very remarkable about him, just the standard rumours of links to al-Qaeda you get with anyone who's been in Pakistani intelligence. But he was flagged yesterday because he works with that American financier, Malachi Zorn. The one the ex-PM's now—'

'I know who Malachi Zorn is,' Grantham snapped. 'What does this Razzaq do for him?'

'Runs his personal security operation, which appears to be pretty extensive. I mean, it's not just bodyguard duty. Zorn effectively has his own private intelligence network.'

'So I gather. What was Razzaq doing in Mykonos?'

'Well, that's what we haven't yet worked out, sir. He came in on a private helicopter yesterday morning, and from his phone-traffic it looks as though he was talking a fair amount to people from that TV production company, the one that caused all the fuss at that restaurant.'

'Does Zorn have any interests in media or TV?'

'Not that we can see, sir, no.'

Grantham got out of bed, went downstairs to brew a very strong cup of tea, then made two more calls before getting dressed. The first was to Piers Nainby-Martin, telling him to shift the investigation into Malachi Zorn up a notch, paying particular attention to the life and times of Ahmad Razzaq.

The second call was to Samuel Carver.

'This is Grantham. I want a word with you.'

'Why?' The word was more of a heavy, lazy grunt. Carver had not been awake for long.

'Mykonos. I'm wondering why you were running away from that restaurant. And there's a Pakistani gentleman I think you might have met . . .'

There was silence down the line. The next time Carver spoke he sounded decisive and fully alert. 'I assume you're talking on an encrypted line?'

'Of course.'

'Right, then . . . can you get on the six forty-five BA flight out of Heathrow this morning?'

'Yes.'

'Then I'll see you by the Rousseau statue at ten. It's on its own little island, halfway across the Pont des Bergues. And Grantham . . .'

'Yes?'

'Tell me you've not been sat on your arse behind a desk for so long that you've forgotten all your fieldcraft.'

'You realize you're talking to the Head of the Secret Intelligence Service . . .'

'That's what I'm worried about.'

'Piss off, Carver. I'll be there. And I won't be followed.'

'Then we've got a date.'

'Seems like old times . . .'

Grantham put the phone down. He and Carver had always had a strong streak of mutual antagonism, mixed with a dash of grudging respect. Neither man was afraid to tell the other exactly what he thought. And so far that had been the basis of an unusual, highly unofficial, but productive working relationship.

He drove himself to the airport and used a personal card to buy the ticket when he got there. As he contemplated his in-flight breakfast, Grantham realized to his surprise that he was smiling. His professional life nowadays was essentially political: an endless round of meetings, committees and reports to ministers. It was good to get out in the field again. It felt like a day off.

13

The Old Town, Geneva

Carver made his way up on to the roof of his building and looked around. The Old Town of Geneva, based on a Roman settlement that dated back more than two thousand years, had originally been surrounded by high walls that kept invaders out, but also penned the town's citizens in. With land at a premium, and unable to expand outwards, they instead crammed their homes and businesses into tall buildings that were packed as tightly as possible into the confined space. So it was easy for Carver to make his way over the roofs of neighbouring structures to the far end of the block, and then down on to a street that ran at right angles to his own, completely out of sight of anyone watching his building.

Checking to see that no one was following, he made his way to the rue de la Corraterie, where he picked up a Number 3 bus over the Pont Bel-Air, across the River Rhône to the modern heart of the city. After a few blocks, he hopped out of that bus, crossed the street and got on to a Number 9 that went back across the river on the Pont du MontBlanc, the last bridge on the river before Lake Geneva itself. Carver took care to get a seat on the right-hand side of the bus. As it made its way slowly across the bridge he took out a pair of miniature binoculars and looked across the narrow expanse of water that separated the bridge he was on from Rousseau Island. There was the bronze statue of the great eighteenth-century philosopher, sitting on its stone plinth. And there, just a few metres away from it, was the familiar figure of Jack Grantham, a little stockier than he had been when Carver had last seen him, perhaps, with his hairline somewhat receded. But the air of impatience, a humming energy detectable even at a distance, was unmistakable. Carver scanned the area around Grantham and saw no one who looked remotely like a fellow MI6 agent or a hostile tail. A few minutes later, he had got off the bus, walked halfway across the Pont des Bergues and on to the little island, and was strolling towards Grantham.

They made their introductions. Grantham looked pointedly at his watch. 'It's seven minutes past ten,' he said. 'You're late.'

Carver ignored him. 'So what's the big deal about Mykonos?' he asked.

Grantham's fingers played over the screen of his iPhone. He handed it to Carver, showing him a photograph of a familiar face.

'Tell me what you know about this man,' Grantham said.

'He called himself Shafik, said he was ex-Pakistani intelligence,' Carver replied.

Grantham gave a satisfied little grunt, as if his expectations had been met. 'Well, that was half-right. His real name is Ahmad Razzaq, but he is, as he said, an ISI old-boy. Made quite a name for himself with our American cousins, helping them run Stinger missiles to the Mujahedin forces fighting the Soviets in Afghanistan. But, like so many of his colleagues, he kept on helping his old chums when they mutated into the Taliban, which didn't go down so well. Still, he's not in that game any more.'

'There was a woman, too – the one in the restaurant who pretended to get shot. She works for Shafik, or Razzaq, or whoever the hell he is. She gave her name as Magda Sternberg, but told me to call her Ginger. She's quite a piece of work. You should check her out, too. Could be interesting.'

'Maybe,' said Grantham, tapping a note into his phone. 'But back to Razzaq – what did he say he did for a living these days?'

'Security consultant for financial institutions.'

Grantham raised his eyebrows quizzically. 'Security consultant, eh? Now there's a job description that can mean almost anything.'

'I've done a bit of it myself.'

'My point exactly. And what was his interest in you?'

'What do you think?'

Something close to a smirk crossed Grantham's face. 'You know, for a man who keeps telling everyone how much he hates his work, you seem to have a hard time retiring.'

'He set me up. Got me on the hook for a murder charge. Sacrificed one of his own men to do it, too.'

'Unscrupulous bastard,' said Grantham admiringly. 'So who's the target?'

Carver paused for a moment before he replied, 'OK . . . I might as well tell you, since I have no intention of taking the job. He wanted me to take out an American, some kind of financial trader. The name he gave me was Malachi Zorn.'

Grantham frowned. His grey eyes looked at Carver with a new intensity. 'Zorn was the target?'

'That's what I just said, yes.'

'So why did Razzaq want him taken out?'

Carver shrugged. 'He said Zorn was costing his clients too much money. What's so unusual about that?'

'Simple . . . Ahmad Razzaq does not work for any financial institutions. He works for Malachi Zorn.'

Razzaq had lied. Well, that was to be expected. In Carver's world deceit was standard operating procedure; honesty was the real surprise. 'OK, then, Razzaq's some kind of double agent,' he said. 'Or he's been planted on the guy with the intention of getting rid of him – an inside job.'

'I doubt that,' said Grantham with a shake of his head. 'Razzaq's been with Zorn, at first as an occasional consultant, then as an employee, for almost five years. If he was only there to get rid of him, surely he'd have done it by now?'

'Unless someone has got to him recently.'

'I can't see why. Zorn pays very well. There'd be little financial incentive to betray him.'

'How about blackmail? A man like Razzaq is bound to have dirty secrets in his past.'

'And a man like Zorn is almost certain to know what they are already. Besides, I don't get the impression Zorn gives a damn about that kind of thing. He makes his own mind up and acts accordingly. He's not interested in social or political conventions, or what anyone else thinks – not unless he can make money from it. Razzaq could have wiped out whole villages or buggered orphans by the score; Zorn's not going to worry.'

'So that leaves only one possibility,' said Carver.

'What's that?' asked Grantham, frowning again in puzzlement.

'Simple: Razzaq is still working for Zorn. He's doing what Zorn wants.'

'Don't be ridiculous. Are you trying to tell me Malachi Zorn wants to die? The man has just set up an investment fund worth a minimum ten billion quid.'

'Yes, I know.'

'So you know he's coming to London for the big public launch party?'

'Yes.'

'Did you know that your old friend Alix is one of the guests?'

This time Carver really was caught off guard, unable to stop the momentary look of shock in his eyes. Grantham relished his discomfort, always glad of an opportunity to get one over on a man who had often got the better of him.

'Thought not,' he said.

'Doesn't make any difference,' Carver retorted. 'The party's not going to take place because Zorn has to be dead by then. Razzaq was very insistent about that. No way was Zorn going to make it to the party.'

Grantham frowned, his momentary triumph over Alix forgotten as he took in this new information. He looked out across the lake towards the Alps, as if seeking some answer hidden among the distant, snow-topped mountains. 'I'm sorry, maybe I'm missing something. What possible reason could there be for Malachi Zorn to come over all suicidal, now of all times?'

'I have no idea. And what's more, I don't care, because I'm not going to be the one that does it. I'm not taking the job.'

'Really? I thought you had no choice. You have a murder charge hanging over you.'

'That's happened to me before, in case you've forgotten,' said Carver. 'But I'm still here, aren't I? I'll deal with Razzaq, whoever he's working for.'

'About that murder charge ... the other one ...' Grantham began.

'What about it?'

'I have a file, you know. I compiled it in the months after you and I first met. Did a little digging around. Had some colleagues in France look through CCTV footage. Checked your movements, looked into a few Panamanian bank accounts and shell corporations, that kind of thing.'

'I can't say that surprises me,' said Carver.

'And although I never quite found a smoking gun – or should that be a shining laser? – I did put you there or thereabouts, as they say.'

'She died in an accident,' Carver replied flatly. 'There's been an inquest. It's official.'

'Oh, I agree. And there's nothing to be gained by raking over that old ground. But I'm sure you know what did for Al Capone. It wasn't the racketeering, or the corruption or even the Valentine's Day massacre—'

Carver completed the sentence: 'It was tax evasion.'

'Good,' nodded Grantham, 'I thought you'd get the point. The fact is, you've made a lot of money over the years, Carver, and you've paid sod all in tax. That's very antisocial. The Revenue would be most upset.'

'It's none of their business. I've not lived in the UK for years.'

'Come on, you're smarter than that. You've been paid money by lots of people in lots of different tax jurisdictions. Unless you've signed the appropriate forms, which I very much doubt, you will now owe tax, plus interest, in all those jurisdictions. That's a lot of pissed-off authorities. Once they start digging over your affairs and finding out who paid you the money, well, those'll be some seriously pissed-off clients. They'll want to shut you up. Not nice.'

'Unbelievable. First Razzaq, now you ... so much for my holiday.'

'That's life.'

'And don't tell me ... You can make all this grief go away if I do what you want. So what's that?'

'The same thing Razzaq wanted,' said Grantham, as if it were the most reasonable thing in the world. 'Tell him you'll assassinate Malachi Zorn.'

Carver contacted Razzaq within the hour and told him he was accepting the Zorn assignment. His conditions were straight-forward. Half the fee was to be paid up front to a Panamanian bank account. Carver would not start work unless and until he received notification from the bank that the funds had been received. He needed a detailed itinerary for every day and night of Zorn's visit to the UK, as well as registration numbers of the cars he would be using. Detailed plans should be supplied of both Zorn's residence and offices, including electric circuitry, plumbing, air conditioning and security systems. Once he had these, Carver would not make contact of any kind with Razzaq, and certainly not with Magda Sternberg, alias Ginger. The first that either of them would know of the hit would be when they heard about it on the news or witnessed it with their own eyes.

His terms were accepted in every respect. In return, Razzaq had only the two conditions he'd listed before, but he repeated them with special emphasis. 'It must be done before Friday, the first of July,' he said. 'And it must be public.'

14

Chinatown, London

Ahmad Razzaq operated on a strictly need-to-know basis. Although Ginger Sternberg was aware that Carver had been hired to assassinate Malachi Zorn, he saw no need whatever to explain the underlying thinking behind that, or any of the other tasks he had assigned her. Ginger, for her part, knew that she was not entirely trusted, and, although the gaps in her knowledge frustrated her, she did not resent Razzaq's caution. After all, she knew perfectly well that he was right to be that way. She was, indeed, entirely untrustworthy.

Before Carver had even left Mykonos, she had contacted another of her clients to inform them that he had been invited to assassinate Zorn. No sooner had Carver accepted Razzaq's offer than she confirmed the news. She was summoned at once to a meeting to discuss this new development. She made an excuse to Razzaq, and by Saturday evening she was in London, sitting in a small room above a dim sum joint in Gerrard Street, right in the heart of Chinatown, where the ends of the street are marked by red ceremonial gateways, the mini-supermarkets advertise their wares in Chinese script, and half the restaurants have ceremonial lion statues standing guard outside their doors.

Ginger was taking tea with a Chinese businessman. Like her, he was in his early forties, but, thanks to an unlined face and slender build, looked a least a decade younger. He was dressed for the weekend in Emporio Armani jeans and a lightweight summer cardigan, no shirt underneath. His name was Choi Deshi, though he now went by the westernized name Derek Choi. It was public knowledge, thanks to his regular appearances in gossip columns and glossy magazines – invariably with a beautiful woman on his arm – that Choi owned a number of successful restaurants and clubs, as well as a growing portfolio of retail and domestic property developments. It was less well known, however, that he had begun his career as a member of the unit known to native Chinese as Zhong Nan Hai Bao Biao, or 'the bodyguards from the Red Palace': the agents who protect the lives of China's most senior leaders. For the past dozen years, however, since his arrival in London and his swift climb up both its business and social strata, he had been what the Chinese term a 'deep-water fish': in other words, a foreign-based undercover agent of the Guoanbu, or State Security Ministry.

It was the Guoanbu that had supplied Choi with the seed money for his commercial empire, and they had also used him as the front-man for placing a two-billion-dollar investment in the Zorn Global fund. In Beijing's eyes, this was an extremely worthwhile invest-ment, both because there was a very good chance that Zorn would succeed in generating a massive return on their money, and because the methods by which he operated – principally aggressive, highly leveraged short trades that profited from economic downturns – were deeply damaging to western economies. The West might be unwilling to accept that it was in a fight to the death with China for domination of the next few hundred years of world history, but Beijing was very much at war.

Choi, like Razzaq, saw no need to share any of his underlying thinking with Ginger Sternberg. Just as she had only cared about the money he had offered her to keep him informed of Razzaq's activities, so his discussions with her never strayed far from the practical consequences of the information she provided.

'I presume you will supply me with a description and photographs of this man, Samuel Carver. But for now tell me this: how good are his chances of success?'

'Very good, in my opinion,' Ginger replied. 'After all, Zorn's own head of security is plotting to have him killed. He's bound to leave gaps in his boss's protection.'

'So you say, but you and I both know not to take anything at face value. Leave Razzaq to one side for the time being. How dangerous is Carver himself?'

'Extremely dangerous, that's why he was hired. He was a highly decorated officer in the British Special Boat Service, and his record as a private operative is outstanding. I assume your superiors know, even if you do not, that he was responsible for the death of President Gushungo in Hong Kong last year . . .'

She was pleased to see by his frown that this was news to Choi. She had the advantage over him for once, and wanted to rub it in: 'It happened on Chinese territory, after all.'

'I thought Gushungo was killed by jewel thieves,' Choi countered, his outward equilibrium swiftly restored. 'If I recall correctly, there were several million dollars' worth of uncut diamonds in the house. They disappeared at the time he was killed.'

'I am sure that is the impression Carver intended to give. But he now holds a five per cent stake in a mine sold to foreign investors by Gushungo's successor, President Patrick Tshonga. He didn't have to pay for those shares. They were his reward for a job well done.'

Choi looked thoughtful. Gushungo had been the dictatorial president-for-life of the southern African state of Malemba. Under his rule, a fertile country, rich in natural resources, had been reduced to a state of crippling poverty, barrenness and starvation.

When the nations of the West increasingly shunned the Gushungo regime on the grounds of its relentless disdain for its people's human rights, Beijing saw a vacuum to be exploited for its long-term advantage – and sought to cultivate a friendship with the old despot. With his death, and replacement by a democratic, UN-approved leader, that opportunity had been lost.

'If Carver killed Gushungo then he is certainly a man to be reckoned with. But he is also a man who has caused my government considerable inconvenience. If he kills Malachi Zorn and thereby wrecks his investment fund, he will have dealt us a second blow. That is clearly unacceptable.'

Ginger smiled. 'Yes, I would think so . . .'

'Has Carver revealed how he plans to undertake his mission?'

'No. He refused to have any further communication with Razzaq once the deal was agreed, and the initial fee deposited in his account. Razzaq put him under surveillance, of course, but he managed to lose the men who were tailing him. Since then, however, a delivery boy has been seen taking food to his apartment, so we assume he's in Geneva.'

'Unless that is a smokescreen.'

'Yes,' Ginger agreed, 'it could be. But he will certainly have to be in London some time tomorrow, I should think.'

'You do not know where he will be staying?'

'I'm sorry, no.'

'It does not matter. We will find him.'

'That may not be easy. He goes to great lengths to remain un-detected. His phone calls go through a number of relays and different numbers; he regularly uses satellite handsets so as to avoid the usual means of tracking via mobile network cells.'

'If he uses a satellite phone that only means that he can be pin-pointed with absolute precision.'

'If you have access to the satellites through which his calls are routed, yes.'

'My point exactly,' said Choi. 'So, we can assume he is some-where in London. What were the parameters of his assignment?'

'Primarily, to kill Zorn before the public launch of the Zorn Global fund.'

'Which is when?'

'Friday evening. It was also specified that the killing had to be public: something that couldn't be missed.'

'A news event . . .'

'Exactly.'

'I presume that you provided him with Zorn's itinerary. What public appearances is he making?'

'A few media appearances,' Ginger said. 'But those will be in closed studios, or within the grounds of the house Zorn has rented. Carver has the plans of the house, but I don't expect him to strike there.'

'Where do you think he will strike?'

'Wimbledon. Zorn is going to the tennis on Monday, Wednesday and Friday. I made a point of emphasizing that, and putting the idea firmly in Carver's head. He will certainly want to prepare his operation as well as he can in the limited time available, so I don't expect him to do anything until Wednesday.'

Choi nodded. 'I agree. This is already an extremely tight schedule. He will not want to rush it any more than he absolutely has to. That is how mistakes are made. So . . . Wednesday or Friday . . . thank you very much. That is very useful.'

'And my money?'

'Will be deposited in your account as always.'

'With a bonus if you succeed in killing Carver?'

'I don't believe I mentioned any such possibility.'

'Of course not.' Ginger fixed him with a brittle, humourless smile. 'You didn't have to. And I don't have to say that I will expect a success fee in the event that the attack on Zorn is prevented . . . However it's prevented.'

'Noted,' said Choi. 'And now I'm sure you must be busy. My people will show you out.'

Choi watched Ginger Sternberg as she left the room. She was undeniably attractive for a western woman, and it amused him to see the arrogance with which she used her sexuality, presuming that no man could resist her. It would, he thought, be enjoyable to turn the tables on her one day, so that she was the one who begged and pleaded. That had not, he imagined, happened very often in her life, if at all. She had great power, and it had corrupted her and made her lazy, very much like the West itself. Both would be made to grovel.

First though, he had to deal with Samuel Carver. It would give him great face if he were seen to dispose of a man who had been the cause of such irritation. He would, of course, seek guidance from Beijing, but he had no doubt what his instructions would be. Samuel Carver had to die so that Malachi Zorn might live. And he, Choi Deshi, would personally ensure that the task was accomplished to his superiors' satisfaction and his own personal glory.

15

The Old Town, Geneva

Carver spent the twenty-four hours following his deal with Razzaq deep in thought. He ran through possible identities and disguises; spent hours memorizing the junctions and landmarks on key roads; compared a number of indoor and outdoor locations; and considered all the many different ways of ending a human life at his disposal.

For a while he even toyed with the idea of sabotaging the private jet that would carry Zorn from New York to London. The timing was crazy, though: it would mean hiring a jet of his own to cross the Atlantic in order to reach Zorn's plane before it took off. It was too soon, anyway. He and Grantham alike both needed to know more about what Zorn was up to. And Carver needed flexibility, a little wriggle room in case he had a sudden change of plans. Nothing about this job felt right, and he had no intention of getting caught with his pants down if Razzaq, Zorn, or some other player as yet unknown started changing the rules of the game.

He ended up concentrating his attention on Wimbledon,

searching out every piece of information he could find about the All England Club and the suburban townscape that surrounded it. Looking at the aerial views of the tennis complex, and correlating them with the official maps available on the tournament website, he noticed an entrance gate on Somerset Road, just behind the press and broadcast centres. It was not listed among the spectator gates, and seemed to be an access point for trucks servicing the tournament's insatiable demand for food, drink and merchandizing. To the left of the gate, the road disappeared into the mouth of a tunnel. It didn't take long to discover that this led to an unloading bay below Number One Court before rising back up to an exit on to Church Road, on the far side of the club. Carver reckoned there had to be some way of distributing all the deliveries from the unloading bay to the places where they were needed without interfering with the crowds above ground. That meant more, and smaller tunnels. So now he had the possibility of underground ways into, out of and around the All England Lawn Tennis Club.

He also looked into the debenture tickets Zorn had bought. Their original owners had paid £27,750 for the right to buy a Centre Court ticket for every day of the Championships over five years (Number One Court debentures cost roughly half the price for the same period.) They were the only Wimbledon seats that were legally transferable, and could be sold at any price the market would bear. With each seat came perks: a dedicated entrance to the show courts, private bars, restaurants and so on. If Zorn had these tickets, Carver had to have them, too. He phoned a ticket agency.

'We can do you a debenture ticket. When do you need it?' the man from the agency asked.

'Monday, Wednesday and Friday.'

There was a soft whistle. 'Blimey, that'll cost you. I mean, the best price we've got for the men's semis on Friday is, hang on . . . $6,758. In pounds that's—'

'Don't bother, I'll take it,' said Carver. 'And I'll take the other two days. And I want Number One and Number Two Courts as well, all three days.'

Now the whistle became a chuckle as the agency man worked out what he was about to sell. 'You planning to be in three places at once?'

'I'm planning to be wherever I need to be.'

'Fair enough, but there's a problem, yeah? They don't do debentures for Number Two Court. So there ain't no tickets on sale for that.'

'Yes, there are.'

'No, there's not. See, that's not legal.'

'I'm sure it's not,' said Carver. 'But if I'm willing to pay the same price for Number Two Court tickets as for Centre Court ones, I reckon someone will want to sell me them. I'll pay cash, if necessary. So, can you help me?'

'Well, obviously, selling you them tickets is a criminal offence, as such . . .' There was a pause and Carver could sense the battle between greed and fear going on in the man's mind. Eventually, as he thought it would, greed won.

'I'll see what I can do.'

It would take Carver most of Saturday night to finish his planning. But first he wanted to know more about the business his target was in. His financial affairs were handled through a private bank in Geneva. It placed customer service at the very top of its priorities. So when Carver called his personal manager, Timo Koenig, and asked him if he could spare an hour or so for a drink, the fact that this was a Saturday evening did not deter Koenig – openly at least – from saying yes.

'Great, meet me at seven in the bar of the Beau Rivage,' said Carver.

The Beau Rivage was an old-fashioned grand hotel on the banks of Lake Geneva. It had been quite a while since Carver had visited it. The last time, also, he'd had a meeting with a bank manager, and he'd been with Alix. Things hadn't worked out too well for them that night. Carver saw no need to tell Koenig about it . . . let alone how much worse they'd worked out for the banker.

16

Hôtel Beau Rivage, Geneva

Carver bought the drinks. A beer for himself and a martini for Koenig, a well-preserved fifty-year-old, kept trim by tennis and skiing, whose idea of casual weekend attire consisted of immaculately pressed jeans, a Ralph Lauren polo shirt, and a cotton jumper so crisp and clean that that it appeared to have only just been unwrapped from the store tissue paper. Carver had not shaved all day, and he'd seen no reason to change before he went out. He felt like a vagabond by comparison, but that didn't bother him in the slightest. 'What do you know about a man called Malachi Zorn?' he asked.

'Not a great deal,' said Koenig. 'I have never had any reason to do business with him. But he made his fortune shorting Lehman's, no?'

'You tell me. How does a guy like this work? For example, you say he shorted Lehman's. I know that means he bet against them. But how?'

'Mm . . . good martini,' said Koenig, savouring his drink before answering the question: 'CDSs . . . sorry, credit default swaps . . .'

'Which are what, exactly?' Carver asked.

'A credit default swap is a way that an investor can make money out of someone else's loss. You might say it is an insurance policy taken out on something you do not necessarily own.'

Less than a minute into the conversation, and already Carver felt like he'd walked into an alternative universe. 'That sounds like me taking out insurance on your car. Why would I want to do that?'

Koenig smiled, as though what he was describing was the most normal thing on earth. 'Well, you might decide that was a good investment if you knew that I was a terrible driver who was almost certain to crash.'

'Or if I knew I could make you crash . . .' Carver said.

Koenig clearly thought he was joking. 'Ah, well, that would be cheating!'

'If you say so.'

'In any case, a default swap is just like a regular insurance policy,' Koenig continued. 'You buy a certain amount of cover for a fixed premium, over a given period – usually ten years – and it pays out in the event of loss. The premium is often very low. If you wanted to take out a credit default swap on a very safe, AAA-rated corporate bond, for example, it might only cost you fifteen thousand dollars a year for ten million dollars of coverage. So your downside is fixed: over the course of a decade the maximum you will ever spend is a hundred and fifty thousand dollars. But if the company collapses and its bonds become worthless, then you will make ten million dollars. Those are very good odds. And because the length of the term is so long, a default swap is very useful when you are sure that a collapse of some kind will occur at some point, but you don't know exactly when.'

'But what's in it for the other guy, the one who's selling?' Carver asked.

'Ah, well, he gets a guaranteed income, based purely on a promise,' said Koenig, to whom this was clearly a perfectly reasonable proposition. 'He does not have to spend any money of his own.

He just collects your premium every year for ten years, and hopes that he never has to pay out. In most cases, he will be right. He will end up with a hundred and fifty thousand dollars for doing absolutely nothing. But sometimes, particularly in times of crisis, an unexpected, apparently impossible, failure occurs and he loses his bet. The market was certain that Lehman's was safe, because it was too big to fail, and so it was very cheap for Monsieur Zorn to buy billions of dollars of credit default swaps. When Lehman Brothers collapsed, he collected those billions, and, of course, the banks that had sold him those swaps lost the billions they had to pay him.'

'That wouldn't make him too popular.'

'Not if he did it more than once, certainly,' Koenig agreed. 'A bank is like a casino. The management do not mind the occasional jackpot. That encourages the other gamblers. But if someone creates a system for winning, and gets the jackpot again and again . . . well, then they are asked to leave the casino.'

'Yes . . . and they aren't always asked politely,' said Carver. 'So these swaps, are they the only way Zorn makes his money?'

'I had no idea you were taking such an interest in finance, Sam. May I ask why you are so fascinated by Malachi Zorn in particular?'

'His name came up in conversation.'

Koenig gave Carver the chance to say more, accepted that no further information would be forthcoming, and then smiled as he said, 'You are very discreet. You would have made an excellent Swiss banker! OK . . . get me another martini and I will try to explain.'

Carver bought a second round of drinks and settled back for Koenig's tutorial.

'So, Zorn . . . Well, I imagine he's using a great many different financial vehicles. His aim, though, will always be to leverage his money to the greatest possible extent, so that he gets the maximum possible return.'

'The impression I got was that he bets on failure most of the time,' Carver said.

'In that case, another way to go is "put" options. Basically, that gives him the right to sell a quantity of a stock or a bond at a particular price, on or before a particular date. So, imagine a company that is doing well. Its shares cost ten dollars, and the price is very solid, very steady . . . But for some reason, Zorn thinks to himself, "These shares are overvalued, they must crash. Soon they will be worth much less." So he buys the option to sell these shares at eight dollars. Financial institutions will sell Zorn these options, because they see no reason for this price to go down. If they are right, the price holds steady, and Zorn loses all the money he has spent buying the options. But if the share crashes – say to three dollars a share – Zorn exercises his options, sells at eight dollars, and pockets five dollars a share profit.'

'Which the bank has to pay for?'

'Effectively, yes.'

'So what is Zorn paying for these options?'

'Ah, Sam, that is a very complicated question . . . But it can be reduced to a pair of very simple elements: time and risk. The greater these are, the more an option costs. Imagine, for example, that you want to buy "put" options on the price of a house, betting that its value will decrease. A six-month option on a house made of straw will cost you much more than a week-long option on a house made of brick.'

'Unless you know that the big bad wolf has a wrecking ball.'

'Precisely . . . in any market, exclusive information is the most valuable commodity of all.'

Carver took a long drink of his beer, using the time to get his head around what he had just learned. 'You know, what I really don't get about any of this,' he said, putting his drink back down on the table, 'is what's the point of it all?'

'It's business. It makes money. What other point does it need?'

'But it doesn't make money, does it?' Carver pointed out. 'You said it yourself. Every time there's a winner on a trade, someone else loses the exact same amount. So nothing new is created. Oh, no . . . wait . . . Something tells me that if a trader does a deal to sell one of those swaps, or "put" options, he puts that down as new business and he gets a slice of that business as his bonus. Am I right?'

'Sure,' Koenig agreed. 'Bankers' pay is based on a percentage of the profits they generate, so yes, in theory . . .'

Carver was feeling the excitement that comes when you suddenly get an insight into something new. 'OK . . . so then a couple of years go by and – uh-oh – turns out that swap was a bad idea. Lehman's go bust. Now that swap Zorn bought has cost millions, even billions . . . does the guy who sold the swap, or the option or whatever it was, pay for that loss? No, of course he bloody doesn't! He probably doesn't even work at the same place any more. But the bank certainly has to pay.'

'Of course, it comes off the balance sheet.'

'Exactly! So the bank's profits fall, or maybe it makes a loss. Either way its shares lose value, so the shareholders lose money . . . and those shareholders are mostly pension funds who invest the money for ordinary people who don't have a clue about any of this. So now those pensions are worth less . . . and basically what's happened is that poor people have lost money so that rich idiots can gamble with their cash and never have to take any of the losses themselves.' Carver shook his head in surprise. 'Razzaq was right, after all . . .'

'I'm sorry, who is Razzaq?'

'Someone I was talking to. He said Malachi Zorn's deals ultimately made ordinary people poorer. And he was right. He just forgot to mention that all those other bastards' deals have exactly the same effect.'

Koenig laughed nervously, trying to defuse the intensity in the air. 'Calm down, Sam, really . . . I have never seen you like this before. My God, it's a good thing you don't have a gun on you right now. This bar is full of investment bankers. You might try to shoot someone!'

'Yes,' said Carver. 'I just might.'

Custer County, Nebraska: six months earlier

Seen from the air, the valley that stretches to the north-west of the town of Broken Bow looks like the remains of tiles on a crumbling wall. The mottled, dusty-brown and olive-green earth is dotted with perfectly square fields, in which sit circular splashes of emerald caused by the rotating water sprayers that irrigate the cultivated land thereabouts. The dusty, dead-straight roads that bisect the flat valley floor even criss-cross one another like grouting.

Of course, that's only in the summertime, when the corn is growing. In the middle of winter, the rock-hard earth is as dark as bitter chocolate, dusted with sugar-white snow. Jed Rogers grew corn on land that ran along County Route 92, land that his father and grandfather had farmed before him. He had been a local celebrity for the best part of twenty-five years, ever since his final two years at high school, when he'd quarterbacked the Broken Bow Indians football team and been voted Homecoming King. Maryjane Rogers had been his pretty blonde queen. The eldest of their three children, Jed Jnr, was only in his sophomore year at Broken Bow High, but already folks were saying he'd inherited all his daddy's talent and more besides. And his two little sisters were just as cute and pretty as their mom. The Rogerses were a popular family, good people. They worshipped at the First Presbyterian Church, and never missed a Sunday service. They contributed generously to local charities, and Maryjane was the kind of PTA stalwart who could always be counted on to help out at school events or bake a tray of cookies at a moment's notice.

Custer County, like much of rural Nebraska, has less than half the population it did a century ago. There are barely eleven thousand souls spread across its two and a half thousand square miles. In a place like Broken Bow, people know one another and lend a helping hand when they can. So when Jed Rogers was found in his barn, with the back of his head blown off by the shotgun he'd placed in his mouth, his death was not officially noted as a suicide, but as an accident. No one wanted Maryjane and the kids to lose the insurance money. And it wasn't as if the insurance company had really been cheated or anything. Jed Rogers was suffering from Huntington's disease. There was no hope of a cure. All he'd done was spare his family the pain and expense of caring for him as his mind slowly decayed into dementia and his fine, strong body fell apart.

Sometimes it was right and proper to turn a blind eye to the truth.

Sunday, 26 June

17

Lambeth, London SE1 and Chinatown

Carver flew to London on Sunday, taking the 12.15 a.m. British Airways flight. He had no intention of staying anywhere that required payment by credit card, so Grantham had arranged a one-bed apartment for him: a safe house halfway between Waterloo Station and the Imperial War Museum, a couple of miles from MI6 headquarters.

'I'm sorry if it's not your usual style,' said Grantham, sarcastically. 'The public-spending cuts have shot our interior-design budget to pieces.'

Carver had been in some pretty rough billets in his time. His sanity had been all but destroyed in a blinding white torture chamber. But this place took some beating for sheer, gut-churning awfulness. The walls and woodwork had been painted in borstal tones of rancid cream, murky green and excremental brown. The windowless bathroom had grime-encrusted units surrounded by floor-to-ceiling tiles that gave all the warmth and comfort of a municipal public toilet. Carver did not feel housed so much as institutionalized.

'I'm going to take pictures and tell my decorator to give me just the same effect at home,' he replied.

'Just as soon as you've sorted out Malachi Zorn,' said Grantham.

'Yes,' replied Carver. 'Just as soon as that.'

Thanks to technicians in Beijing, who had hacked into the systems through which Carver placed his calls, Derek Choi had been able to have his target tracked from the moment he landed at Heathrow to his arrival at the surprisingly modest apartment where he was staying. This was, Choi noted, situated on the top floor of a development shaped like a hollow square. Vehicle access was only possible through a single arched entrance, and the apartment, which had windows on two sides, overlooked both the road that ran up to the arch and the inner courtyard to which it led. Access to the place was via an external door, followed by a narrow flight of stairs that led up to the front door of the flat itself. It was, in other words, a very easily defended position, and though it would be possible to overwhelm Carver by sheer weight of numbers, the casualties that would be sustained, plus the time that such an attack might take and the unwanted attention it would inevitably attract, made it unrealistic to hit him there.

Another unexpected problem had also arisen. A second man had accompanied Carver to the apartment, and then left alone. Photographs of this man appeared to identify him as John Morley 'Jack' Grantham, the Head of the British Secret Intelligence Service. This raised an obvious question: why would such a senior official be acting as an accessory to the assassination of a prominent American? Had Grantham gone rogue? Or had the British identified the threat to their economy posed by Malachi Zorn and decided to remove him by covert means? Both these matters required further consideration, and it would also be necessary to consider the possible consequences of eliminating Carver if he were, in fact, a British asset with highly influential connections. Choi was therefore given instructions to maintain the closest possible watch on Carver, but not to take any further action until ordered to do so. In the meantime, however, he was to prepare detailed plans for Carver's elimination. So far as both Choi and his masters were concerned, this was just a postponement: the fundamental need to kill Samuel Carver before he killed Malachi Zorn remained as pressing as ever.

18

Carn Drum Farm, the Cambrian Mountains, Ceredigion, Wales

Dave Smethurst plunged his hand into a large plastic bin filled with icing sugar. He lifted it up again, letting the bright white grains slide through his fingers. 'Almost any kind of weapon you can think of can be improvised if you know how,' he mused as he looked at his now empty palm. 'That's why that whole de-militarization process in Northern Ireland was such bollocks. PIRA were laughing their heads off.'

'PIRA?' asked Brynmor Gryffud.

'Provisional IRA. They knew, and we knew, they could make everything again for themselves the next day. Take this icing sugar. Bags of energy in it, and exceptionally small particles, see? That means it actually coats that stuff over there, the ammonium nitrate,' he nodded at a pile of garden fertilizer bags, 'in a very fine powder. That aids the reaction between the two of them. If we mix this properly, you're going to end up with an explosive more powerful than military-grade TNT.'

Smethurst was not an idealist. This was just another job to him, a means to make a few bob from the skills he had acquired as an ammunition technician, Class 1. That was the unassuming name given to any soldier who was qualified to test and maintain all forms of army ordnance – from rifle clips to anti-aircraft missiles – and, more importantly, to deal with all types of explosives. After six months of initial training at the Army School of Ammunition, followed by an upgrading course two or three years later, an AT Class 1 knew everything worth knowing about all the various ways of making things go bang. He was equally qualified to make a bomb of his own, or dispose of someone else's. In a twenty-year career in the forces Dave Smethurst had done his time in the streets of Belfast and Basra before spending his last six months in Helmand Province, Afghanistan, disarming Taliban bombs with the sweat streaming down his back and bullets smacking into the dirt tracks and stone walls all around him. The way he saw it, he'd given his country everything he owed it, and then some. From now on he was looking after number one.

He and Gryffud were standing in an old hay barn on Carn Drum Farm, thirteen hundred acres of bleak but spectacularly beautiful Welsh uplands about ten miles south-east of Tregaron, in the county of Ceredigion, that had been in the Gryffud family for generations. The land hereabouts was traditionally used for sheep farming, forestry and field sports. There were black and red grouse nesting on the hillsides, and salmon, sea trout and brown trout in the rivers and pools that watered the valleys between them. More than one local businessman had told Gryffud that he could double his income if he opened the farm up for corporate shooting and fishing parties.

Gryffud had always refused. He was adamantly opposed to blood sports, and would not even keep sheep, preferring to let the grazing land revert from grass to the heather that naturally flourished there. He funded the estate with a combination of environmental grants, holiday lets of the old farmworkers' cottages, and guided walking tours for ramblers and birdwatchers: the red kites that soared above the landscape with their beautiful russet, black and white plumage always had the twitchers purring with delight.

The recent arrival of a party of eight guests had caused no comment from any of the locals who had happened to see them driving towards Carn Drum. They were only too happy if Big Bryn could make some money from his farm. Better it stay in the hands of a local boy, even if he did spend far too much of his time in London, than be bought by a foreigner. They might have felt rather differently, however, had they known what was going on there on this particular weekend.

The group's three female members were hard at work, mixing the sugar and fertilizer with which Dave Smethurst had been toying. They were following two different recipes, each involving slightly different proportions of the two ingredients. One was designed to burn as an extremely high-energy fuel. The other was the explosive. The work was delicate. A single spark would be enough to blow the barn and everyone in it sky-high. So the three women had been working in an atmosphere of fierce, near-silent concentration, an atmosphere that was shattered as one of the trio looked up at Gryffud, grinned, and said, 'Hey, baby, have you been talking about how to spend my money?'

Her name was Uschi Kremer. The heiress to a Swiss industrialist's vast fortune, she was both the source of the group's funds and the motivating force that had taken them from conventional acts of protest to the brink of violent action. Her gentle but relentless pressure had steered Gryffud away from his traditional, harmless acts of attention-seeking towards something far more extreme. And when the final decision to act had been made, she had even managed to persuade him that it had all been his idea. Her behaviour, though, was casual to the point of indifference. This morning, for example, she had appeared twenty-four hours after everyone else, without apology for her late arrival, secure in the knowledge that they literally could not afford to do without her.

Gryffud forced a smile. 'Have no fear, Uschi, we won't waste a penny of your cash.'

'I don't care if you do.' She laughed. 'It was all made by thieves and bastards anyway!'

'If you don't give it one, I fucking will,' Smethurst muttered beneath his breath.

Gryffud gave a grunt of disapproval. There was no denying Kremer was as hot as the fiery red hair that was now all but hidden by her simple cotton scarf. There wasn't a scrap of make-up on her face, and she was dressed in a simple khaki T-shirt and jeans. But the way those cheap clothes clung to every one of her body's long, slender curves was as revealing as the most elegantly cut designer gown. Her freckled skin glowed with a tan acquired on a short break in the Mediterranean. 'I took the family jet,' Uschi had teased, knowing how annoyed Gryffud would be. 'But don't worry. I bought a few more thousand hectares of jungle to make up for it.'

Every man on the farm was affected by her presence at a primal, pheremonal level. They worked that bit harder, spoke more assertively and laughed more loudly in her presence. The other two women knew, and resented it. The result was an atmosphere of sexual tension that was dangerously volatile: a potentially fatal distraction from their mission.

'Keep up the good work,' Gryffud said distractedly, and went off with Smethurst to the tractor shed, fifty metres away across the farmyard, where the four other male group-members were at work.

The shed had been split into three discrete zones. In one a collection of thirty-two high-pressure gas-cylinders had been lined up in two groups. Fourteen of the cylinders were the size of large domestic calor-gas tanks: roughly 120 cm tall with a 36 cm diameter. The other eighteen were small enough to fit inside them. One of the men was working with a plasma torch, cutting off both ends of the larger cylinders so as to transform them into open tubes. The smaller cylinders merely lost their bases.

At the next workstation two group-members were constructing a crude steel framework, split into twelve compartments – four long by three wide – like an oversized wine rack. Each compartment was big enough to take one of the large cylinders, with a little room to spare. The whole structure was about as big as a coffin, but twice as deep.

The fourth member of the group was perched on the roof of a white Toyota Hiace camper van that looked far older than its X-registration plates suggested. He, too, had a plasma torch, and was using it to cut a large rectangular hole in the vehicle's roof. The concrete floor behind the van was piled with the cupboards, bed, cooking gear and chemical toilet that had been stripped from its now-empty interior. Only the old window curtains remained, discreetly drawn to prevent anyone looking in.

Every single one of the Vehicle Identification Number stickers and tags scattered about the camper van had been located and either removed or rendered illegible. The plates belonged to a completely different car that had been bought at auction two weeks earlier, disposed of, and then reported stolen.

'This is another old PIRA trick,' said Smethurst, looking at the scene before him. 'The way they hit 10 Downing Street is the way we're going to blow a large hole in Pembrokeshire.'

Back at the hay barn, Uschi Kremer sighed theatrically. 'I need a cigarette,' she said.

'Not here!' one of the other women cried in alarm. 'You'll kill us all.'

Kremer laughed. 'Thanks, but I'd already worked that out for myself! Don't worry. I will make sure I am much too far away to set fire to anything here. Would either of you care to join me?'

The other two grimaced. Neither woman smoked, and if there was a choice between watching Uschi Kremer have a cigarette or having a good talk about her behind her back, they both knew which they preferred.

Kremer knew it, too. 'Please yourselves,' she said with a sly smirk.

Five minutes later and four hundred metres away, she got out her phone and speed-dialled Derek Choi's number. 'It's me,' she said. 'I just wanted to let you know that everything is going well.'

'Are you confident that these people are capable of executing their plan?'

'Yes. The planned initiative far exceeds what would be required to create the desired effect. If we only achieve a twenty-five per cent success-rate, that will still have a major effect. If the rate is one hundred per cent … well, then there will be a fireworks display that the whole world will see.'

'We Chinese invented fireworks, of course,' said Derek Choi.

'I promise you never saw fireworks like these,' Uschi Kremer replied.

Beverly Hills, California: five months earlier

In the luxuriously appointed office of his surgical suite, its walls lined with framed certificates proclaiming his medical proficiency, and large colour photographs illustrating his artistry with a scalpel, Dr Arpad Karvakian was dictating a letter to his personal assistant Sherilyn, who was herself a walking advertisement for his work.

'I am sure you will agree that the operation has been a complete success,' he said. 'Do not be alarmed ... no, forget that, it'll only alarm him ... do not be concerned ... yeah, that's better, concerned that, ah, there is considerable bruising under the eyes and swelling to the forehead, nose and jaw. This is an inevitable result of surgery, and will subside considerably over the next six weeks. Any remaining swelling ... no, any small amount of remaining swelling, will disappear entirely within four to six months. The surgery involved some reduction of the bossed area of the skull across the brow, implants to the cheekbones and also reshaping of the jawbone and chin. These procedures, as well as the mid-facelift, may impact upon nerves in the affected areas, causing a degree of numbness. Again, this is completely normal, and the regular range of sensations will gradually return over time. In general, the healing process appears to be going exactly as I would expect, and provided that all the protocols I have suggested are observed there is no reason to be concerned in any way. I hope you agree that the results are everything you desired. Yours ... etc. Got that?'

'Uh-huh,' Sherilyn replied. 'But I still don't understand. This was the guy with the cancer, right ... ?'

Karvakian nodded in confirmation.

'So what's he doing having his face fixed, when he's not going to live long enough to enjoy it?'

'I don't know, sweetheart. Maybe he's hoping that death won't recognize him when the time comes.'

Sherilyn giggled. 'Or maybe he just wants to look cute at the funeral.'

6, Gresham Street, London EC2: the following day

The Wax Chandlers' Hall has stood on the same site in the City of London since 1501. Originally built as the home of the Worshipful Company of Wax Chandlers – the merchants who sold the fancy beeswax candles used in royal palaces and aristocratic stately homes – it was burned down in the Great Fire of London, bombed out in the Blitz and rebuilt five times in total. The wax chandlers don't shift so many candles these days, but they do good business renting out their hall for business meetings, product launches, parties and receptions, along with every type of food and drink any client could require, from elevenses to a banquet.

On a freezing afternoon in late January, with the pavements crusted in hard-packed snow and more falls forecast overnight, an elegantly dressed Indian businessman arrived for an appointment with a senior member of the hall's management staff. His card gave his name as Sanjay Sengupta. He explained that he represented the interests of a very prominent, but very discreet Bangalore-based industrialist, specializing in computer manufacturing and software, who was interested in establishing a European base in London. A firm of City headhunters would soon be hired to find candidates for key executive positions in this new venture. They would come up with a shortlist of individuals whom Mr Sengupta's client would interview in person in late June or early July, when he was in any case planning to be in England for social reasons. To this end, he wished to hire the entire Wax Chandlers' Hall for three full days, evenings included.

'My principal will not be requiring more than very light refreshments for himself, his assistants and the interview candidates,' Mr Sengupta explained. 'He appreciates, however, that this will cause you considerable loss. He is therefore willing to compensate you. Let us assume that the profit margin for yourselves and your caterers is thirty per cent. We will pay you, in addition to the hire cost of the building itself, thirty per cent of the full

cost of food and drink, lunch and dinner included, for one hundred people.'

There is, of course, no such thing as a free lunch, particularly in the catering trade. So when a slick operator acting for an unnamed client suggests a deal of improbable generosity, requiring minimal effort from those who will be paid, suspicions are bound to be aroused. Sengupta, however, was able to provide copious references in India, the UK and the US. When he paid half the total cost up front, the money went through without any problems at all. After all, the days when India required British aid were long gone. Indian entrepreneurs today owned Jaguar and Land Rover cars, Typhoo tea and almost all of the UK's steel production. If one of their number wanted to hire a City hall, who could possibly object?

Monday, 27 June

19

Long Island, New York, and Wentworth, Surrey, south-east England

Malachi Zorn left Italy immediately after his dinner party and headed back to the States. He'd agreed to be the subject of the next edition of *HARDtalk*, BBC World's interview show, and the producer wanted to tape the conversation with him on Zorn's own territory. So the interview took place in the office of his house on Lily Pond Lane.

It went well, and Zorn spent less than thirty-six hours at home before flying to London, landing at Farnborough. The airport is thirty-five miles south-west of London, but only thirteen miles from the Wentworth Estate in Virginia Water, Surrey, a development of luxury homes scattered around the famous Wentworth Club and its three golf courses. Zorn had rented a newly built mansion there, valued at fifteen million pounds, for the summer. As he was driven past the wrought-iron gates and along the curving driveway that led to the front door Zorn grimaced. The building possessed exactly the kind of showy extravagance he most despised, from the classical portico that attempted to give its facade the grandeur of a stately home, to the shiny marble floors that were as vulgar as a Baghdad brothel and as slippery as an ice-rink. But it looked like the kind of place where a man of his wealth should reside, and that alone would serve to reassure both the media and his investors.

He went to bed early, taking an Ambien to counteract the jet lag, then rose at four in the morning. Half an hour later he was in the study, sitting before an array of screens that were an exact replica of the ones in his office back home in East Hampton. One of the screens was linked to a live TV feed. At 4.30 a.m. London time, the week's first showing of his *HARDtalk* interview began. The host, Stephen Sackur, began by taking Zorn through a brief account of his early life and more recent business success. Then, about halfway through the conversation, he turned to the new fund.

'Can you tell us what your investment strategy will be?' Sackur asked.

Zorn laughed. 'Nice try, but you know I can't do that! Would the chief executive of Coca-Cola tell you the secret recipe? But I guess I can give you an idea of the way I see events panning out in a few key areas.'

Sackur's high forehead wrinkled in an earnest, slightly puzzled-looking frown. 'What kind of areas?'

'Well, Stephen, it's no secret that I gave evidence before a congressional committee a few months back, and that I warned of the dangers posed by large-scale eco-terrorism. I guess I hoped that I could send out a warning to oil companies, utilities and public authorities to be more vigilant. But that didn't seem to work so well . . . Can't win 'em all, I guess.'

'Maybe the threat is not as great as you fear?'

'Sure, that's a possibility. But I'm not buying it. My belief is that terrorism is a business like any other. When one guy comes up with something that works – you know, that gives him a competitive advantage – all the other guys have to play catch-up. That's how ideas spread, how markets evolve. Well, the various Islamic forces around the world have been the market leaders in terror for the past ten to fifteen years. From a terrorist point of view things like suicide bombs, IEDs—'

'Improvised explosive devices, like the ones used in Afghanistan . . .' Sackur interjected, for his audience's benefit.

'Exactly . . . the use of passenger jets as weapons of mass destruction . . . all these have been incredibly effective innovations.'

'That almost sounds as though you approve of them.'

'Not at all. I'm no friend of Al-Qaeda, believe me. I'm just stating a fact. These methods have achieved the aims all terrorists share: to kill, attract publicity, create an atmosphere of panic and fear and to force governments into, ah, excessive countermeasures that end up harming the exact same liberties we're all trying to protect. So it figures that other people who are hostile to the West and what it stands for – democracy, consumer capitalism, continuous growth, all that good stuff – will pick up on these terror methods and start using them, too.'

'And you think that ecological campaigners will start to do this?'

Sackur's voice contained a note of scepticism. Zorn, however, chose to ignore it.

'Sure.'

'And are you putting your money, and your clients' money where your mouth is?' Sackur asked.

'Absolutely,' said Zorn, relishing the effect that his words would have, and knowing that there was much more to come. 'I can tell you that I've taken a number of short positions that reflect my opinions.'

'I'm sure investors will be very interested to hear that. So let's cover another subject on which I'm sure they will welcome your insight. This week you'll be coming to the UK. What is your view of the state of the British economy? The government is pursuing policies that have attracted support from some commentators and business leaders, but also tremendous opposition from trade unions and special interest groups, as well as their political opponents. Where do you stand?'

Zorn's shrug conveyed an impression of relaxed impartiality. 'I don't stand anywhere politically. To be honest with you, Stephen, I'm not interested in political parties or ideology. I'm interested in situations as I see them, and the opportunities that confront me. But just to pick up on my earlier comments, I guess if I were talking to the British Prime Minister I'd advise him to take a real good look at the security of his national energy supplies. The UK is very vulnerable to external disruptions. Power-generating capacity has been allowed to decline drastically, relative to need. Plus, for political reasons the UK is way overcommitted to wind-power, which strikes me as just about the dumbest idea imaginable. I mean, the wind stops and you're screwed . . . ah, can I say that?'

Sackur grimaced. 'Not really, but—'

'Well, anyway . . . the UK has to import most of its oil, its natural gas and increasingly its electrical power, which is cabled in from France. I mean, come on! Check out the history you have with the French. Are you sure you want their hand on the light switch?' Zorn laughed engagingly, drawing a smile out of Sackur before adopting a much more serious expression again. 'But that's the story all over. British Energy, the nuclear power station operator, was sold to Electricité de France. A consortium of German companies is building four more nukes. And the designs they're using will be either French or Japanese. So basically you've lost national control of your own power grid. To me that's a disastrous situation. Britain is wide open to its very own 9/11, and when that attack comes, it—'

'Not "if" it comes?'

'No, Stephen, I believe that this is a case of "when", and any major terrorist event will have consequences that go way beyond the actual incident itself. I can see major falls on the Footsie, led by the energy sector, instability in the price of oil, downward pressure on sterling, and knock-on effects in all the nations that have bought into the UK energy market. With the economic situation as fragile as it is, well, I have to say that I'm a bear on Britain, and also on specific sectors of both the US and European economies . . .'

Zorn had seen all he needed. He closed the screen and gave a grunt of satisfaction. This time there was no danger of the message failing to get through. The financial public relations firm he had retained to publicize the launch of his fund had emailed a press release, along with a three-minute extract from the interview containing all the key lines, to a carefully chosen list of news organizations, columnists and bloggers. Within minutes of the interview's opening, the tweets had started. Now Zorn began adding fuel to the fire through his own newly opened @malzorn Twitter account.

'Are u saying I shouldn't be investing in #globaloilcorps?' one follower asked.

Zorn replied, 'Put it this way, I'd get out of @BP_America (again) if I were you! Or go short.'

Another follower gleefully remarked that, '@Number10gov must be sh*ttin bricks after #zornhardtalk.'

Zorn grinned, thought for a moment, then typed, 'Just my way of giving the PM a Monday morning wake-up call – get him out of bed real fast today!'

Looking at his screens, he saw that the Asian markets were already putting pressure on international oil corporations with significant UK investments, as well as multinational gas and electricity providers. Sterling lost ground against both the euro and the dollar. When the FTSE index opened at 8.30 a.m. it was sixty-five points down. Oil, however, was gaining: up five dollars a barrel in early trading.

'Excellent,' murmured Malachi Zorn, lying almost horizontally in his chair, his feet up on his desk, sipping a cup of fresh coffee. 'Just excellent.'

A newsfeed was crawling like a ticker tape across the bottom of one of his screens. An item caught Zorn's eye, and he flipped forward in his chair, leaning towards the screen to get a closer view.

It seemed that more of the money that the fraudster Bernie Madoff had stolen from his clients had been found. There were indications that it might amount to as much as five billion dollars. Zorn stretched back in his chair again, and grinned.

'You know the big mistake you made, buddy?' he murmured, as if speaking to Madoff in his prison cell. 'When they came for you, you were still around.'

20

Carn Drum Farm

'It's a nice bit of land you've got here, Taff,' said Dave Smethurst, giving an appreciative nod as he gazed at the magnificent Welsh landscape, its wild beauty only magnified by the dramatic shafts of morning sunlight that pierced the thick, charcoal-grey clouds like beams from a 'Super Trouper' spotlight.

'I know,' Gryffud said, looking out at the hills he loved with all his soul. 'If I ever wonder why I'm doing all this, I just come out here and witness the glory of what nature can do in the absence of mankind . . . and then I know what I'm fighting for.'

'Yeah, right,' said Smethurst, with flat indifference to Gryffud's oration. Then he added, 'We're going to fuck up some of this nature good and proper, you know that, right? And not just here, neither.'

Gryffud grimaced. 'That's unavoidable. I wish there was any other way at all of doing this. But since there isn't, we have to accept that it's a necessary sacrifice for the greater good.'

'Collateral damage, eh?' said Smethurst. 'I know all about that.'

Gryffud caught the snide tone in his voice. 'Are you saying I'm no better than some fascist American general? Is that it?'

'I'm saying I don't give a shit. There's no justification you could give me I haven't heard before. It's all bullshit, if you ask me. But it's none of my business, is it? I'm here to do a job, collect my money, keep my mouth shut and fuck off. And that's what I'm going to do.'

'You don't care about the future of the planet, then? I don't understand how anyone can have that attitude. And if that's how you feel, I wonder if you're really the right man for the job.'

Gryffud glared at Smethurst. He was a good six inches taller, and several stone heavier than the former soldier. But the smaller man just grinned at him.

'Calm down, Taff. I don't care about the planet because it's got fuck all to do with me. It's been here for billions of years, and it'll carry on for billions more when I'm gone. But I do care about my trade. I'm the dog's bollocks at what I do, right? And I'll do a better job for you than any other bastard you're likely to find. That's why I'm the right man for the job.'

Gryffud nodded grudgingly, reflecting as he did so that it had not been him who had found Smethurst. That, too, had been Uschi Kremer. She'd been given his name, she said, by a friend of a friend.

'OK,' Gryffud said. 'Let's get on with it. How do you want to proceed?'

They were standing on the hillside above a cwm – the steep, curved head of a glacial valley – that fanned out as the land fell away before them.

'Basically, the target as a whole covers an area of about fifteen hundred metres by nine hundred, which is way too big for us. So I think we should concentrate on a smaller area, about two hundred metres by one hundred, in the south-west quadrant. That's got two advantages, right? Number one, it's full of juicy targets, and you should be able to set off some nice little chain reactions that'll do far more damage than your actual strikes. And number two, it's the area of the facility that's closest to the launch site. The place you picked is a kilometre from the refinery. That's at the absolute extreme limit of the range I can get from these things.'

'There's no alternative. All the land closer to the refinery is owned by National Petroleum, and there are regular security patrols.'

'But the place you've picked is safe, right? 'Cos we're proper fucked if anyone catches us with this little lot in the van.'

'Don't worry. The property's derelict. Some developer from London bought it, thinking he could convert it into holiday cottages, but he couldn't get planning permission. Now he can't sell it, and he's letting it rot. Believe me, nobody goes there.'

Smethurst seemed satisfied with what he'd heard. 'Fair enough. Right then, I've set up a proving ground so we can get all our trajectories worked out as precisely as possible. The target area is just over there . . .'

Smethurst pointed at a small, flat patch of land at the bottom of the main slope, with hills rising all around it like an auditorium around a stage. Then he went on, 'And the launch site is eleven hundred metres over there to the south-east.'

'So what are you doing?'

'Obviously, what I've got to do is work out the basic characteristics of the projectiles, the propellant and the launchers, yeah? I need to know how far the little bastards go at any given trajectory; how long it takes them to get there; how much fuel to use; and how long I have to set the mortar fuses. Once I know that, all I have to do is plot the angle and distance from the actual launch-point to the specific targets you'll be aiming to take out. Then I work out the right combinations of fuse, launch-angle and propellant . . .'

'Sounds complicated,' Gryffud said.

'Don't you worry, pal, I've got programs on the laptop to do all that.'

'And you're confident we can do something that will really make people sit up and ask questions?'

Smethurst grinned and slapped the big man on the back. 'Fuck, yeah, Taffy-boy. I wouldn't be here if I wasn't.'

21

The All England Lawn Tennis Club, Wimbledon, London

The second Monday of Wimbledon is regarded by many tennis lovers as the best day of the whole tournament. Weather permitting, the last sixteen in both the ladies' and men's competitions all play, so there are top seeds on court all day long. Sadly, not all of them are worth watching.

The opening match on Centre Court featured the women's world number one, a sturdy-thighed Swede who had spent the past ten days wandering around Wimbledon Village in her time off without once being recognized. Five minutes and three games into the first set, with half the seats still waiting to be filled by ticket-holders who were more interested in finishing their lunch, she was already flattening a patently inferior Bulgarian. The Bulgarian, however, was winning the decibel battle. As her grunts and shrieks echoed around London SW19, Zorn turned to his guests and said, 'If I want to hear a noise like that I'll go rent some lesbian porn.' He took out his phone and went online to the BBC's Wimbledon home page. To Zorn's delight a match on Court Two had been done and dusted as quickly as this one was likely to be. 'OK, Come with me. I've got something better.'

Zorn was entertaining two investors and their partners as his guests today. One was Carlos Castizo, the heir to a Colombian drug-cartel fortune, who, like a Latin American Michael Corleone, was engaged in giving his family's enterprises a sheen of legitimate respectability. The other was Mort Lockheimer, the former head of asset-backed bond trading at a now-defunct Wall Street bank. Lockheimer's trades, specifically the vast sums he had wagered and then lost on subprime mortgage bonds – in the mistaken belief that property prices could only go up – were arguably the single biggest factor in his former employer's demise. He had thereby cost thousands of bank workers their jobs and left shareholders with nothing, but, by a great stroke of good fortune, Lockheimer had actually left the bank about three months before his entire portfolio was revealed to be a ten-billion-dollar liability, rather than the great asset he had claimed, taking a golden parachute of more than a hundred million dollars with him. He had now spent all of that, and more than twice as much again – all of it borrowed – on buying into Zorn Global.

For Lockheimer, this was a win-win deal. He was absolutely certain that Zorn was going to make him a fortune. But more than that, to be an investor in Zorn Global was to be a member of a very exclusive club, one that was talked about with admiration and envy in the smartest, richest circles. Mort Lockheimer had attracted a great deal of negative publicity in the months after his losses on subprime trades were written about in a host of blogs, newspaper articles and even books on the financial crisis. He'd been made to look like a crook. Even worse, he'd looked like an idiot. His wife Charlene and daughters Chelsey and Alissa had been humiliated, and had retaliated by heaping vast amounts of acrid, bitter shit on him. Now he looked like a hero again, or less of a schmuck, at any rate.

Be that as it may, though, Charlene was not happy about Zorn's change of plan. 'What the fuck is he talking about?' she hissed in

Lockheimer's ear. 'I want to sit on Centre Court. Tell him we ain't moving.'

'You tell him,' Lockheimer countered. 'That guy's gonna make us more money than we've seen in our whole fuckin' lives. If he wants to go sit someplace else, that's what we do. And if he asks you to blow him, just get on your knees and start sucking.'

'Screw you, asshole,' Charlene glowered. But even though she was simmering with resentment, she picked up her bag and followed her husband up the steps to the exit. And when Zorn asked her how she was, she put on her broadest, most plastic smile and said, 'Just great!'

To anyone watching Zorn – and someone was – he appeared far more entertained watching the squabbles – for Castizo's twenty-two-year-old mistress was no happier to be moving than Lockheimer's fortysomething wife – than the abysmal tennis being served up on court. It was as if he was confirming in his own mind just how desperate these already wealthy individuals were to give him large amounts of their money. Messing around with their day was as good a way as any to test the depths of their greed. And of course, unlike his guests, Zorn did have a genuine interest in tennis. He'd actually come to Wimbledon for the sport.

Accompanied by Ahmad Razzaq, Zorn led the way out of Centre Court and through all the people trying to get on to Wimbledon's so-called Tea Lawn – in actual fact the All England Lawn Tennis Club's staff car park, dolled up for the fortnight with a bandstand and tables with green and purple striped parasols. There was more muttering from both sets of guests, which only intensified as a posse of uniformed security guards barged their way past, stepping on the toes of one of the women's Louboutin sandals as they went, escorting a dark, thickset, heavily stubbled player.

'That's Hernandez, the number nine seed,' said Zorn, as the black uniforms and white tennis clothes were swallowed up by the crowd. 'Tough guy, plays real hard, never gives up on a ball. But he's up against Arana, and I say the kid wins it in four.'

The path towards Number Two Court narrowed, cramming

spectators making their way there even more tightly together. The court was a plain concrete bowl, whose only concession to show court glamour was its padded seats. There were no celebrities to be spotted, no royal box to gawp at. Zorn could not have cared less. Oscar Hernandez was the established player, but Quinton Arana was a nineteen-year-old qualifier on a mission. The son of a blue-collar family from a Pennsylvania mining town, he'd already taken two seeded scalps in the first week, and he was gunning for a third. Zorn watched a couple of ultra-competitive rallies, filled with fizzing ground strokes, applauded both players as they chased down seemingly lost causes, gave a loud, 'Yeah!' of delight, and declared, 'Now this is what I call tennis!'

22

Carver heard every word. His seat was to the side of the court, ideally placed to observe Zorn and his party in the front row, behind the nearest baseline. The collapsible umbrella on his lap concealed a directional microphone. The khaki canvas fishing bag next to it contained a hidden camera. It had not been detected in the derisory bag-check to which he'd been subjected at the entrance gate, nor had there been any body-search or scanner, a fact that would make his life a great deal easier later in the week. The camera was sending pictures back to the iPad that was also in the bag, along with a rolled-up copy of that day's *Herald Tribune* newspaper, a V-neck cotton sweater from J. Crew, and a packet of throat lozenges. Carver was dressed in an all-American summer uniform of stone-coloured chinos, pale-blue Ralph Lauren shirt, and dark-blue, single-breasted Brooks Brothers blazer. He had padding on around his abdomen to give him a softer, fatter gut, and his normally clean-shaven chin and short, dark hair were now hidden beneath somewhat longer, wavy blond hair and a beard to match. Aviator shades covered his eyes. All the while that he kept

Zorn under surveillance he kept turning the same questions over and over in his mind: asking himself what Zorn was really up to in London, and why someone wanted him dead so badly. He had nothing against Zorn, personally. In fact, he was impressed by Zorn's disdain for the smart seats. It spoke well of him as a man. On the other hand, Carver had paid more than three thousand pounds for his Centre Court ticket. It seemed a pity to waste it.

Zorn seemed to feel the same way. After an hour on Court Two he relented and, to smiles of relief all round, led his party back to Centre Court. As he walked into the most famous tennis arena in the world, Carver was struck by its intimacy. The stands held fifteen thousand spectators, yet the players on court seemed almost close enough to touch. It was easy, too, to pick out individual spectators, Zorn included, in the crowd. From an assassin's point of view, Centre Court was a gallery full of sitting ducks. That very intimacy, however, meant that it offered precious few positions where a marksman could lurk unseen and take his shot unobserved.

Another practical problem struck Carver the moment he walked into the stands. The gangways between the rows of seats were accessed by entrances, each of which was guarded by two armed forces personnel – one from the army and another from the navy – to make sure that spectators only entered or left the court during breaks in play. These guards were unarmed, but they were, nevertheless, trained fighting men, and their presence only added to the difficulties that Centre Court posed.

Zorn and his guests, meanwhile, were no more aware that Carver was surveying them there than they had been on the walk out to Court Two. At four o'clock they went to the Courtside Restaurant, reserved for debenture ticket holders, for afternoon tea. Tables at the restaurant were limited to six guests. Razzaq slipped away so that Nicholas Orwell could take the final place at the table. The security chief left the group, Carver thought, with the relieved air of a busy man who was glad to be able to get back to work.

Sitting alone, Carver appeared to bury himself in his newspaper, which he was holding in front of him at the table, angled upwards to make it easier to read. The paper concealed the iPad on which Carver was scrolling through the pictures he had taken that morning. Zorn, he noticed, had been wearing an earpiece. That wasn't necessarily suspicious: he had every reason to want to keep discreetly in touch with his business affairs. But there was something else Carver spotted, and when he saw it, he immediately went back through every other picture he had taken to make sure that he had not just been fooled by a trick of the light. The answer was no. This was no trick – not of the light, at any rate.

Carver slipped the iPad back into his bag with a smile of deep satisfaction on his face. He had just worked out why he had been hired to kill Malachi Zorn. Now it was just a matter of deciding what, precisely, he was going to do with the discovery he had made. By the time he got up from the table to follow Zorn and his party back to their seats he had formulated a plan of action. He now knew the time, location and method by which he would hit Malachi Zorn.

When Zorn left Wimbledon shortly after five thirty, apologizing to his guests that his business commitments made his departure unavoidable, Carver was fifty metres behind Zorn's dove-grey Bentley on a motorbike. He had by now learned all that he needed to know, but it never hurt to go the extra distance when preparing for a job, so Carver followed his target all the way back to Wentworth.

It had not crossed his mind to be concerned that the multinational crew of waiters and waitresses had included a young Chinese woman among the Poles, Australians and Spanish. Nor had he attributed any great significance to the fact that a couple of times during the day the faces in the crowd, either watching the tennis or trying to make their way from one part of the All England Club to another, had included a slightly older Chinese male, respectably dressed in a lightweight summer suit and tie. Carver's mind was focused on his job as the perpetrator of one killing. He was not thinking of himself as the target of another.

23

Whitehall, London SW1

Sir Frederick Greenhill, Chairman of the Joint Intelligence Committee, looked around the table. 'So, any other business?'

The question was a formality. The agenda for the meeting had been completed. A couple of the senior intelligence officers and civil servants who comprised the committee membership began gathering up their papers. But then Cameron Young, the Prime Minister's political advisor, and his personal representative on the JIC, spoke up: 'Yes, there is one thing, actually.'

Young did not look much like the slick corporate types, with their sharp suits and self-satisfied expressions, who constituted the majority of the Prime Minister's closest associates. He had pale-ginger hair, a fleshy face, and a bushy drooping moustache – which gave him the slightly morose, doggy air that had long ago inspired his nickname: Fred Basset. This particular hound, however, had claws and teeth worthy of a Dobermann. Young had qualified as a barrister before becoming a political operator. He possessed intelligence and ambition in abundance, not to mention an independently wealthy American wife who had become one of London's leading political hostesses. He was not a man to be crossed.

'As I'm sure you'll be aware, the American financier Malachi Zorn is formally launching a new investment fund in London at the end of this week,' Young continued. 'Many of the world's richest and most influential individuals have placed very large sums of money in this fund, and will be attending the launch party, as will the PM himself. He sees this event as a tremendous vote of confidence in the government and in UK plc, and he wants the world to know about it.'

'Is that wise?' asked Sir Charles Herbert, the Foreign Office's man on the committee. 'Some of the individuals in question are not necessarily people with whom the PM would want to be associated. The provenance of their fortunes is not always as respectable as one might wish.'

'I'm sorry?' asked Young with a frown.

'He means the money's dirty,' snapped Jack Grantham, whose duties as Head of MI6 included attendance at JIC meetings.

'Then we will make sure that the PM is not photographed standing next to any of them,' said Young, with an almost imperceptible air of impatience. 'But he has to make an appearance. There's just going to be too much money and too much power in the room to ignore. And of course, Mr Orwell will be there.'

'Well, we wouldn't want him hogging the front pages while the PM sits at home at Number 10 . . .' Grantham mused.

'No, we certainly would not,' Young agreed. 'The question that concerns me, however, is this: what are the security implications of this event in particular, and Mr Zorn's presence here in general? I'm sure many of you will be aware of the interview Mr Zorn gave to the BBC World programme *HARDTalk* yesterday. He gave a public warning to the UK government that we were at risk from attacks by eco-terrorists. Firstly, let us just establish the facts of the matter. Do you have any reason to believe he's right, Dame Judith?'

The successor to Agatha Bewley as Head of MI5, Dame Judith Spofforth, was not given to dithering. Her reply was immediate, all the facts at her fingertips: 'Not at the moment. We keep a weather eye on the most extreme ecological and animal rights groups, of course. They tend to go in for nasty, frequently illegal, but essentially small-scale activity: harassing executives that work for companies of which they disapprove, digging tunnels on the sites of planned motorways, and so on. But there's no sign any of them have any major stunts in mind.'

Cameron Young turned to Euan Jeffries, the Director of GCHQ. 'Euan?'

'I must say, I agree with Dame Judith. We're not seeing any significant traffic that indicates planning for an attack of that kind.'

'Jack?'

Grantham thought for a second. To anyone else in the room, it looked as though he was sifting through intelligence data and analysis in his mind, weighing up the threat to the UK. In fact, he was thinking about Ahmad Razzaq and his contract on Malachi Zorn. Strictly speaking, he ought to mention it – the PM would go ballistic if Zorn came to any harm on British soil. But the fact was, Grantham had not been asked about threats to Zorn. He'd been asked about eco-terrorists.

'No,' Grantham said. 'Not a dicky bird.'

Young nodded encouragingly. 'Well, that's reassuring. Nevertheless, the PM believes that we have to be seen to respond. He does not relish the prospect of doing nothing and then standing up in front of Parliament – or, even worse, *Newsnight* – when a bomb goes off somewhere. He is also keen to have an initiative to take to this launch. Congress ignored Mr Zorn. We will not make that mistake.'

Dame Judith cast her sharp eyes in Young's direction. 'May one ask what you have in mind?'

'We need a high-profile event of our own, a proper eco-terrorism summit: senior figures from the intelligence, defence and energy communities; a couple of top energy executives; scientists who can discuss the possible implications of a blown-up oil rig, that sort of thing.'

'Clearly you will want to make an announcement within the next week or so,' said Sir Charles Herbert, with diplomatic smoothness. 'But surely there's no rush over the summit itself. As I'm sure you'll know, these things take many months to organize. In fact, I dare say everyone will have forgotten about the idea long before anything can be done.'

Cameron shook his jowly head. 'No, the PM is adamant. An announcement is not enough. He wants to be seen taking swift, decisive action. It's got to be put together immediately: tomorrow, in fact, nice and early so it dominates the whole day's news cycle. So I'd be very grateful if all the relevant bodies would rustle up a few of their brightest stars. To save any interdepartmental wrangling, we'll coordinate it all from the Cabinet Office. And let me emphasize in the strongest possible terms, the PM wants a real spectacular.'

The men and women of the Joint Intelligence Committee were, by definition, highly experienced, unflappable individuals who weren't given to panic. But even they had a hard time concealing their shock at what Young had just proposed.

'Where were you thinking of holding this meeting?' Sir Charles Herbert asked, hoping that a moment's consideration of the practicalities would swiftly scupper the PM's hare-brained scheme. 'It's going to be hard getting one of the major London conference venues at such short notice.'

Cameron Young was not deterred. 'No, we don't want anything like that. We have to have maximum media coverage, so we need a photogenic backdrop.'

'Well, maybe you should try an oil rig, then,' suggested Jack Grantham, wondering to himself just how mad this was going to get.

He, too, had underestimated Cameron Young. 'No, we considered that option. But it's always a nightmare getting people to and from rigs, and they can't cater for the number of visitors we had in mind.'

'And just think what would happen if the weather got up, and you suddenly found several chopper-loads of dignitaries stuck on a rig overnight with all the media jackals,' said a man from the Ministry of Defence. 'Doesn't bear thinking about.'

'Precisely,' said Young. 'We need a controllable environment. And we think we've found just the one . . .'

24

Wentworth

Carver watched as Zorn's Bentley disappeared behind the gates of his mansion. He rode back up the road a few hundred yards, then pulled into a lay-by, took off his helmet and checked his phone. There was one missed call: Grantham.

'Learn anything?' the MI6 man asked when Carver got through to him.

'Yes.'

'Anything you want to share with me?'

'Well, I have one question. Zorn's never been married, right?'

'No.'

'Thought so. Just checking.'

'You want to tell me why?'

'Not yet.'

'Have you worked out what you're going to do: method, time, location and so forth?'

'Yes, pretty much.'

'And . . . ?'

'And as soon as I've finalized everything, and worked out exactly what I need, I'll tell you.'

'Big of you,' Grantham said. 'Meanwhile, Zorn's not going to Wimbledon tomorrow, correct?'

'That's right. What of it?'

'I've got another little job for you.'

'Just because I'm not tracking Zorn tomorrow doesn't mean I won't be busy,' Carver objected. 'I've got a lot to prepare, and bugger all time to do it in.'

'You help me, and I'll lend a hand with that. I have ways of saving you a lot of time. Access to resources, you might say.'

'We'll see about that . . . what do you want?'

'Zorn's given some interview to the BBC. He says the next big thing is energy terrorism – eco-loonies blowing up oil rigs and so forth.'

'That old chestnut. I spent half my time in the SBS freezing my tits off in the North Sea, climbing on to oil rigs and pretending to kill terrorists who'd occupied them. I'll bet they still train for that. But we've never had a single terrorist on a single rig.'

'Be that as it may, the PM's got his knickers in a twist. He's decided to hold some bloody stupid summit meeting tomorrow morning . . .'

'So what do you want from me?'

'I need you to go. Strictly speaking this is a domestic issue, so our Security Service friends are being annoyingly territorial and saying it's their responsibility, not ours. That means I can't send anyone on an official basis. But I need someone there, someone I can trust.'

'And you think you can trust me?' Carver asked, with just a hint of amusement in his voice.

'Not much.'

'But what's the point? What can I achieve there?'

'I don't know,' Grantham said, with an exasperation that was principally directed against himself. 'But this meeting wouldn't be happening if it wasn't for Malachi Zorn. I'm not sure he planned for it to happen: I don't care how brilliant he is, he couldn't have predicted that the PM would respond to his interview this way. But he wouldn't be going on about energy terrorism – and this isn't the first time, apparently – if he didn't have a bloody good reason for it.'

'So this is basically an unknown element in a plan that's still a total mystery. Is that what you're saying?'

'Yes, if you want to put it that way.'

'And you have no idea what good it will do me, or you, if I'm there?'

'Correct.'

'Well, if I go, you'd better give me precisely what I need for the Zorn job. And some of it you won't like.'

'Well, naturally, the Service can never condone violence, torture or the harming of soft, furry animals . . .'

'Naturally . . .'

'And there's one other thing,' Grantham added.

'You don't know when to stop, do you?'

'That's why I'm where I am, and you're not. It's to do with this Magda Sternberg woman . . .'

'Yes?'

'We've been doing some digging. She's an elusive girl, our Magda. But my people think she's Polish. If she's who they say she is, she was born Celina Novak. And here's the interesting bit that you might be able to help me with. She was sent to Russia to be trained by the KGB.'

'So what?' asked Carver. 'Lots of kids from Warsaw Pact nations spent time in the USSR. It was the communist answer to finishing school.'

'Yes, I do know that,' snapped Grantham impatiently. 'What interested me were the dates. It seems that Celina Novak was quite the young beauty. So her training appears to have involved teaching her to take advantage of her natural assets . . .'

Carver had an unnerving premonition of where this was going. 'Don't tell me . . .'

Grantham laughed. 'Oh yes, the dates match perfectly. Celina

Novak was an exact contemporary of the young Alexandra Petrova.'

'And you want me to ask Alix about her?'

'Well, you know her better than anyone else.'

'It's been a while.'

'Nonsense. She'll greet you like a long-lost friend.'

'Doesn't she have a man in her life? That Ukrainian who's investing in Malachi Zorn – isn't he the reason you spotted her at that party?'

'Dmytryk Azarov? I don't think that true love is running too smoothly at the moment. According to the gossip columns he's holed up at the Ritz with a series of, ah, "mystery companions".'

Carver sighed. 'I'll put in a call.'

'Thought you might,' said Grantham. 'Meantime, I'll email you instructions for tomorrow. And when you're ready, send me your shopping-list, I'll see what I can do.'

25

'So the Prime Minister blinked,' said Ahmad Razzaq, as he stood
admiring the view from the window of Zorn's study, entirely
unaware of Carver's presence less than five hundred metres from
where he stood.

'Sounds like it,' his boss agreed, barely looking up from his bank
of trading screens. 'He's ordered some kind of instant anti-
terrorism conference. Orwell heard about it this afternoon.
They've asked him to go along. Downing Street wants the US
Ambassador to attend, too. And the EU Energy Minister is in town
to give some speech tonight. I heard the Prime Minister called her
personally to get her to come along.'

Razzaq turned his head towards Zorn. 'Maybe Orwell should go.
He can tell us what they talk about . . . and also where this event is
taking place. I cannot get a location out of anyone.'

'Me neither.' Zorn nodded. 'But Nicholas Orwell . . .' Zorn
pursed his lips as he thought for a moment. 'Yeah, you could be
right. He was going to do breakfast with Karakul Sholak, the
Kazakh—'

'Who is himself a terrorist.'

'Yeah, he's a rich one, and that's all that concerns me. Ah, what the hell, his money's in the bag. I'll tell him Orwell's been called away on top-secret government business, and promise he'll hear all about it at the launch party. That should keep him happy, right?'

'Absolutely . . . now he will be able to stay in bed all the longer with his whores.'

Zorn gave an indifferent shrug of the shoulders. 'Again, that doesn't concern me. OK . . . so I'll call Orwell, tell him to say yes to the invitation. He's not going to object, not with the number of TV cameras they're going to have pointing in his direction.'

Razzaq frowned. 'I cannot understand it. Orwell was Labour. The Prime Minister is Conservative. Why give publicity to an enemy?'

'Because he wants to show the world that this is not a party-political issue. So he invites an opponent. But he picks Orwell, who can no longer hurt him politically. Plus, the more Orwell is seen as a world statesman, the smaller he makes the current Labour leader seem. No, it's a smart move.'

'And while they have their meeting, we will be showing the world what eco-terrorism really looks like.'

Zorn got up and walked towards the window. 'They all set down there?'

'Yes . . . but there is still time to call this off. Many people are going to die. Are you sure you wish to go ahead?'

The two men were standing side by side now, looking out at the vivid green lawn, across which the shadow cast by an ancient cedar of Lebanon was spreading.

'What, you think I don't have the stones for this?' Zorn asked, with a genuine note of surprise in his voice.

'It is not easy to have that many deaths on one's conscience,' Razzaq answered.

A lazy smile spread across Malachi Zorn's face. 'What makes you think I have a conscience?' he said.

26

Carver looked at the phone in his hand, wondering what he was going to say. It had been a couple of years since he'd last spoken to Alix, just a handful of words snatched at the funeral of a mutual friend. There hadn't been a chance for a proper conversation: he'd been there with another woman.

He wasn't even sure if the number he had for her would still work. He dialled it. Well, at least there was a ringtone. But no one was answering. He heard the phone ring three, four, five times, and was just formulating a voicemail message in his mind when she took the call, sounding brisk and a little hurried: 'Hello, Alexandra Vermulen.'

The sound of her voice still thrilled him. They'd been apart for more than a decade, yet even now there was no other woman in the world that could get to him the way she did. But there was a stab of jealousy in him, too, that she should be using another man's name as her own. That was another thing Carver had never quite got used to. 'It's me,' he said.

There was no need for any further identification. He knew that his voice would be as instantly recognizable to Alix as hers was to him. Now he waited to hear her reaction. There was a hesitancy, almost a brittleness, as she said, 'Hello . . .'

'Look, I'm sorry to call you out of the blue. But you might be able to help me . . .'

Did he imagine it, or was there a sigh before she asked, 'Is this a business call?'

'Yeah.'

'I suppose it was too much to hope that you might just want to speak to me.'

Carver rolled his eyes to the ceiling and took a deep breath. Bad start. Try again.

'Come on, Alix, you know it's not like that.'

'So what is it like?'

Silence fell on the line, neither knowing what to say next, but not ready yet to hang up. It was Carver's move. He made it.

'Can we start again, here? I would really like to see you. Full stop. Also, you might be able to help me with something important. Is there any chance we could meet up this evening? It doesn't have to be for very long if you're busy. Maybe we could have a quick drink?'

There was another pause. Carver could sense the debate in Alix's mind as she weighed up the pros and cons of taking this further. Finally she said, 'OK, Sam, we can meet. There's a party at the Muscovy Gallery in Cork Street this evening. They're opening an exhibition of Soviet propaganda posters. I'll get your name put on the guest list. Be there in an hour.'

'Thanks, I appreciate it.'

'Yes,' she said, 'you should.'

27

Kensington Park Gardens

Alix had taken the call in her bedroom, where she'd been getting dressed. She'd decided hours before what to wear to the opening: a white silk blouse and slimline midnight-blue cigarette pants with strappy high-heeled sandals. The look was simple, elegant, respectably attractive. She had put the clothes on, chosen a necklace and some bangles, and satisfied herself that the whole outfit worked. Now she looked at herself in the mirror once more, almost in disbelief that Carver had called and that somehow she had agreed to see him again. Why had she done that? Why couldn't she just let go of the past and say no?

If she'd not had that argument with Azarov they'd have gone to the party together, and she would have had the perfect reason to turn Carver down. As it was, her so-called lover was still sulking in the Ritz, doubtless surrounded by hungry young women who'd be only too willing to take his mind off his troubles at home. So was that all she was doing now: getting her own back?

She found herself wanting to change her clothes completely. Alix told herself that she would not be dressing for Carver. She was not trying, still less hoping, to seduce him. She wanted it to be perfectly clear that she was a successful, independent woman who could do – in fact had done – very well without him. But she also wanted to look marvellous.

She went through several options before settling on a simple tobacco-coloured silk dress. The apparent modesty of its length was offset by a perfect cut that subtly showed off every inch of her body, caressing the curves of her breasts and hips. She tied the halter neck that held the dress in place, and let the loose ends of the bow fall, brushing against her naked back.

Now she examined herself in the mirror. Objectively, she knew she was in amazing shape: her scales and her dress size did not lie. But that did not make her any less critical of the flaws she could see in every part of her body. As she straightened her back to pull in her already flat stomach she wondered what Carver would see when he looked at her. Would she still be, to him, the beautiful young woman he'd once loved, or would the evidence of all those passing years, so obvious to her own eyes, destroy any illusions he might still have?

She imagined Carver standing next to her. Even in her heels she would still be an inch or two shorter than him. She lifted her chin as if looking up at him and was relieved to see how her jawline was tightened. For a second she stared herself in the eye, and as she did a memory came to her of her first day in Carver's apartment. It had been a refuge for them, a haven after a night of violence and danger. He had looked at her with a frown of concentration on his face and said, 'Your eyes. There's something just a tiny bit uneven about them.' The words had stung her like a whip. In an instant she had become that ugly duckling again, the butt of so many cruel taunts about her crazy cross-eyes. Even now she could feel the shock of having her deepest, most private insecurity so forensically stripped bare.

Carver had seen her pain at once, sensed her vulnerability, and apologized profusely. 'You have amazing eyes. They're beautiful, kind of hypnotic. I can't stop looking at them, and now I know why.' She had forgiven him. After all, his mistake had been the result of looking past the glossy surface of her and seeing the real woman within – and how often had she wished men would do that?

She'd been wearing Carver's old grey T-shirt, sitting curled up like a cat in one of his huge armchairs, its leather scuffed and softened by age, basking in the warmth of the sun that streamed through the window. She had felt so comfortable there; so right, and yet so surprised that she had somehow allowed herself to lower all her professional defences.

And then she recalled the feel of him as they had made love, and the memory was so intense that she cursed herself for letting it into her mind. As she picked up her handbag and made her way towards the front door she told herself once again that she was not doing any of this for Samuel Carver. She was doing it for herself. Yes, that was it.

28

Whitehall

The Prime Minister wanted a spectacular, and once the word got out to the highest reaches of the civil service that there was going to be an event that would provide massive publicity and a jolly day out, the biggest problem for the hard-pressed administrative officials at the Cabinet Office became the need to limit numbers. By early evening a plan was coming together. Support staff, press officers and media would be packed on to coaches at six in the morning, ready to set off on a magical mystery tour to a destination that, for security reasons, none of them would be given in advance. They would be followed by a flotilla of TV outside broadcast vans and trucks. But by far the fastest, most reliable way of getting VIPs from London to the chosen location would be by helicopter. That meant using 32 (Royal) Squadron, based at RAF Northolt in West London, which had two of its three Augusta Westland AW109E Power Elite choppers available, each of which could seat six passengers. There were, therefore, twelve VIP seats available . . . and at least ten times that number of people who were absolutely convinced they deserved them.

29

Cork Street, Mayfair, London W1

Alix looked around the gallery at the socialites and art-lovers crammed together to celebrate the art of a totalitarian system that would have shot them all in the blink of an eye. It was, she thought, becoming harder with every year to tell the Russians apart from the rest, as wealth and consumption became entitlements to be taken for granted, rather than novelties to be wallowed in as greedily and flagrantly as possible. She wondered how many of them, like her, were former members of the KGB. Plenty, in all probability: the Committee for State Security's grip on the upper reaches of the new capitalist Russia was almost as tight as it had been in the old Soviet system. She made her way into the crush of bodies, through an invisible cloud of competing scents and aftershaves, searching for Samuel Carver.

And then she saw him, standing no more than ten metres away. He was looking at an image of a young woman in a red-spotted blouse standing in front of a silhouetted factory, brandishing a gun in her raised right fist. The slogan on the poster, in bold Cyrillic script, read, 'Women workers, take up your rifles!' Carver was regarding it with a wry smile on his face: she had a feeling he wouldn't feel too threatened by anything that girl was likely to do. Alix ran her eyes down her former lover's body, appraising him. He was still as lean and taut as ever, but the lines on his face were a little deeper, and there was the hint of grey at his temples. These signs of age merely served to make him look more attractive, and she cursed the unfairness of the differing ways time affected men and women. She took a couple of steps towards him, and he must have sensed her approach because he turned and greeted her with a broad, boyish smile that made her heart leap. Damn him!

'Would you like me to translate?' she asked, sounding cooler than she felt.

'Sure, go ahead,' he said, his eyes fixed on hers.

She pretended to look at the image with exaggerated concentration, using the time to pull herself together before she answered, 'So . . . what it says is: what am I doing here?'

'Appreciating your country's great history . . .'

'It's not so great.' Alix ran her eyes around the other posters on the walls, with their repetitive images of Lenin – one arm always extended towards his people: soldiers, workers and noble, sturdy communist women. 'Everything in this room is a lie.'

Carver's expression lost its amusement. 'Everything?'

Alix shrugged. 'I don't know, you tell me. What am I doing here?'

'Like I said, business . . .'

'Is that all?'

'Yes,' Carver said, adding to the number of lies. 'I need to know about a woman who currently goes by the name of Magda Sternberg. We think she used to have another identity.'

'Who's "we"?'

'Me, Grantham . . . MI6.'

'Ha! You're working for Grantham now?'

'Let's just say we're helping each other out.'

Alix felt calmer now. Maybe this really would just be business. Maybe that would be better. 'I see,' she said. 'OK, this Magda

Sternberg . . . the name means nothing to me. Why should I know her?'

'Because it's possible that you trained together. We think she used to be called Celina Novak.'

That name! It took all her years of experience to conceal the shock of it. Alix felt herself taken back to a time when she was still a gauche, provincial teenager, her eyes only recently cured of their squint, her teeth still in the braces that would create her perfect smile. She thought of Celina Novak, the spoilt, vicious daughter of senior officials in Poland's ruling United Workers' Party, sent to Russia to be trained by the KGB. She remembered the absolute contempt and disdain with which Celina had regarded her, and felt a sudden rush of the humiliation that used to be her overpowering emotion. It took an effort to control her voice as she said, 'Do you have a picture?'

Carver held up his phone. On its screen was an old black and white identity photo of a uniformed cadet, her beautiful face set hard as flint.

Alix nodded.

'Have you met her?' she asked.

Carver turned his head away from her and cast his eyes towards the poster again. 'Professionally,' he said, still not looking at Alix.

'Then you'll know she likes to destroy the lives of everyone she meets.' She wondered what Carver was trying to hide.

Now he turned back to her. 'But not yours . . .'

'I had powerful protectors. I was luckier than I knew.'

Carver frowned. 'What happened to the ones who weren't lucky?'

'There was a girl called Dasha Markova. She hanged herself . . .'

Alix could not bear to tell the whole story of how Markova had committed suicide after months of psychological torture inflicted by a gang of classmates recruited and led by Celina Novak. She, Alix, had been part of that gang. She'd felt thrilled that Celina had finally allowed her into the inner circle after all the months in which she had herself been excluded and tormented. And, yes, she'd been relieved that someone else had now been the target. The shame of it had only grown over time.

'Celina can make you do anything,' Alix said, her voice barely more than a whisper, so that Carver had to strain to hear her over the noise of the gallery crowd.

Her words seemed to affect him, though, because he grimaced.

'So what happened to her? Did she get kicked out?' he asked.

Alix gave a bitter smile. 'No, she graduated with honours.'

Carver mimed the opening of an envelope: 'And this year's winner of the Stalin Prize for psychopathic cruelty is . . .'

Despite herself, Alix could not help but laugh.

Carver said nothing, just looked at her.

Nervous about what he was seeing, she asked, 'What is it?'

'Your smile.'

Just the way he said it told her that his feelings had not changed. But maybe she was fooling herself. She realized her pulse was racing. Her mouth was dry.

'I need a drink,' she said.

'Sure.'

A waiter was passing by, his tray laden with glasses of champagne. Carver stepped over to him, took two and offered one to Alix.

She reached for it. Her fingers brushed his, and it was as if an electric circuit had been completed as the energy surged between them. It was all she could do not to drop the glass.

They looked one another in the eye and felt the connection again.

'Let's get out of here,' Carver said.

'I haven't had my champagne,' Alix replied.

'Don't bother. It's not the real stuff.'

'Well, I always want the best stuff there is. Don't you?'

'You know I do,' he said.

Less than a minute later they were hailing a cab.

30 _____

Carn Drum Farm

The weapon had specifically been designed to be as simple as possible. 'The fewer parts there are, the less there is to go wrong,' Smethurst had said. 'People always try to get fancy, you know? Doesn't matter if they're the Paddies or the Pentagon, they can't resist fucking it up with unnecessary complications.'

He'd made sure there would be none of that.

A metal plate had been welded to the base of each of the larger cylinders, with a small hole in the bottom for an electric wire. The wire was passed through the hole into the cylinder, and one of the igniters was attached.

Twelve of these cylinders were placed inside the metal frame-work, which had already been welded to the floor of the camper van. They were each arranged at fractionally different angles, according to instructions given by Dave Smethurst, who supervised the entire process and checked the results with extreme care. He had spent two hours test-firing shells from that remote cwm, far from prying eyes, then processed the results and determined an individual trajectory for each of his projectiles.

Only when the cylinders were positioned exactly as he wanted them were they filled about one-third deep with the fuel mix of icing sugar and fertilizer, just as an old-fashioned muzzle-loading cannon would have been filled with its load of gunpowder.

The result was a multi-barrel launcher, filled with propellant. All that was missing was something to propel.

That wouldn't be long in arriving.

Under Smethurst's direction, two of Gryffud's men had removed the valves from a dozen of the smaller cylinders. The explosive mix was poured in through the hole where the valve had been, then the fuse and detonator assembly was inserted and the hole resealed.

The small cylinders were placed in the big ones, like one Russian doll inside another, so that the fuse wire from the bottom of the shells nestled in the fuel mix.

The wires from the bottom of each of the launch cylinders were connected to a junction box, along with a thirteenth wire which led to a large plastic jerrycan filled with petrol. The junction box was in turn connected to a timer located by the passenger seat.

The rear door of the van opened vertically. When the multiple launcher was complete and loaded, the door was lowered and welded shut. Then the open top of the camper van was covered with a large sheet of paper, lacquered to improve its strength and water-resistance, and sprayed white to match the van. It was sealed to the roof with clear vinyl tape. Only the closest inspection would reveal that anything had been done to the roof. Only a torrential downpour would break through the lacquered, painted paper. This, too, was another old IRA ploy.

The weapons had been made and loaded. The mission was ready to go.

31

London

Grantham called while Carver and Alix were in the cab. 'So, did you speak to your old girlfriend?' he asked.

'Yes.'

'And . . . ?'

'And you were right. Magda Sternberg and Celina Novak are one and the same person. And she was just as tricky then as she is now: manipulative, sadistic, totally cold-blooded. "Celina can make you do anything," was the way Alix put it.'

Carver put a hand over the phone and mouthed 'Grantham' at Alix, who shook her head with a rueful sigh.

'Don't tell me you're getting lovey-dovey with her again . . .' Grantham asked, almost as if he'd seen Carver's gesture.

'Not with Ginger, that's for sure.'

'You know that's not who I meant.'

'No comment.'

'Unbelievable. Some people never learn . . . Well, if you don't mind me interrupting your true romance, I have details of tomorrow's operations.'

'Fire away.'

'You're on the list for this absurd publicity stunt, sorry, this vitally important meeting on energy security. You'll be Andy Jenkins, a member of the Ministry of Defence support staff. There'll be a few of them around.'

Carver was having a hard time paying attention to what Grantham was saying. Alix's hand was making its way up his inner thigh. Grinning, he swatted it away, then did his best to focus on business.

'Support staff? Sounds like another way of saying non-uniformed special forces.'

'Your words, not mine,' said Grantham. 'But it shouldn't be too far out of your comfort zone.'

'So where do I have to be, and when?'

'Cardiff Gate services on the M4. There's a motel there called the Ibis. Go down tonight. Check in under any name you like. In the morning, all your Andy Jenkins documentation will be waiting at reception. Your contact will be called Tyrrell.'

'Is that a first or second name?'

'It's the only name you're getting. He'll be waiting for you in the motel car park at 7.00 a.m. in a 58 Reg, metallic-grey Audi A4.'

'And then what?'

'Get in the car and go with friend Tyrrell to your destination.'

'But what is my destination?'

'An oil refinery.'

'On Milford Haven, presumably,' said Carver, thinking of the nearest major installations to Cardiff.

'That's one presumption, yes. But anyway, keep your eyes open. Check out as much as you can. See if it helps you in any way to find out what the hell Zorn's up to. When you get back we can discuss what you plan to do about him. Assuming you know.'

'Oh, I know what I'm doing,' said Carver. 'I just don't know if it'll work.'

He ended the call and looked at Alix.

'Were you talking about me just then?' she asked, with a spark of humour in her eyes. 'When you said you didn't know whether it would work?'

'Of course,' said Carver. 'What else could I possibly be talking about?'

'I can't imagine,' she murmured, leaning towards him and gently putting her hand back between his thighs.

32

Lambeth

'Sorry about this,' Carver said as he opened the door to his flat. 'It's not exactly five-star.'

'But you're in it,' Alix said, gazing at him.

'Yes I am.'

'Then I love it.'

He took her in his arms then, holding her body against him with the fierceness of a man who never wants to let go. He felt himself get hard, and the press of her hips as she responded to it. The scent of her – not just her perfume but her skin, her hair, even her breath – filled his senses as intoxicatingly as any drug. He covered her mouth with his, and kissed her with a decade of pent-up longing and frustrated desire.

Alix needed the strength of his arms around her. Without them she might not have been able to stand upright. After all this time she was still not immune to him, still failing to retain her self-control as sensations buried for years flooded back with all their old overwhelming power. She felt her body mould to his without any need to think what she was doing. There was no artifice, no tension, just the knowledge that she felt so close, so intimate and so absolutely known to this man that she could barely tell where she ended and he began. The softness of his lips, the rasp of his chin, the way his tongue entered her mouth, the taste of him, the smell of him . . . It was ecstatic and yet also destabilizing. All her resolution, her determination to remain strong, independent and separate, dissolved. They stumbled through the flat, their lips still locked together, their arms entwined as he led her into the bedroom.

Carver kicked open the door, and only once they were standing right beside the bed did he let go of her. Alix stepped back from him, and in a single fluid movement reached behind her neck, pulled at the bow and let the dress fall to her feet. She stood there in her knickers and her heels, and the sight of her stopped him dead. All this time he'd been imagining what it would be like to see her again, and still he wasn't prepared for the reality of it. He shook his head in disbelief, and with deep seriousness said, 'My God, you're so beautiful.' And then he was kissing her again, and her fingers were prising open the buttons of his shirt, undoing his belt, unzipping him and slipping under the waistband of his underpants.

As she took hold of him she giggled and said, 'Hello, old friend.'

Laughing, he wrapped his arms around her again, lifted her off her feet, and they tumbled together on to the waiting bed.

Alix gave a little gasp of pain the moment that Carver entered her, followed by a long, sighing moan of pleasure. The physical sensation of him filling her was matched by an overwhelming rush of emotion, a profound recognition of how different she felt making love with Carver than with any other man she had ever known. The intimacy between them was deeper, their connection more intense. He had always made her feel completely vulnerable, and yet totally safe from harm: she could feel anything, do anything, be anything with him. He could kiss or stroke her with gentleness, almost delicacy, one moment, then overpower her with raw strength the next. And to her amazement, nothing had changed. She knew, with absolute confidence, how wonderful it was going to be, and any intention she might have had of hiding her true feelings was swept away. She wanted him to know the effect he was having on her, and she felt a profound desire to give all of herself to him.

He was looking down at her now with intense concentration, as if he were reading and constantly responding to every one of her desires and emotions. Yet he seemed also to be toying with her longing for him. Sometimes he drove into her so hard and so deep that she wondered how she wasn't torn apart, only for him to withdraw almost completely, teasing her and moving his hips away from hers as she struggled to get him back before he plunged into her again.

And all the time he was kissing her, stroking her and murmuring in her ear, his defences as abandoned as hers, telling her how he had longed for her, how incredible it felt to be with her and in her again.

She came with a sudden, hot burst of ecstasy that made her cry out. He had not taken his eyes off her face, and the half-smile that played around his lips told her of the pleasure he had taken in her orgasm. But she knew that he had held himself back. Now she needed Carver to come, too.

'I know what you want,' she said.

Carver didn't need an explanation. Alix slid out from under him and knelt on the bed with her back to him. For a second he just looked at her perfectly rounded arse, her slim waist, the arch of her back, and the mane that tumbled around her shoulders. Then he leaned forward and wrapping his left hand around hers pushed it against the headboard.

'Take my hair,' she said. He heard the arousal in her voice, and his right hand took a firm hold of her hair, making her gasp. He nibbled at one of her earlobes, feeling her shudder of delight. His chest pressed against her back, and he felt the hot sweat between their skin. Then he took her again.

Up until now, he'd been taking his time with Alix, reading her responses as his cues until she came. As incredible as it had been to be making love to her again, part of him had remained detached, bringing the same cool precision to sex as he did to death. But this time his only concern was for his own pleasure. He was going to fuck her, and that was the beginning and end of the matter.

'Do it,' she said.

Now there was no teasing, no variation, no great subtlety. Now he just went at her in a hard, steady, driving rhythm. As he grew more excited he covered her neck and shoulders with kisses whose fierceness increased until he was biting at her skin with quick, sharp little stabs of his teeth. Her moans became louder and higher, and Carver gave a deep animal groan as he felt himself swell still more inside her. He knew she felt it, too, by the way she responded, pushing against him, wanting more and more of him.

Carver felt his orgasm build inside him, the feeling becoming stronger, surging through him, closer and closer to the edge, until at last, with an explosion that felt like someone had just fired a bullet of pure sensory euphoria through his head, blowing his brains out of the back of his skull, he came.

33

They lay in bed, their bodies still slick and glowing, grinning in post-coital smugness. Alix felt as though she had been defined anew by the experience of being with Carver again. 'This is who I am,' she thought, 'and where I'm meant to be.' No one else had ever been able to make her feel this way. And yet the fear still gnawed at her that they had not been able to make their relationship last before: why should this time be any different? She should be wise, and get out now, and yet she could not help wanting him more than anything she had ever wanted in her life. Having him next to her only reminded her of the emptiness of her life without him.

She began to say something, trying to express how she felt, but then stopped herself.

'What is it?' Carver asked.

'Oh . . . nothing,' she said.

He looked at her again, and then kissed her face with infinite tenderness. 'It's all right,' he said. 'I know.'

They kissed again. He stroked her cheek, then ran his fingers through her hair. 'I've got to go soon,' he said.

'More business?' This time there was only understanding in her voice.

Carver gave a rueful grimace. 'Afraid so ... It's nothing too serious. I have to go to some ridiculous anti-terrorism summit.'

'Is this anything to do with that woman – the one you were asking me about?'

'Not directly, but there is a connection.'

Alix propped herself up on one elbow, a serious look in her eyes. 'What kind of connection?'

Carver wondered what he should tell her. He trusted her implicitly. Yet she was supposed to be living with one of Zorn's investors. She might have divided loyalties. On the other hand, she might also know something about Zorn, something that would help unravel the mystery of the American's true intentions.

'She works for a guy called Ahmad Razzaq. He's Malachi Zorn's security chief, but it's not clear where his real loyalties lie. There's a lot that's not clear about Zorn.'

'I agree,' she said, surprising him. 'I assume you know I've been living with Dmytryk Azarov.'

'Sure ... but it really wasn't any of my business—'

'It's OK, you don't need to be defensive. That's over, anyway. I don't think I'd be here if it wasn't.'

'So what ended it?'

'That's what I was coming to. We argued about Zorn. And I agree with you. There's something wrong about that guy. Did you know that none of his fancy offices have leases longer than three months?'

'Maybe he's worried his business won't pan out?'

'Ha! Have you met Malachi Zorn? That man isn't worried about anything. Every cent he earned he got by backing his judgement against the world. So if he's only got short leases—'

'It's because he's not planning to stick around. He's only renting his house here, too.'

Alix nodded, relieved that Carver had taken her point. His trust in her judgement was an affirmation of the bond between them.

'You and me,' he said, shaking his head in wonder as if reading her mind. And then again, 'You and me.'

'Mmm . . .'

'You think it can work this time?'

She smiled, thrilled that he, too, was thinking about their future. 'I don't know, Sammy . . . maybe we can be smarter this time.'

'You know I don't let anyone call me Sammy.'

'You let me.'

'Yeah . . . I do . . . but then, you're not just anyone, are you?'

He kissed her again, and then, before she could stop him, got up out of the bed.

'I really do have to go,' he said.

Waygal Valley, Afghanistan: two months earlier

Corporal Chico Morales, a section leader in C Company of the 502nd Infantry Regiment, did not claim to be any kind of expert on theology. But he knew one thing: if God had been on the side of the Islamic insurgents in Afghanistan, he would sure as shit have taught them to shoot straight. Since he'd begun his tour of duty in the Waygal Valley in eastern Afghanistan, Morales had lost count of the number of contacts with the enemy when the men of 'the Deuce', as the 502nd was known, had been outnumbered, out-gunned and in serious danger of defeat. And in every case, the single biggest factor in his getting out alive had been the Afghans' obsession with 'spraying'n'praying'. They didn't fight as coordinated units, concentrating their fire on specific targets. They just blasted away in every direction, each man for himself, and hoped to Allah that some of their bullets actually hit an enemy.

Even so, they could still make a damn nuisance of themselves. Give a handful of insurgents a bunch of AK-47s, throw in some rocket-propelled grenades or a .50 calibre rifle, and give them a wall or a boulder to hide behind, or a gully to lie in, and they could, at the very least, pin you down for fifteen to twenty minutes.

Then the 'Punisher' arrived in Afghanistan. And that changed everything.

Punisher was the nickname that its first awestruck users had given to a device the US Army categorized as the XM-25 Individual Airburst Weapons System. Simply put, the XM-25 was a semi-automatic grenade launcher rifle. But that was like saying that, simply put, a Bugatti Veyron was a car. The truth was, the XM-25 was unlike any other hand-held weapon on earth. It simply removed the concept of cover from the battle-field. And as Morales and his buddies all agreed, it looked frigging cool while it did it, like some kind of mean, black sci-fi ray gun.

The way it worked was this: on top of the rifle there was what looked like a regular telescopic sight, but was actually a computerized fire-control system, accurate up to seven hundred metres. If the insurgents were hiding behind a wall, you just pointed the gun in that direction. The Punisher calculated precisely how far away the target was, and then transmitted that information down the barrel of the gun to a high-explosive 25 mm grenade. But of course, the wall wasn't the actual target; the insurgents hiding behind it were. So you, the soldier, used a button by the trigger to add a metre or two to the range, and the grenade adjusted itself to that, too. Then you fired, aiming just above the wall, and the grenade shot away, went over the wall, and then exploded in the air behind it, blowing the enemy away. Use an armour-piercing round and you didn't have to go over a wall or an enemy vehicle; you could go straight through it. Man, it was a beautiful thing to behold.

So far the Punisher was still in its field-trial phase of development. There hadn't been more than a couple of dozen in the entire Afghanistan theatre of operations. But those guns had been game changers. There were four grenades in a Punisher's magazine. Fire them all, and the fight just ended. Engagements that used to last twenty minutes were over in less than five. US casualties dropped to zero. Soldiers in the units that had been selected to test the XM-25 would beg to be allowed to use it, like kids fighting over a new toy. Today it was Morales's turn and he hated to admit it, but damn he was excited.

Morales belonged to a platoon that had recently arrived at COP (Combat Outpost) Wanda, a brand-new installation near the village of Aranas. It was situated on a bluff, looking down the valley to the Waygal River. The only way in or out was by helicopter. All their supplies came in by air. The first day there, as Morales looked at the hills all around him, knowing that the insurgents were out there somewhere, just waiting to attack, he'd felt like he was living in a twenty-first-century version of Fort Apache. But today he had the Punisher. Today his motto was, 'Bring it on.'

Morales woke shortly after 4.00 a.m. and took up his post at

Observation Post Highpoint, a lookout a short way from the main body of the COP. Morales and the other men in his eight-man section had built Highpoint themselves. With their trenching tools they'd dug up what meagre quantities of dirt could be prised from the rocky terrain, and used them to fill, or in some cases part-fill, the collapsible steel and nylon HESCO containers that acted as their fortifications. The observation post's location provided superb views across the Waygal Valley for miles around. But as Morales was about to discover, this long-range visibility came at a price. A ravine ran down the side of the hill and came within thirty metres of the HESCO barricades, passing so close that the HESCOs created a blind spot for the men behind them, who were unable to see down into the bottom of the ravine. Not that they were aware of that just yet.

Shortly after dawn, the observation post came under small-arms fire from an insurgent position behind an outcrop of boulders atop a ridge about three hundred metres away. This was no big deal. The insurgents always preferred to move at night and attack with the first light of day. Morales ordered his men to return suppressing fire. They didn't have to take anyone out just yet. They just had to keep them in one place long enough for the Punisher to do its thing.

'Say hello to my leetle frien,' Morales joked as he pressed the control that charged up the XM-25 and made it ready for use. Like his men, he had focused all his attention on the hostile position on the ridge. He had no idea that a dozen insurgents had made their way up the ravine during the night; not until the first grenade exploded inside the observation post, killing two of his men and wounding a third. Another grenade took out a fourth soldier. Morales himself was not targeted by the blasts. He and his remaining three troops were left for the Afghan fighters, inheritors of a guerrilla warfare tradition that dated back to the days of Alexander the Great and beyond, who scrambled over the HESCOs like pirates boarding a ship, armed with rifles, pistols and razor-sharp knives.

Morales had no means of protecting himself. The XM-25 was a fantastic weapon so long as its grenades exploded far enough away not to harm the soldier who had launched them. But at this kind of hand-to-hand range it was pointless: just a high-tech way of committing suicide. So Chico Morales never even fired a single round before he died, his throat sliced open by a curved steel blade. But in his last few seconds two thoughts crossed his mind. The first was that the insurgents had attacked in a way he'd never seen before: like trained professional soldiers. The second was that he could have sworn he heard someone shouting orders to them. And those orders had been given in English.

One of the insurgents stood over Morales's body, even as the last few spurts of blood from his carotid artery were soaking into the earth around his corpse. He reached down and prised the XM-25 from Morales's fingers.

'Cheers, mate,' the insurgent said. 'I'll be having that.'

Tuesday, 28 June

34

Carn Drum Farm

Bryn Gryffud and Dave Smethurst left at four in the morning, driving the camper van; Uschi Kremer had already left in a separate vehicle late the previous night.

The remaining members of the Forces of Gaia had all woken early to see Gryffud and Smethurst off. Some of them went straight back to bed, others were gripped by a combination of anticipation, tension, anxiety and downright fear as the seconds ticked by. They brewed coffee, paced around the farmhouse kitchen, or made futile attempts to get some rest. All but one, though, stayed within Carn Drum farmhouse.

The exception was one of the two remaining women, Deirdre Bull. The closer the time came to the moment when the group would finally engage in direct action against the forces destroying the environment, the more troubled she became. Neither she nor any of the other members of the group had been told what the precise target would be – this, they had been told, was for their own protection as well as operational security – but she knew they were engaged on an act of destruction. And it made little sense to Deirdre to fight one act of ecological vandalism with another. When she'd gone to Brynmor Gryffud to voice her concerns, he had assured her that the good they were going to do in the long run far, far outweighed any short-term cost.

'Gaia understands,' he had assured her, knowing that Deirdre had an essentially religious view of the environmentalist cause. But Deirdre was still not entirely convinced. She had needed to get away, to be by herself, so that she could feel a sense of communion with the earth goddess and come to terms with what was going on. So around forty minutes after the camper van had set off on its journey south, just as dawn was breaking, she put on her green wellies and her cagoule – decorated with vivid, two-tone pink spots against a white background. Then she slipped out of the back door of the commune and, following a path that ended just a few metres from the house, headed off alone into the hills.

After she had walked for a few hundred metres Deirdre turned around to look back at the farmhouse down below her on the floor of the valley. The sun had begun to rise over the hills to the east and it was steadily spreading across the valley, replacing the soft-grey darkness with dazzling bright colour. Deirdre frowned as she saw two large, black vehicles heading at high speed along the drive that led to the house. From where she was standing they looked like vans of some kind, but as they got closer to the farm she could see that they were in fact four-by-fours. As a matter of principle, Deirdre knew as little as she could about any form of motorized transport. But the sheer intensity of her disapproval of these large, cumbersome, gas-guzzling vehicles, which so profoundly offended her socialist as well as environmentalist instincts, meant that she had absorbed some information about various makes and models. These, she suspected, might be Range Rovers – the worst of the lot, to her way of thinking.

As she watched, puzzled, yet somehow mesmerized by what she was seeing, one of the cars drove past the main house into the farm-yard behind it. The other pulled up right in front of the farmhouse itself. Men got out of the vehicles, all dressed in black, their faces invisible behind balaclavas. They fanned out, surrounding both the front and back doors like malevolent wraiths. Each of the men was carrying something, held out in front of him, though Deirdre could not see what it was. She had a horrifying suspicion, however; one that she could not name, but that was tightening her belly and constricting her throat until she could scarcely breathe.

A man walked out of the front door of the farmhouse. From the shock of blond hair Deirdre recognized Tobyn Jansen, her favourite of all the male members of the group. She adored him for his commitment to the cause, his apparently effortless ability to make her laugh, and – though this she found hardest to admit, even to herself – his strongly muscled, golden-haired forearms.

Jansen stood in the open air for a moment, facing the four men who were lined up in a half-circle around him. He seemed to be saying something, though she could not hear what. His gestures, though, conveyed their own meaning: at first conciliatory, then increasingly indignant, and then desperate as Jansen seemed to plead with the men, then threw his hands up in a desperate but futile gesture of self-protection.

Deirdre saw a series of bright flashes. Tobyn Jansen staggered back before falling to the ground, and it was almost at the instant that the back of his head hit the foot of the farmhouse front door that the sound of gunfire reached Deirdre Bull's ears. And then she started screaming.

35

Ronnie Braddock was a former paratrooper. He'd done his time in Iraq as a soldier, then again as a private contractor, bodyguarding administrators and businessmen for an American corporation that was less a commercial business than a private army. Now he was running his own crew, and after that Afghan job it was good to be working on home ground for once, instead of some fly-ridden shit-hole filled with stinking ragheads. The assignment had turned out to be easier than expected, too.

Braddock's lads had come to the farmhouse pumped up, expecting opposition. They'd been told the occupants were members of a terrorist group. That suggested they'd be violent, determined, even willing to die for their cause. In the event, though, the five that they encountered inside the house were almost disappointingly easy to dispose of. They were unarmed, and unable to defend themselves. Even the men failed to put up a fight.

'Eco-warriors, my fucking arse,' said one of the attackers, disdainfully kicking a corpse.

'There's one missing,' said Braddock. He didn't like to see

anyone losing concentration, just because it had all been a stroll so far. 'We were told four men and two women. Well, we took four men down all right. But only one woman. Where's the other?'

'Maybe we were given the wrong numbers.'

'Is that what you want to tell Razzaq? "There was only one woman, so we thought you'd got it wrong?" Fuck off.'

'What do you want to do, then?'

Braddock snapped out his orders: 'Take the lads who were in your car. Search the house, top to bottom, every bloody inch of it. Attics, cellars, cupboards, the lot. You know what to do if you find her. The rest of us are going for a little drive. This lot were nature lovers . . .' He made it sound like some kind of perversion. 'Maybe she went outside.'

'Out there? You'll never find her. She could be fucking anywhere.'

'Bollocks. We're not exactly talking special forces, are we? What we're talking about is some useless, hysterical bitch who's wandering round in circles, pissing herself with fear. If she's out there, she's as good as dead already.'

36

Up on the hillside, Deirdre Bull had managed to crawl through the heather to a low outcrop of rock, behind which she was now hiding, barely able to think straight for the shock of what she had witnessed. As the men went into the farmhouse and further bursts of gunfire echoed around the empty landscape every instinct told her to run, to put as much distance between herself and the danger as possible, as fast as she could go. But fear seemed to render her immobile. She kept imagining eyes, glaring through the farmhouse windows, scanning the landscape, waiting for any sign of movement. It took her several minutes just to remember that she had her mobile phone with her, stuffed into a pocket of her cagoule. But did she dare use it? Her brain told her that no one could possibly hear her. Her fear would not allow her to believe it.

She'd not taken a single further step when four men came out of the house and got into the Range Rover by the front door.

The big black car started moving. At first Deirdre was relieved. That surely meant they were going to drive away the way they had come. But then she realized that they were taking a different course, heading towards the path. And then they were on it, driving directly towards her.

Now Deirdre Bull moved. She dashed from behind the rock and started scrambling straight up the hill, away from the path, which cut diagonally across the slope. She could hear the engine of the Range Rover now as it picked up pace. She knew without even turning around to look that she had been spotted. The chase was on.

Deirdre was thirty-four years old, reasonably fit, but no athlete. She was further hampered by wearing wellington boots. Her breath was becoming more laboured with every few strides that she took. Her feet, made clumsy by the loose-fitting rubber boots, were struggling to get a proper purchase on the hillside. Still she kept going upwards as fast as she could, fighting through the pain in her thighs, her calves and her gasping, protesting lungs. Her eyes were focused on the ground immediately around her. She did not dare look around, for fear of what she might see, or even up, for fear of how far she was from safety. So she was unaware that the escarpment up which she was struggling was actually the side of a long, narrow ridge that ran like a spur from a much larger hill.

Nor did she know that her struggles were the cause of great amusement in the Range Rover, whose driver and passengers were laughing uproariously as they drove up the path to a point directly beneath the fleeing woman. One of the men put on the voice of a TV sports commentator to describe her ascent, 'Oh, I say,' he pontificated. 'She covered the last fifty metres in a shade under thirty seconds. That's quite remarkable! But you have to ask, how long can the plucky little tree-hugger keep going before someone goes and puts her fucking lights out?'

Ronnie Braddock was not amused. 'I'll put your fucking lights out if you don't shut the fuck up.' He was sitting up front, next to the driver. 'Stop the car,' he ordered.

The engine died, and now there was only the sound of the wind rushing across the hillside. Braddock got out of the Range Rover and walked round the front of the car until he was crouching beside

179

the bonnet on the driver's side. He rested his left elbow on the bonnet so as to steady himself as he lined up his sleek, futuristic-looking Steyr AUG A1 sub-machine gun on the back of the fleeing figure some two hundred metres beyond and above him. It was a tricky shot, uphill, with a constantly varying crosswind. And then Deirdre Bull contrived to make it much easier.

One second she was fighting her way up an increasingly steep and treacherous slope, the next she was grasping at fresh air as she reached the top of the escarpment. Directly in front of her the ground fell away even more steeply, leaving her looking down on to a dizzying drop. She straightened up as she fought to stop herself falling down it. And for that brief moment her head and upper body were presented in perfect silhouette.

Braddock smiled beneath his black balaclava and fired off his first round. It missed. He swore under his breath, then smiled as he saw the woman turn round to look back in the direction that the shot had come from. His grin broadened and twisted across his face as he sensed the panic and terror with which she must now be over-whelmed. Twice more he pressed the trigger in quick succession, and this time he hit. The bullets tore into the upper left-hand corner of her torso, spinning her round. And then the woman stumbled over the edge of the escarpment and vanished from his sight.

It took the hunters a couple of minutes to make their way to the point where Deirdre Bull had fallen. Her body was clearly visible far below, the jaunty pink and white cagoule standing out from the grass and bare earth around her.

'Right, that's her done,' said Ronnie Braddock. 'Time we got the fuck out.'

37

Rosconway, Pembrokeshire, Wales

Brynmor Gryffud was at the wheel of the camper van. He drove steadily through the heart of rural Wales, staying well within the speed-limit at all times – with the underpowered Hiace weighed down by its deadly cargo he had little choice in the matter – and reaching the town of Pembroke by 6.00 a.m. From there he headed due west, taking the B4320 towards Angle, a seaside village that is a popular stopping-off point on the spectacular Pembrokeshire Coast Walk that runs around the far south-west corner of Wales. A couple of miles short of Angle Gryffud turned right down a lane towards the village of Rosconway, which had virtually all been demolished, or simply abandoned, when the refinery was built. Only the old parish church still stood intact, as a memento of what had once been a thriving little community. It was now shortly before six thirty.

Just before the lane reached the church Gryffud came to a gate. Beyond it the semi-derelict shells of some old farm buildings stood around a yard, hidden by thick, overgrown hedges from the casual view of any passers-by. The camper van turned off the lane into the old farmyard. Bumping and shaking over the rutted ground, it passed through a gaping hole in the walls of a roofless old barn. As the van entered the barn, moving at little more than a crawl, Smethurst was looking at a GPS location finder, about the size of a stopwatch.

'Forward about five metres,' he said, his eyes fixed to the flickering digits on the readout. 'Left a bit ... stop ... wait a second.'

Smethurst took another look at the GPS, which also doubled as a compass.

'Right, we're on the right spot,' he said. 'But we need to line the van up three more degrees to the north-west. Just reverse a fraction, then go forward again, right hand down.'

Gryffud did as he was told.

'Bollocks!' Smethurst hissed to himself. 'That was one degree too much. Try it again, but this time left hand down. Only a fraction, though. That's all we need.'

The van shifted. Smethurst cursed again, and delivered an even more precise set of instructions. Gryffud did his best to follow them to the last millimetre. Finally Smethurst was satisfied. 'That'll do,' he said. He set the timer to go off in four hours. When that was done he turned to Brynmor Gryffud and said, 'Right, Taff, time to go.' It was now 6.41 a.m.

The two men walked out of the farmyard and turned right, back up the lane towards the Angle Road, a distance of about one and a half miles. They walked at a good, hard pace, aiming to arrive at seven o'clock exactly. They had been standing by the roadside for less than a minute when a BMW pulled up next to them. The driver's window lowered to reveal Uschi Kremer's smiling face.

'Hello, boys! Fancy meeting you here!' she said.

38

Cardiff Gate Services, M4, Wales

At that exact same moment, Carver, too, was hitching a ride. He'd woken at 6.15 a.m. and pulled open the window to see a grey, but dry morning. He'd showered, dressed and had a full English breakfast before heading out into the car park a minute before seven. The Audi was waiting for him. He tapped on the passenger window and it slid down to reveal the lightly tanned face of a man in his early thirties, whose cheerful smile and upper-class accent were in sharp contrast to the steely look in his eyes. Carver knew that look. He saw it in the mirror on a regular basis. The only difference was that his eyes were green and his stare – when he chose to use it – was, if anything, even steelier and colder than the one now appraising him.

'You Tyrrell?' Carver asked.

'Ah, you must be Jenkins.'

'That's right, Andy Jenkins.'

'Then you'd better climb aboard.'

Carver got in the back of the car. He was dimly aware of

suppressed laughter from the massive, shadowy figure in the driver's seat.

'Something amusing you?' Tyrrell asked.

'Bollocks he's called Andy Jenkins, boss,' the driver replied in a South London voice. 'His name is Pablo Jackson . . . isn't it?'

Carver laughed. 'Not for a while . . . How are you, Snoopy?'

'That'll be Company Sergeant Major Schultz to you, boss. I'm a warrant officer these days. Gone up in the world.'

'You know each other?' Tyrrell asked, his curiosity piqued in particular by Schultz calling the newcomer 'boss', the special forces equivalent to 'sir'.

'You could say that,' Carver replied. 'We served together, a long time ago.'

'He's one of us, boss,' Schultz told Tyrrell. 'And one of the best, too.'

39

Carn Drum Farm

Deirdre Bull was not dead. Not quite. She opened her eyes, emerging from unconscious oblivion to a skull-splitting headache and an overwhelming desire to be sick. It took a second or two to register further sources of agony from her shoulder, her left arm, her ribs and her right leg. Neither the arm nor the leg would move. She propped herself up on her right arm, gasping with the pain that this simple movement sent shooting through her body, and saw jagged fragments of bone poking through the bright nylon arm of her cagoule and the dark-stained denim of her jeans. She almost fainted, slumping back to the ground again. Then she remembered: her phone. She fumbled in her pocket for the little handset, lost her grip on it as she pulled it out of the cagoule, and felt the panic rise in her as her hand fumbled blindly across the ground before touching the phone again. She held it up to her face so that she could see what she was doing, and then with her one working thumb tapped out the three digits 9 . . . 9 . . . 9.

'Help me,' she whimpered. 'Please help me. I've been shot. I'm hurt really badly. And the others . . . I think . . . I think . . .' But before she could complete the sentence she had fallen unconscious again.

It took a combined force of police and volunteers from the Brecon Mountain Rescue Team the best part of three hours to locate Deirdre Bull. By that time the carnage at Carn Drum farmhouse had been discovered. Deirdre herself was in a critical condition. She had multiple fractures, and although the bullets that had hit her had miraculously avoided doing any damage to her heart or lungs, there was a strong chance of internal organ damage caused by her fall. She had lost a great deal of blood, and was slipping in and out of consciousness. Just as she was loaded into the rescue helicopter that was going to take her away to hospital she gripped the arm of the paramedic nearest to her, stared him right in the eye and hissed, 'The attack . . . You've got to stop the attack!'

40

RAF Northolt, Hillingdon, West London

At 8.30 a.m. a dozen individuals began to assemble for a flight that would carry them some two hundred and forty miles due west and last an hour and forty minutes.

The PM had banned any Cabinet members from the conference, for the simple reason that he did not want any possible pretenders to his position attracting the publicity it would bring. Nevertheless, there was still an impressive Whitehall turnout. The Home Office, Ministry of Defence and Department of Energy and Climate Change each sent a minister. The Director of Special Forces, who was overall commander of the SAS and SBS, attended, as did senior officers from MI5 and Scotland Yard. As keen as ever to maintain its green credentials, the government had also reserved VIP seats for a representative from Greenpeace and a professor from Imperial College, London, whose special subject was the long-term effects of man-made environmental disasters. Last, but by no means least in their own minds, came Nicholas Orwell, the EU Energy Minister Manuela Pedrosa, and Kurt Mynholt, the second most senior diplomat at the US Embassy in London, whose Senior Foreign Service rank was equivalent to that of a three-star general.

That made eleven passengers. The twelfth was Nikki Wilkins, a twenty-nine-year-old Cabinet Office representative, selected on the grounds of competence, intelligence, people skills and – though no one dared suggest this openly – fresh-faced good looks that made any man, no matter how powerful, just that bit more eager to please her. Wilkins's job was very simple: she had to corral her high-powered passengers on to the choppers, and make sure they had been given all the tea, coffee and biscuits they required and were happy with their seats. Then she had to get them all off again at the far end, in the gaze of the cameras, looking like confident, purposeful men and women who were ready to protect the nation against terrorist threats to its fuel and power supplies.

In short, Nikki Wilkins was both a hostess and a minder. Or as her boss had told her, 'You'll be matron.'

Right now, though, she wished she were an octopus.

She was doing her best to herd the VIPs on to the two helicopters. She would be in the first craft along with the British government ministers, Nicholas Orwell and the EU politician; the members of the group, in other words, who had the strongest desire to be seen by the TV cameras. Those who were happier to remain anonymous would travel in the second helicopter, attracting far less attention at the rear of the VIP party.

As the choppers fired up their engines the noise was so deafening that she was forced to direct everyone by hand gestures. Unfortunately, Wilkins's right hand was occupied holding her phone close to her ear as she talked to her increasingly frantic colleagues already at their destination. But she could not hear a word that was spoken to her without clamping her hand over her other ear. Frantically, she tried to alternate increasingly desperate waves at the milling VIPs with five-second bursts of telephone conversation, with the result that no one, least of all Nikki Wilkins herself, had any clue at all about what the hell was going on.

Her situation was a microcosm of the whole operation. It was as if an orchestra was trying to improvise an entire symphony without a proper score, let alone a single rehearsal. At the site of the meeting itself, local police had only just arrived to set up a security perimeter. A couple of the TV vans, one from the BBC and the other from *Channel Four News*, had become detached from the convoy of vehicles making its way west, and were now hopelessly lost. No one seemed to know what was more important: maintaining security, in which case the TV people could not be told where to go, or gaining maximum publicity, in which case they had to know.

Calls bounced back and forth between Whitehall and the officials who were already in position at the site of the energy security meeting. Finally someone, somewhere made a decision. 'Rosconway . . . Just tell them to put the word Rosconway into their satnavs and take it from there.'

41

Rosconway

Carver, Tyrrell and Schultz arrived at the refinery a few minutes after the helicopters had left Northolt. Along the way Carver had learned a bit more about Major Rod Tyrrell, to give him his full rank and name, or 'Rodders', as he was known to his men. He and Schultz had served together in Iraq, Afghanistan and a smattering of other trouble spots. They were two tough, experienced fighting men and they talked to one another with an ease that downplayed, but never entirely ignored, the difference in their ranks. It was obvious to Carver that Tyrrell had earned Schultz's complete respect. The battle-hardened sergeant major was well over six feet tall, with biceps like boiled hams and the gnarled, bulldog features of a rugby front-row forward. He had precisely zero patience for weakness, incompetence or bullshit of any kind. So if he was impressed by a la-di-da 'Rupert' – as the men referred to their officers – that was all Carver needed to know.

'What a shambles,' Schultz said disgustedly, as they drove past a minimal, painfully inadequate security check into a car park filled with randomly placed vehicles. People were milling around in various stages of aimlessness, confusion and phone-clutching panic, while security men wearing high-visibility yellow tabards over their black uniform jackets tried desperately to impose some kind of order.

'An absolute clusterfuck,' Tyrrell agreed. 'But look on the bright side. If the good guys haven't had enough time to get organized, then neither have the bad guys.'

Schultz laughed. 'You always were a logical bastard, boss.'

'Hmm,' Tyrrell murmured, casting a sharp, narrow-eyed look at the pandemonium. 'Let's just hope that I'm also right.'

42

Willie Holloway needed this like a hole in the head. It was tough enough being the operations manager at the National Petroleum refinery on any normal day, let alone this one. He ran an installation that was supplied by gigantic supertankers that had to be guided up the waters of Milford Haven without running down any of the scores of yachts and pleasure craft that flitted to and fro throughout the summer months, apparently oblivious to the leviathans passing between them like elephants through ants. The massive ships were filled with cargoes of crude oil that were an environmental disaster just waiting to happen. Virtually every stage of every process undertaken at the refinery itself produced substances that were capable of poisoning human beings, blowing them to smithereens or both. The finished products were then stored in giant tanks that were potentially some of the biggest Molotov cocktails in the world.

Now this had been dumped on him. Barely sixteen hours had passed since head office had called Holloway to say that his refinery had been given the huge honour of hosting an instant conference on the risks of terrorist attacks. That meant he had to cope with more than a hundred people arriving on some magical bloody mystery tour. He knew what they'd be like – a bunch of puffed-up ponces, all convinced that they should be allowed to go wherever they wanted and do whatever they wished – none of them with any experience at all of the oil industry. It was his responsibility to get them all through the day without compromising their safety, or the refinery's. And just to make matters worse, everything he did would be noted and judged by the senior executives from UK headquarters, who would be National Petroleum's official corporate representatives at the event.

At least he'd finally been given some outside help. Three casually dressed men had introduced themselves to him as envoys from the Ministry of Defence. Two carried military identity cards that gave their names as Sergeant Tom Croft and Major Hugh Gould, without specifying the unit to which they belonged. The third introduced himself as Andy Jenkins and said he was a civilian advisor.

Willie Holloway had no doubt at all that all three names were false. He had spent enough years working in oil-rich parts of the world that were a lot less pleasant than this corner of the Pembrokeshire coastline to know special forces when he saw them. And he wasn't going to turn down their offer of help.

'Delighted to be of assistance,' said Rod Tyrrell after Holloway had shaken his hand. 'Let's take a look at a plan of this place. See how we can get through this without too much risk of total disaster.'

Carver said nothing. Until further notice he planned to keep his eyes and ears open and his mouth very firmly closed.

43

Carn Drum Farm

In London, the Metropolitan Police have a dedicated Counter Terrorism Command, designated SO15, which deals with threats to the capital city. The Dyfed-Powys police, however, are not so well-equipped to fight the forces of terror. Why should they be? Their patch, which covers a great swathe of south-western and central Wales, has one of the lowest crime-rates in the entire UK. Back in the seventies, outraged Welsh nationalists set fire to the occasional English-owned holiday cottage, but since then, the area has been notable for its lack of antisocial behaviour. So the slaughter at Carn Drum Farm was totally outside the experience of any of the officers who first attended the scene of the crime. They searched the entire property for bodies, but once it was clear that these were all confined to the farmhouse and its immediate surroundings, little attention was paid to the outbuildings, so no one initially realized what the inhabitants of the farm had been up to during their stay in the country. In any event, there was no one whose training or professional experience would have equipped them to detect an improvised bomb factory.

To make matters worse, the force, which includes Pembrokeshire, was already stretched to the limit providing officers to police the unscheduled, unplanned event at the Rosconway refinery. The Chief Constable and a number of senior officers had also decided to attend the event. So when reports of the terrible events at this isolated hill farm first started arriving at the force HQ in Carmarthen, their significance was by no means clear. Were the deaths the result of a burglary that had spiralled into deadly violence? Was this some kind of cult mass suicide? No one knew, and since it can take days, if not weeks, to process the results of forensic examinations of violent crime scenes, especially ones as complex and large-scale as this appeared to be, there was as yet no evidence at all to suggest any terrorist aspect to the crime.

Nor did Deirdre Bull's warning cause any alarm bells to ring. When she begged the paramedic, 'You've got to stop the attack!' he just nodded reassuringly.

Then, as she slumped back on to her stretcher, he turned to a colleague and said, 'Bit late for that.' He naturally assumed she was referring to the attack on the farmhouse. What other attack could there possibly be?

44

Rosconway

Willie Holloway's problem, as he explained to Tyrrell, Schultz and Carver, was that just when he had the greatest need for totally watertight security around the refinery, he actually had less capacity than usual to provide it. The four men were in Holloway's office on the second floor of one of the bland, low-rise administrative blocks from which the plant was managed. A series of ground-floor conference rooms had been hurriedly commandeered to act as the working venues for the participants at the morning's conference and the reporters who were covering the event.

'Half my lads have become car park attendants,' Holloway grumbled. 'They're all standing at the gates, checking IDs and getting everyone spaces.'

'What about the local police?' asked Tyrrell.

'They've set up roadblocks. Nothing's got closer than a mile to here since about eight this morning. As soon as it got light we were out patrolling the fields around the plant.'

'So there is some kind of buffer-zone around the place?'

'Sure. I'll show you . . .' Holloway walked to a wall of his office, on which was a large, framed Ordnance Survey map of the refinery and its surroundings. The plant had been sited on a headland. It was criss-crossed with streets whose names revealed the American origins of the refinery's parent company: First, Second, Third and Fourth Avenues intersecting with Refinery Street, State Street and Ocean Drive.

'As you can see,' Holloway said, 'almost two-thirds of the perimeter of the plant backs directly on to the sea, and we own all the land between the furthest storage tanks and the water. The coastline here is pretty rocky. There's anywhere between thirty and fifty feet of cliff for most of the way around. I've got people patrolling the cliff tops, and there's a couple of boats offshore, keeping an eye on things. Facing the other way, we've got all the land within around seven to eight hundred metres of the perimeter fence.' He ran his finger around the limit of the refinery's land. 'Everything inside that line we searched earlier. If anyone's there, all I can say is they're bloody well hidden.'

For the first time since he'd arrived, Carver spoke: 'But you didn't patrol outside your actual property?'

Holloway gave an exasperated sigh. 'Look, there's a limit, you know? I've had this dumped on me from on high, and I'm doing the best I can.' He looked at his watch. 'Shit! . . . The VIPs are due here any minute, and I've got to make sure we've got everything ready. One of the ministers wants to make an opening statement to the media, and his people say he has to stand right by the distillation columns. They want powerful pictures for the TV. So can I leave you gentlemen to get on with, well . . . whatever you want to do?'

'I think we'll tag along, if that's all right with you,' Tyrrell said. 'Come on, Sergeant . . . and Jenkins?'

'Give me a minute,' said Carver. 'I just want to take another look at this map.'

He watched the others leave the room, then turned his attention back to the refinery layout, and the land around it. Why was Zorn making such an issue of energy terrorism? Did he know something no one else did – did he have advance warning, perhaps, of a planned outrage? 'Well, then,' Carver thought, running with the idea. 'Suppose he were attacking a refinery – this one, for example – what would he do?'

One option was to come in from the sea. Carver could get past Holloway's boat and foot patrols without too much trouble. He'd once beaten the combined forces of the US Coast Guard and Secret Service to attack the President's seaside holiday compound. But then the target had been a single individual, not a giant industrial installation. So how much damage could he do here? There was a limit to the amount of explosive anyone could haul up a cliff-face. A few well-placed C4 charges would certainly make a hell of a bang, but they'd struggle to do the kind of serious, long-term damage that sent a message no one would be able to ignore. For that you'd need a lot more explosive, and that meant some form of transport, either by land or by air.

Well, if anyone really wanted to recreate 9/11 with a death-dive into an oil refinery or nuclear power station there was not a lot Carver could do about it. So what about a truck-bomb? It would have to get past the roadblocks. And even though a truck could deliver a massive amount of explosive, it only delivered it to one place and made one very big hole. But the refinery covered a huge area. It could surely survive a single bomb, no matter how big.

No, the way to attack a place like this was to mount some kind of spectacular: hit it more than once. An image came to his mind of black and white film from the Second World War – Russian 'Katyusha' rocket launchers, mounted on the back of trucks, blasting a fusillade of projectiles at the German lines. Like so many Russian weapons, Katyushas were very basic, very brutal and very easy to copy.

He looked at the map again. If he had a rocket launcher, where would he put it?

There weren't too many options. Anyone using home-made devices would want them as close as possible to the refinery, without actually getting on to its own, well-defended, regularly patrolled property. They'd also need cover behind which to hide: trees, walls, even low hills. But there didn't look to be much of anything near the refinery. The land was flat, with only the odd copse of trees marked on the map, and virtually all the buildings in the area fell within the refinery's property. There was just one farm close by whose buildings might fit the criteria Carver had set himself.

He walked around Holloway's desk, sat by his computer, and called up a satellite picture of the area. He zoomed in on the farm, frowning as he peered at the screen. The buildings seemed unoccupied, even derelict. One was missing its roof. Even from the aerial shot it was obvious that the farmyard was overgrown, the stone or tarmac long since lost beneath a cover of vegetation. Well, if he were going to launch anything, Carver thought, that's where he'd do it from. He looked at the broken-down buildings for a few more seconds. 'Yes, that's the place,' he muttered to himself. And then he, too, left the room.

45

Mid-air, en route to Rosconway

The two Augusta Power Elite helicopters packed with VIPs took off six minutes late, but the pilots put the hammer down and made up time along the way. 'Don't worry, everyone, we're going to arrive bang on time,' the RAF lieutenant at the controls of the lead craft assured his passengers. Nikki Wilkins passed the news on to her colleagues on the ground.

'This could get interesting,' she was told. 'We're still a couple of TV crews short. *Channel Four News* should make it in time, but God only knows where the missing BBC lot have got to.'

'Do you want us to slow down, then?' Wilkins asked.

'No. Get here on time. You're due at ten forty, right?'

'That's the time I was given, yes.'

'Right then, let's try to stick to the schedule if we possibly can. If the BBC don't get their own pictures, that's their problem. They'll just have to take a feed from someone else.'

'What's it like there, though – apart from all the madness? You think this is going to work?'

'Well, that depends … if the TV people all turn up, and if there isn't some God-awful cock-up, this is a great place to do it. You've got this huge industrial complex – you know, all steel and concrete and flaming chimneys – set against this stunning coastline. And the weather looks pretty good. Plenty of blue sky, fluffy clouds, bright sunshine. I think we're going to get some spectacular pictures.'

'That sounds great,' said Nikki Wilkins. 'Full speed ahead!'

46

Wentworth

Malachi Zorn had been unable to contact Nicholas Orwell during his helicopter journey. The total embargo preventing anyone revealing the location of the conference or reporting from the Rosconway refinery applied even to ex-Prime Ministers. But that embargo ended at 10.25 a.m. Immediately reporters began filing their first scene-setting stories via TV camera, microphone, mobile phone and laptop. They described the awesome scale of the refinery, the hubbub of the hastily improvised conference, and the status of the people who would be attending. This, it was agreed, was a remarkable response by the Prime Minister, and though critics would surely be quick to suggest that he was showing signs of panic (Opposition politicians and spokespeople, glued to their TV screens, immediately began drafting precisely such suggestions), there could be no getting away from the speed and seriousness of his actions.

Zorn was, as always, tracking the news channels. It took him a few seconds to grasp what he was seeing. 'Of all the oil joints, in all the countries, in all the world, they walk into mine,' he murmured. He frowned as he digested the reality of what was about to happen. This was going to be what was known as a Black Swan Event, a totally unpredictable occurrence with massive consequences. Except that he, alone of all the world's investors, actually could predict what was going to happen within the next fifteen minutes.

The adrenalin started to pump through Zorn's system, sharpening his mind as it began to process all the possible permutations of events and reactions that could take place over the next few hours. He'd skied black runs, free climbed sheer rock faces without anything but his hands and feet to keep him from falling hundreds of feet, and sailed through storms in the Southern Ocean when the waves had towered over the mast and icebergs had loomed out of the darkness like frozen ghosts. But no fight against the natural elements thrilled him as much as the moments when he took on the market and risked everything he had on his ability to beat the odds.

Zorn realized that Orwell was in very great, possibly fatal danger. He felt no personal concern whatever for the ex-Prime Minister's well-being. But Orwell's death would seriously complicate plans for the rest of the week: though Orwell did not yet know it, a vitally important role had been set aside for him at the Zorn Global launch on Friday evening. There was, though, nothing to be done about that now; even if Zorn had been able to get through to Orwell, it would have been impossible to give him a reason to turn the helicopter around without giving away what was about to happen at Rosconway. So his fate was sealed. And it would, Zorn now realized, be very useful if someone so famous and so closely associated with his fund should be among the casualties. Yes, this was actually an extraordinary stroke of luck.

Very quickly, and taking even greater than usual care to cover his traces, Zorn did everything he could to increase his exposure in all his most highly leveraged trading positions. He staked his own capital and every last cent that his investors had given him, and did it in such a way that his wins, or his losses, would be many, many times the value of what he had put in.

As he always did at moments like this, Zorn looked at the picture of his parents that went everywhere with him. 'OK, Dad, Mom, here we go. I'm going to make them all pay, I promise. I'm so close now . . . So wish me luck, guys. I'm going all-in.'

47

Rosconway

Carver found Tyrrell and Schultz staring despondently at a podium set up in front of a massive steel column, ringed by gantries and pipes. It looked like a rocket on a launch pad. More columns, chimneys and buildings rose behind it. Massive steel pipes wove between them, and ran past the small open space where the minister would address the media. A crowd of journalists and civil servants milled around, waiting for the show to begin. Willie Holloway, meanwhile, was having a heated argument with a pink-faced young man in a pinstriped suit who seemed unhappy with the positioning of the dais. Carver saw a look of undiluted loathing on Holloway's face as he caught a braying, arrogant voice declaring, 'I don't give a damn about your ridiculous health and safety rules. The minister has to have the optimum backdrop. You'll just have to move it.'

The SBS men were no happier. 'Look at this,' Schultz moaned, waving in the direction of the columns. 'Fucking firing positions everywhere. Enough cover to hide a fucking regiment. Even a fucking para could get a shot off before we could stop him.'

'Well, I wouldn't put it quite like that, but I can't say I disagree,' Tyrrell said, giving Carver a nod of greeting. 'How familiar are you with the way these things work?' he asked.

'I know more about mining and ore extraction.'

'Well, you heat the crude up to about six hundred degrees centigrade, till it vaporizes, then stick the gas in these distillation columns, where it separates into different petrochemicals. They all condense at particular levels of the column: the higher up you go, the finer the product. And here's the bit that we need to worry about: every one of those petrochemicals has different properties of flammability, explosiveness and toxicity.'

'In simple English, having a bloody great media bunfight at a refinery is like having a barbecue at a fireworks factory,' said Schultz.

'Well, you lads enjoy the party,' said Carver. 'Can I have the keys to the car?'

'Off to the pub, are you, sir?' asked Schultz, smirking.

'No, just curious about something Holloway and his lads might have missed.'

Tyrrell frowned. 'Anything I need to know about?'

'Not yet,' said Carver. 'Just want to take a look around the area.'

Tyrrell looked at him searchingly. 'That's all you're doing?'

'Positive.'

'Well, if you come across anything suspicious, give me a call.'

'Will do . . . So, the keys?'

'Catch,' said Snoopy Schultz.

Carver plucked them from the air one-handed, and headed for the car park.

48

Blackpole Retail Park, Worcester

Shortly after 10.30 a.m. Uschi Kremer pulled into the parking lot of a McDonald's restaurant located within a soulless shopping centre on the northern outskirts of Worcester. She had driven hard from Rosconway, cutting across South Wales and up into the English Midlands, avoiding motorways, tolls and the CCTV cameras that came with them.

'You can turn your phones on now,' she said, oblivious to Brynmor Gryffud's notional status as group leader. 'In fact, I think you should use them. Call some friends, or maybe, Bryn, you could check in with your office. Keep it nice and light, everything very normal. OK?'

'I'm bursting for a piss,' said Smethurst, getting out of the back of the car, closely followed by Gryffud.

'If you guys do that, then make your calls, I will get you some food,' said Kremer, walking beside them towards the golden arches. She gave them both a cheeky smile. 'So . . . you want to go large?'

'Looking at you, love, I'm getting large already,' Smethurst replied.

'Really? I didn't notice,' Kremer said, putting him in his place. 'So, Bryn, are you hungry?'

'I won't have anything, thanks,' said Gryffud. 'I don't want to give McDonald's any money. I don't approve of their impact on the environment.'

'Oh, fuck off,' Smethurst sneered. 'In case you haven't noticed, you're about to blow an entire fucking refinery to pieces ... and you're worried about having a Big Mac? You'll be telling me meat is murder next.'

'He's right,' said Kremer, pausing for a moment outside the restaurant door. 'It is important that we are seen here, a long way from South Wales, acting like ordinary people. Really, if you think about it, this is part of your mission.'

'Well, if you put it like that . . .' Gryffud conceded.

Kremer took their orders, collected and paid for the food, and spent a minute at a side counter, putting milk and sugar in the men's coffees. It would have taken a very acute observer indeed to notice that two of the miniature plastic pots of milk that she used had not been supplied by the restaurant.

Back at the BMW she settled into the driver's seat, then turned to the two men. 'One Big Mac with large fries for you,' she said, reaching into a brown paper bag and handing two cartons to Smethurst. 'And one Big Tasty with bacon and regular fries for you.'

Gryffud took his food, and then a moment later his cup of coffee. 'You not having anything?' he asked Kremer.

She laughed. 'And ruin my figure? Never!'

'Good thing I don't have a figure to ruin, then,' said Gryffud. 'I'm starving.'

The men ripped great bites from their burgers, grabbed fistfuls of fries, and then washed the whole lot down with gulps of scalding coffee. They ate and drank greedily, saying nothing. And then they started gasping for breath as the cyanide that Kremer had slipped into their drinks got to work, shutting down their bodies' ability to use oxygen, and attacking their hearts and brains. Smethurst, being much the smaller, lighter man, was the first to fall into a coma. Gryffud was able to look imploringly at Kremer and gasp, 'What have you . . . ?' before he passed out. Both were dead by the time Kremer had driven out of the parking lot.

It was now 10.36 a.m.

49

Rosconway

Carver pulled into the deserted farmyard just before 10.37 a.m., a little under three minutes before Dave Smethurst's home-made launchers were due to fire their shells at the oil refinery.

On the way in he passed a long, low brick shed. There was a gaping hole in its roof, about a metre square, as though a meteorite or a cannonball had fallen from the sky and punched its way through the slates. Directly opposite him stood the remains of a traditional farmhouse, flanked on either side by stables, sheds, a small piggery and a large barn. He got out of the car without any great sense of urgency. He didn't seriously expect, let alone fear, that he would find anything. He just wanted to get a sense of what might be possible. And it was good, too, to get away from the farcical chaos and disorganization of events at the refinery and go somewhere quiet and peaceful where he could think undisturbed.

He looked around the yard. As his eyes came to rest on the barn, he had to squint into the sun, which was shining directly at him. So it took him a couple of seconds to register that the object just visible inside the derelict building was the front end of a vehicle: a van, by the looks of it. Carver frowned and strode across the yard towards the barn. As he got closer, he could see that it was an old Toyota Hiace camper van.

Carver's immediate reaction was embarrassment: he'd stumbled into a place where some holidaymakers were trying to find themselves a little privacy. Maybe he should let them enjoy it. Then he thought, 'Who wants to go on holiday in the shadow of an oil refinery?' The number plates caught his eye: they couldn't have been more than ten or eleven years old. But the van looked less up to date: a late-eighties model, even. No innocent holidaymaker drove a car with false plates.

Now, suddenly, he felt the first small shots of adrenalin coursing through him, tightening his stomach and sharpening his reflexes as he approached the van. The interior was dark, the curtains of the side windows drawn. There was no noise or any other sign of life. Carver walked around to the rear of the vehicle. Something caught his eye. He stepped closer and tilted his head to one side as he looked along the vertical line between the door and the body-panel. It had been welded shut.

Carver had told Tyrrell he'd call if he found anything suspicious. This certainly qualified. He pulled out his phone, pressed the number, and then waited frustratedly as the rings at the far end went unanswered. Carver could imagine the rising noise-levels at the refinery. He could hear helicopters getting closer. The VIPs were on their way. When the voicemail came on he said, 'This is Carver. Call me. I've found something you should see.'

Ninety seconds had passed since Carver had driven into the farmyard.

It was clear to him now that there was something in the van that someone did not want discovered. He wasn't going to wait around for backup before he found out what it was. He ran back to the Audi, opened the boot, and pulled up the felt lining to reveal the spare wheel. In the middle of the wheel a plastic tray held the tools needed to put it on the car, including a tyre iron. Carver picked this up and went back to the barn.

He was sprinting now, driven by an instinct that something was badly, urgently wrong.

Inside the van, the timer had run down to twenty seconds, and counting . . .

Carver dashed up to the van and smashed the tyre iron against one of the side windows. The effect was minimal, just a small crack in the glass. He swung his arm again, putting all his strength into it, then repeated the blow again and again, battering the toughened glass until it first cracked into a spider's web of fracture lines, and then, at last, a hole appeared.

Carver needed to make it bigger, and the small head of the tyre iron wasn't up to that job. He used his own elbow, jabbing at the glass until a great section of the window gave way.

Now he reached into the open window and pulled the curtain open. He looked in and his eyes widened as he saw the gas cylinders, arranged like giant test tubes in their metal rack. Carver knew exactly what he was looking at. He gripped the sides of the window frame, ignoring the fragments of broken glass that still clung to them, and was about to pull himself up and through the window when there was a sudden blast of blinding light, deafening noise and burning heat, and as Carver flung himself to the ground he realized that he'd been beaten.

Dave Smethurst had set the four-hour timer at 6.39 and 42 seconds, precisely. And so at 10.39 and 42 seconds an electrical signal was sent by the timer to the junction box inside the Toyota Hiace, and then on to the twelve launch tubes. Twelve igniters sparked into life, causing the ammonium nitrate to decompose, releasing a large quantity of oxygen. This reacted with the hydrogen and carbon in the icing sugar to produce an intense, barely controlled burst of energy, concentrated within the high-pressure tubes. This sudden flare of light and flame ignited the fuses at the bottom of each shell, and blasted the shells through the skin of paper stretched across the roof of the camper van and up into the clear blue sky.

Five seconds later the thirteenth fuse set off the igniter in the jerrycan of fuel that Smethurst had left inside the van. It, too, burst into flame, engulfing the interior of the vehicle and destroying any trace of fingerprints or DNA, leaving just a scorched and blackened metal shell.

Carver picked himself up from the floor of the derelict barn, momentarily deafened by the force of the explosion. He screwed up his eyes, gave his head a shake to clear it . . . and then sprinted desperately to his car.

50

The choppers were just making their final approach to the refinery, barely five hundred metres from their destination. Their crews' attentions were entirely concentrated on the landing ground that had been marked out for them in a field directly opposite the main gates. A reception committee of officials and media representatives had formed up there in a ragged semicircle. From her window seat, Nikki Wilkins could see the cameramen jostling for the best position and raising their lenses to the sky. As the helicopter swung round to come into land, she spotted a sudden, dazzling flash of light from the ground, away to her left. She turned her head towards it, and had just enough time to register the billowing plume of flame and smoke before something punched into the side of the helicopter and sent it staggering off course like a dazed boxer stumbling across the ring. The next thing Wilkins knew, the cabin was spinning round and round and she was screaming out in terror as the air all around her was filled with scorching flame and red-hot shards of metal.

The explosive-filled steel gas-cylinder that hit the Power Elite was bigger than the shell from a Challenger 2 battle tank. It obliterated the cockpit window, decapitated the pilot, missed the co-pilot by a whisker, and exited the far side of the helicopter, taking a mass of glass, metal, plastic and electrical wiring with it, like a through-and-through bullet tearing the flesh from its victim's back. It did not, however, explode. There was still a tiny fraction of the fuse left unburnt, and until it triggered the detonator, the sugar/fertilizer mix would remain inert.

Its momentum somewhat slowed by its impact with the helicopter, the cylinder veered off course, flattened the arc of its trajectory, and hit the second helicopter amidships.

Now it exploded.

A millisecond later, the United Kingdom's special forces had been left without a commanding officer, and MI5 had lost its deputy director. The fireball that consumed them had been captured live on television. But this was just the start of the catastrophe.

As the cluster of people by the landing site ran for cover from the shrapnel that fell like red-hot hail from the sky, the co-pilot of the first helicopter desperately fought for control of his craft.

And then the whole world seemed to go up in flames, as the other eleven cylinders hit their targets.

The pipes, towers and storage tanks of an oil refinery are double-skinned to prevent any leaks. But even two thin sheets of steel are no protection against an explosive shell impacting at close to the speed of sound. The tanks that each hold millions of gallons of oil and petrol are clustered in twos and threes within brick and concrete berms, designed according to safety regulations that demand they can safely contain a hundred and ten per cent of the capacity of the biggest tank. But those regulations do not account for what happens when all the tanks are breached at once, and a torrent of flaming liquid overflows those concrete defences like lava escaping a volcano. Refinery staff are trained to evacuate their workplaces quickly and safely in the event of an emergency, and await the arrival of local fire brigades. But evacuation attempts are futile when there is no place of safety; when death waits at every turn, and any attempt at rescue will be far too little, too late.

Armageddon had come to Rosconway. The air was torn asunder by a terrifying conflagration of thunderous noise, light, heat – and blasts of explosive pressure that picked up cars and trucks, sent people flying, and obliterated the mighty structures of the refinery in a series of explosions that seemed to go on and on in a never-ending wave of destruction.

The explosive shells were damaging enough in themselves. But their greater purpose was to set free the pent-up power that was locked in the refinery itself. The giant storage tanks, the distillation towers, the miles of pipes that carried a multitude of petrochemical substances around the complex: all now became locked in a deadly chain reaction as the fires of hell engulfed them.

51

Willie Holloway had been trying to tell the arrogant little tit of a ministerial aide, for the umpteenth time, that safety really was an important issue at an oil refinery. He was shouting even louder than before, just to make himself heard over the hubbub of the chattering people all around them, and the whirring clatter of the incoming helicopters. Then the noise of the rotors was obliterated by a metallic crash, immediately followed by a thunderous explosion. Holloway looked up to see a single helicopter spiralling down from the sky. All that was left of the other chopper was a boiling cloud of fire and thick black smoke.

A second later one of the projectiles hit the distillation tower that rose from the ground no more than fifteen metres behind him, and the gigantic explosion that followed wiped all traces of Willie Holloway, the aide and everyone anywhere near them from the face of the earth.

Tyrrell and Schultz were about a hundred metres away, walking down the road towards the administrative blocks, where they were due to have a discreet and hopefully unobserved meeting with the Director of Special Forces. A razor-sharp shard of steel, roughly the size of a frisbee, hit Major Rod Tyrrell just above his right ear, sliced the top of his head off, and killed him instantly. Schultz was unharmed, but the sheer force of the blast picked him up and threw him to the ground. By the time he dragged himself to his feet, the air was filled with choking, billowing smoke that reeked of burning oil, and the ground shook from the relentless barrage of explosions as one refinery unit after another burst into scorching flames or blew itself to smithereens.

Holding a handkerchief to his face to give himself the most basic protection against the fumes, Schultz broke into a stumbling, coughing run as he tried to get away from the inferno. Amidst the thunder of explosions and the clouds of smoke he neither heard nor saw the stricken helicopter until it scraped over the roof of one of the office blocks just ahead of him, dislodging scores of roof-tiles as it went, crashed on to the road surface, and came skidding towards him in a screeching mass of tangled metal and shattered glass.

Schultz flung himself out of the way, somehow managing not to be shredded by the mangled blades of the helicopter rotors. The chopper kept going in the direction of the stricken, blazing distillery towers, before coming to rest by the side of the road, no more than a few metres from a ruptured pipe that was pouring some kind of burning liquid on to the ground. The petrochemical flowed across the tarmac, flaming like the brandy on a flambéed steak, creating a pool of fire that was spreading wider and wider. And the shattered helicopter was right in its way.

If anyone had managed to survive the crash they were about to be incinerated.

Schultz did not stop for a second to worry about his own safety. He ran straight to the helicopter. The door of the passenger compartment was half-open. Schultz pulled at the hot, twisted metal and managed to widen the gap so that he could force a leg and part of his upper body into the cabin. He swept a hand back and forth in front of his face, trying to clear away the smoke to see if anyone had survived. His first impression was that they were all dead, or at the very least unconscious: no one was moving or crying out for help, and there simply wasn't time to check them individually for any signs of life. He realized that he recognized one of the faces: Nicholas Orwell, the former Prime Minister, was staring at the ceiling of the cabin with lifeless, unblinking eyes. And then Schultz saw a hand – a woman's hand – move a fraction. She was trying to reach out to him, and through the roar of the flaming refinery he heard her voice very faintly beg, 'Help me . . . help me, please.'

Schultz squeezed his way further into the compartment. He could see her now, strapped into a chair to his right. Her face was covered in blood that had come from a deep gash on her forehead, where a flap of skin had peeled away, exposing the bone of her skull. More bone was visible on one of her legs, where a compound fracture had stabbed through the skin below the hem of her skirt. Schultz was relieved. Neither wound was fatal. Unless there were any nasty surprises that he could not yet see, the woman was not going to die just yet.

But if he couldn't get her and himself out of the chopper fast, it wasn't going to make much difference what her wounds were like. They were both going to be burned to a crisp.

He reached for the clasp of her seat belt and pressed the button to release it. Nothing happened. He pulled at the belt. Still it would not loosen. Schultz stayed calm. He and Tyrrell had come to the conference in civilian clothes and, in theory, unarmed. Schultz, however, was not a man who liked the idea of being defenceless. So he'd strapped a KA-BAR fighting knife with a seven-inch chromium steel blade to his lower right leg. He took it out and started sawing at the tough, webbed nylon of the safety belt.

The smoke in the cabin was getting even thicker. The air was roasting hot. Schultz could not see the burning liquid outside, but he didn't have to. He knew it had to be a metre at most away from the side of the fuselage. He kept sawing, working his way through the unyielding material until only a few strands were left.

One last swipe of the blade and the belt came free. Schultz reached for the woman and hauled her up over his right shoulder in a fireman's lift, hearing her moan in pain as her shattered leg was so crudely manhandled.

That was all right. Pain was good. It meant she was still alive.

He shoved his left arm and shoulder against the half-open passenger door and managed to create just enough space to get himself and the woman through. As he poked his head out Schultz could see the first flames from the burning chemicals licking against the helicopter. Any urge he might have had to be delicate with the woman disappeared. All that mattered was getting her out. She gave another whimper as he bumped her against the door frame, and he could feel her chest rising and falling against his as she sobbed in agony.

The flames were rising around them as Schultz gave one last heave. Then he heard the door crash shut behind him as he and his human burden staggered out of the helicopter. He found himself standing on a tiny island of bare tarmac, surrounded by a sea of fire. It was impossible to judge his bearings. All he could do was look back at the now-burning chopper, try to picture where it had ended up, relative to the road he had been on, and then plunge blindly into the flames.

52

Carver spun the car round, put the pedal down, and raced out of the farmyard. When he hit the lane he did a handbrake turn to wrench the car through ninety degrees, then accelerated again as he drove towards the refinery. Up ahead the sky itself seemed to be ablaze, as the entire horizon filled with night-black smoke pierced by geysers of yellow, white and orange flame.

It took him forty seconds to reach the road that ran alongside the refinery's main security fence. He was met by a scene of total carnage and devastation.

The field where the VIPs were supposed to land held the smouldering wreckage of the blown-up helicopter and the bodies of those who had died in it, or been hit by pieces of falling wreckage. Survivors were standing in small dazed groups: shadowy figures who were visible for a moment or two before being swallowed up again by the drifting, choking smoke. A man was striding up and down, jabbering at people and pointing towards the refinery as if giving orders, but no one was paying him any attention. Two uniformed security men were standing like lovers, one hugging and consoling the other, who was weeping at the horror of what he had seen. A TV cameraman was looking at the nightmare in front of him, his camera held uselessly down at his side. There was no point in him filming anything: the rest of his team, and the truck in which they'd come to Rosconway, had been obliterated. A solitary outside broadcast van painted in BBC livery had pulled up on to the grass and a female reporter was speaking to camera, turning back every few seconds to look at the scene she was attempting to describe. She started at the sound of another explosion, and cowered for a second, before pulling herself together, straightening up and looking at the camera again.

Carver drove as close to the conflagration as he could, then got out of the car. On foot he made his way towards the fire, surrounded all the way by dead and wounded people, abandoned vehicles, and random bits of torn and twisted metal, blown or fallen from who knew where. Holloway, Tyrrell and Schultz had been somewhere in there, and were now almost certainly dead. If he had got to the van sooner, they might still be alive. He stared at the volcanic fury of the blaze, feeling overawed and utterly insignificant in the face of its sheer scale.

Then Carver caught a glimpse of a familiar silhouette, outlined against a wall of fire. Schultz was alive. He was staggering out of the inferno, and there was someone over his shoulder. Carver saw the big man stumble, overcome by the heat and the smoke. Schultz took a few more paces, and then his knees buckled beneath him and he toppled to the ground, letting go of whoever he was carrying, so that their body rolled off his shoulder and fell helplessly, defencelessly, on to the tarmac.

Carver ran towards the two prone bodies, ignoring the terrible, roasting heat and the poisonous rasp of the chemicals in the air. He found Schultz apparently unconscious on the ground. A woman was lying beside him, her face bloodied, her leg broken. Carver knew that he would be able to carry her away to safety, but Schultz was another matter. He weighed sixteen or seventeen stone: too much for Carver to drag with one arm if he was holding the woman with the other. Desperately, Carver grabbed Schultz's chest and shook him. Then he gave his face three or four stinging slaps. Schultz blinked, groaned and tried to focus his eyes on Carver.

'Get up!' Carver shouted, his throat burning with the effort, still so deafened by the earlier explosion that he could barely hear his own words.

Schultz just looked at him uncomprehendingly.

'Get up, Sergeant Major!' Carver repeated. 'That's an order!'

The air was getting even hotter, if such a thing were possible, and Carver could barely breathe. He felt dizzy, there was a rushing sound in his ears, and his vision was blurring.

He could just make out the blurred outline of Schultz's body as the SBS man tried to get up. Carver got down on one knee, reached for the woman and lifted her over his shoulder. It took every ounce of strength and concentration he still had to be able to push up with his legs and get to his feet again. Then he reached out for Schultz.

'Grab my hand!' he croaked, his parched vocal chords now barely able to summon the means to speak.

Carver felt Schultz's hand grip his wrist. Somewhere in the distance he heard the tortured scream of failing metal, and the remnants of a distillation tower appeared out of the flame, loomed over the three stranded humans, and toppled towards them with the slow, stately, but crushing inexorability of a felled redwood tree.

Carver wrapped his fingers round Schultz's arm and pulled him upright. The two men broke into a ragged, shambling run as the top of the distillation tower crashed down, smashing into the road at exactly the point where they had been huddled less than ten seconds before.

Carver kept moving, driving himself forward, one desperate step after another. In the near delirium of overpowering heat and oxygen starvation, he felt as though he had been transported back a quarter of a century to the beastings he'd endured as he fought for selection to the SBS: forced marches with full packs in which every man had to complete the course, even if his mates had to drag him over the line. Back then his enemies had been the cold, the rain and the biting wind of the Brecon Beacons, the very opposite of the forces tormenting him here. But the principle was the same. You kept going when every fibre of your body was screaming at you to stop. You kept going when you thought you would die if you took a single step more. You kept going until you got to the end.

And suddenly Carver was aware that the air was a fraction cooler, and that the smoke had cleared away. He came back to reality to find himself back out on the road beside the refinery. Schultz was standing next to him, coughing and dry-retching. There was a small patch of cool, green grass a few metres away, so Carver walked over to it and laid the woman down. He took off his tie and wound it around the woman's broken leg to give the shattered bone some small degree of support. He noticed she still had her name badge pinned to her jacket. It read, 'Nicola Wilkins, Cabinet Office.' Carver put his finger to her throat, just below the jawbone, and felt a faint, fluttering pulse.

'Congratulations,' he murmured. 'You survived.'

53

Wentworth

The British Prime Minister had wanted a television spectacular. To Malachi Zorn's delight, what he got was a live horror show.

It had all been caught on camera: one helicopter exploding in mid-air; the other in its death-spiral to the ground; the flaming debris raining down upon spectators; the slaughter on the ground; the screams of reporters as they realized that they, too, were as vulnerable as anyone else; the roar of the flames, the volcanic thunder of the explosions, and then the darkness as one by one the TV crews were added to the casualties, their equipment was destroyed and their broadcasts died. For a minute there was nothing but blackness from Rosconway, and panic in the studios of TV channels whose presenters were realizing that they had just witnessed the deaths of old friends and colleagues along with all the other casualties.

Then the lost BBC van arrived, and a single feed from Rosconway supplied footage that was sent around the world – footage that sent global financial markets into a frenzy as traders tried to digest the implications of a major US oil corporation suffering a terrorist attack on supposedly friendly soil. It showed an attack that had killed three members of the British government, an EU minister, a senior US diplomat, Nicholas Orwell, and, if rumours already surfacing on the internet were to be believed, the Director of British Special Forces.

Just as on 9/11, the financial implications were immediate, and felt throughout the global economy. Oil prices spiked. So did gold, as investors sought a safe haven. The pound plummeted. Investors started dumping UK government bonds. The Bank of England had not yet raised interest rates, but it could only be a matter of minutes, and that would add further downward pressure to the UK economy. The FTSE index in London plunged almost eight per cent as energy stocks, already softened by recent comments made by Malachi Zorn, collapsed. Insurance companies were hit as the multi-billion cost of rebuilding the refinery became evident. The shares of airlines, airport operators, hotel corporations and online travel agencies on both sides of the Atlantic fell as the markets decided that US travellers, nervous of threats to their safety, would stay away from Britain. Defence stocks, however, rose. It was reasonable to assume that the British government's savage defence cuts might now be reversed. And since, as Zorn had also pointed out in his BBC interview, Britain's energy supplies were dominated by foreign-owned corporations, the knock-on effects were felt on the bourses of Europe. And with the New York Stock Exchange due to open at two thirty in the afternoon, UK time, they would hit Wall Street like a tsunami rolling across the Atlantic.

There was an atmosphere of stunned, speechless despair at 10 Downing Street. There was frenzy in financial institutions. But at Zorn's hired mansion on the Wentworth estate there was only the exultant laughter of a man for whom Christmas Day has come earlier, and more joyously, than he could have dreamed possible. This was the single biggest financial coup of all time. He had made tens of billions of dollars, pounds, euros, yen and Chinese yuan.

Now all he had to do was collect it. If 9/11 was anything to go by, the markets would soon be shut down. He had just a few minutes, maybe less, to get out of all his positions, collecting his winnings on the way. There wasn't a second to lose.

54

Kensington Park Gardens

Alix could see Dmytryk Azarov's lips move. She could hear the words he was saying. She knew – because he'd made a point of emphasizing this fact, as if to prove her importance to him – that he'd cancelled an important business meeting to be with her. But he was wasting his breath, because she felt so totally disconnected from him that none of it made any difference. He was as distant from her, and as unimportant, as the reporter on the screen of the television that was on, but ignored, in the far corner of the sitting room.

'Don't believe what they say in the papers about these women I was supposed to be seeing,' Azarov was saying, working himself up into a fever of righteous indignation. 'These . . . what do they call them? . . . party girls, who claim that I slept with them. It is all lies. These women just want money, and journalists are vermin who will spread any slander to sell their filthy rags . . .'

He felt he had to persuade her, that much was obvious. But Alix didn't care if he'd slept with one party girl, or ten, or one hundred.

Her head was filled with Carver. Her body was still sending reminders that he had been inside her, like pulsing echoes of their lovemaking.

'All the time I was away, all I thought about was you,' Azarov went on. 'You were in my dreams. I missed your body next to mine . . .'

He didn't realize that all he was doing was making Alix think of Carver's body next to her. The memory of his touch was so vivid that it sent a little shiver through her, and made her catch her breath.

Azarov saw that tremor of emotion, and, of course, mis-interpreted it. 'You feel the same way, too! I knew it!'

Alix managed a wan smile as Azarov launched into another declaration of his passion for her. She was wondering how and when she was going to extract herself from Azarov's life. She couldn't possibly mention Carver. Irrespective of his own behaviour, Azarov did not take kindly to women who betrayed him, or the men with whom they slept. He would want revenge, and that frightened Alix, not just for Carver's sake but also Azarov's. He would not know what he was taking on.

She wondered where Carver was now. She knew what it meant when he disappeared the way he'd done last night. He was work-ing. And she knew what that led to, too: violence, danger, secrecy and the constant worry of never knowing where he was and when, if ever, he would come home. By making love to him, and making herself so vulnerable to the effect he had on her, she had let that back into her life. She'd broken a vow she'd made to herself and . . .

Alix realized that Azarov had fallen silent. He was looking past her with an expression of total incredulity on his face. 'Mother of God,' he gasped, regaining the power of speech.

Alix turned to follow his staring eyes, and saw the television screen go blank, before the picture cut back to a pair of presenters trying to maintain some semblance of professional self-control.

'What's going on?' she asked.

Azarov walked across to the remote control that was sitting beside the television, and rewound the picture. Alix watched explosions fall in upon themselves to leave intact metal towers and tanks. One helicopter flew backwards from the ground up into the sky, and another was magically reconstituted in mid-air. Then Azarov pressed play and the action was repeated, this time in the correct direction and at the right speed, ending in that terrible blank, dead screen. And as she watched Alix knew, with an intuitive certainty she could not possibly explain, that Carver was there. That blazing oil refinery had been the destination he had been heading for when he had left her lying in his bed.

He was there. And now, so soon after she had found him, Alix feared she had lost him for ever.

But while she worried about the personal cost of what had happened, Azarov was already working through the financial consequences. 'This is exactly what Zorn said would happen. It's almost as if . . . no, that's impossible.' He looked at Alix, talking to her now less as his lover than as another businessperson. 'Do you think he knew this would happen? Or that he made it happen?'

Whatever Alix's differences with Azarov, she shared with him the instinctive Russian belief that behind any disaster there was always a conspiracy. 'That's possible, of course it is,' she said, her mind now fully engaged in the question. Carver had talked about Zorn, linking him to the woman she had known as Celina Novak. Now she could see connections starting to form in her mind between a string of previously separate elements: her mistrust of Zorn, her conviction that Carver had been at the refinery, and now the suggestion that Zorn had somehow been the instigator of the disaster there.

'What will you do if Zorn really did plan all this?' she asked Azarov. 'I did warn you that I thought there was something suspicious about his scheme.'

Azarov grinned. 'And I told you that a man should not pick up the dice unless he has the balls to lose everything on a single roll. I am very happy that I placed my money on Zorn. He has certainly rolled the dice. Surely, too, he will win.'

A picture of Nicholas Orwell appeared on the screen, as a presenter's voice announced that he was missing, believed dead at the scene.

Now Azarov laughed out loud. 'So he was willing to let his closest ally die to help his plan succeed. Ha! This Zorn is a man with iron in his soul.'

'You didn't answer my question,' Alix insisted. 'What are you going to do?'

'And you asked the wrong question, my beautiful darling. It should have been: what are we going to do? And I will tell you. We have been invited to go to the tennis at Wimbledon tomorrow with Malachi Zorn. If he still goes – and he will, I guarantee – then we will go with him. I want to take another close look at this man, and I would like you to do the same. I want to know exactly what he is made of, and a woman's eye will see what a man's does not. You know the saying: keep your friends close and your enemies closer. I do not yet know whether Malachi Zorn is my greatest friend or my most bitter enemy. But either way, I will stay close.'

Dmytryk Azarov was by no means the only one of Malachi Zorn's investors to be glued to the TV news. In his suite at Claridge's, chosen at Charlene's insistence because it had been designed by Diane von Furstenberg, Mort Lockheimer was cheering every horrific element of the disaster unfolding before his eyes. He had watched Zorn's BBC interview and been puzzled by the way so much of it had been devoted to the risk of energy terrorism. Now he got it. Zorn had obviously been given some kind of inside in-formation that an attack was imminent – either from the perpetrators or through leaks from the security forces; Lockheimer wasn't bothered which. Zorn must have set up a bunch of short positions, just like he'd done so many times before. Now he was watching them all pay off in spades. And if Zorn was getting rich, so was Lockheimer.

Lockheimer was at least forty pounds overweight. His entire body was covered in a thick mat of black and grey hair, and the only thing covering it right now was a white towelling bathrobe. 'What did I tell you!' he exclaimed, grabbing Charlene in a gleeful bear hug. 'That little fucker Zorn just hit the fuckin' jackpot. Didn't I say you should blow him . . . didn't I?'

Charlene looked at her husband appraisingly. 'He made us a lot, huh? Millions?'

'Tens of millions, baby!'

She reached down and started undoing the knot of the towelling belt that was holding her husband's robe together. 'Well, in that case, sweetie, why don't I just blow *you*?'

55

Rosconway

The Cabinet Office staff had arranged for a St John Ambulance crew to be present at the conference, just in case anyone tripped over a pipe, or was taken ill. Somehow they had survived the blast with their vehicle intact. But Carver only had to take one look at the chalk-white skin and dazed eyes of the amateur volunteers to know that they were too traumatized by the overwhelming violence that they had just witnessed to be of any help. It made little difference: he and Schultz knew enough about basic battle-field medicine to tend to Nikki Wilkins's immediate needs. They climbed up into the ambulance and commandeered the splints, bandages and morphine shots they needed to stabilize her broken leg and head injury, and reduce the pain of the wounds. Then they carried Wilkins, still unconscious, back to the Audi, laid her out along the rear seat, and strapped her in as best they could.

'Drive,' said Carver. 'Head for Pembroke. There's got to be a hospital there.'

They were less than a mile down the road, still travelling

beneath a pall of smoke that was spreading across the sky as far as the eye could see, before Carver had gone online and found both the location of the South Pembrokeshire Hospital and directions for getting there. He was about to offer Schultz his condolences for Tyrrell's loss – nothing too overwrought, just a simple acknowledgement that a good man had gone – when the phone rang. It was Grantham. His first words were: 'You're alive.'

'Don't sound so disappointed,' Carver replied.

'You know, for once, I might actually be pleased to hear your voice,' said Grantham. 'So what the hell just happened?'

'Someone stuck a dozen home-made mortar barrel tubes in an old Hiace van, loaded them with explosive shells, and blew the shit out of an entire refinery. And I should have stopped them.'

'How?'

'I wasn't at the refinery when the shells hit. I was at the launch site.'

'What do you mean? Had you found out what was happening?'

'No, I'd worked out what might happen. I didn't think there'd actually be anything there.'

'Well, that's as clear as mud.'

'Sorry . . .' It struck Carver that he might not be as out of it as that St John Ambulance crew, but his mind was still reeling as it struggled to process what he had just experienced. It was time he pulled himself together.

'All right,' he said. 'Here's how it was done. The van that contained the mortars was parked inside an old barn, at a deserted farmyard about a kilometre from the refinery. The weapon was set to a timer, along with some kind of incendiary device – petrol by the smell of it. The moment the mortars fired, the van was burned out, removing all trace of the people who'd driven it or worked on the weapon. This was a professional job, straight out of the old IRA manual.'

'Really? You think there were Paddies involved?'

'Maybe . . . but it could just as easily have been one of ours. Anyone who served in Ulster during the Troubles, or even did bomb disposal work on this side of the Irish Sea, would have seen things like this.'

'But how could they have known about the conference today?'

Carver thought for a moment: no, it was out of the question. 'They couldn't,' he said, definitively. 'Look, this was a totally last-minute event. No one had any warning. That's why it was such a dog's breakfast. The organization, the security, the media coverage – it was all a total joke. But this attack was the exact opposite. It was very carefully calculated. Whoever hit the refinery had every single one of those launcher tubes calibrated to the last millimetre, the last bloody fraction of a degree. Each of those things hit a target. And making the launch tubes, the framework to hold them, all the projectiles . . . getting hold of the explosives . . . no, there wasn't anything last-minute about that. I'd say weeks of preparation, even months, went into this.'

'So what are you saying – that it was just a bloody coincidence? I'm not buying that.'

'Why not? Stranger things have happened. But even if it was a coincidence that the attack and the conference were planned for the same place at the same time, I don't think there was anything remotely coincidental about the time and place of the attack itself. Come on . . . someone blows the crap out of a massive oil refinery the day after Malachi Zorn's told the whole world that eco-terrorism is the big new threat . . . What do you think?'

'I think it's a bit bloody adjacent, certainly.'

'Exactly, so what are the markets doing right now? Let me guess: oil price rocketing, stocks crashing, pound through the floor . . .'

'All of that and more,' Grantham agreed. 'It's a total nightmare. The economy was weak to begin with. An event like this could send it over the edge.'

'Meanwhile Zorn's cashing in. He's got to be. The whole thing was a set-up.'

'Except for Orwell . . . how do you explain that? Are you seriously saying Zorn deliberately sacrificed his own right-hand man?'

'I don't know,' Carver admitted. 'He could have done. The amount of money he stands to make, my guess is he'd do just about anything. But you're right ... I don't have any concrete link between this and Zorn.'

'I might be able to help you with that,' Grantham said. 'Early this morning, hours before the refinery was hit, someone went to a farmhouse in the middle of Wales, miles from anywhere, and executed four men and a woman. According to the locals, they'd been staying there for the past few days. The police are searching the place now. They've found evidence of a bomb-making factory: a couple of kilos of home-made explosives, plus several discarded gas canisters of various sizes, steel girders, welding equipment—'

'Exactly what you'd need to make the set-up I saw,' Carver pointed out.

'Precisely.'

'But everyone was killed. What good is that?'

'Not everyone. One of them got away, a woman, name of Deirdre Bull. She tried to make a run for it. Whoever attacked the farmhouse tracked her, shot her, and left her for dead. But she lived. In fact, she's lying in the intensive care unit at Bronglais General Hospital, Aberystwyth, right now. Oh, and here's an interesting titbit: when she was rescued she even told the paramedics they had to stop the attack . . .'

'What? She told them about Rosconway?'

'No such luck. She just mentioned an attack. They thought she meant the one on the farm.'

'Christ, has she been interviewed yet?'

'Apparently not. The local coppers have been told she's not well enough to talk.'

'Oh, bollocks to that!'

For the first time the hint of a smile entered Grantham's voice. 'That's what I thought, too. Why don't you get up there, see if you can get in for a word with Ms Bull? Play at being Andy Jenkins, pillar of the MoD, a while longer. I'll have a word with the local police chief, appeal to his sense of patriotism at a time of national emergency, so you shouldn't have any trouble from him.'

'What about the medics?'

'Oh, just use your natural charm, Carver. How can they resist?'

'I'd better get going. It's got to be a two-hour drive to Aberystwyth, minimum.'

'No need. There's an airport at Haverfordwest, just the other side of Milford Haven from where you are now. They've got a helicopter charter outfit there. Get a chopper, go to the hospital, get Bull to link this to Zorn, and then get back here to London. We need to discuss what to do about Zorn. And speaking of that particular devil, he's about to make a public statement, live on every TV channel known to mankind. I'd better see what he has to say for himself.'

Carver put away the phone and turned on the car radio, tuning it to *Radio 5 Live*, and heard the voice of a news reporter saying she was outside the mysterious American billionaire Malachi Zorn's Surrey mansion, and was expecting him to appear at any moment.

'Zorn?' asked Schultz, as they entered the outskirts of Pembroke. 'Is that the bastard you said was responsible for what just happened?'

'Yeah.'

'I'd like to tear that fucker limb from fucking limb.'

Carver looked at Schultz. He'd planned on doing the Zorn job alone. But there was a lot to be said for having the massive SBS man on his side. He thought about his plans and the specific ways in which Schultz might improve them. Yes, it could certainly work.

'Suppose I helped you do that?' he asked.

'You taking the piss, boss?'

'Never been more serious. Listen, no one knows whether you're dead or alive right now . . .'

'Nah, suppose not.'

'And it's going to be days before they work out the final casualty lists. So you could just disappear off the grid, couldn't you?'

'The CO's not going to like that. I'm a company sergeant major.

I'm supposed to set an example, do my duty, not piss off on private jollies.'

'Don't worry about that. The man I was just talking to is a very influential individual. If I ask him to square it for you, trust me, there won't be a problem.'

Schultz pulled up at a red light and gave Carver a long, searching look. 'What exactly was it you said you did for a living, boss?'

'I didn't say.'

'But we're going after this Zorn geezer?'

'Yes.'

'And you know a bloke who can just call up Poole, get my CO on the line, and tell him what to do?'

'Yes.'

The light turned green and Schultz drove away. 'And what exactly do you want from me?'

'Drop the girl at the hospital and get me to the airport at Haverfordwest. Then head for London. Give me a number and I'll call you. We'll be doing the job tomorrow. We're going to need someone else, too, someone we can trust. And I mean, absolutely. One word of this gets out—'

'Don't worry, I've got the right man. He was in the Service, got out about six months ago. Just about to fuck off to Iraq with one of them Yank security companies.'

'And he's good?'

'One of the best.'

'Then that'll do me.'

'And we're going to take this Zorn bastard out?'

'Well, Snoopy,' said Carver, 'just you wait and see.'

On the radio the presenter was saying, 'And now let's cross back, live, to Surrey, where we are about to hear an official statement from the man who predicted a tragedy like today's, and who was a close personal friend of the late Nicholas Orwell. I can see on my monitor that the statement is about to begin. So this is Malachi Zorn . . .'

56

Wentworth

Malachi Zorn's PR people had advised him to wait a few hours before he faced the media. It was worth taking time, they said, for their best writers to craft a statement. He had said no. 'I don't want a crafted statement. I just want to go out and speak from the heart.' The PRs had protested, but at the same time, he had seen their minds working out how to use his determination just to go out and speak his mind on behalf of a departed friend as a story in itself. It was a nice human touch: the media would gobble it up. Of course, he'd had hours to contemplate his reaction to Orwell's likely demise, and months to think about the refinery's destruction. So there was very little that was spontaneous or off the cuff about what he was going to say. Nor was it an accident that the few rough notes – 'NB: VICTIMS most important . . . Nicholas counsellor, contributor, friend . . . human not financial tragedy . . . business as usual,' and so on – scrawled on the sheet of paper in his hand had been written large enough to be picked up by zoom lenses. Even the hesitation with which he opened had been considered in advance.

'Ahh . . .' Zorn grimaced nervously and cleared his throat as he ran his eyes over the crowd of reporters in front of him, hoping to give as many of them as possible the impression that he had looked directly at them. He felt a momentary shock of alarm as the thought struck him that Carver might be out there in the crowd, ready to fire the bullet that would blow his brains out. The image didn't frighten Zorn. It thrilled him: the shot of physical danger spiced up his financial gamble like a splash of chilli oil. He coughed to hide his excitement, and then began: 'I want to make a short statement about today's tragic events at the Rosconway refinery in Wales.'

Zorn looked down at the notes, as if seeing inspiration and re-assurance from them, though he knew perfectly well what he was going to say. 'My first and, ahh, deepest thoughts are for the victims of this terrible atrocity: the dead, the wounded, and all the loved ones who are feeling such loss and anguish at this dark hour. There will be much talk of the political and economic consequences of what has happened, but you know, we must never forget that this is a human tragedy that touches us all.'

He gave another look around his audience, drawing them in, making them complicit in what he said. He saw no sign of Carver, just one or two reporters who actually nodded back at him. Good: they were hooked. Now to gently reel them in.

'Of course, no one person's life is of any greater value than another's. But I hope you will allow me to pay a special tribute to my colleague and dear friend Nicholas Orwell. I got to know Nicholas very well over the past few months, as he and I worked together on the development of the Zorn Global fund. To the British people, he was of course a strong and greatly admired leader . . .' Total bullshit, of course: Zorn knew perfectly well the contempt in which Orwell was held by many, if not most of his former electors, but no one wanted to be reminded of that now.

'But to me, he was a fine man, a wise counsellor and an in-valuable contributor to this venture. Above all, he had an incredible gift for relating to other people, and winning their trust and understanding. Nicholas made all our investors feel like true partners in a fund whose purpose is to unite people from different nations, different cultures and different generations in a single enterprise spanning the world we all share. We will all miss you, Nick, but I know that wherever you are, you will be delighted to hear that we will not be defeated or downcast by your tragic loss. Zorn Global is already trading, and its public launch will take place as planned on Friday evening.'

The last sentence had, as Zorn had intended, caught everyone's attention. After all the obligatory tributes, here was a nugget of hard news: Zorn Global was going ahead whether Orwell was there or not. That he, the host, might also be absent, too, would not occur to anyone.

He continued, 'Now, as many of you know, I have for many months warned that an event such as today's might occur. In fact, I discussed it on the BBC World show *HARDtalk* earlier this week. It is also no secret that my security concerns have influenced the investment decisions I have made, both on my own account and on behalf of Zorn Global and its clients. You know, even within the past hour I've already seen speculation on various financial web-sites suggesting that I may have profited to the tune of tens of billions of dollars from what happened at Rosconway . . .'

As the phrase 'tens of billions of dollars' was jotted down in dozens of notepads, Zorn took on the voice and demeanour of a stern, high-minded headmaster, disappointed by the conduct of a few unruly pupils. 'I am not prepared to dignify such speculation with any official comment. It is simply not appropriate to consider personal gain at a time like this; people's lives are far more important than financial profit or loss.'

If it was not proper to consider personal gain, the clear impli-cation was that there had been some . . . and the words 'tens of billions' were already on the record, just waiting to be attached to it. Now Zorn added a political dimension. 'But I can say that I have already spoken to the British Prime Minister and the Chancellor of the Exchequer, and assured them both that, at a time when I am enjoying the hospitality of the United Kingdom, I have no intention of harming its economy. I have therefore divested myself of all my short positions in UK-listed corporations, UK government bonds and sterling.'

Fighting hard to contain his amusement, Zorn contemplated the sheer panic that would be seizing the trading rooms of banks and hedge funds as they digested the news that he'd got out of all his positions. They would be racing to do the same as the market rebounded. The way things were now, if he said he was going long, everyone would want to pile in and do the same. And, of course, he'd already taken the fresh positions that anticipated such a move.

Now it was time to show he wasn't just about making money. He could give it away, too. 'I am sure that this great nation will swiftly and completely recover from the blow it has been dealt today, just as it recovered from the Blitz and the bombs of 7/7. And to do my bit in assisting that process, I will be setting up a fund to aid victims and their families, to which I will be making a personal donation of a hundred million dollars.'

There was actually a gasp from the crowd at the size of the donation. Maybe in time they would figure out that it was far less than one per cent of his personal profits. But for now the headline figure would be all that anyone cared about. Zorn caught the eye of a young woman to one side of the crowd. She worked for his PR agency, and she was gazing at him as adoringly as a thirteen-year-old girl worshipping a teen idol. He gave her a flash of his best, most dazzling smile, then returned to his speech.

'Finally, I would like to say that I have absolute faith in the ability of the UK authorities to track down the perpetrators of this appalling crime, and bring them to justice. We all have a duty now to assist in this investigation in any way possible, to do everything we can to support those who have been affected, and to carry on with our lives as normal. Terrorism must not be allowed to win. I will be carrying on with my schedule exactly as I had planned, and I advise everyone else to do the same. Thank you.'

At once there was a clamour of questions from the media, and a forest of hands shooting up, seeking his attention. But Zorn paid no attention to them. He simply gave a couple of brisk nods, turned on his heels and walked back into his rented house.

Another stage of his plan had been triumphantly completed.

57

Bronglais General Hospital, Aberystwyth

It was 1.15 p.m. when the helicopter landed on a patch of open ground on the western edge of the University of Aberystwyth campus, close to the National Library of Wales complex. The hospital was just a couple of hundred yards away, and Carver was already out of the helicopter and walking across the grass, past groups of startled students, before the pilot had cut the engine. He made his way to the intensive care unit, flashing his 'Andy Jenkins' Ministry of Defence pass at the receptionist, and walking straight by. A young, uniformed female PC was stationed outside the room where Deirdre Bull had been taken.

'My name's Jenkins,' Carver said, showing her the pass. 'I need to speak to Deirdre Bull.'

'Oh no,' she said. 'That won't be possible. No one's been allowed in there. Not even us.'

'I understand,' said Carver. 'But my boss has spoken to your boss. And I mean your Chief Constable. Go ahead and check.'

The policewoman had a brief conversation on her radio. 'Well, that seems to be in order,' she said. 'But it's not really a police decision. You'll have to ask Dr Fenwick. He's the one who can help you.'

'I see. And where can I find Dr Fenwick?'

'Right here,' said a voice from behind Carver's back.

Fenwick was a short, black-haired man. He placed himself between Carver and the door to Deirdre Bull's room, and glared at him like a surly guard dog. 'I'm not at all happy about you, or anyone else, speaking to Ms Bull,' Fenwick said. 'She's suffered very serious injuries and considerable loss of blood, followed by a lengthy operation. She's a very sick woman indeed.'

'Well, I'm very sorry for her,' said Carver. 'But this is a matter of national security.'

Fenwick looked at him disdainfully. 'National security is not my concern. Patient welfare is.'

Carver gritted his teeth. Fenwick was no more than five feet eight inches tall, mildly overweight, and presumably untrained in any form of combat, whether armed or unarmed. The temptation to give him an educational slap was all but overwhelming. But Grantham had told him to use his charm, so, fine, he'd try that. Well, up to a point he would, anyway.

'You've heard about what happened at Rosconway this morning?'

Fenwick grimaced impatiently. 'Yes. What of it?'

'We believe the woman in that room there may be able to give us vital information about who was responsible. The death toll's over two hundred, in case you hadn't heard. Hundreds more injured. So if patient welfare is your concern, perhaps you'd like to tell all the people who are sitting in hospitals all over Wales, waiting to discover if the men and women they love are going to be all right, why this woman is so bloody precious. I was at Rosconway, Dr Fenwick. I saw it happen. So please, do me a favour ... don't talk to me about patient welfare.'

It might have been Carver's oratorial skills that did the trick, or just the intensely intimidating coldness of the gaze he fixed on

Fenwick. But in any event, the doctor briefly relented: 'All right, but make it quick. Now,' he went on, regaining a little self-confidence and looking right back at Carver, almost daring him to try something, 'I'm going to observe you. If you are in any way hostile or threatening to this patient – if you so much as raise your voice – I'm ending it, immediately. And I'm her doctor. So I don't care who you are, or what you're really up to. As long as you're in my hospital what I say goes. Got it?'

'Absolutely. Let's do it.'

Fenwick opened the door, and led Carver into the room. Deirdre Bull was lying with an arm and a leg in traction. Her head was bandaged. She had an oxygen mask on her face and a drip attached to her right arm. A monitor beside her bed tracked her pulse, blood pressure, temperature and respiration. She looked at them blearily through heavy, barely open lids, spaced out on painkillers that would be making it almost as hard for her to think straight as to move.

Carver's spirits sank. The woman was even more wrecked than he had feared. But she was the only surviving member of the terrorist gang that anyone had been able to find, so if he couldn't get anything out of her, there wasn't anywhere else to go.

58

Fenwick took up station at the head of Bull's bed and motioned to Carver to sit in a chair positioned halfway down the mattress. Carver was about to speak, but Fenwick raised a hand to stop him. 'Leave it to me,' he said.

Fenwick bent closer to Bull's head. 'Hello, Deirdre, there's a gentleman here who'd like to have a word with you,' he said, in an unexpectedly gentle voice. 'You don't have to talk to him if you don't want to. But if you do, don't worry, I'll be here all the time to make sure you're all right.'

Bull tried to focus on Carver. 'Uh ... who are you?' she asked, sounding as though each word was an effort.

'My name is Andy Jenkins,' Carver replied, with what he hoped was an ingratiating smile. 'I work for the Ministry of Defence. I'm not a policeman. I'm not interested in collecting evidence against you. I just want a quiet, private chat – off the record. Do you understand?'

'Not sure. Why d'you want to chat?'

'It's a matter of national security. You'd be helping us keep people safe. And I'm sure you want to help ...'

She looked uncertain. 'Well, yes, suppose so.'

'Good. Well, then, when they found you this morning, you told the paramedics, "You've got to stop the attack" . . .'

Bull looked at Fenwick for confirmation. 'Did I?'

'I believe so,' he said.

'Yes,' Carver underlined, wondering when exactly Fenwick had known about a possible attack, and hoping for his sake that it hadn't been before ten thirty. 'So were you talking about the attack on Rosconway refinery – the one that happened today?'

'Dunno . . .'

'What do you mean, you don't know?'

Bull struggled to formulate the words. 'I've never heard that name . . . what was it?'

'Rosconway.'

With more certainty she said: 'No, I've never heard that before.'

'But you knew there was going to be some kind of attack somewhere?'

'Yes, but I didn't know where it was going to be,' Bull argued, finding it a little easier, now, to talk. 'All Bryn told us was that the target was a place that was harming Mother Earth.'

'I see. Who's Bryn?'

She sounded surprised he didn't know. 'Bryn Gryffud, of course. He's . . . well, not the leader, because we don't believe in that kind of hierarchy . . . but he's the founder of the Forces of Gaia, our group. It was his farm we were staying at.'

Carver caught Bull's eye and held it as he said, 'Did Bryn get you all to fit up a Toyota Hiace camper van with a dozen home-made mortar tubes, firing explosive shells, set on some kind of timer fuse?'

Bull nodded, too ashamed to acknowledge what had happened in actual words, and Carver saw Fenwick frown as he looked at her, the reality of what she'd been involved with starting to sink in.

'I was there when the mortars went off, Deirdre,' Carver said. 'Right there, standing by the van. Couldn't do anything to stop it. I don't feel too good about that. Thing is, I saw what those shells did. They killed two hundred people, Deirdre: innocent people, just going about their lives, doing their jobs, loving their families. Did they all die for the sake of the planet?'

She'd been biting her lip as he spoke, trying to retain some self-control. Now her face crumpled, and tears filled her eyes as she sobbed. 'Oh God ... oh God ... I worried something bad might happen ... I prayed to Gaia because I was worried we were doing the wrong thing. But Bryn sounded so convinced, and I, well, we all, we just believed him, and—'

'Because he's a good man. Yeah, I get it.'

'Where is he? Is he all right?'

Carver shrugged. 'How should I know? He's not exactly advertising his whereabouts.'

Bull sniffed, and then muttered, 'Thanks,' as Fenwick pulled some tissues from a box by her bed and handed them to her. 'It's all that bloody woman's fault,' she continued, wide awake now, wiping her face with her working hand. 'She's the one who put the idea into Bryn's head ...'

'What woman?' asked Carver, frowning.

'Uschi ... Uschi bloody Kremer ...' Bull's voice rose in intensity, filled with bitterness and pain that had nothing at all to do with her physical wounds. 'It was so obvious – the men only went along with her because they wanted to get into her knickers.'

The last thing Carver wanted was to be diverted by an angry woman's sexual jealousy. 'OK ... take it easy. I know you didn't want anyone to get hurt.'

'No! I don't believe in violence! I—' Her words were cut short by a gasp of pain. 'My chest hurts so much,' she whimpered, her eyes filling with tears again as she slumped back against her pillows. 'Everything hurts ...'

Fenwick turned to Carver. 'I'm sorry, but this isn't doing her any good at all. If you carry on like this, I'm pulling the plug.'

'Just give me a minute,' Carver pleaded. 'This won't take long ...' He took a second to gather his wits, then focused on Deirdre Bull once again. 'I'm sure you'd like a chance to make things better. To try and put things right . . . as much as they can be put right, obviously.'

She nodded miserably. 'Yes . . . please . . . I never meant to do any harm.'

Carver glanced across at Fenwick, and was relieved to get a nod of approval. 'All right . . .' he continued. 'Have you ever heard of a man called Malachi Zorn?'

Bull looked puzzled. 'No . . . should I?'

'I don't know . . . He's an American, works as a financier.'

'Well, no wonder I've not heard of him. He's obviously the kind of man I despise. I don't want to know about people like that.'

Carver tried again: 'Or how about a Pakistani man called Ahmad Razzaq? He's middle-aged, wears a moustache, quite distinguished-looking. Sometimes calls himself Shafik.'

'No . . . I don't know anyone like that at all.' She sounded more confident now, as though her ignorance somehow established her innocence.

'You haven't even heard their names mentioned by other people . . . people like Bryn?'

'No.'

They seemed to have reached a dead end, and Fenwick sensed it, too. 'Well, that settles it. She can't help you. I think we should call this a day.'

Carver tried not to let his desperation show. He was sure he was close to a breakthrough, if only he could find the right button to push. Something Bull had said had rung a bell, but he'd missed it, failed to make the right connection. It was there, though, some-where: he knew it. He fixed an ingratiating smile on his face and spoke to Fenwick and Bull together. 'Wait, let's just take it nice and easy ... a few simple questions. Nothing to get excited about. Is that all right?'

Fenwick looked at Bull.

She nodded.

He gave Carver a shrug that said, 'Be my guest.'

'So . . . How many of you were there in the group?' Carver asked.

Bull closed her eyes, picturing her old comrades in her mind. 'Ahh . . . six of us at first, then Dave Smethurst and that Swiss bitch joined . . .'

'Kremer?' Carver asked, thinking: 'Her again.' Bull nodded. Kremer loomed so large in Bull's memories of the group. Maybe he should stick with Kremer: see where that took him.

'So when was that?'

'About four or five months ago, I suppose. Though even then, she was never really part of it like the rest of us. She was always flitting in and out, leading this disgusting, privileged life . . .'

'So she's rich?' he asked, a bell just starting to ring, very faintly, in the back of his mind.

'Her family's stinking rich. That's what she said, anyway, and the way she behaved, I believed it.'

'And you people weren't violent before she arrived, four or five months ago?'

Bull gave a feeble shake of the head, wincing at the effort. 'No . . . I mean, we believed in direct action as a way of making our point. But no one ever got hurt. We were just trying to attract people's attention to what was being done to the planet.'

'Then along comes Uschi Kremer and says . . . ?'

'Well, she never said anything to us women. But she was always whispering with Bryn, or taking him off to dinner . . . I'm sure he slept with her. She was certainly making it very obvious she was available.'

'So she's attractive?' The bell was ringing louder now.

'If you like that kind of thing. Personally, I think it's cheap and vulgar. But you know what men are like . . .'

'We fall for that kind of thing . . .' Carver said, as it all tumbled into place: the woman who could seduce men at will, who'd always been able to make anyone do anything she wanted. Could it really be her?

'Describe Uschi Kremer,' he asked.

Bull gave a little 'Huh!' of disapproval. 'Well, she's older than she likes to admit, that's for sure. The way she acts, you'd think she was in her early thirties, maybe even her twenties. But if she's a day under forty, I'd be surprised. If you really look at her, close up, it's much more obvious.'

Fenwick was leaning forward a little in his seat now, aware that something had changed. There was a new atmosphere of expectation in the room.

Carver already knew the answers when he asked, 'Height, weight, eyes, hair colour?'

'Oh, well . . . she's a couple of inches taller than me, I suppose, and I'm five foot six. But she's very slim. If she weighs much more than nine stone I'd be amazed. She's less than that, even. She's a redhead, so she's got that colouring. You know, blue eyes . . .'

'Freckled skin?'

Bull started, surprised. 'Yes, that's right.'

'Quite full lips: you know, pouty . . . sexy . . .'

Now she gave a puzzled frown. 'I suppose so, yes, if that's what you think is sexy. But how do you . . . ?'

Carver raised a finger to his face. 'A little groove, on the end of her nose . . . just here?'

'Yes . . . yes, that's right. Do you know her?' Now Bull was displaying the anxiety of someone who suspects that they may have been the victim of an elaborate practical joke. Fenwick, too, was looking at Carver as if he was trying to spot the trick he was playing.

Carver got out his phone, put the black and white photo of Celina Novak on screen, and held it up so that Bull could see it. 'Well, you tell me . . . is this her?'

'Yes! That's Uschi all right, though she looks a lot younger there.'

'Thank you, Deirdre . . . thank you very much indeed.'

'Really . . . have I helped?'

'Oh yes. A lot.' Carver nodded at Fenwick. 'Thanks, doctor. Couldn't have done it without you.' He got to his feet. 'I'll be on my way,' he said.

59

Paxford, Gloucestershire

On the fringes of a village on the northern edge of the Cotswolds, where the last boxy little houses of a newly built estate met the first drab fields of farmland, stood a run-down scrap metal site. Its single-page website was dotted with contemporary, eco-friendly buzzwords like recycling and reclamation. But that didn't alter the reality of a grimy, litter-strewn graveyard for abandoned cars and piles of metallic junk – from shopping-trolleys to radiators and old library shelves – run by three oil-stained, boilersuited men fuelled by PG Tips and nicotine. None of them were present as Uschi Kremer – alias Magda 'Ginger' Sternberg, alias Celina Novak – drove up the dusty lane that led beneath the arch of a long-abandoned railway and turned in through the scrapyard gates, ignoring the sign that said the yard was closed. The two black Range Rovers were waiting for her. Braddock was leaning against one of them, smoking. As she drove up, he threw the cigarette on the floor and ground it under his heel. The driver of the other Range Rover got out and walked towards his boss.

'This is Turner,' Braddock said as Ginger emerged from her car.

She did not bother to shake their hands or say hello. 'There's no one else here?' she asked.

'No. Gone to lunch,' Braddock replied.

'And when are they coming back?'

'When they've pissed away the five hundred quid I gave them down the bookies and the pub. We've got a while.'

'OK.' Ginger looked around the yard, noting the CCTV cameras at the gate and by the front door to the Portakabin that served as an office. 'What about these?'

'All off. The video-machine's not working. Something seems to have gone mysteriously wrong with it.'

'Good. Then let's get on.'

She opened up one of the rear doors and pulled away the blanket that had been covering the bodies of Gryffud and Smethurst. Braddock turned away in disgust at the stench that emanated from the corpses. Ginger looked at him contemptuously. 'Their bowels evacuated at the moment of death,' she said, speaking with a technician's precision. 'A man like you should be used to that.'

'Shit still stinks, however much you're used to it,' he said. Then a thought struck him. 'I'm not having that fucking smell in my car!'

Ginger looked at him with utter contempt, then gave an impatient sigh. 'All right, let's clean it all up.'

There was a standpipe outside the Portakabin, with a bright yellow hose attached to it. Braddock and Turner pulled the two bodies out of Ginger's BMW, before they and the car's passenger compartment were drenched with water, rinsing away all the filth. Braddock took a roll of green plastic sheeting out of the back of the Range Rover and cut off a couple of metres of it, which he then laid on the ground. The two men dragged Brynmor Gryffud's body on to the sheet, then rolled it over twice, so that the body was entirely wrapped in plastic. Braddock used gaffer tape to secure the package, and then he and Ginger hefted the body into the back of one of the Range Rovers.

The process was repeated for Dave Smethurst's remains.

'Good thing I've got blacked-out windows,' Braddock said, breathing heavily as he closed the tailgate.

'If you drive sensibly, there will be no problem,' said Ginger bluntly, wasting none of her charm on him. 'You are confident that the bodies will be disposed of securely?'

'Oh yeah,' Braddock assured her. 'This bloke Gryffud was obsessed with the environment, right?'

'Yes.'

'Well, he'll love what's going to happen to the bodies, then . . .'

'Just so long as no trace of them is ever found.'

'It won't be, trust me.'

'Huh . . . So, now we deal with the car. Can you operate a fork-lift?'

'I can't . . . but he can.'

Turner got behind the controls of the scrapyard's forklift. There was a compactor on the far side of the yard. It consisted of two massive steel slabs, supported by hydraulic lifts at either end. The forklift picked up the BMW and carried it across to the compactor. The car was slid on to the bottom slab, side-on, then given another couple of prods with the forklift's two sharp prongs to make sure it was as far in as possible. Braddock pressed the button that operated the compactor, and the whine of the hydraulics combined with the sound of crumpling metal as the top slab descended with grinding inexorability, reducing the BMW to a mechanical sandwich filling. Braddock pushed another button, the two slabs parted again, and the forklift removed the crushed remains of the car and placed them on a pile of other flattened vehicles.

Ginger watched the proceedings from the passenger seat of the second Range Rover while she made a call to Derek Choi.

'Do you know any more about the project we discussed?' he asked.

'No, I've been busy on other affairs.'

'But you still anticipate activity tomorrow?'

'I'm sure you heard the speech that our mutual friend made. The original schedule is being maintained, with a higher public profile than ever. So my original estimates still hold true.'

'I agree. And I will proceed on that basis. Incidentally, your friend Samuel had company last night – a woman, Alexandra Petrova Vermulen. I believe you are old friends.'

Ginger caught the taunting edge to Choi's voice, and was infuriated to realize that he had succeeded in getting to her. Of course, she did not want Carver. She had only seduced him for professional reasons. It wasn't personal. So why did it annoy her so much to think of that pathetic little bitch Petrova getting her claws into him?

She had not even mustered a reply when Choi said, 'Please contact me immediately if you receive any further information. Goodbye.'

Ginger used the five minutes between the end of the call and Turner's return to the car to refresh her make-up, though she only applied her lipgloss and mascara with a fraction of her full concentration: the rest was devoted to Alexandra Petrova and what she would do to her if she ever got the chance. Turner gave her a lift to Moreton-in-Marsh Station, where she took the train back to London. She sat in the first-class compartment in a foul mood. With just a couple of sentences Derek Choi had ruined what should have been a triumphant day. She would not forget or forgive that, either.

An hour later Braddock drove his Range Rover up a broad track, deeply rutted by the tracks of heavy vehicles, that ran like a disfiguring scar across the side of a once picturesque hill. At the top of the hill a massive pit had been dug, a wound to the landscape made worse by the continuous slurry of concrete being poured into it from a line of giant truck-mounted mixers. This despoliation of the countryside was largely subsidized by government funds, despite the blatant flouting of every known planning regulation pertaining to conservation areas and Sites of Special Scientific Interest. (A scattering of rare orchids and several species of butterfly had once added their fragile beauty to the hilltop, only to be obliterated by the first few scoops of the digger's bucket.) But then, the destruction of the environment didn't seem to matter if its end result was a gigantic, noisy, bird-shredding wind turbine. That this was made of steel and rooted in concrete – two substances whose manufacture generated vast amounts of CO_2 – was neither here nor there. Nor did anyone seem to care that the turbine, like virtually all others, would be very lucky to operate at more than ten per cent of its full capacity, and would require constant backup from oil- or gas-fired power stations to make up for the times when the wind ceased to blow. Wind turbines were magically going to cut greenhouse gases, keep temperatures down, lower sea levels, and prevent polar bears from falling off melting icebergs. Therefore they were good.

Braddock owned the farm on which the turbine was being erected, and was collecting a substantial subsidy accordingly. It made him laugh, getting paid to wreck the landscape just so a bunch of sandal-wearing, lentil-eating eco-twats could feel better about the environment. The fact that turbines were such obvious cons only made it even funnier. And bunging a couple of dead Greens into the hole, so that they could spend the rest of eternity under thirty feet of concrete, supporting a propellor on stilts, well, that was fucking hilarious.

As the Range Rover went back down the hill again, minus the bodies that had been in the back, there was a smile all over his face.

60

Aberystwyth

'You'd better get someone to put a guard on Deirdre Bull's bed,' Carver said to Grantham, making the call as he walked across the hospital car park. 'And I mean more than just a local plod in a skirt. Because the moment Zorn or Razzaq twig that she's alive, they're going to need her silenced.'

'Really? So she talked?'

'Oh yeah – we've got our connection. The attack was carried out by a bunch of eco-freaks called the Forces of Gaia. Their leader was one Brynmor Gryffud. They were into peaceful protest until a mysterious woman, calling herself Uschi Kremer and pretending to be a Swiss heiress, showed up. She used her powers of seduction to persuade Gryffud that the only way he was going to change anything was through violence. You want to know what this woman looked like?'

'Let me guess,' replied Jack Grantham. 'Redheaded, older than she looks, borderline psychopathic?'

'Got it in one. Looks like I wasn't the only one that got

Gingered. She works for Razzaq. Razzaq works for Zorn. Zorn needed a terrorist outrage. She got it for him.'

'Fair enough, I'll buy that.'

'Good,' said Carver. 'And while you're at it, there's a few other things I need you to buy.'

He was within sight of the green space where the helicopter was waiting for him by the time he had finished outlining his plans.

'And you want me to make this possible?' Grantham asked.

'You and whoever else it takes, yes.'

'You're not giving me a lot of time. It won't be easy, getting hold of some of the stuff you want.'

'Don't see why not. It's all available off the shelf. And the modifications I need could be carried out by any half-decent mechanic.'

'Maybe, but it means going public. I won't even contemplate something like this unless my arse is not just covered, but armour-plated. This has to be signed off all the way to the top.'

'Does that mean going public about me, too?'

'As long as you're the man who's going to do it, yes. But don't worry, I'll be discreet. I'll emphasize the bits of your record that make you look like an acceptable individual.'

'And you'll bury the ones that don't?'

'Got it in one.'

'Good luck with that.'

'Forget it,' said Grantham. 'You're the one who's going to need all the luck. You're taking a hell of a risk with this. If it turns out you were wrong, don't expect me or anyone else to protect you.'

'I never expect anyone to protect me,' said Carver. 'Except me.'

61

Whitehall

Two hours later, just as Carver was coming in to land at Northolt, Jack Grantham was making his presentation to an emergency meeting of the Joint Intelligence Committee. Cameron Young, the prime ministerial representative who had proposed the conference plan barely twenty-four hours earlier with such determined self-confidence, now had an air of desperation as he struggled to find some way of pulling his master from the deep lake of excrement into which he had just been tipped. His present problem was trying to decide whether the Head of the Secret Intelligence Service was a man who could enable some sort of miraculous recovery, or whether the outrageous plan that he had just outlined would only serve to make the Prime Minister's plunge even deeper.

Dame Judith Spofforth, Head of MI5, was in no mood to accept the kind of risk that was being proposed. 'I suppose I don't have to point out that Mr Grantham's plan...' She placed particular emphasis on the 'mister' as if to emphasize Grantham's lack of a knighthood. '... is not only entirely inappropriate, coming from a department whose responsibility is intelligence-gathering outside the borders of the United Kingdom, but also illegal in more ways than I even care to consider.'

'We don't want to tread on our friends' toes,' said Grantham. 'We're just trying to propose a solution to a problem that affects us all. And, incidentally, we first gathered the intelligence that led us to suspect Mr Zorn's motives in a number of locations including the United States, Italy and Greece, none of which are exactly domestic. And every single one of the leading suspects in the conspiracy that we believe we have uncovered is a foreign national. So I would argue that we do have reasonable grounds for involvement. As for the legality of the whole thing, this country didn't have any trouble finding a legal justification for an Iraqi war based on intelligence that many of us knew was, to put it bluntly, absolute bollocks. So how difficult can it be to find a good excuse to do this? Malachi Zorn has waltzed into this country and made complete fools of us all. And he's done it by killing a great many people, including ones we all knew. I think we have a right to let him know that we won't stand for that kind of thing.'

'In the end it all comes down to this man Carver,' Young interrupted, putting an end to the turf war. 'You're asking me to place an enormous amount of faith in the quality of his information, the accuracy of his interpretation of that information, and, above all, his ability to pull off what appears to be little short of a public execution. That's a very great deal to ask.'

'It wouldn't be the first time we've had to trust in him,' Grantham replied. 'A few years ago he asked me – and Dame Judith's predecessor, Dame Agatha Bewley, come to that – to believe that there was a threat to the life of President Lincoln Roberts from an assassin called Damon Tyzack. The President, you will recall, was making his first visit to this country, giving an open-air speech in Bristol. Both the US Secret Service and the Metropolitan Police dismissed Carver's concerns out of hand. Luckily, Dame Agatha and I did not. That is why Damon Tyzack's remains are currently rotting away at the bottom of the Bristol

Channel, whereas President Roberts is still alive and well and sitting in the White House. I'm sure he'll be happy to give Carver a character reference.'

'And you believe Carver's on the right track now?' Young asked.

Grantham did not answer immediately. His reputation was on the line here, just as much as Carver's. If the plan worked out, they might, if they were very lucky, get some grudging thanks. If it failed, they would certainly be vilified.

'Yes,' he said. 'I think he is.'

'In that case,' said Cameron Young, 'I can't see that we have any other option. The Prime Minister needs to turn this situation around fast. Let's see if Mr Carver can help him do it. You may go ahead with your operation, using whatever resources are required.'

Young looked at Grantham with a sad half-smile, as though he regretted having to utter the next few words. 'Although you must understand that, in the event of failure, this conversation never happened. Her Majesty's government cannot possibly be seen to be associated with any activities that do not meet the strictest standards of legality.'

'Of course,' said Jack Grantham. 'I quite understand.'

62

Chinatown

In his private office above the dim sum restaurant, Derek Choi was holding a video-conference with a senior State Security Ministry official in Beijing. Another intelligence officer, a political analyst based at the Chinese embassy in London, was also party to the conversation.

'Today's events are highly significant,' said the ministry man. 'It is clear that we had greatly underestimated the effect of Mr Zorn's self-fulfilling prophecy. Based on what your source within the Forces of Gaia told us, Comrade Choi, we predicted that the refinery would suffer severe damage, which would swiftly be made public.'

Choi maintained an impassive expression, though his guts seemed to twist like noodles round chopsticks as he heard the implied criticism of his information.

'It was, of course, impossible to predict that the actions of these amateur saboteurs would have such a remarkable effect,' the official continued, easing Choi's tension with every word he spoke. 'What is the current position of the British government, in your opinion, Comrade Jian?'

'Squatting with their pants down, fertilizing the paddy fields with their shit,' the analyst sneered, provoking laughter in the other two men. 'As the British themselves say, they are running around like chickens without heads. The Prime Minister is in a state of shock. He has suffered a catastrophic loss of face, and neither he, nor his ministers, nor their officials, have any idea what to do to regain it.'

'This makes the position of Grantham all the more interesting,' the official in Beijing observed. 'We regard him as a worthy opponent, one who does not lose his nerve. And he seems to have foreseen the danger posed by Zorn in a manner that other, more gullible fools did not.'

'In that case,' Derek Choi observed, 'will he not be even more keen to use Carver to remove Zorn?'

'That is a reasonable assumption, yes.'

'Should we not therefore do our best to prevent that happening, since the effect of Zorn's actions will now be even more to our financial profit and political gain than we could ever have imagined?'

'Again, there is merit to that argument. What is your opinion, Jian?'

'I agree with your assessment of Grantham. He is clear-sighted. He sees things as they really are, not how he would like them to be. And he has the courage to act while others are still weeping and wringing their hands. If he believes it would be advantageous to eliminate Zorn he will not hesitate to do so.'

'And you still believe that this will happen tomorrow at Wimbledon?' the official asked Choi.

'My considered view is that Carver is more likely to attack Zorn close to the tournament site, rather than within the All England Club itself,' Choi replied. 'If he were killing by means of stealth, it would be relatively simple to poison Zorn's food or drink and then be gone before the poison started to take effect. But he has been told that the killing has to be highly visible. This suggests a bomb, perhaps, or a shooting. Of course, Wimbledon is broadcast to more than one hundred and eighty nations, so if Zorn were to die in front of the TV cameras that would certainly provide visibility. But there would also be a high risk of collateral damage from crowds of people being caught by the bomb-blast or an innocent spectator walking into the line of fire. Then he must consider the issues of access and escape. In the panic that would follow such an assassination, the crowd would act unpredictably, posing a danger in itself, and certainly making it difficult to make a swift, unimpeded getaway. For all these reasons, I anticipate an attack carried out on the roads leading to or from the tournament. I have already ordered both Carver and Zorn to be placed under observation, and have contingency plans in place should we need to act swiftly. If we do not, then I plan to eliminate Carver while he is watching the tennis.'

'But Comrade Choi, I thought you said that this was not a suitable place for an assassination,' Jian said.

'For the kind of assassination Carver must carry out, yes, that is quite correct. But we can be more subtle. Let us suppose a group of civilized middle-country persons, anonymous amidst a sea of strangers, and lost in their own conversation, bump into an English barbarian. He is jostled for a few seconds. Perhaps there is a brief flash of anger. But then there are polite apologies, tempers cool, everyone goes on their way. The men from the middle country are soon lost in the crowd. It is as if nothing ever happened. Then, a few minutes later, the Englishman is taken ill. By the time he dies, my men and I have left the tournament. By the time an autopsy reveals that the Englishman's heart attack was caused by poisoning, all the men but me will have long since left the country. I will of course be above suspicion, for why would a brilliant entrepreneur stoop to the murder of a stranger? And should anyone ask, I will have a dozen witnesses confirming my presence at a business meeting that lasted all day.'

'Very good, Comrade Choi,' the man from the State Security Ministry said. 'You will of course send me written details of your plan for examination and comment. But in principle we are agreed. Carver will die tomorrow.'

63

Kensington Gardens, London

They met on the path that runs beside the Long Water in Kensington Gardens, just another two lovers snatching a few furtive moments together at the end of a working day.

'I was so worried about you,' Alix said. 'As soon as I saw it all happening on the news, I just knew you were there, and I thought . . . I'm sorry . . .' She rummaged in her handbag for a tissue to wipe away the tears that had caught her by surprise. 'Dammit,' she muttered, trying to manage a smile, 'I was hoping to look pretty for you!'

With the same delicacy of touch that could be so arousing when they were in bed, but now just made her feel loved and comforted, he gently stroked a tear away from her cheek. 'You always look pretty – much better than pretty,' he said. Then he took her in his arms and she rested her head against his chest, hearing the strong, steady heartbeat that reassured her more than any words of his could do.

Alix sniffed, cleared her throat and, embarrassed by the

weakness that she had just displayed, tried to snap back into a steadier, more professional mindset.

'So what really happened?'

'There was a very effective, professional, calculated assault on an oil refinery that just happened to cause a ton more collateral damage than the people who planned it expected.'

'And who did plan it?'

'In theory, a group called the Forces of Gaia. In practice, your old friend Celina Novak, calling herself Uschi Kremer, put the idea into their heads.'

Alix frowned. 'You said she was working for that guy Razzaq . . .'

'Yes.'

'Who works for Zorn . . . You mean, this was all his idea?'

'Got it in one. This whole thing was basically a financial scam. Zorn sticks a pile of money into the market, placing it all on bets that will pay off if there's a disaster. Then he gives the market jitters by saying, "The eco-terrorists are coming!" Then they come. Then he cleans up . . . only in this case he does even better than he ever dreamed of because half the government is taken out along with the refinery.'

'So Azarov was right,' Alix said. 'As soon as he saw the news – as it was all happening – he said that Zorn must be behind it.'

'I thought that was over, you and Azarov.'

'As far as I'm concerned it is. But I said I would do one last thing with him. We're supposed to be going to Wimbledon tomorrow, as Zorn's guests . . .' She stopped and shook her head. 'I can't believe it. I have to smile at the guy and act like nothing has happened, when all the time I know what he has done. Anyway, Azarov wanted me to pay close attention to Zorn. He said my woman's eye might spot something that his male one could not. Why are you smiling?'

'Because I just had exactly the same idea as Azarov,' he said. 'There's a couple of things I need to know. And you could tell me the answers . . .'

*

An hour later, and six miles south-east across London, Carver was in a pub off the Walworth Road with Schultz and his oppo, an ex-lance corporal called Kevin Cripps. There were three pints of London Pride on the table, and whisky chasers for Schultz and Cripps. Carver was carrying out an impromptu mission briefing using Google Earth shots of Wimbledon on his phone screen to set the scene, and an assortment of coasters, pepper pots and cigarette packets to represent elements of the action he was describing.

'Think you can do it?' he asked them at the end.

'Can you get all the kit by tomorrow morning?' Schultz replied.

Carver nodded.

'Even the Krakatoa?' Cripps sounded sceptical.

'Absolutely.'

'In that case, boss, it's a piece of piss,' said Schultz.

64

Wentworth

The last of the reporters had long since left Malachi Zorn's rented mansion. Now he and Razzaq were left in peace to consider their next moves.

'What are you going to do now that Orwell is dead?' the Pakistani asked. His religious principles did not permit him to consume alcohol, but he had a fat Cohiba cigar, fresh from Havana, to assist him in his thinking.

'On Friday night, you mean?'

'Yes. That was going to be his finest moment. Who is going to take his place now?'

Zorn was drinking red wine. He swirled it in the glass, savouring the bouquet as he thought about his reply. 'Good question. I need to think this through. My first instinct is to go ahead as planned. We just need another way to get the guests in the room.'

'Do we? Do you? Isn't what you already have enough?'

'Enough is a word I don't recognize, Ahmad. There's no such thing as enough.'

'Sometimes there has to be. There are points when the wisest course is to accept that one cannot have everything one wants. Having enough is better than losing it all.'

'What makes you think I will lose anything?'

'It is not so much that I think you will, as that I fear you might. Let us take this from the beginning. You wished to take revenge for the deaths of your parents. Correct?'

'That was one of the motivations, yes,' Zorn agreed, pouring himself some more wine. 'Another was . . . just victory, I guess. I want to win. That's the American way.'

'Indeed it is . . .' Razzaq let out a long stream of aromatic smoke. 'But Americans should know by now that one day's victory can be the next day's defeat.'

'This has nothing to do with defeat,' Zorn said. 'There is a class of people that I hate. I want to beat them at their own game. I want to hurt them, to crush them. I want them down on their fat, piggy knees. And since they value money more than anything else, the best way to do this is to take their money, multiply it many times, and then steal it from them so that I am richer than they can ever be. And you'll be rich, too, Ahmad, don't forget that.'

Razzaq laughed. 'I never forget that! But let us look at the way in which you set about achieving your ends. First, you entice investors to give you enormous sums of money. You create a situation in which they are pleading with you for the chance to hand over hundreds of millions – even billions – of dollars. They are like turkeys begging for Christmas.'

Now Zorn's face was split by a schoolboy grin. 'I know, aren't they?'

'And of course, Orwell was the perfect man to help you do this. He always had the ability to persuade himself that the best possible course of action was whatever he happened to be doing at the time. He fooled himself first, before he fooled anyone else. Tell me, what did he do with the money you gave him?'

'He gave it right back to me to invest in Zorn Global, of course – his own fee and the charity money!' Zorn replied gleefully. 'My bet is he was planning to make a huge profit on all of it, give the charity the original five mill, and keep the rest for himself. I've already had messages from his lawyers. Sure as shit they want to know how much money there'll be for the estate.'

Razzaq nodded. 'Without any doubt that is what they want. So, Orwell helped you get the money. Then you found a way of multiplying it many times over. And by complete chance this turned out to be more successful than even you could have imagined. I am assuming that today's events have returned a much bigger profit because of the deaths of Orwell and the rest.'

'That's a fair assumption, yes.'

'All right. But it has also caused you a problem which we need to assess. The plan originally called for you to be assassinated prior to the public launch of the fund. Then I would persuade Orwell to host the event in your memory. I say, "persuade" but of course it would have been simple. He would have loved that chance to be the centre of attention.'

'Oh yes, I can see him now, giving them all his big, fat Nicholas Orwell grin . . .' Zorn agreed.

'And the investors would all come to the Goldsmiths' Hall pretending that they were doing it in your memory, but in reality because they wanted to know what was going to happen to their money.'

'Sure . . . the contracts they signed when they invested their money specified that in the event of my death, they would receive all the money they had invested, plus eighty per cent of any profits. And after Rosconway, they'd all figure that would be eighty per cent of a helluva lot . . .'

'So they would come to toast your memory and their even greater good fortune. And we'd kill them all.' Razzaq stubbed the cigar out in the ashtray by his side, punctuating his words with downward jabs as he said, 'Every . . . last . . . one of them.' He sat back in his chair and went on, 'But now Orwell himself is dead. So I ask you, how will any of the investors be persuaded to attend?'

'Perhaps you could say that you were going to make the big announcement?' Zorn suggested.

'Ha! You forget that I know what is going to happen. I am not that foolish a turkey! And that is why I ask you now whether it would not be simpler to cut this whole project short. You already have enough money to last a thousand lifetimes. I assume that you can make sure that your investors never see a penny of it ever again.'

'Of course. Hell, the damn money doesn't really exist to begin with. There's no pile of gold, no giant suitcase of cash. It's just digits, you know, bits of data that get switched from one server to another. It can vanish into the ether any time.'

'And so can you,' said Razzaq. 'So my advice is, do it now. Disappear. Go. Vanish.'

'Well, that's good advice. Don't get me wrong, Ahmad, I appreciate your concern, and I can see the sense of it.'

'But . . . ?'

'But I'm not ready to call it quits. This game has a few more twists and turns just yet. We're only in the third quarter, and there's still a lot of time on the clock. I want to see how it plays out.'

Razzaq frowned. 'So you want to go ahead with our plans? You don't want me to call Carver off, for example?'

'No, I don't. I want him to go ahead and carry out the assassination.' Zorn emptied his glass, put it down, and then said, 'Wait till I'm dead. I think the game could look a whole lot better then.'

Wednesday, 29 June

65

Putney, London SW15

It was past 11.00 a.m. before Carver got the call from Grantham. 'We got everything you asked for. The van's a white Transit, with "McNulty Brothers Builders" written on the side. It's parked on the rooftop level of the Putney Exchange multi-storey car park, in the far south-west corner. The door's unlocked. The keys are in the plastic B&Q bag in the passenger-side footwell. So's that Krakatoa thing you asked for. The rest of the kit's in the back of the van. Leave your car as near as you can with the keys in the ignition. We'll have someone waiting to take it away.'

'Thanks.'

'Don't thank me, Carver. You're still screwed if this doesn't work.'

'What else is new?'

Carver hung up and immediately put in a call to Schultz, telling him to meet by the van in exactly one hour's time. Then he texted Alix: 'On my way. Keep me posted.'

A minute later he got her reply: 'Latest update. Standing in bra and panties, deciding what dress to wear. Want to look my best for you, haha!'

Carver laughed. 'Dress code update,' he texted. 'U will be thrown out of Wim if turn up in bra and knickers. But would not be thrown out of my bed.'

Alix wrote again. 'Down boy!! Gotta go xxx'

Carver grinned, then closed the window. There was nothing wrong with having a few jokes before you went into action. But it was time for the laughing to stop.

It took forty-eight minutes to make his way in the Audi through heavy South London traffic to the Putney Exchange Shopping Centre. He wound his way up through the multi-storey car park to the open expanse of the rooftop level. The van was exactly where Grantham had promised it would be. Carver found an empty space nearby and left the keys as Grantham had told him to do. He had barely got to the door of the Transit when he heard an engine start up behind him, and seconds later the Audi was driving past on its way to the exit.

He opened the Transit's passenger door. The B&Q bag was sitting on the floor in front of the passenger seat. Carver reached in, picked the bag up and looked inside. Aside from the keys it contained a couple of plastic garden pegs linked by a short length of green nylon twine; a thin disc of copper about 15 cm in diameter, beaten into a shallow cone; a packet of Polyfilla that had been opened and then resealed with a bright yellow plastic clip; and a series of grey plastic components. These comprised a short, open-ended tube whose diameter was a fraction greater than that of the copper disc; a couple of locking rings, similarly sized; a plastic disc, again as wide as the cylinder, to which a tightly looped length of electrical wire was attached; and four rigid plastic sticks, each about 30 cm in length. Anyone looking into the bag would assume that they all fitted together to form some kind of plumbing device.

Carver cast his eye over it all, muttered, 'Good,' to himself, then closed the passenger door again and walked around to the back of the van. He opened up the rear cargo-bay doors just enough for him to see inside, without enabling anyone else to glimpse what was there. This time his reaction was a little more effusive: a broad smile and a murmured, 'Excellent.'

He closed the doors and made his way to the driver's seat. Two minutes later there was a rap on the window. Schultz and Cripps were standing outside. Carver lowered the window, then handed them the B&Q plastic bag. 'There you go.'

Schultz looked inside and grinned broadly. 'Lovely jubbly,' he said. He and Cripps walked back to their car, an old Mazda 626 saloon. Carver rolled up the van's window and started the engine. Two minutes later they were all on their way.

Meanwhile, on the crowded approaches to Putney Bridge, the Chinese agents trailing the silver Audi were asking themselves why it was heading north, back over the river towards Central London, in the opposite direction to Wimbledon. It was only when they were on the bridge itself and able to accelerate enough to bring their car alongside the Audi that they realized Carver was no longer at the wheel. The string of obscenities that followed was equalled only by Derek Choi's fury when the news was relayed to him.

It took Choi several minutes to obtain the latest tracking data for Carver's phone signal. That, at least, was moving in the right direction. So his destination had not changed, even if his method of transport had. And once he got to Wimbledon, there were only a limited number of gates by which he could enter. Choi calmed himself. Nothing had really changed. Carver was still on course for his death.

66

Wimbledon

Azarov's other car was a Rolls-Royce Phantom. It nosed its way into the area of the Wimbledon Park Golf Club that was rented out every year to the All England Club and used for car parking and corporate entertainment marquees, and proceeded with a barely perceptible purr towards the spaces reserved by Malachi Zorn. Zorn was waiting there to greet them. He opened Alix's door himself, standing to one side as she smoothed down her skirt, then swung her legs together out of the car. Zorn held out his hand and she took it, rising gracefully to her feet till she was standing beside him on the close-cropped grass.

'Such a gentleman!' she said, looking up at him from coyly downcast eyes. He laughed and then held her hand to his lips, kissing it with a playfully exaggerated smack, as if to underline that he was an informal American, just kidding around with this ancient European custom.

'*Enchanté, mademoiselle,*' he said.

'*Tu es trop gentil,*' she replied, slipping into French without a second thought. She smiled at Zorn again, much to his delight, and this time the smile was genuine. As she and Azarov walked arm in arm towards the gates of the All England Club, Alix was truly happy. She already knew the answer to the first question Carver had asked her in Kensington Gardens.

Carver saw Alix making her way to her seat half-a-dozen blocks away, and his mind flashed back to another summer's day, more years ago than he really cared to remember, and the sight of her in another silk summer dress. He only had to close his eyes for a moment, and he was back at that table at the Eden Roc restaurant, looking out across the sun-sparkled waters of Cap d'Antibes. He could see her on the deck of General Kurt Vermulen's yacht, the wind pressing her dress against her body, outlining every curve. He'd watched as she'd kissed Vermulen, thinking it was just an act, and not knowing until it was too late that she had fallen in love with the general and would soon become his wife. Now Vermulen was dead, another entry on Carver's personal casualty list, and there was Alix once again, in a summer dress, looking just as beautiful – and with another man.

He watched as she sat down, said something to the thuggishly handsome man to her left, and laughed at his reply. Was that Azarov? Carver wondered. They looked pretty friendly for a couple who'd all but called it a day. Alix reached into her bag and, still half listening to the man, pulled out her phone and started tapping on its screen.

A few seconds later Carver's phone buzzed. It was a text from her: 'Re: Zorn. U were right. Ax'

Immediately, Carver tapped out a message to Schultz. 'Mission is go. Be in position by 16.00. Wait for my signal.'

Then he texted Alix back. 'Thanks. You look amazing.' Carver smiled as he saw her glance up and search for him in the crowd. She didn't find him, but he knew that when she sat back, crossed her legs, tossed her head and ran her hands through her hair she was putting on a show just for him.

He sat back to watch the tennis. Quinton Arana had made it into the quarter-finals. Zorn wasn't going anywhere while the American kid was on court. As long as he had a great seat on Centre Court, Carver thought he might as well enjoy it.

Arana won in five. Zorn and his guests took time out in the third set to grab a late lunch. Carver did not go with them. He did not want to be spotted in the restaurant. And if for any reason Zorn decided to leave, Alix was on the lookout and would tell him: that had been the second favour he'd asked her. But Zorn wasn't ready to go just yet, because he and his group returned for the second half of the match, cheering every point Arana won and politely applauding his opponent's successes. At the end of the match Alix got up, as did the other woman in the party, and made her way out again. Carver was pondering the apparent inability of women ever to go to the ladies' room without company when he got another message.

'Need to see you. Meet at deb holders' entrance. Now! Ax'

Something had gone wrong. Why else would she be texting? Carver rose from his seat and headed for the exit.

67

A mile or so away from the All England Lawn Tennis Club the old Mazda saloon pulled into a parking space on Southside Common, which, as its name suggests, runs along the south side of Wimbledon Common. The space was just beyond the junction with Murray Road, a typically leafy Wimbledon street filled with large suburban homes, where the average property won't leave change from two million pounds.

'There you go, boss,' said Kevin Cripps.

'Cheers,' Schultz replied, hefting his massive bulk out of the cramped passenger seat and on to the grass verge that ran beside the road. About ten metres away across the grass was a tarmac path that followed the line of the road. On the far side of the path stood a pair of park benches about twenty metres apart. One of the benches was directly in line with the space where the Mazda had parked. Schultz made for it. He was carrying the B&Q bag that Carver had given him. While Cripps settled himself lower in the driver's seat, as if about to take a nap, Schultz stood beside the bench and looked around. Yes, this was the place all right.

He got down on his haunches, screwed up his eyes and stared intently past the Mazda to the far side of the road, where a row of trees screened the traffic from the Common. Schultz plotted an imaginary line from his position, through the Mazda, to a tree directly behind it. From the B&Q bag he took the two garden pegs, linked by twine. Just by his feet there was a large clump of dry, wispy grass. Schultz forced one of the pegs down into the earth just behind the clump, placing it at one end of the imaginary line. Then he placed the other peg in the ground, making sure that the twine was good and taut.

Schultz took another look: both pegs, the car and the tree were all perfectly in line.

Now he sat down on the bench and very carefully examined the car and the tree, noting their relative positions when seen from this fractionally different angle. He went back to the pegs and made another sighting from there. Then he checked the view from the bench again. Now he was satisfied.

The first part of the job was done.

68

Derek Choi was sitting at a table on the Tea Lawn, not far from the bandstand, which gave him a view of Centre Court debenture holders' entrance. Two of his restaurant workers, both agents of the State Security Ministry, were with him. A female voice sounded in his ear: the agent he had stationed in the stands of Centre Court. 'Carver has got up from his seat. He is leaving the stadium.'

Choi switched to another line. 'Attention! The target is in motion. Prepare to move on my signal.'

On the Aorangi Picnic Terrace, the grassy slope otherwise known as Henman Hill or Murray Mount, a trio of young Chinese adults – two men in jeans, T-shirts and bomber jacket, and a woman wearing a singlet, miniskirt and Converse Hi-Top trainers – calmly got to their feet. All three were registered as students at a language school in Central London. One of the men pointed at the action on the giant screen fixed to the outside of Number One Court, directly opposite the terrace, and said something that made the girl laugh as she brushed a few leaves of grass from her skirt. The sound of her laughter made a man sitting nearby turn around and then fix her with a stare of frank appreciation as he took in her long black hair, prettily smiling face, pert breasts and long bare legs.

She was carrying a squashy leather shoulder-bag, big enough to carry her phone, her make-up, a knitted top in case it got cold, and all the other random items that any young woman needs. It also contained an EpiPen – like the one used by diabetics to inject themselves with insulin, except that this was filled with deadly toxin – and a loaded QSZ-92 9 mm pistol, produced by a Chinese state arms factory. Not so many young women need those.

Choi was wearing dark glasses that hid eyes now entirely focused on the debenture holders' entrance. He saw Carver emerge from Centre Court. Choi waited for a moment to see where his target was heading, but Carver stood still. He was waiting for something, but what? Choi saw him glance at his watch, betraying his tension. Then another figure appeared in the doorway, a woman. Choi recognized Petrova, the Russian who had been with Carver two nights earlier, and whose name had so infuriated the Sternberg woman. Choi frowned. Had Carver really set up some kind of romantic assignation, right in the middle of an active operation? Or were the two of them working together? It made no difference. Carver was exposed and standing still. He would never be more vulnerable. It was time to move.

Without betraying the slightest suggestion of urgency, Derek Choi rose unhurriedly from his seat. He took a couple of twenty-pound notes out of his wallet and placed them under one of the teacups under his table. 'Time to go,' he said to the other two men at the table, who also stood up. Then Choi spoke into his microphone, a single word: 'Go!'

69

Carver was not, for once, pleased to see Alix. 'What is it?' he asked her impatiently.

She smiled flirtatiously and kept the happy, carefree look on her face as she said, 'Zorn just said he was about to leave.'

'Couldn't you just text?' he said, smiling back.

'It was easier to say I needed the bathroom. And you're better placed out here. When he goes, he will come out of this door, right there, and you will see him. Besides,' and now the phony flirting gave way to a much more serious emotion, 'I wanted to be with you. Just for a minute or two . . .'

Carver was about to reply when he saw her frown. She stepped closer to him, nuzzled her lips against his ear, and, making it look as though she was giving Carver her full attention – even though her half-closed ice-blue eyes were focused at a point beyond his left shoulder – she said, 'There's a man by the bandstand looking at you. He looks Chinese: quite tall, slender build, black designer jeans, black jacket, dark glasses . . .'

'Chinese?' Carver asked quizzically, wondering what interest anyone from the Far East might have in him. He'd made some serious enemies in Thailand, but that had been a long time ago. And they'd all been dead when he'd left them.

'You're sure he's not just looking around, watching the world go by?' he asked.

'No. This looks like surveillance.' She frowned. 'There are two other guys with him, very similar style of clothes – jeans, jackets, but more casual – he's talking to them. They both looked this way, too. OK, now they're moving towards us, fanning out.'

'Are they armed?'

'I can't be sure, but they certainly could be. Under those jackets . . . sure.'

'Take my hand,' Carver said. 'They could be coming for you, not me. Let's see how interested they really are.'

Gripping her tightly, he turned on his heel and started walking towards St Mary's Walk, the path that cuts right through the Wimbledon site from north to south. It begins at the top of Aorangi Terrace, and plunges downhill all the way to the far end of the club grounds, passing virtually every court and building of any significance as it goes.

Carver and Alix moved quickly, with the purposeful strides of people with an urgent appointment to keep, forcing their way past slower movers with brusque words of warning or apology. They reached St Mary's Walk at a point about two-thirds of the way along it. To their left, it continued down past the new mini-stadium of Court Number Three, and a gaggle of outside courts, to a tented village of shops and eating places. Carver went the other way, up a steep flight of stairs. Here the path ran like the floor of a canyon between the looming bulk of Centre Court on one side and the zigzag facade of the Millennium Building on the other. This was where both the press and the players had all the facilities they needed to work and relax, and the mini-theatre where both sides met for pre- and post-match interviews.

Carver stopped at the top of the stairs and looked back. The three Chinese were heading his way, forcing their way past the people at the foot of the steps thirty or forty metres away. He tightened his grip on Alix's hand. 'Let's go.'

Ahead of him the crowd became even thicker. A knot of fans stood immobile in the middle of the path, clutching cameras, video recorders and phones, and gazing up at a covered footbridge that ran over their heads between the Millennium Building and Centre Court. They were waiting to see a star player walk along it, going to or from a match, and they glared crossly at Carver as he forced his way through.

He heard a gasp from Alix.

'What is it?' he asked.

'Look,' she said. 'Up the hill . . . more of them.'

Carver grunted to show that he'd spotted three more Chinese, one of them female. They might be completely innocent, but he couldn't afford to risk it. He and Alix were caught almost exactly halfway between the two groups. He glanced at one, then the other, before giving a sharp tug on Alix's hand.

'Change of plan,' he said.

He turned towards the Millennium Building and made for a gap in its facade, past the plate-glass windows behind which the world's tennis journalists were sitting at their desks, splitting their attention between TV and computer screen as they filed their latest reports. Now Carver came to a small courtyard, hemmed in on all sides by high white walls. He felt Alix flinch as she took in their claustrophobic surroundings. 'Don't worry,' he said. 'Through here.'

He made for a door in the far corner of the courtyard, that opened on to a stairwell.

'Down,' he said. 'We're going underground.'

70

One good thing about looking the way Schultz did: if you sat down at one end of a park bench, no way was anyone else going to sit at the other. Certainly not without asking very politely.

He heard a voice in his ear. It was Cripps. 'You need a hand with the fireworks, boss?'

'No worries, Kev, I've got this fucker well sorted.'

Schultz had delved into the B&Q bag and taken out the squat grey plastic tube, the shallow copper cone and a locking ring. He placed the cone at one end of the tube, the point facing inwards so that the external surface was concave. Then he screwed the locking ring on to the tube until it pressed tight on the copper, to keep it securely in place. Then he turned the tube over so that the open end was facing him.

Next Schultz got out the bag of Polyfilla and undid the clip that had been placed over the open corner. He then held the bag upside down, over the grey tube, and poured out the contents of the bag – in actual fact, high-explosive RDX powder – tamping the floury white particles down as he went, to make sure they were tightly packed into the tube. When the bag was empty, he placed the plastic disc over the open end of the tube as a backplate, and secured it with the other locking ring. The looped wire was now on the outside of the backplate.

Schultz now had a closed canister, not much bigger than a beer can, filled with explosives, with a fuse wire at one end and copper at the other. This was a Krakatoa, a weapon that arguably produced more bang per buck than any other on the planet. It struck Schultz that this was essentially a smaller, smarter version of the mortars that had been used to attack the refinery. Good to think that the man behind the attack would be getting a taste of his own medicine. It was just a pity Carver's orders had been so specific: hit the engine, not the passenger compartment. Schultz would have liked to atomize the bastard. But orders were orders, even when they were crap.

There were four small open tubes on the side of the newly formed canister. Schultz took the four plastic sticks from the bag and inserted them in the tubes. Now the canister had legs to stand on.

Schultz undid the wire tie holding the loops of the fuse wire together, and unwound it. Holding one end of the wire in his hand, he placed the canister on the ground, lining it up with the pegged string.

'Oi, Crippsy! Wake up, you idle bastard!' Schultz said.

There was a laugh in his ear. 'What do you want, boss?'

'Take a look out your passenger window. Can you see the Krakatoa?'

Cripps grunted as he shifted his position. 'Hang about . . . Yeah, if I look for it I can see something through the grass, and obviously I know what it is, right? But no other fucker's gonna have a Scooby.'

Schultz chuckled. 'No, not till they get it right up the Aris. Then they'll fucking know all about it.'

71

One thing you can count on in any combat situation is that nothing will go exactly according to plan. The ability to adapt to changing circumstances, and improvise accordingly, is therefore vital. Derek Choi was no soldier, but he was well versed in the need to think on his feet. Carver had slipped his original trap. But now he might have run right into another.

For Choi, too, had been studying plans and photographs of the All England Club and its surrounding area. When he saw Carver disappear into the media centre stairwell, and then take the stairs heading down, he knew exactly where he was heading. He snapped out a series of orders to his most trusted subordinate: a thickset, shaven-headed tough called Lin Zhuang. 'You and the others will be the hunting dogs and I will be the hunter. Follow Carver and the woman. Drive them towards the unloading bay. I will be waiting to snare them. If you kill them first I will not be displeased. Understand?'

Lin nodded.

'Then go.'

Lin and the other four agents raced away down the stairs. Choi turned on his heels and went the other way. He ran about a hundred metres, and then he, too, headed down into the depths of the earth.

72

There was a small landing at the bottom of the stairs, with a single, duck-egg blue door, which had a round glass porthole. Carver took a look through it, then pushed it open with his shoulder, glancing back up the stairwell as he did. The sound of scurrying footsteps was clearly audible, coming from above them. The Chinese were on their way.

Carver raised his gun to cover the stairs as he gestured for Alix to go through the door. He followed her into one of Wimbledon's underground service tunnels. The door was positioned close to a right-angled bend, so that the tunnel ran away straight ahead of them and to the right. The concrete floor was shiny and slick from the constant passage of feet and wheels. The walls were made of bare breeze blocks. A couple of doors, painted in the same duck-egg blue, were set into the right-hand wall. The nearest one had a sign next to it that read, 'Ball Boys and Girls'. The one beyond it displayed one word: 'Pilates'.

On the left, two massive black pipes ran all along the bottom of the wall, with metal racks above them that were used to carry countless, loosely hung strands of multicoloured wire. A number of smaller red-painted pipes were suspended from the ceiling, along with yet more wires. They were all held in place by metal frames like horizontal ladders, from which hung a line of harsh white neon strip lights that ran as far as the eye could see.

'Let's go,' said Carver, running down the tunnel up ahead.

Alix followed him, her heels clattering against the concrete floor. As they rounded a left-hand corner Carver gestured at her to stop and get to the side of the tunnel, just behind him. He took up a position by one of the pipes, wishing that Schultz were down in the tunnel with him, instead of sitting on a bench by Wimbledon Common. Give the two of them a couple of sub-machine guns and a bunch of grenades, and they'd have the Chinese sorted in no time. Doing it solo was a little more complicated.

Carver was as close as he could get to the angle of the corner, leaning slightly out into the tunnel to get a view of the door from the stairs. It opened and one of the Chinese stepped through it, holding his gun out in front of him. He stopped for a moment, saw no one else in the tunnel, and lowered his gun as he relaxed a fraction, and that was when Carver stepped out and fired the two shots that killed him.

Carver put another two rounds through the porthole to discourage the men waiting the other side, then immediately turned – and almost ran right into a squat, white, open buggy that was coming down the tunnel towards them. Thanks to its electric motor the buggy was virtually noiseless. In fact the loudest sound coming from it was the music seeping from the earphones of the skinny, acne-faced lad at the wheel. He seemed lost in what he was hearing, his attention long since dulled by the constant repetition of trips up and down the same stretch of tunnel. He barely registered Carver's presence until he was two metres away, and then his dull working day suddenly got a whole lot more exciting. He slammed on the brakes and came to a halt within a few centimetres of Carver, who simply put a foot in front of the buggy, leaned forward, and used one hand to shove his gun in the young driver's face, while the other ripped the earphones from his head.

'Get out, now,' said Carver. 'That way.'

The driver nodded frantic agreement, then scrambled across the seat towards the wall where Alix was standing.

'Now hold out your hands in front of you,' Carver told him.

From round the corner came the sound of the door to the stairs being kicked open.

Carver pulled a pair of the yellow plastic handcuffs from his trouser pocket and gave them to Alix.

Now a voice could be heard barking out orders in Chinese.

Carver nodded at the wall and said, 'Tie him to those racks.'

There were distant footsteps, getting fainter – men running down the tunnel in the wrong direction. Then more commands.

Alix nodded and slipped one of the handcuff loops around the driver's left hand, tightening it hard enough to make him wince.

More footsteps, coming in their direction.

Alex passed the cuff around the back of one of the upright struts that supported the wire racks, then took the driver's right hand and secured it.

As she did so, Carver got behind the wheel of the buggy and executed a quick three-point turn, so that it was facing back the way it had just come. He slid across the seat so that Alix could get behind the wheel.

'Floor it,' he said.

The buggy trundled away, gradually picking up pace towards its top speed of sixteen miles per hour. Carver turned around in his seat so that he was facing backwards, half-kneeling with one knee on the seat, his weight pushed forward so that his thigh was braced against the vertical seat-rest. He reached around to the small of his back and took out his gun. Then he held it out in front of him, sighting at a point in the middle of the corner round which the Chinese were about to appear.

The footsteps got louder.

The kid tied to the wire-rack was darting his head from side to side like one of the spectators on the courts up above them, staring with terrified wide eyes at Carver, then back towards the sound of the approaching footsteps. He started desperately trying to clamber up and over the pipes to give himself a little cover.

'OK,' Carver told Alix, 'hit the brakes.'

The two fastest Chinese came racing around the corner. The first almost skidded to a halt as he spotted Carver up ahead, aiming a gun directly at him, and there was almost a touch of slapstick about the way the next runner crashed into him, nearly knocking him off his feet. But that comedy moment saved the first runner's life. It meant that Carver's first shot missed him, and the second hit him high on his right shoulder, smashing into the joint between the shoulder blade and the upper arm. The impact knocked him backwards. He screamed in agony and his gun dropped from his limp, useless arm. But he was still alive.

Carver didn't have time to finish the first target off. The second was already steadying himself and bringing his gun to bear on the buggy. Carver went for a head shot. Two more quick-fire rounds hit their target, splattering a mess of scarlet blood and grey brain matter against the stark, bare breeze blocks.

Eight rounds used, seven left in the magazine. Three men down . . .

No, make that two.

The man Carver had wounded was struggling to his feet. He switched his gun to his left hand, and staggered forwards.

Carver winced as he killed him with a pair of shots to the chest, almost resenting his victim for forcing such a clinical execution rather than being smart enough to count himself lucky and stay down.

He pointed his gun up at the neon strip lights and fired off the rest of his rounds, throwing that section of the tunnel into semi-darkness. Then he released the magazine, slammed in a new one and passed the gun to Alix. 'Get round the next corner, then wait for me,' he said. 'If I don't come for you, shoot whoever does.'

Carver got out of the buggy and she drove away. He jumped up and grabbed hold of the framework that ran along the ceiling, carrying the red pipes, wires and shot-out neon lights. Then he swung his legs up into the framework, and pulled his body up until he was lying flat alongside the pipes and wires, hoping that the thin metal struts that supported them would take his weight as well; hoping, too, that he had taken out enough lights to hide his presence from the other Chinese, who must now have realized that they had gone in the wrong direction, and be doubling back his way.

Carver reached down to his leg and slipped the knife from his ankle sheath.

More voices came, two of them, one higher-pitched than the other. Their words were indecipherable, but the questioning tone was clear. They were calling out for their mates, and wondering why there was no reply. Seconds later the owners of the voices came into view: a shaven-headed, thickset guy who looked like he could handle himself, and a slip of a girl in a sexy little mini. They both glanced at their dead comrades. The girl visibly flinched, then pulled herself together, advancing down the tunnel at a slow, steady pace beside the man. They had their guns in front of them, alert to the slightest sound or movement.

They were almost directly under Carver now.

Then there was a strangled cry for help, the sound of a man too terrified to be able to raise his voice. The buggy driver slid back down the pipe towards the tunnel floor and the two Chinese turned in his direction, presenting their backs to Carver. The girl swung her gun until the barrel pointed directly at the wide-eyed scream-ing driver, her face clenched into flint-eyed immobility as she put three shots in a tight grouping right in the centre of his skinny torso. They blasted bloody chunks out of his back as they passed right through him.

The sound of the firing was still echoing around the tunnel as Carver slipped down from his hiding place, his feet hitting the concrete directly behind the shaven-headed man. His left hand clamped over the man's mouth as the knife in his right cut into the flesh of his neck and, in a single sweep from left to right, severed the windpipe and the carotid artery, sending a spray of blood pluming through the air in a downward arc. The man fell dead at Carver's feet.

The young woman turned round to meet this unexpected threat, and Carver threw himself at her, reaching out for her gun with his empty hand and stabbing the knife up towards her guts.

The knife never got there. Carver felt the woman's slim hand clamp against his wrist, her grip surprisingly powerful, crushing enough to cut off the supply of blood to his hand and weaken his grip. So now they were locked in a stalemate, each able to prevent the other from using their weapon, but unable to make an attacking move without releasing the grip that was keeping them safe. They stumbled into the centre of the tunnel, turning around in a fatal dance in which each partner was trying to kill the other. The woman was the first to make a move, bringing her right leg round in a scything kick towards the side of Carver's left leg.

Carver evaded the kick, pulling the woman's much lighter body with him and taking advantage of her fractional loss of balance to spin her around and then hurl her at the far wall. The woman's skull hit the breeze blocks with an audible crack, stunning her so that she stood groggily, leaning back against the wall and presenting her body to Carver front on.

A second later the knife that Carver had thrown was embedded in the woman's delicate, slender throat, and her body was sliding, stone dead, to the hard, cold floor.

Carver waited for a second to see if anyone else was coming, but there was only silence. He stepped across to the corpse and took the gun from the lifeless right hand. Then he sprinted down the corridor toward Alix. Less than a minute had passed since they'd entered the tunnel, and the only un-silenced shots had been the ones that had killed the buggy driver. They would actually serve to keep anyone else away: nowadays no unarmed security men, or even police officers, would advance towards a suspected gunman. The health and safety culture that put the reduction of risk far ahead of the doing of duty would see to that. But that would not prevent the authorities from setting up a security cordon. Unless he and Alix got out fast, they'd be trapped underground like rats in a blocked drain.

He was going flat out round the bend: so fast, in fact, that he slipped and went skidding and scrambling to the floor, accidentally saving his life as the bullets intended for his upright body slammed into the breeze blocks behind him.

Carver tucked his head into his shoulders, turning his fall into a roll, then got straight to his feet, his gun in front of him. He was just about to fire in the direction from which the firing had come when he caught sight of the shooter.

It was the sixth Chinese, the one in the black designer gear: the leader.

He was standing behind the buggy.

He was not pointing his gun at Carver.

He was holding it against the side of Alix's skull.

73

Derek Choi could hear more voices echoing down the tunnel, British voices, getting closer. Yet he made no attempt to escape, nor did he bother shouting threats or demands at Carver. As long as he had the Petrova woman at his mercy, Carver could do nothing. In the meantime, Choi was happy to let the time go by until they were all discovered. Carver's death was really only a means to an end. The ultimate objective was to prevent him getting out of Wimbledon, so that Malachi Zorn could escape. If Choi and Carver both ended up in custody, that aim would be accomplished. Choi carried a diplomatic passport, and his immunity would keep him safe. Carver, though, would have a lot of explaining to do. He might have powerful friends, but they would not help him if the police were conducting a multiple murder investigation. Carver would be left alone to face his fate: the bizarre British obsession with correct procedure would see to that. He would be rotting in jail for the rest of his life.

Carver could see that Alix was looking straight at him. She glanced down for an instant at her feet, then straight back at Carver with a look on her face that said, 'Shall I?'

He gave a fractional nod of the head, then switched his eyes back to the gunman, stared at him hard and shouted out, 'Oi! You!'

That got his attention.

At that moment Alix brought up her right knee and then slammed it down again, driving the point of her heel into her captor's foot, then, as his grip on her loosened, throwing her body down too, and leaving him exposed.

Carver finished the job with two more kill shots.

He ran to Alix. 'You OK?'

She nodded angrily, furious with herself. 'I'm sorry. I wasn't looking behind me and—'

'Doesn't matter. Let's get out of here.'

They ran back up the tunnel, past the corpses strewn across the scarlet-smeared concrete, till they got to the door marked 'Pilates'.

Carver stopped beside it. He wiped the handle of his gun, then threw it away. He took a deep breath to settle himself. He looked at Alix. 'We're drunk. We're idiots. All right?'

She gave him a wry smile. 'Whatever you say . . .'

He pushed open the door and as they went through put his arm around her and slurred, 'You really are bloody shexy. You're worth every penny.'

Alix gave him a dig in the ribs with her elbow, and then in a heavy Russian accent giggled, and said, 'You English men. So funny. But so small.'

They had found their way into a large treatment room. A track-suited female instructor was giving instructions to a pair of male players, who were lying face-down on mats.

'Lift your heads and your feet and hold the stretch . . .' she said. Then she saw Carver and Alix and snapped: 'Who are you? This is not a public area.'

'We're looking for the bogs,' said Carver with drunken amiability. 'My friend Natasha.'

'Oksana,' said Alix.

'Well, whatever she's called she's bursting for a piss.'

'Get out!' shrieked the instructor. The players were getting to their feet, looking as though they were ready to remove these drunken intruders personally.

Carver raised his hands palms out, appeasingly.

'S'all right,' he said. 'We'll be moving along. D'you happen to know the way to Centre Court?' He grinned stupidly. 'We have ama-a-azing seats.'

'That's the way out, mate,' said one of the players in an Aussie accent, pointing at a door on the far side of the room. 'Up the stairs. Out the door at the top. You'll be right opposite the court. Time to go.'

'But you can stay,' said the other player, giving Alix a cheeky grin.

She gave him a withering stare.

Carver took her hand and said, 'Come on, darling. I need another drink.'

They followed the tennis-player's instructions and found themselves back out on St Mary's Walk, just another couple in the crowd. It took a few minutes to make their way round to the debenture holders' entrance.

'I'll see you later,' Alix said, giving Carver's arm a squeeze.

'I'll call you,' he said.

Carver followed her as she went off towards Zorn's seats. Ahmad Razzaq was still there. Dmytryk Azarov was still there.

Malachi Zorn, however, was gone.

74

Carver ran like hell, racing back down the stairs, out of Centre Court and back across the Tea Lawn to the nearest exit gate. As he came out on to Church Road he heard police sirens in the distance, but getting louder. By now the carnage in the tunnel must have been discovered. He could imagine the panic as Wimbledon's officials tried to work out how to respond. Should they carry on as normal, with the possibility of a gunman on the loose, or terminate proceedings for the day, risking panic as tens of thousands of fearful spectators tried to leave the grounds?

Not his problem. And at least it would keep the police fully occupied while he got on with his business. If he could get on with it.

He speed-dialled Schultz as he ran across Church Road between the crawling lines of departing spectators and homeward-bound commuters and dashed into the car park.

'Any sign of Zorn?'

'No, boss.'

'Let me know if you see anything.'

'Haven't you got him in view?'

'Lost him . . . long story.'

The fractional silence before Schultz next spoke was enough to tell Carver how unimpressed the big sergeant major was by that news. 'So what do you want us to do?'

'Nothing. Just keep your eyes open. The moment you see anything, let me know.'

'Right, boss.'

Carver could see his Transit up ahead. But there was no sign of Zorn's Bentley. 'What's the traffic like there?' he asked.

'It's moving,' said Schultz. 'I mean, it's not going quick, but it's moving.'

'Shit.' He didn't want Zorn in a moving vehicle. He wanted him stuck in a traffic jam, going nowhere.

'OK. Keep this line open. If you see anything, shout.'

Carver did a quick calculation. From the moment he met Alix outside Centre Court to the time he saw Zorn's empty seat couldn't have been more than five minutes. Unless Zorn had decided to leave at the precise moment Alix saw the Chinese, he was unlikely to have had more than a two- or three-minute head start. Unlike Carver, he would not have run to his car. Nor could Zorn have done what Carver did next.

He opened up the rear doors of the Transit and leapt up into the cargo bay. A Honda CRF250X trailbike, a skinny, long-limbed red whippet of a machine capable of racing over virtually any terrain, from the wilderness to the urban jungle, was standing there with a helmet hung from its handlebars. A gun was clipped to its body, just ahead of where Carver's right knee would be resting. A grenade was clipped to the left.

Carver pulled on the helmet, released the clips that held the bike to the floor of the van, pressed the ignition button, and drove the bike straight out the back of the van. Its shock-absorbers easily handled the impact as it landed on the grass outside, and then it spun on a sixpence as Carver pointed it towards the direction in which his quarry was travelling. But he didn't head for the car park exit on to Church Road. Instead he revved the engine to a furiously loud chainsaw buzz as he steered between the lines of parked vehicles, racing over the grass, dodging pedestrians, squeezing so tightly between cars that his handlebars seemed to brush the paint-work on either side; all the time following the line of the road and keeping one eye out for any sign of Malachi Zorn.

Next door to the debenture holders' car park was an area given over to the marquees used for corporate hospitality. Carver kept going, ignoring the outraged shouts of drunken businessmen as the nimble Honda zipped between the huge white tents. A man in a waiter's uniform emerged from one of them, pushing a trolley laden with crates of empty wine bottles. He looked up in wide-eyed terror as Carver bore down on him, and let go of the trolley, which tipped over, spilling crates and bottles across Carver's path. He slalomed and skidded through the sudden avalanche of glass and plastic, fighting to retain control as the rear wheel spun against the grass, before rocketing forward again as it regained traction.

He passed the last tent and headed into another one of the giant car parks, turning towards the exit this time and riding past a line of cars patiently waiting to leave, before forcing his way through the exit and left on to the road. As he passed the end of the tournament grounds, the road rose again up towards St Mary's Church. The traffic was beginning to move a little faster. Carver swept past the church on to a road that ran between ranks of large suburban houses – hiding behind high brick walls, thick shrubs and trees, as if concealing their cosy, complacent prosperity from the passing hordes. He peered ahead, trying to spot the dove-grey Bentley. No joy. Then he heard a voice in his ear: 'I've got visual contact, boss. He's turning into Southside Common. Got to be less than two hundred metres away from me, maybe one fifty. What do you want me to do?'

'Let him get closer. Jam the road. Then wait for my signal. On my way . . .'

'Got it, boss.'

By Carver's reckoning he was about four hundred metres from

the turn into Southside Common. He needed to be there fast: fifteen seconds, twenty at most. He upped his pace still further, running flat out between the lines of traffic. Up ahead a bus had stopped, blocking the cars behind it and bringing the traffic to a crawl. Carver didn't hesitate. He mounted the opposite pavement and kept moving, dodging metal bollards, waste-paper bins and another bus stop, muttering, 'Sorry,' as a mother pushing a stroller screamed and scrambled herself and her baby out of his way. On the far side of the bus the road was a little clearer, and Carver swung back down on to the tarmac. The houses on either side of the road were getting much smaller: little terraced cottages with lines of shops, galleries and estate agents scattered between them. He swung right, across a mini-roundabout and on to the crowded high street of Wimbledon Village, cutting up a yummy mummy in a BMW X5 and receiving a loud blare of the horn in exchange.

Almost there. He could yet make it. But only if Schultz and his mate did their bit.

75

Schultz spoke to Cripps. 'You hear that, Kev? Get to work, son. Just act like a twat. Shouldn't be difficult.'

'Ha-ha! I'm on it.'

Southside Common is a two-way street. For much of its length parking is allowed on either one or the other side of the road, but never both. So the traffic is inevitably slowed somewhat, as it has to swing first one way and then the other to get round the parked cars which form a series of bottlenecks. Cripps was halfway along one of these bottlenecks. And now he was going to put a cork in it.

Cripps looked in his rear-view mirror at the line of traffic coming towards him from behind. He could just see the Bentley, five cars back.

Another line of traffic was coming towards him in the opposite direction, slowing down to allow for the narrowed road where Cripps and the other cars were parked.

There were no obvious gaps in either line.

Cripps started his engine and signalled right. Without waiting for any response, he then swung the Mazda out into the traffic. The two cars nearest him slammed on their brakes. They came to a halt, barely a hand's breath away from either side of Cripps, who had now got his car almost broadside across the road. The cars behind them braked, bumped into one another, blew their horns and flashed their lights. In a matter of a few seconds, a calm and steady flow of traffic had been reduced to chaos. Cripps grinned sheepishly at the drivers on either side of him and mouthed the word, 'Sorr-eee . . .' Then he put the car into reverse and attempted a three-point turn. Except that the road was too narrow and the cars around him too close to allow it.

So now he started shuffling the car back and forth, nodding idiotically at the driver in the car closest to him, who was screaming, 'Turn the fucking wheel!' through his windscreen and miming extravagant turning gestures. Cripps just ignored him, shuffling his car back and forth so that neither he nor anyone else could get anywhere.

In the Bentley, the chauffeur turned round to Malachi Zorn and said, 'Sorry about this, sir. Some idiot's trying to turn round in the middle of the road. Shouldn't be long, and we'll be on our way.'

Carver sped past dinky little restaurants for ladies who lunched, and fancy fashion boutiques for those who shopped. He ignored two red lights on pedestrian crossings and left a trail of startled, angry citizens in his wake. Up ahead he saw the Wimbledon war memorial, an obelisk topped by a cross that stood by the left-hand turn on to Southside Common. A line of cars was waiting to make the turn, but no one was moving. The traffic had come to a grinding halt. Carver kept going past the cars, barely slowing at all. He bore left past the memorial. The common was almost upon him. Time to get things moving.

One of the drivers being blocked by Kevin Cripps had got out of his car, and was walking angrily towards the Mazda. Cripps watched him come, smiling at the thought of the shock the man would get if he tried to pick a fight. Then he heard a voice in his ear.

'This is Carver. Move!'

Now Cripps turned the wheel. In a couple of seconds he had floored the gas, turned hard right, and was racing away down the road, missing Carver by millimetres as he came the other way, gunning his bike down the middle of the road.

Schultz narrowed his eyes as the traffic started to move. In his hand he held a detonator switch, connected to the wire that led to the Krakatoa. One car came past the empty space where the Mazda had been. Then two . . . three . . . four . . . now he could see the Bentley. It was nosing forward cautiously, the chauffeur conscious of both the bulk and value of the car he was driving. The last thing he wanted to do was scratch the bodywork.

Now the Bentley was almost filling Schultz's line of sight.

Schultz pressed the switch.

The high-explosive powder blew, destroying the grey plastic canister. At the same time, the intensely focused heat and power of the blast worked a terrible magic on the copper disc, transforming it into a slug of near-molten metal that speared through the air and hit the front of the Bentley with the force of an artillery shell. It punched a hole the size of a fist in the car's side-panel, then smashed into the engine with a brutal power that instantly reduced a marvel of precision engineering to mere shrapnel and scrap metal.

The shock waves from the blast ripped through the car, shattering every window.

The Bentley was stopped dead in its tracks. The car behind ran straight into it, causing a slow-motion pile-up as it, too, was rear-ended. The cars coming the other way had also stopped again, to the sound of more screeching brakes and crashing metalwork.

Schultz gave a nod of appreciation at the effect of his work. Then he got up from the park bench and calmly walked away. As he went he switched calls to another line.

'Ambulance,' he said. 'Now.'

*

Carver reached down and released the gun that was clipped to the side of his bike. His eyes were fixed on the Bentley just a few metres away. The chauffeur was slumped over the wheel, unconscious, but there was movement in the back of the car. Carver slowed, then braked to a halt as he came alongside the Bentley's passenger compartment. He could see Zorn quite clearly through the shattered window. He looked dazed, but he was pulling himself together, shuffling along the rear seat, reaching for the door handle, trying to get out of the car. Carver stuck his gun-hand through the window. He took careful, considered aim. And then, as Zorn shouted, 'Please! No! Don't!' he fired.

And then, for good measure, he unclipped the grenade, pulled the pin and threw that in as well.

The bright yellow emergency ambulance had been waiting at the far end of Murray Road, about five hundred metres from the crash. The moment the driver got the signal from Schultz, he turned on the siren and flashing blue lights and sped away up the road, across the Ridgeway towards Southside Common. Estimated time of arrival: a little over thirty seconds.

Carver had the bike moving before the grenade blew. The blast went off behind him as he gunned the bike across the road, between the trees that bordered the common and on to the open grassland beyond. The terrain was made for a trailbike, and the Honda sped away with the enthusiasm of a racehorse given its head and pointed at the finishing line.

For a good fifteen seconds, no one dared get out of their cars. Then the first door opened and a balding middle-aged man climbed out. Tentatively, looking from side to side as if he feared some new threat might suddenly appear, he made his way towards the crippled Bentley. With nervous darts of his head he looked at the mangled bonnet and engine compartment, and the driver still motionless at the wheel. He bent down to peer at the back passenger seats. He took one look at the blood-drenched body and the gore that the grenade had spattered all over the creamy leather seats. And then he wrenched his body to one side, bent almost double and threw up all over the road.

The man was still standing by the Bentley, dazed by the shock of what he had seen, when the ambulance arrived. He was ushered to one side by paramedics, who immediately forced their way into the car and removed Zorn's inert, blood-soaked body, placing it on a stretcher and wheeling it to the ambulance. The driver came next.

The paramedics worked very fast. They did not seem to be too interested in the finer points of patient care. They just got the two victims into the back of their ambulance as quickly as possible and then set off again – lights flashing, siren wailing – so that they had been and gone within little more than a minute of the crash taking place. By the time the fire and police teams got there, the car was empty.

Malachi Zorn had just vanished from the face of the earth.

76

Parkview Hospital, Wimbledon

Under any normal circumstances, the victim of a violent, potentially fatal attack on Southside Common would be taken three miles across the South London suburbs to St George's Hospital, Tooting. A teaching hospital that has won national awards for its standards of care, St George's has an accident and emergency department that sees around a hundred thousand patients a year. It is open every hour of every day, has a resuscitation area for critically injured patients, and is staffed by four consultants, forty junior doctors and around fifty nursing staff. But when the ambulance carrying Malachi Zorn raced away from the scene of the assassination attempt, it did not drive east towards that waiting A & E. Instead it double-backed across Wimbledon Common, before turning north and then dashing less than a mile towards a smaller, private hospital that had no emergency facilities at all. It did, however, boast a much more significant speciality: extreme discretion. And in the case of Malachi Zorn, a billionaire financier attacked by an impromptu black ops team unofficially commissioned by Her

Majesty's government, privacy and silence were far more significant priorities than quality of treatment.

By the time that the ambulance drove through the hospital
entrance and into a forecourt hidden from inquisitive passing eyes
by a tall, thick hedge, Carver had already arrived, parked his bike
and was waiting to greet it. He followed the paramedics as they
rolled the gurney carrying Zorn's blood-soaked body across the
tarmac, past the plain-clothed policemen standing guard by
the front door, and into the hospital itself. There was no one at all
in the reception area, except for a single doctor. He was dressed in
a suit, rather than scrubs, and he was not waiting to carry out a swift
examination of his patient's injuries, as one might have expected in
a case of this kind. There was no attempt to administer drugs and
fluids or blast the motionless figure back to life with shocks from
defibrillator pads. Instead he just raised the blanket that had been
covering Zorn's face, gave a quick, brisk, businesslike nod and said.
'Take him to Room 68, top floor,' before following the gurney, the
paramedics and Carver into the lift.

The atmosphere was oddly calm as they rose three floors to the
top of the building, just the usual mix of self-conscious silence and
uneasy attempts to avoid one another's eyes. Then the doors
opened, and the doctor stepped out first with a brisk 'This way,' as
he strode away down the corridor. Room 68 was at the end,
occupying one corner of the building. It had that three-star-hotel
look so beloved by private hospitals: all pastel walls and patterned
curtains, with two visitors' chairs and a flat-screen TV on the wall
opposite the bed. The chairs were occupied, and the TV was on as
Zorn was rolled into the room, lifted off the gurney and placed
upon the bed, still in his bloodied clothes, uncovered by any
blanket.

'Ah,' said Jack Grantham, switching off the TV and getting to his
feet, 'the moment of truth.'

He stepped close to Carver, and in little more than a whisper
said, 'Six bodies in a tunnel underneath Centre Court, and a
home-made bazooka disturbing the peace of the leafy, Tory-voting

suburbs. That's a bit extreme, don't you think? Even by your standards.'

Then, as the paramedics left the room, Grantham turned back towards the bed, assumed the cheerful demeanour of a drinks-party host greeting his guests, and said, 'Good afternoon, doctor, my name's Grantham. I work for the Secret Intelligence Service.'

'Good afternoon, Mr Grantham,' replied the doctor. 'I'm Assim. Hmm . . . your face seems familiar. There was some publicity at the time of your appointment, I believe.'

Grantham grimaced. 'Yes, we're not as secret as we used to be . . . More's the pity.'

Assim frowned inquisitively at the man who had risen to his feet from the second chair, and was now standing at the foot of the bed, tugging nervously at his moustache. 'And you must be . . . ?'

'Cameron Young. I work for the Prime Minister. Look, can we get on with this, please? I need to report back to Number 10 as soon as possible.'

'This is Carver,' said Grantham, paying no apparent attention to Young as he completed the introductions.

'So what is your position?' Assim asked, shaking Carver's hand.

'Self-employed,' Carver replied. 'A private contractor, you might say.'

'I see,' said Assim. 'And you are responsible for the fact that Mr Zorn is with us here this afternoon?'

'Yes, he's here because of me,' said Carver. 'But he isn't Malachi Zorn.'

77

Dr Assim looked puzzled. A slow, sly grin spread across Grantham's face. And the tension on Cameron Young's face was replaced by a look of appalled surprise.

'What the bloody hell do you mean? Of course it's Malachi Zorn. Just look at him!' Young exclaimed.

'All right,' said Carver, 'I will.'

He went to the side of the bed. 'Malachi Zorn is five feet ten inches tall and weighs around a hundred and seventy-five pounds. Looks about right, wouldn't you say? He has dark-blond hair: check. He has hazel eyes.' Carver reached over and lifted an eyelid to reveal a sightless eye. 'Check. His facial features look remarkably like these ones here.'

'Yes, because he's Malachi bloody Zorn!' Young interrupted.

'Except,' Carver continued, unperturbed, 'that Malachi Zorn is a lifelong bachelor. He's never even got engaged, still less married. That means he's never worn a ring on his wedding finger. So how do you explain this?'

Carver lifted up the body's left hand and separated the fourth finger from the others. 'Look,' he said.

'Look at what?' asked Young. 'It's a finger, what's the big deal?'

'Look at the colour of the skin, just here, at the base of the finger. It's paler than the rest, like skin that's been covered for years by a ring. And if you look very closely, you'll see that the skin is slightly indented, which is what happens when you wear a ring for a long time. Now, the skin is beginning to get some colour, and the indent is much less than it would have been when the ring was first removed, so I'm guessing it's been a couple of months since he took it off. But even so, this man was married. So he can't be Malachi Zorn.'

'That's it?' asked Young incredulously. 'That's your entire reason for thinking this isn't Zorn? I never heard anything so ridiculous! The whole point of this lunatic exercise was to strike back at Malachi Zorn because – or so you claimed, Grantham – he was a mass-murderer who had wreaked appalling damage on the UK economy. And now you're telling me that we got the wrong man?'

'I'm not telling you that,' said Carver. 'I got the right man. Well, the man I meant to get, anyway. Could you examine his face, please, doctor? Look out for signs of recent plastic surgery.'

Assim glanced around, seeking confirmation. 'Go ahead,' Grantham said.

The doctor stooped over the head of the supposed Malachi Zorn, and ran his fingers along the hairline, around the right temple, parting the first few strands of hair to reveal the skin beneath. 'Hmm . . . very interesting,' he murmured to himself. He turned on the reading light above the bed to give himself more light. 'Yes, there is clearly some scarring here,' he said. 'And it would be consistent with a temporal incision for an endoscopic rhytidectomy. That's to say: a mid-face lift.'

Assim leaned back a fraction, turned his head slightly to one side, and narrowed his eyes, focusing on the man's nose. He took a tissue from a box beside the bed and rubbed it along an area of the bridge of the nose that had not been spattered with blood. 'Concealer,' he said, lifting the tissue to reveal a smear of flesh-coloured make-up. Then he looked again, moving his head to view the nose from a series of different angles before pressing his fingers delicately on the area that he had been examining.

'There's some very slight residual swelling, as one might expect from surgery carried out four or five months ago,' Assim said. 'It's barely perceptible and the discolouration is very slight, and easily covered up with a minimal amount of make-up. But it's certainly there.'

He turned the head to one side and looked behind an ear and underneath the jaw, on both occasions wiping the concealer away to reveal faint scars. 'Yes, there's no doubt that this man has undergone a number of surgical procedures. I'd need to X-ray him, of course, to be completely certain. But I would not be surprised to find evidence of work on his jawbone, his chin, the bossing of his skull, his cheekbones and even the orbital rims around his eyes. In each case it would have been possible to reduce the mass of the bone by shaving or grinding it, or to augment and/or reshape a particular bone with fillers and implants of various kinds. Wait a moment . . .'

Assim took a look at the crown of the man's head. 'Yes, he's had some hair transplantation, too. It's really first-class work, so it's as imperceptible as one can get. But it's there all right. You might want to get a dentist to take a look at the teeth, too. It's not my field, of course, but given what else has been done to this man, it's reasonable to assume that his teeth were included in the overall makeover.'

'Are you telling me that this man, whoever he is, has been given the face of Malachi Zorn?' Young asked.

'I suppose I am, yes,' Assim replied.

Young glared indignantly at Grantham and Carver. 'And you didn't see fit to tell me about this deception?'

'It would only have confused matters,' Grantham said. '"Let's kill the bad guy" might not be a politically acceptable plan, but at least it's a simple one.'

'Zorn has informers everywhere,' Carver added. 'It wouldn't

have bothered him at all if he'd known that the government was helping me kill him, in the belief that the target was genuine. In fact, he'd have been delighted. It would make his death official, which is exactly what he wanted. But if he'd known we'd discovered he was using a double, that would have changed everything.'

Young ran a hand through his hair and gave a baffled sigh. 'I'm sorry. Why would it change things?'

'Because Zorn wants the world to think he is dead. But if the victim is just someone who looks very much like Zorn, and we know it, that's no good to him.'

'Yes, but why is it so important to him to be dead?'

'Because dead men can't be tried for killing hundreds of people or stealing billions of dollars and pounds. Cops don't chase dead men. Angry billionaires who've just been massively ripped off don't hire hit men to go after corpses. Dead men are safe.'

'Ah, yes . . . I see,' said Young. 'So now what?'

'Well, the first thing to do is to switch on the television,' Grantham said.

The set flickered back to life. It was tuned to *Sky News*. A banner was rolling across the bottom of the screen. It read, 'Breaking news: billionaire financier Zorn believed dead in South London attack.'

'Excellent,' said Grantham. 'Time to send in the troops.' He took his mobile phone out of his pocket, pressed a button and said, 'You're on.' Then he looked around the room at the other three men and said, 'Have I forgotten anything?'

'Yes,' said Carver, 'why don't we wake this poor bastard up?'

78

Wentworth

The black-uniformed SAS men slipped over the walls of Malachi Zorn's rented mansion like vengeful wraiths. Immediately before the start of the operation they had been informed that Zorn was almost certainly the mastermind behind the refinery attack that had killed the Director of Special Forces. He had been responsible for the sudden death of a man who was not only their ultimate commanding officer, but also a former colonel of the regiment. The eight men assigned to capture Zorn were grimly determined to get him by any means possible. And if he happened to get hurt in the process, so much the better.

The man on screen was a sports reporter. He spent ten months a year covering the various injuries, transfer deals, disciplinary issues and sexual shenanigans with which Premiership footballers filled their days. For two weeks in midsummer he became an instant expert on tennis, reporting on Wimbledon. But now all hell had broken loose in the streets less than a mile from the tournament, and suddenly he'd swapped thigh strains and broken strings for hard-core news reporting.

'I don't know if you can see behind me the burned-out remains of the Bentley limousine that is believed to have been carrying the controversial American financier Malachi Zorn,' he was saying.

'Yes, Barry, we can see it,' said the newsreader in the studio. 'But is there any more information about what actually happened here?'

'Yes there is, Kate. This was a very public assassination attempt, carried out in front of lines of cars all stuck in a traffic jam – a jam that may even have been created as a means of trapping Zorn. From what eyewitnesses are saying, a car pulled out into the middle of the road, stopping the traffic in both directions, before suddenly driving away at high speed. Seconds later there was a huge explosion that disabled the Bentley.'

'Was that some kind of mine, like the IEDs we've become so familiar with in Afghanistan?'

'Possibly. Some witnesses, however, are describing a rocket or bazooka being fired at the car. All we know for certain is that the Bentley was disabled. Very soon after that, a man approached the stricken car on a motorbike, fired a gun into the passenger compartment and then lobbed a grenade into it. One eyewitness who saw the interior of the car is still too distressed to speak. It's safe to say it was not a pretty sight.'

'And what about Mr Zorn? Do we know whether he is dead or not?'

'That's still hard to say, Kate. Certainly it seems very unlikely that anyone could have survived this attack. But he might have had one stroke of luck. A London ambulance was nearby and rushed to the scene. Mr Zorn's body was taken from the car and driven away within a minute or so of the incident. It's thought that his head may have been covered by a blanket, suggesting he was already dead, but I'm getting conflicting reports on that.'

'So where is he now?'

'We're not sure, Kate. There's been no word from any of the local hospitals. Meanwhile, in another extraordinary development, rumours are sweeping the tennis world that there has been some sort of incident in the tunnels beneath Centre Court, possibly involving gunfire and multiple fatalities. I have to stress, though, that these are unconfirmed . . .'

With a press of a remote control the screen turned to black.

'What do you think? Am I now officially dead?' asked Malachi Zorn.

'How could you not be?' Razzaq replied. 'Carver blew up your car, then used a gun and a grenade to carry out the actual hit.'

'The grenade bothers me,' Zorn said.

'Why so?'

'If that grenade went off inside the car, how come the ambulance men were able to put the body on a stretcher? It should have been torn to pieces by the blast.'

Razzaq frowned. 'True, though a blast can easily be blocked or deflected. A table-leg saved Hitler from von Stauffenberg's brief-case bomb, after all.'

'I guess,' said Zorn. 'But I'll still be happier when I see some spokesperson standing outside a hospital, saying how tragic it is that I passed away.'

The SAS team had divided into two four-man patrols, which were now approaching both the front and rear of the building. Surveillance of the property with highly sensitive parabolic micro-phones and thermal-imaging binoculars had detected the presence of two adult males in the room that Zorn was believed to use as an office. The two men were still in place as the troops reached the building and flattened themselves against the walls. They weren't going in through any of the mansion's doors. They didn't need to. Simultaneously they placed coiled rings of explosive cord, whose blast was tamped and focused by black rubber tubes of water up against the brickwork. The moment the signal was given, the cord would be detonated. Even before the smoke had cleared, the SAS would be in the building and racing towards their quarry.

*

Zorn was going back over the news report in his mind, its in-consistencies nagging at him, like an itch that would not go away. 'That ambulance . . . we're supposed to believe that, what? It just happened to be down the road, with nothing better to do? No way, that's just not possible.'

'What are you saying here?' asked Razzaq.

'I'm saying maybe the whole set-up was fake. Maybe Carver double-crossed you. Either that or the Brits got to him.'

'But that would mean that they knew it wasn't you in that car.'

'Not necessarily. They could have figured out the connection to Rosconway.'

'Impossible! How?'

'I don't know. But if they did, they'd have plenty of reasons to come after me.'

Razzaq did not reply. He wasn't paying attention to Zorn any more. He was looking at an image on one of Zorn's screens. It showed security camera footage: shadowy figures in black combat fatigues and helmets placing something on a wall. There was a sudden flare of white light and then the picture disappeared in a snowy blizzard of interference.

'They're coming after you now,' said Ahmad Razzaq.

Modern explosive devices combine violence and precision. The tamped detonator cord generated a combination of noise, blast and total surprise that delivered all the shock and awe any attacking force could desire. And it left a hole as neat as a laser-beam through steel. The SAS troops poured through with their guns raised and ready to fire. They took just seconds to race from their entry points to Zorn's study, and when they got there they blew out the lock and kicked open the door so fast that they barely had to break stride.

Eight heavily-armed members of the special forces, faceless behind their balaclavas, goggles and helmets, shouting at the tops of their voices and ready to respond in an instant to any threat burst into Malachi Zorn's study . . .

. . . and found the property's gardener and his assistant cowering behind a leather sofa, while the latest action from Wimbledon played on a massive flatscreen placed on the opposite wall.

'Mr Zorn said we could be here,' the gardener pleaded, raising his hands in surrender.

'Honest,' said his assistant.

Zorn had watched the attack play out. 'So now we know,' he said. 'They're on to me. But Jesus, don't these jerks know how much money I've made? And can't they figure out what that means? Anyone who's got billions in the bank, there's a good chance they're smart enough to see things coming. And it's a friggin' certainty they can afford more than one damn house.'

79

Parkview Hospital

The man with Malachi Zorn's face looked blearily around the room, trying to summon up the focus to make head or tail of the surroundings and the men looking down at him from the far end of the bed. One of the men, who had an olive-skinned, Middle Eastern appearance, detached himself from the group and came closer. 'Hello,' he said, 'my name is Dr Assim. Don't worry, you're in hospital and you're quite safe. Now, can you tell us who you are?'

The man frowned and screwed up his eyes as he gathered his wits and then replied, 'My name is Malachi Zorn.'

Assim smiled. 'It's all right. You don't have to do that any more. We know you aren't Mr Zorn. Who are you, really?' A look of fear entered the man's eyes, a shock so palpable that Assim placed his hand on his wrist and assured him again, 'It's all right. You're in no danger.'

The man looked at Assim for a moment, then his lips twisted into a bitter laugh as he said, 'Sure I'm in danger. I'm a dead man. That's the whole point . . .'

'What do you mean?' Assim asked. 'The whole point of what?'

'Wait.' The man grimaced as he struggled into a sitting position. 'I'll answer your questions . . . maybe. But first you answer mine.'

'What would you like to ask?'

'Well, for a start, how come I'm still alive? I . . . I can remember an explosion at the front of the car. Then glass smashing right by me, and a gun coming through the window . . .' He looked down at his own body and began patting at his chest and stomach. 'And my clothes . . . they're all covered in blood, but I can't feel any wounds. How did the blood get there?'

Dr Assim took a step back. 'Mr Carver, perhaps you could help here?' he said.

'Sure. I was the guy who fired that gun at you. Sorry about that. It must have been a shock.'

'Not really . . . I'd been expecting worse,' the man replied.

Carver gave a wry smile. 'Yeah, that makes sense. You were set up to take a bullet. What I actually fired at you was a tranquillizer dart, like the ones they use on wild animals on nature programmes. Then I threw a special effects grenade into the car. Made a lot of noise and splashed a load of pig's blood all over you and the interior of that Bentley, but it looked a lot worse than it really was.'

'And you didn't want to kill me?'

'Have you ever done me any harm?' Carver asked.

'Not as far as I know.'

'Do you plan to do me any?'

'Er . . . no.'

'Then why would I want to kill you?'

'Because—'

'Because a man called Ahmad Razzaq paid me a lot of money to kill Malachi Zorn. That's true. But you aren't Zorn, so as far as I'm concerned, you aren't my target. Now, since I've been good enough to keep you alive, why don't you tell me who you really are?'

The man sighed. 'Alive? Trust me, it's a temporary reprieve . . . a few months: six, maybe nine if I'm lucky. Cancer. You'd have found it if you'd looked any closer, doc, believe me. But anyway, my name . . . yeah . . . my name is Michael A. Drinkwater. The "A" stands for Abraham, if you can believe that.'

Grantham got his phone out again and tapped a text to his office, ordering a search for any information on a Michael Abraham Drinkwater.

'How old are you?' he asked, looking up from his screen.

'Thirty-seven. My birthday's August the twenty-third. Should make that at least.'

'Home town?'

'Pensacola, Florida.'

'Navy brat?' asked Carver, thinking of the US Navy's flight-training base there.

Drinkwater nodded. 'Sure, my daddy flew Tomcats, though he was mostly flying a desk the years he was stationed there. You in the service?'

'Royal Marines, a long time ago,' said Carver. 'So, tell me about Zorn. How did that work?'

'You mean, apart from waking up every morning and seeing someone else's face in the mirror?'

'I mean now, this week. How much of it was you?'

'That was Zorn – the real one – on that BBC interview. He gave a press conference at his place after ex-Prime Minister Orwell was killed. But that aside, if you ever saw Mr Zorn outside his house or his office, that was me. I was going to go to Wimbledon on Friday, too, and there was going to be some kind of fancy reception that evening, but I was told not to worry about that.' Drinkwater gave a gentle smile. 'I was going to be dead by then.'

'How did Zorn recruit you?' Carver asked.

'He made me a deal. Well, his people did . . . I was at work. I'm a CPA – I guess you guys would just say "accountant". It's not exactly exciting. Anyway, these guys came to my office one day in January, near the end of the month. They said they wanted to make me a deal. They said I could make sure that my family would be well provided for. They knew my wife's name, my kids' names and ages, everything. I said, "Are you trying to sell me insurance?" and they laughed and one of them said, "I guess you could call it that." '

'So what was the deal?'

'All I had to do was agree to impersonate the guy they were working for – they didn't tell me his name, not at that time – and my family would receive two million dollars, cash. Invest it conservatively, and they'd be pretty much guaranteed a hundred grand a year for ever. They said they knew that would appeal to me, in my situation. I mean, it was obvious they knew everything about me – my personal finances, my medical records, you name it. So I said, "What's the catch?" One of them said, "Well, you've gotta have a bit of surgery." And the other one said, "Then you've gotta die. But what the hell, huh? At least this way it'll be quick." '

'Remarkable,' said Cameron Young, almost purring with satisfaction. 'Truly remarkable.'

'What do you mean, "remarkable"?' asked Drinkwater indignantly. 'What kind of word is that for those bastards?'

'I apologize, Mr Drinkwater. I meant no offence,' Young replied. 'But I can't help admiring the way Zorn's mind works. And, if you'll excuse the inappropriate sentiment, I also can't help feeling he took a considerable pleasure in conceiving the choice with which you were presented. You knew that you were mortally ill, facing a very painful death, and yet you must have harboured, indeed may still harbour, the hope that somehow you might be spared. All you had to do – and I appreciate that "all" is a very loaded word here – was accept the inevitability of your fate, lose a few last months of life, and you would receive a swift end, courtesy of Mr Carver here, knowing that your family was secure. It's elegant, don't you think?'

'No,' said Drinkwater. 'I damn well don't. And I wouldn't have taken the deal, either, except for the next thing they told me. Seems I was the third guy they'd approached. The other two had said no. And they were dead already, with not a single cent for their wives and kids.'

'Well, at least you're still alive.'

'Yeah I am . . . and now we've got a problem.'

'Really?' asked Young.

'Yeah, really,' Drinkwater insisted. 'See, the second half of that two million was payable on my death. And thanks to you jerks I'm still alive. So the way I see it, you owe me a million dollars.'

Young looked appalled. Carver burst out laughing. But Jack Grantham was looking at his phone screen with a face as grim as a gravestone. 'That's not our only problem,' he said. 'I just had a message from Wentworth. Zorn got away. Seems the little bastard saw us coming.'

80

Cheapside, Berkshire, and Parkview Hospital

'So now what?' Razzaq asked, as a Chinook carrying eight very dis-gruntled SAS men back to Hereford clattered overhead, its occupants totally unaware that the target they had so spectacularly missed was just a few hundred feet beneath them.

'So now the game has turned around, just like I said it would,' said Zorn, making it sound like a fascinating prospect. 'And it's kind of interesting, y'know?'

'I'm not sure I do,' confessed Razzaq.

'Well, let's just play around with a few scenarios. Suppose Drinkwater is dead. I don't believe he is, but let's stay with me on this. If he's dead, then the Brits can tell the world that Malachi Zorn is dead. And who's going to contradict them? The only person who could do that would be me. And I'm not exactly going to advertise my existence right now.'

'Of course,' Razzaq agreed. 'But that's exactly what you wanted. Everyone thinks you're dead. You've got the money. That's perfect!'

Zorn shook his head. 'No, it would be perfect if everyone thought I was dead. But the Brits know I'm not. So they can come after me. And if they get to me they can kill me, and they don't have to worry about it, because the rest of the world thinks I'm dead already. Got it?'

'Yes,' said Razzaq, 'that is a problem.'

'In theory, yes, but, see, I don't think Drinkwater is dead. I don't think a government, or anyone working for it, or even with its knowledge, goes right ahead and deliberately kills the wrong target.'

Razzaq looked unconvinced. 'You're still assuming they knew that you were using a double. We don't know that for sure.'

'Why else would they have raided the Wentworth house?'

'They could have been looking for evidence.'

'No!' Zorn insisted. 'If the Brits knew that I ordered the Rosconway attack, and if they also thought I was in the car, all they'd be looking for in the house would be evidence on paper or in computer files. So they'd send in the cops, or maybe some spooks from MI5. If they sent in special forces, it's because they were looking for me and they were ready to use force.'

'That makes sense,' Razzaq conceded, 'although it is still possible that they might have been allowing the possibility of resistance from other people: myself, for example.'

Zorn grinned. 'No, Ahmad. You would never be that stupid. You would have called them first and offered to cut a deal.'

Razzaq burst out laughing. 'I will not even pretend to deny that! You know me too well.'

'So, let's get back to Michael Abraham Drinkwater. Let's assume he's alive and the Brits have got him. What's the first thing we know for sure?'

Razzaq smiled. 'Once again, they can still kill you.'

Zorn was not the slightest bit offended by Razzaq's amusement. 'You got it! And why can they kill me?'

'Because once they produce Drinkwater and say that he is you, the rest of the world believes you are still alive. So how can you possibly be dead?'

'You got it in one. Outstanding! So, look at it from the Brits' point of view. If they think it through the same way we did . . .'

'They might not. Maybe they're not that clever.'

'Their politicians might not be,' Zorn agreed. 'But don't tell me there aren't people in the intelligence community who can't see the way this plays out.'

'Certainly there are such people in the Security Service and the Secret Intelligence Service. And if Carver somehow managed to discover that you were using a double, then he may also have realized that he can now kill you – the real you – with impunity. Assuming that he wants to, of course. Mr Carver is surprisingly picky about his targets for a man who makes a living as an assassin.'

'He might not have a choice,' Zorn pointed out. 'You recruited him through blackmail. What's to stop them doing the same thing? But I'm not so worried about that. I was always going to disappear when all this was over, but . . .'

'. . . but there's another way you could play it,' Carver said.

He, Grantham and Young had commandeered one of the hospital's consulting rooms. Grantham had immediately placed himself behind the desk, in the doctor's position. Carver and Young were sat in the chairs opposite, like patients. Grantham had just been setting out the strength of their position. 'This Drinkwater idiot is our ace in the hole,' he said. 'Of course, the wife and kids may need a bit of handling. Perhaps I can persuade the Americans to stick them inside the witness protection programme, or something. Give them new names. Make them disappear where no one will ever find them. We can't have the missus pointing at our new Mr Zorn and saying, "Hey, that's my hubby!" '

'Then there's the whole issue of Drinkwater's cancer,' Carver pointed out. 'If he really is going to be dead in months, that means he comes with a sell-by date. But there's another way you could play it.'

'What other way?' Young asked, dreading the answer.

'Well, the traditional intelligence way of operating is based on the idea that you absolutely don't want other people to know what you're doing.'

'Yes, Carver,' said Grantham, 'that's why we're called the Secret Intelligence Service. The clue is in the name.'

'Right, and that makes you strong in one way. But it also limits your resources. There's only so many minds working on any one problem: the people directly under your command, and whatever allies you can find in other agencies who can be trusted to keep your secrets.'

'You're joking. I don't trust anyone,' said Grantham.

'Exactly. Right now, you're looking at Zorn as a problem you and a very few other people have to solve. But the other way to crack a problem is to be as open as possible. Give it to anyone who wants to play with it, take it to pieces, or fix it in any way they want.'

All Young's worst fears had been realized. 'I'm sorry, Carver, but are you seriously suggesting we throw open all the United Kingdom's most valuable secrets and let any Tom, Dick and Harry *play* with them?'

'No, but I am suggesting a way that you could get a lot of very powerful help to deal with Malachi Zorn.'

81

'It's really very simple,' Carver said. 'In case you haven't noticed, Malachi Zorn is trying to pull the biggest heist in history. It's robbery, fraud, mass-murder, you name it, all wrapped up in one package. He rips off some of the richest people in the world. He makes mugs of everyone who's had anything to do with him. And at the end of it he ends up with some completely insane amount of money. But what's he going to do? Everyone's going to be after him. Unless they think he's already dead . . . That's why he wanted me to kill him – or appear to. It's a disappearing trick.'

'Tell me something I don't know,' Grantham said. 'Like where he'd disappear to.'

Carver held up his hands in exaggerated bafflement. 'How the hell should I know? He's probably bought himself a Pacific island, or a stretch of Amazon jungle, or maybe he's paid off an African dictator to give him protection. Does it matter?'

'It does if we've got to find him.'

'Which is why I'm saying you should get some help. You've got yourself a handy replica Malachi Zorn. He's proved that he can fool people, including some of Zorn's investors, into thinking that he's the real thing. So let him announce that he's magically survived the attack, and that the launch of Zorn Global is going ahead as planned. Then, when all the people Zorn has stolen from are together in one place, you tell them the truth. That this poor bastard is a bloke called Drinkwater and that the real Zorn is still somewhere out there, with God knows how many of their billions. Then just stand back and see what happens. My guess is they'll find Zorn soon enough.'

'Well, that's one way of doing it,' said Grantham. 'But you've missed an obvious alternative – well, obvious to any normal person, anyway.'

'What's that?'

'Call the police. As you said, that Deirdre Bull woman can tie your old friend Magda Sternberg to the Rosconway attack. And you, Carver, can tie Sternberg to Razzaq. His links to Zorn are easily established, connecting Zorn to Rosconway. Now we have Drinkwater as proof of Zorn's attempt to evade prosecution – that's a conspiracy to murder.'

'Not if I refuse to give evidence,' said Carver. 'Come on, Grantham, you of all people don't ever want me anywhere near a witness box.'

Cameron Young raised an eyebrow and made a mental note to discover what it was that Carver knew that Grantham would never want made public. Grantham himself, however, was undeterred.

'Doesn't matter,' he said. 'There's still Drinkwater, and even the dimmest juror won't miss the fact that he's walking around wearing Zorn's face. If the police can get Razzaq and/or Sternberg in custody, one of them's bound to start talking in exchange for a lighter sentence. Meanwhile, get the best forensic accountants the taxpayers' money can buy, and start them working through the money trail. Let's try sorting something out the proper, legal way for once.'

Now Young entered the conversation, easing his way in with a contemplative 'Hmm' before starting to speak. 'I completely sympathize with you, Grantham, and of course you're right that this is evidently a conspiracy. But take it from a former barrister, conspiracy cases are a nightmare to prosecute. It may be quite clear to us how the whole thing was put together, but that's a very long way from saying it can be proven beyond reasonable doubt in a court of law. All the evidence so far is either hearsay or circumstantial. There's no smoking gun, no email from Zorn ordering the attack, let alone a bomb with his DNA or fingerprints on it. He will be able to hire the best lawyers his huge wealth can buy. Meanwhile one of our key witnesses may very well die of cancer before the case even comes to court. A second witness may herself not recover from her wounds, and even if she does, her admitted involvement in a terrible crime would clearly give her a motive to lie about Mr Zorn in exchange for favourable treatment. And a third key witness is a former Royal Marines officer who appears, if you will excuse me, Mr Carver, to have spent many years behaving in a way that does little credit to his former regiment. If I were acting for Mr Zorn in that case, I would be very confident indeed of securing a not guilty verdict.'

'I see,' said Grantham sullenly. 'Well, then, we'd better take the Carver option . . . again.'

'Ah, well, that may also be a problem,' said Young. 'This is, I'm sure you will both agree, a very embarrassing situation for a great many influential people. Mr Zorn has, to be blunt, conned his investors. But they don't know that yet and I'm not sure we want to be the ones to tell them. After all, these are some of the world's richest men and women. They wouldn't enjoy looking foolish in public.'

'So what?' Carver asked. 'There are millions of people out there who'd be only too happy to see a few rich bastards taken down a peg or two.'

'Possibly,' Young conceded. 'But those rich bastards would not appreciate the government that let that happen, would they? And they aren't Zorn's only victims. Every one of his trades required a counterparty . . . or to put it another way, each of his bets required a bookie who took it. So when he made money, someone else lost it. And by someone else I mean either multinational financial institutions – banks, in other words – or London and New York-based hedge funds.'

'Once again, I can hear the cheering crowds,' said Carver.

'As can I,' said Young. 'But I can also see the Chancellor of the Exchequer's face when he is told that all these institutions have taken their revenge by quitting London, thereby depriving the Exchequer of tens of billions in tax revenues. And I must also think of the Governor of the Bank of England, who is already fighting hard to save the value of the pound without raising interest-rates to the point where they cripple the UK economy. One more straw could easily break the camel's back. This country has been limping for years. Do you really want to bring it to its knees?'

Carver shrugged. 'That's not my problem.'

'No, but it is mine. It seems to me that if we expose Zorn we will play right into his hands. The end result will be to destroy the market. And that is exactly what he wants.'

'Really? I thought he said today that he was putting his money back into the market.'

'And you believe him? I must say, Mr Carver, I would not expect you to be so naïve. And I have two last considerations. The first is that my boss, the Prime Minister, publicly placed a great deal of faith in Malachi Zorn. If it transpires that he was backing the greatest fraudster of all time that will not, to put it at its absolute mildest, look good. In fact, it could bring the government down. So now we have a ruined economy and a broken Prime Minister. And the cherry on top is that a senior member of the royal family regards Mr Zorn as a personal friend.'

Grantham shook his head disgustedly. 'Oh great!'

'Quite so,' Young agreed, making it plain that he shared Grantham's frustration with the limitless ability of that family's members to make life difficult for those who served them. 'They have met at numerous functions. Mr Zorn has dined at this royal personage's country home and given generously to certain charities which the personage supports. He has also made certain of his properties around the world available, discreetly, to the personage's spouse and children . . . and various extra-marital partners.'

Grantham frowned. 'Why didn't I know that already?'

'Before your time. I'm sure you would have been informed if the issue had ever arisen again. Suffice it to say, for now, that the palace would not be happy to see Mr Zorn's nefarious activities widely publicized. Which means, Mr Carver, that we will have to alter your plan somewhat.'

'So what do you want?' Carver asked.

'In public, we must make sure that the show goes on. For the time being at least, Mr Drinkwater will have to maintain the fiction that he is Malachi Zorn. We need to create a believable media narrative that links the attack on Zorn today with yesterday's events at Rosconway, but without any suggestion that Zorn himself was the perpetrator. As for the Zorn Global launch, it should go ahead, as you suggested, but there will be no public revelations, and the Prime Minister will, I think, be too busy to attend in person. The main aim has to be to keep Zorn's investors – and the financial markets in general – happy. Meanwhile, with the help of the SIS, among other agencies, we will very discreetly take every possible measure to trace and recover as much of Mr Zorn's stolen money as possible.'

'But once Zorn knows that the launch is going ahead without him, he's bound to react,' Carver said.

'Yes, which is why I don't want the PM anywhere near tomorrow's event. And why it will have a very high level of security around it.'

'But then what? You can't keep going for ever with two Malachi Zorns in the world.'

Young nodded. 'I quite agree, Carver. That's why I'm counting on you to make sure, as soon as humanly possible, that there's only one of them.'

82

London and Cheapside

Shortly after 8.00 p.m. a brief announcement from the hospital to which Malachi Zorn had been taken revealed that Mr Zorn had made a remarkable escape. Though suffering from shock, concussion and multiple bruises and abrasions, he was alive and could be expected to make a full recovery. Mr Zorn was resting comfortably. Further statements would be made in due course. Until such time, no comment would be made by any of the hospital staff.

It was now 8.40 p.m. The banner strung up on the back wall of the abandoned warehouse had the 'Forces of Gaia' logo spray-painted on it big enough to be read on even the smallest YouTube screen. One of the three masked men in front of the camera had the same imposing bulk as Brynmor Gryffud, but when he spoke his voice was so heavily treated that he could have been Welsh or Watusi for all that anyone listening could tell. The words he had to say, however, were clear enough.

'The Forces of Gaia claim full responsibility for two acts of war against the industrialists, speculators, politicians, armies and multinational conspirators whose actions threaten the survival of Gaia.

'We believe that the planet and all the organisms on it are linked in a single entity. We call this entity Gaia. We believe that it is naturally self-regulating, naturally healthy and naturally beautiful. Only the actions of mankind can possibly threaten it, and so we fight back against the violence of global warming, the violence of environmental pollution, and the violent exploitation of the world's natural resources for financial profit.

'Our struggle began yesterday at the Rosconway oil refinery. This industrial installation was specifically designed to exploit a precious substance torn from the belly of the earth. Its products pollute and heat the atmosphere. It is therefore a totally legitimate target in our struggle. We regret the loss of life caused by this necessary act of war, but condemn the actions of the government which caused so many unnecessary extra casualties.

'This afternoon, we passed sentence on the man whose provocative, ill-judged remarks provoked that government action, the American speculator Malachi Zorn. His warnings against so-called eco-terrorism were intended solely to inflame public opinion and influence financial markets so that he could profit. Gaia could not allow such obscenity to go unpunished. Accordingly, speculator Zorn was attacked this afternoon. Our only regret is that he some-how managed to survive. Other enemies of the planet will receive less mercy.

'We are the Forces of Gaia. And we will defend the sanctity of this planet to the death.'

The man stopped speaking. He and the two silent figures on either side of him remained rock still. Then a voice from off-camera said, 'Cut!'

The speaker pulled off his black balaclava to reveal the face of SBS Company Sergeant Major Mike 'Snoopy' Schultz. 'What total fucking bollocks,' he said, shaking his head in disgust. 'I couldn't hardly read half of it. What kind of a twat believes shit like that?'

'The kind that bombs oil refineries,' said Carver, who'd thrown away his balaclava and was scruffing his fingers through his hair.

'The real Forces of bloody Gaia can count themselves lucky I never got to them. They were shot, right?'

'That's what I heard.'

'Yeah, well I wouldn't have been that quick about it. Ah, fuck it! At least we got Zorn, eh?'

'Something like that . . .'

Schultz looked at Carver. 'What are you saying, boss? We did get that fucker, didn't we?'

Carver said nothing. Schultz looked at him with a mixture of disappointment and mounting anger. 'Don't say you were bullshitting me. You were never a bullshitter. Don't start now. Seriously, boss. Don't take the piss with me.'

'I'm not taking the piss. It's just that there were . . . complications. Things weren't what they seemed.'

'And you're not going to tell me any more than that?'

'Not now. Not yet. But I'll promise you this: Malachi Zorn will get what's coming to him. You have my word on that.'

'You sound like a fucking politician, boss.'

Carver felt the sense of betrayal behind Schultz's insult. 'I'm anything but that,' he said. 'Listen, you and Cripps did a great job with the Krakatoa. You'll probably get a medal for saving that woman at the refinery. I know how tough it is for you, losing Tyrrell. I know you want payback. But there's nothing more you can do right now. So return to your unit. Get on with the day job. And take it from me, Malachi Zorn will not get away with what he's done. All right?'

Schultz gave a reluctant nod of acceptance. 'Yeah, fair enough, I s'pose.'

'Good. Then I'll buy you a beer before you go.'

Within an hour of being released on Twitter and YouTube, the Forces of Gaia statement had received more than three million hits and been picked up by all the major global news networks and agencies. Among the millions who watched it with interest was Malachi Zorn.

'Very interesting,' he said to Razzaq. 'The British government knows who carried out the Rosconway attack. They know that I've been using a double. They must have made the connection between us and the Forces of Gaia. But they're deliberately obscuring it. You know what that means?'

'No, but I think you're going to tell me.'

'It means they're not interested in due process. If they had any intention of getting me inside a courtroom they'd be getting all the evidence they could to put me next to those dumb bastards in Wales. But I don't think they have that evidence. And even if they did, I don't think they ever want to see me in a witness box. Which can only mean one thing . . .'

'Which I am able to deduce also,' said Razzaq.

'Precisely. They want me dead.'

'My conclusion, also.'

'Well, they're in for a helluva disappointment.'

Thursday, 30 June

83

Parkview Hospital

The media were informed that Malachi Zorn had rested well overnight. He was not yet well enough to give a full-scale press conference. He would, however, consent to a brief one-on-one interview with an ITN reporter, on condition that the resulting material was made freely available to any news outlet that wanted it. The lucky woman who got the job was sent on her way to what she and her jealous colleagues all considered a potentially career-making encounter, with suggestions for questions ringing in her ears.

No one thought of asking Zorn, 'How much are you being paid to do this?' If they had, they might have caught Michael Abraham Drinkwater enough by surprise that he would have blurted out the truth: 'One million dollars.' He had sensed the Brits' desperation, stuck to his guns, and insisted on receiving the second half of the money Zorn was due to pay him. In the end, Young had been forced to give in. And so Drinkwater had gone back into character again.

The interview took place in Drinkwater's room. He spoke from his bed, sitting up, with a pile of pillows behind his back. To add to the drama of the occasion, a bandage had been wound round his head and he was wearing dark glasses to shield him from the glare of the TV lights. There were bruises, cuts and swellings on the left-hand side of his face. They had been put there by a make-up artist.

'When the car was first attacked, it stopped very suddenly and I was thrown forward and hit my face against the seats in front,' Drinkwater explained, as the interview began, using lines given to him in advance by Cameron Young's top writers. 'Guess I should have worn a seat belt, huh?'

He managed a weak, battered smile. 'But you know, it might have saved me. I was right on the floor of the car, between the front and rear seats. So I was sheltered from the rest of the attack.'

'Have you seen the statement released last night by the Forces of Gaia, the terrorists who claimed responsibility for the attack on you yesterday and for Tuesday's atrocity at the Rosconway oil refinery?'

'Uh, no . . . no I haven't. But I heard about that. My doc told me about it.'

'Do you have any message for those terrorists?'

'Well, I guess I wish they hadn't tried to shoot the messenger! And I hope that the police can arrest them, and that justice can take its course. But really I'm not the issue here, and nor are these terrorists. The important thing is that decent, hard-working people died on Tuesday, and they deserve to be remembered. Their sacrifice must be honoured. Their deaths must not be in vain. We need to take the whole issue of energy security much more seriously. I've been saying this for a long time, and it's just terrible, to be honest, to be proved right in this way.'

The reporter put on her most soulful expression and nodded thoughtfully. 'So how did it feel when some people suggested that you had been behind the refinery attack?'

'Well, you know, it wasn't easy hearing that. I lost a very dear friend in Nicholas Orwell at Rosconway. And it was a miracle that

I didn't die yesterday afternoon. You can take it from me, I didn't order anything. I'm a trader. I make deals. I don't kill people.'

'Well, speaking of deals, you were planning to launch your Zorn Global fund here in London tomorrow with a gala reception in the City of London. Will that be going ahead now?'

'Absolutely. I'm alive. I'm in one piece. And I will not give the terrorists the satisfaction of beating me. I'll be there . . .' Drinkwater leaned forward conspiratorially. 'And I'll tell you what, maybe I can fix you an invitation, too!'

Cameron Young was watching on a live feed to his office at 10 Downing Street. 'Cheeky beggar!' he said, to no one in particular. Still, there was no harm in a little humour. If they got through the next couple of days with the markets steady, Zorn Global's investors happy, and the real Zorn satisfactorily dealt with, that million dollars would look like a positive bargain.

Malachi Zorn was watching, too. So far as he was concerned, the information that Drinkwater would be hosting the reception in his place was the best news that he could possibly have been given. He immediately contacted Razzaq.

'The reception is going ahead as planned,' he said.

'I see,' his security chief replied. 'So can I take it that we will be proceeding exactly as we had originally planned?'

'You certainly can,' said Zorn. 'We're going to make a killing.'

84

Wax Chandlers' Hall, City of London, and Cheapside

Malachi Zorn had never been interested in acquiring corporations as long-term investments. He left that kind of thing to Warren Buffett. But for the purposes of his current operation he had spent six months and more than a billion dollars buying controlling shares in a number of fast-growing Indian computer companies. In every case, he hid his presence behind a web of shell corporations, even if the decisions about which businesses to buy were entirely his. He then created a holding company named after its apparent major shareholder, a hitherto-unknown entrepreneur called Ashok Bandekar. Even if he personally remained a mystery to the Indian media – a mystery made all the more intriguing by titbits of gossip about his past and present activities that were released into the blogosphere on a regular basis, and invariably then picked up by the conventional print media – Bandekar's company looked like a typical success story of the new, modern India.

So when the police and security service operatives assigned to cover the Zorn Global launch discovered that Bandekar

Technologies had hired the Wax Chandlers' Hall for three days they saw no obvious cause for alarm. The company itself checked out. The executives invited for interviews by the headhunting company all appeared to be genuine: UK citizens with no criminal records and impressive CVs. The security men who met the interviewees at the front door and checked their identities before letting them in all came from a reputable firm that only hired individuals with spotless records. The receptionist who then made sure that the new arrivals were comfortable while they waited to meet Mr Bandekar had an equally respectable background. And every one of those individuals sincerely believed that they were involved in legitimate business with Bandekar Technologies.

Two anti-terrorist officers, accompanied by a sniffer dog, arrived at the hall and were greeted by Bandekar's aide Sanjay Sengupta and a member of the hall staff, both of whom were highly co-operative. The officers had no reason to know that Sengupta did not actually exist: his identity had only ever been a cover for Ahmad Razzaq. They were shown through the many areas of the building that were not in use. They saw the conference room where the interviewees waited before their appointments. A series of display panels had been set up there, presumably to impress the prospective executives with the scale and ambition of the company they were seeking to join. Each panel proclaimed a different aspect of Bandekar Technologies' activities. A Perspex case in the middle of the room contained an architect's model of the corporate campus planned for a site outside Milton Keynes – the symbol of Ashok Bandekar's commitment to his European operations. A lighting rig on lightweight trusses illuminated the whole set-up. (The flight-cases in which the lights and all the display materials had been transported to the hall were neatly piled in one of the unused rooms.) At the end of the room a door led into a smaller office, suitable for private meetings like the ones Bandekar was currently conducting.

The officers were told they would have to wait for a few minutes before they could see Bandekar himself. He did not wish any of his interviews to be interrupted since that would be unfair to the candidate he was meeting at the time. But it was not long before the office door opened and a well-groomed young businessman in an expensive suit strode out, giving the small group waiting outside a confident, snowy-toothed smile as he passed. A few seconds later, Bandekar himself emerged. He was a large man, whose substantial girth was carried as elegantly as only the finest Savile Row tailoring can manage.

'Come in, gentlemen, come in!' he insisted. 'Have you been offered drinks? Some snacks, perhaps? We have excellent chocolate biscuits.' He patted his paunch. 'Too excellent, perhaps, for my good. Now what can I do for you?'

The officers explained that this was purely a routine check. Their dog panted happily, far more interested in the chocolate biscuits that its nose had detected the moment it walked in the conference room, than in any explosives. It hadn't had the faintest whiff of those. A couple of minutes later, the officers and their dog were gone, escorted out by the hall staffer.

'Well done,' said Ahmad Razzaq to the semi-retired Bollywood actor playing the part of Ashok Bandekar. 'You're doing well.'

'Maybe I should stay as Mr Bandekar,' the actor replied. 'I've spent so long talking about his business I actually think I could run it now.'

Razzaq laughed politely. 'No, that won't be necessary. Just another day, and then you'll be done.'

He left the office and approached the receptionist at her desk. 'You may show in the next candidate now.'

On the way out he could not resist making a detour to the room where the flight-cases were stored. At the very back of the room was a case that had a false bottom. In the secret compartment beneath it were two packages, covered and sealed in heavy-duty plastic wrap. The wrap had been washed in antiseptic bleach, as had the airtight boxes beneath it. The wrapping and washing of each layer had been done by different individuals, neither of whom had touched the contents of either box. And if the sniffer dog had ever smelled those contents, it would have been very interested indeed.

Ahmad Razzaq took the tube from the City to Waterloo, changing trains twice along the way. He was reasonably certain that he was not being followed, but he wanted to make absolutely sure. At Waterloo he caught a train to Sunningdale, losing himself among the commuters crammed into his carriage. From there he made his way to the modest house on the edge of Windsor Great Park where Malachi Zorn was staying. 'It's just me,' he'd said when Razzaq had questioned why his boss had chosen such humble quarters. 'Why the hell do I need anywhere bigger?'

The door was opened by a man with almost shoulder-length black hair and a heavy black moustache. 'I go see if Mr Zorn he can see you,' the man said in a strong Polish accent.

Razzaq kept a straight face as he came through the door and closed it behind him. Then he burst out laughing. 'Very good!' he said. 'You'd have had me fooled if I hadn't seen the look before.'

'Yeah, it's not bad at all,' Zorn agreed. 'And you got me a job at the catering company for tomorrow night?'

'Well, I practically had to buy the company, but yes, you will be reporting for duty, complete with all the paperwork and proofs of identity you need. But still, I must ask you, are you sure this is a good idea?'

'Yeah, I am, absolutely.'

'But the risk of discovery is so great.'

'Sure, but that just makes the challenge even better. Look, I have to know who's turned up at the launch. It makes a big, big difference to my financial calculations. Plus, I've got to admit, I really want to see how close I can get to Drinkwater. I mean, serving booze to myself: how insane is that?'

'It is, indeed, quite crazy,' said Razzaq. 'But if you must attend the reception, can I not persuade you at least to get well away once you leave?'

'No. I want to see it happen. I want to see those bastards go down. I've spent years on this. God, all the time, the planning, the money . . . I admit, all right, it's obsessed me. And I'm not going to sit on my arse a thousand miles away, watching it all play out on TV. I want to be there, in person, front row centre, for the start of the show.'

'Well, you will do it without me. I am leaving in the morning. By the time the first shot is fired I will be safe and sound in Karachi.'

'It's OK,' Zorn assured him. 'I understand. And you've already contributed more than enough. But before you go, will you do one thing for me? Just run through the getaway one more time.'

'Of course, that would be my pleasure.'

Razzaq pulled an iPad from his briefcase and called up a map of the City of London. 'So, the key to the whole plan is the abandoned underground railway tunnel that runs under the Thames from here, at King William Street, to London Bridge Station. The entrance to the tunnel is in an office building called Regis House. It is a little over one kilometre from where you will be, right here. So . . .'

Zorn listened intently. He asked questions, all the time, never being afraid to show his ignorance or go over something more than once; that way, he made sure that nothing was missed. By the time Razzaq left the house, almost two hours later, Zorn was absolutely confident that he could take on the security establishment, just as he had taken in the financial one – and outwit them just as comprehensively.

85

Lambeth

Carver had spent the day at the dismal MI6 apartment. Officially, security for the Zorn Global reception was being handled by the proper authorities, and he would have no part in it. Unofficially, he was still tasked with the job of disposing of Zorn if the chance should ever arise. For all the efforts that were being made to keep tomorrow night's partygoers safe, there remained a strong chance that Zorn would try something. Carver would therefore be there to stop him – terminally if at all possible. So he spent another day reading reports from all the teams carrying out background checks and site visits. He was kept updated on plans for barriers, ID-checks, body-scans and bag-searches. He was given the locations of three spotter-sniper teams who would be watching from high rooftops, ready to take out any hostile threat. And he was reassured that a combination of blocked roads and the City's excellent security camera system would make it impossible for Zorn to create a repeat of the Rosconway attack.

He was just wondering where to go out to find a decent drink and a bite of supper when he got a call from Alix. 'I left Azarov,' she said. 'I couldn't take a another minute of it. So I just packed a bag and left. I'll get someone to collect the rest of my things tomorrow.'

'Do you need somewhere to stay the night?' Carver asked. 'I happen to have a magnificent luxury apartment handy.'

'Hmm ... well, that's certainly very tempting,' Alix replied. 'Your apartment is very magnificent and so elegantly decorated ... But I think I'm going to rough it at the Mandarin Oriental on Hyde Park. I'm sorry, Carver, but as sexy as you are, I'm a girl, and the thought of being two minutes from Harvey Nicks is even sexier.'

'You mean you'd prefer a shop to me?'

'Of course ...'

Carver knew she was teasing, but two could play at that game. 'Well, I'm a boy,' he said, 'and I've got to work. So if there's nothing else you want to discuss, I'd better get back to it.'

'Oh, don't be cross. The only reason I want to go shopping is to get something really great for the party tomorrow. Please tell me you're going ...'

'To the Zorn Global launch?'

'What other party is there?'

'Yes, I'm going. But I don't think you should.'

Carver could feel the atmosphere change as Alix realized he meant it. 'Why not? Don't you want to be with me?'

'I always want to be with you,' he reassured her. 'But maybe not tomorrow night. I'll be busy and ... Look, it's just going to be difficult.'

Carver's words were followed by a silence whose deep Siberian chill was enough to freeze the line. But Alix must have decided on a change of strategy, because she suddenly brightened. 'Well, never mind about the party. We can sort it out tomorrow. Heston Blumenthal has a restaurant at my hotel. I booked a table for two tonight. Interested?'

Carver was there within the hour.

Friday, 1 July

86

The City of London

English summers are unreliable, and even July evenings can be damp and chilly. This one was no exception. Sunshine earlier in the day had given way to heavy grey cloud and blustery showers, so Ronnie Braddock had a raincoat on and the collar up as he arrived for his interview to be Head of Security at Bandekar Technologies. The legitimate aspects of his career, including his exemplary military service record, made him well-qualified for the role, while the illegitimate aspects were not known to anyone except the people who had hired him. And they certainly weren't talking.

Braddock was listed as Mr Bandekar's final interview at 6.00 p.m. on Friday – a last-minute addition to the list. He arrived early, showing his driver's licence to the goons on the door, neither of whom had ever had anything to do with him. When he got to the conference room, he asked the receptionist if there was a men's room anywhere near. 'Pre-match nerves,' he explained, with an embarrassed smile.

He was given directions to the nearest toilet, but when he left the conference room he forgot all about them. Instead he went to the storeroom where the flight-cases had been stacked. He opened the case with the false bottom, and then removed the two shrink-wrapped packages. Using a Swiss Army knife he then cut open the smaller of the two packages and took out the box it contained. Inside the box was a fully loaded Glock 27 subcompact pistol, an AAC Evolution .40 suppressor, and a spare eleven-round magazine. Braddock checked the Glock, fitted the suppressor, then placed the fully assembled gun within easy reach while he dealt with the other package. It didn't take long to be reassured that everything was in order. The XM-25 Punisher grenade launcher that he had gone to such trouble to steal in Afghanistan had made it all the way to the City of London in one piece. It wouldn't be long now before he found out just how good it really was. First, though, there was one other piece of business to attend to.

He put the Punisher back in the flight-case, closing the top. Then he picked up the Glock and held it down behind his back as he returned to the conference room.

'Hello!' said the receptionist cheerfully as she saw him come back in. 'You were gone a long time. You must have been nervous! Well, there's no need to worry. Mr Bandekar's a charming gentleman. Can I get you some tea?'

'Cheers, that would be great, yeah.'

She got up from behind her desk, and as she did Braddock shot her twice: one bullet in the body, and then another at point-blank range to the head before she had a chance to scream.

The suppressor was very effective, but there's no such thing as a total silencer. So Braddock needed to move quickly now, before anyone worked out what was happening. He went straight to the door to the inner office, opened it, and shot the interviewee in the back of his head, blowing a chunk of his brains out through his forehead and on to the desk behind which Bandekar was desperately trying to heave his massive bulk to his feet.

'You'll need more than two, big boy,' said Braddock. So he used four bullets on the portly Indian. Then he went to the window and drew the blind, repeating the process with the conference room windows. He did not turn the lights on, so the room was in semi-darkness as he dragged the three corpses behind the display panels. It was more to get them out of the way than to hide them; the thick trails of blood smeared across the carpet were like arrows leading the eye to the bodies' locations.

Braddock was sweaty, panting and irritable by the time he'd finished shifting Bandekar. He took a minute to cool down mentally as well as emotionally before he returned to the store-room, collected the Punisher and went back to the office. Lifting the blind and peering out, he could see five huge, brightly lit windows across the way. Not long to go now.

87

Ginger Sternberg was not the kind of woman who is easily impressed, but even she had to admit that the Goldsmiths' Hall was a spectacularly appropriate location for a gathering of the very rich. It was right in the heart of the City of London, less than half a mile from the Bank of England, and even closer to the Stock Exchange and St Paul's Cathedral. The main entrance was flanked on either side by massive classical columns that rose the full height of the building. Once inside, she came to a hall whose panelled walls and coffered ceiling were entirely covered in green, grey and white marble. Directly in front of her, a magnificent staircase rose in a single flight of a dozen wide steps before splitting in two to form a shallow Y.

Ahead of her, Ginger heard a woman with a grating New York accent whining at her fat, balding ape of a husband, 'Hey, Morty, I want stairs just like this in our next place.'

'Whatever you want, Charl, whatever you want,' he replied, humouring her.

Ginger wondered what Mort would be getting his mistress while his wife spent her time redecorating: not marble staircases, that was for sure.

A stream of guests were making their way up to the party itself: the men formally dressed in smart suits, the women dazzling in couture dresses and sparkling jewels. Ginger ignored the men and concentrated on her female competition, instantly noting those who were even remotely worthy of her attention, and grading their dresses, accessories, hair, faces and figures. It was an automatic reflex, combining natural feminine curiosity with professional scrutiny: when you had been trained to seduce men for a living, you very soon learned to determine who might beat you to your target. Tonight, of course, her task was very different. But even so, it gave her pleasure to scan the parade of rich men's wives, scattered with the occasional famous face, and know that she could still do battle with any of them. Her hair was blonde for the night. Her dress was a Valentino, in his signature red. Her heels were high enough to make her taller than all but a very few men. Other women might have felt self-conscious, looking down on so many people. To Ginger, that was merely the natural order of things.

She moved with the human tide, up the stairs towards the main Livery Hall where the launch was being held. Waiters and waitresses, dressed all in black, lined the way from the stairs to the hall, holding silver trays laden with glasses of champagne. Ginger took a glass, sipped and smiled to herself as she tasted the deliciously rich, sophisticated, complex flavour so characteristic of the Krug that Zorn liked to serve. Most of the people around her would be dead within the hour. But at least their final drink would be a great one.

The hall itself could have been a banqueting chamber in the palace of a Roman emperor or Russian tsar, so massive were its proportions, so rich the colour scheme of scarlet and gold. More mighty columns supported an even more ornate ceiling, and at the far end of the room a velvet-draped alcove was filled with a spectacular display of gold platters, jugs and cups. The most inspiring sight of all, however, came from the four great crystal chandeliers that hung over the centre of the room. They glittered not with electric bulbs, but with almost two hundred actual candles that cast a soft, warm, golden glow over the hall. The light was extraordinarily flattering, and it gave the whole event, whose sole purpose was to worship at the altar of money, an unexpectedly sensual atmosphere.

It was almost a pity, Ginger thought, that it would all soon be destroyed. Almost a pity: but not quite.

'Would you like some more champagne, sir?'

Malachi Zorn could not resist it. He'd seen Drinkwater across the room, sitting in his wheelchair, playing the same role, but for a new master, and had felt compelled to go right up to his own double. So now here he was in disguise, offering a drink to a man who looked exactly like his real, undisguised self. It was like some crazy hall of mirrors, mixed with a delicious, thrill-ride sensation of fear. If anyone realized what he was doing, he'd be lost. But no one did. The blatantly obvious police protection unit who were attempting to blend into the crowd, despite the unsubtle bulges in their jackets where their guns were holstered, glared at him suspiciously. But they were doing that to anyone who got within ten metres of Drinkwater.

'Back off,' one of them said, as Zorn held out the magnum of champagne so that its neck was tilted upwards over Drinkwater's glass, ready to pour if required. 'Mr Zorn has his own personal drinks with him. Someone should have told you that.'

'No one told me anything,' Zorn replied, grateful that the guests were so tightly packed and the hubbub of conversation and laughter so loud that no one could hear just how lousy his attempt at a Polish accent really was.

There had sure been an incredible turnout. The assassination attempt on Wednesday had made this an even hotter ticket than it had been before. Everyone wanted to be able to say that they'd been to Zorn's public resurrection from the apparent jaws of death. Zorn had spotted a couple of investors who'd privately told him they would not be able to make it. One of them had come all the way from Palo Alto, California, another from Kyoto, Japan. They must have flown in overnight. No one wanted to say no to this invitation.

The celebrity eye candy was out in force, too: a smattering of supermodels, actresses, athletes and rock stars, all enticed by the prospect of a fifty-thousand-dollar stake in Zorn Global, just for a walk down the red carpet, a wave to the paparazzi and a couple of hours of their time. But as entertaining as it was to gawp at beautiful women in revealing clothes, or men with Super Bowl rings and Olympic gold medals, Zorn's real interest was in guests who were far less easy on the eye. With a very few exceptions, the men whose presence he was committing to memory tended to be dressed conservatively, albeit expensively; to be aged fifty and over; and to be deeply dull, if not actually unappealing to look at. But they owned the fashion houses, movie studios, TV channels and sports franchises that kept the celebrities in business. They were the CEOs and chairmen of the banks into which the stars placed their pay cheques. They took the decisions which closed factories in one place, and reopened them thousands of miles away in some cheaper, more convenient location. They were his investors, and it was very important to Malachi Zorn to know precisely who had turned up, because then he would know who was going to die. And once he knew that, he could determine the final few plays in his great game.

'Almost there, Dad!' he whispered to himself.

He put the magnum down on the edge of one of the buffet tables and checked his watch. If they were sticking to the original schedule, he was due to start speaking in ten minutes, or rather, Drinkwater was. It was kind of a pity, really, Zorn thought. He was curious to know what 'he' was planning to say. But there wasn't going to be much of a speech. A minute, two at the most after Drinkwater started speaking, Braddock would go into action. Zorn wanted to be at his screen, ready to react to the first market movements when news of the massacre got out. He couldn't afford to stick around at his party a moment longer.

Leaving the bottle on the table, he turned and made his way as quickly as possible to the staff exit.

88

Carver was wondering what the hell he was doing. The room was so packed that it was hard to see more than a few metres in any direction. The sound of chit-chat and laughter was so loud that it was almost impossible to overhear anything distinct. He could only catch fleeting glimpses of individual guests. A tall blonde dressed to kill in a scarlet cocktail dress caught his eye; him and every other heterosexual male in the room. Something about her nagged at him, but before he could react in any way, the wall of people had closed again and she had disappeared from view. And that was the problem: if anything did happen, it would be virtually impossible to make his way through the press of people fast enough to take the split-second action that might be required.

His phone buzzed: a text from Alix: 'Stuck in traffic but on my way, like it or not haha! Ax'

Carver winced. He'd done all he could to persuade Alix not to come, but she'd never been the type to do as she was told: he wouldn't be interested in her if she were. This time, though, it was serious. Her safety was at stake. He had to think of a way to head her off.

As he was looking at his phone screen, Carver was half-aware of a waiter a few feet away, putting a bottle of champagne down on the table and checking his watch, but he paid him little attention. The human brain is not particularly interested in people or things that are where they might be expected to be, doing what they should be doing. But it reacts immediately to sudden movement: it senses a possible threat and an immediate fight or flight reaction kicks in.

Just as Carver pressed 'send', the waiter started walking away from the table, and that unexpected motion acted like a wake-up call, snapping Carver straight back into an alert and focused state of mind. That waiter had moved like a man who had come to a realization of some kind and made a conscious decision to act on it. That wasn't in itself suspicious. A bored man on minimum wage checks the time, wonders how much more of his shift there is to go, then decides he'd better do some work before he gets a bollocking. But if that were the case, why did the waiter leave the champagne behind? And why did his watch look like a Rolex? It could have been a cheap fake, of course. Or was the watch real, and the waiter an imitation? No one with any half-decent military, police or intelligence training would make such a basic mistake. So the man had to be an amateur of some kind. He could be a reporter looking for a scoop, or a paparazzi with a hidden camera, in which case he was a serious irritation, but posed no immediate danger. Or he could have serious, hostile intent. The attack on Rosconway had been planned by experienced professionals, but executed by gullible beginners, disposable fall guys to be used and thrown away. Was Zorn planning something similar here?

It had taken Carver just a few seconds to collate, analyse and process all this data: considering all the various possibilities, rejecting some, accepting others on an essentially subconscious level. Meanwhile another part of his mind was watching the waiter push and squeeze his way through the crammed guests towards the staff exit. And then the word 'Zorn' flashed into his brain like a neon sign.

No, that was impossible. Zorn was a wanted criminal. He was certainly smart enough to have worked out for himself that there would be an unofficial death sentence on his head. It would be an act of utter foolhardiness to walk into a room filled with armed men employed by the government he had publicly humiliated, and with the wealthy, powerful men he'd secretly ripped off. Either that or the act of a supremely confident, even arrogant man, convinced of his own superiority over the common herd, and addicted to the challenge of pitting himself against apparently overwhelming odds and winning.

The waiter had not looked like Zorn, but the differences were superficial: long dark hair instead of short and blond; a heavy moustache where Zorn was clean-shaven; heavy-rimmed glasses for a man with twenty-twenty vision. The height and built, though, were entirely consistent.

There was no guarantee whatever that the waiter really was Malachi Zorn. He could turn out to be completely legitimate. This could all be an example of Carver's excessive paranoia. But Carver's willingness to see potential danger in even the most innocent circumstances had helped keep him alive all these years.

Before he had even finished thinking the problem through he was already on the move, easing his way past dark-suited men and brightly dressed women, murmuring brusque apologies as he went, following the waiter like a hunter tracking his prey.

89

The Goldsmiths' Hall occupies an entire block of the City of London. Its main entrance is on Foster Lane, and the rear facade, on which can be found the Assay Office, which officially tests and grades the purity of precious metals, backs on to Gutter Lane. Malachi Zorn, however, left the building by a side entrance, which opened on to Gresham Street. He turned right and walked across Gutter Lane and then turned right again into the entrance to the Wax Chandlers' Hall. This, too, occupies a small block of its own. And its eastern facade runs along Gutter Lane, directly parallel to the rear elevation of the Goldsmiths' Hall.

Armed spotters from the Anti-Terrorist Squad watched him all the way, noting that his appearance matched that of one of the catering staff assigned to the Zorn Global launch: a Pole by the name of Jerzy Kowalski. They saw him approach the private security guards manning the front door of the Wax Chandlers' Hall and be granted admission.

'Typical fucking Pole,' grumbled one of the spotters. 'Got a second job tonight.'

'Good luck to him,' the man on the other end of the radio link replied. 'Our kids are too lazy to get off their arses. Not the Poles' fault if they're prepared to graft.'

'Better call it in, anyway.'

They alerted the command centre, but it was purely a formality. The man was leaving the reception. If he'd left anything nasty behind him he wouldn't have popped next door. He'd have got as far away as possible as fast as he could manage.

Carver couldn't believe it. One minute he'd been following the waiter across the hall, the next he'd run straight into an impenetrable scrum of people that seemed to have materialized out of nowhere. A legendary supermodel was deep in conversation with the multi-billionaire owner of a Premiership-winning football club, and even in this exalted company their overwhelming combination of celebrity, sex appeal and stupendous wealth was enough to draw a crowd. Carver couldn't get through the mob, so he'd had to go around it, and by the time he'd done that the waiter had disappeared. He might have stayed in the main body of the hall, but if he had it would be almost impossible to find him. So Carver took a chance and went through the staff exit into the barely controlled chaos required to provide five hundred guests with a constant supply of drinks and canapés. He tried to look through the hubbub for the bespectacled, moustachioed waiter. But the man he was hunting had gone.

A ripple of anticipation spread across the hall. One of Drinkwater's minders had stepped behind the wheelchair, and was now pushing it across the room towards a stage that had been erected at one end, just in front of the treasure display, while his colleagues marched ahead, clearing the way. The MC for the evening was a famous newsreader. He was picking up a twenty-thousand-pound fee for making a two-minute introduction written for him, he thought, by

Zorn's PR team. In fact it had been composed by the Prime Minister's speechwriters, and then vetted in painstaking detail by the Attorney General. It was vital that the newsreader's bland platitudes and insipid jokes contained nothing that might in any way create a legal liability for the government, as and when its deception was revealed. Now the newsreader made his way to the front of the stage, his progress broadcast to the guests by two large screens on either side of the room. He glanced at the autocue to his right, and gave a quick, throat-clearing cough to confirm that his mic was working. Beside him there was a small podium, approached via a ramp and equipped with another mic on a low stand. This was where the man he believed was Malachi Zorn would make his speech.

On the floor of the hall, Ginger looked over the heads of all the shorter, lesser mortals to check the progress of the wheelchair and its entourage. Drinkwater would reach the stage in around a minute, she reckoned. It would then take another minute or so for him to be correctly positioned, and for the mic to be adjusted so that he could speak into it with ease. Ginger allowed another two minutes and thirty seconds for the newsreader's introduction, and the applause that would certainly follow. All in all, Drinkwater would begin his speech in approximately five minutes.

She took her phone out of her evening bag and sent a three-word text. It read: 'Go in five.'

She waited for the one-word reply: 'Roger.'

And then she turned on her heels and made for the exit.

90

Damn the London traffic! Damn the security controls everywhere! Alix was stressed enough as it was, her emotions torn between her longing to see Carver and anxiety about what might happen if she came face-to-face with Azarov at the reception. She could only hope that the presence of so many other people would force him to control his temper. Just to make matters worse, she was running way late. And then she was literally running, heading down the road in her high heels as she gave up on the logjammed traffic, paid off her taxi-driver, and made a dash for it, praying that her high heels would not give way under her or catch in the gap between two paving stones. Suddenly the lightweight summer jacket and nylon stockings she'd put on in recognition of the chilly weather seemed horribly superfluous, doing nothing but make her hotter and sweatier, and adding to her feeling of physical discomfort and emotional fluster as she arrived – breathless, her chest heaving – at the entrance to Goldsmiths' Hall. Her invitation was checked, her name ticked off a list, and her body and bag were both scanned before she was allowed into the entrance hall. A uniformed doorman was waiting for her at the foot of the main staircase.

'The reception is in the Livery Hall on the first floor,' he said, looking at her with avuncular sympathy. 'But if madam would like to take advantage of the cloakroom facilities, they are downstairs to your right.'

Alix smiled weakly, and just about managed to say thank you before scurrying away to get rid of her coat and try, if it was remotely possible, to repair the worst of the damage to her face and hair.

'My God, you look terrible,' she muttered half a minute later, as she placed her evening bag beside one of the ladies' room basins and gazed miserably at her reflection in the mirror.

And then behind her she heard an instantly recognizable voice from the past: 'Oh no, darling, you don't look terrible. You look much worse than that.'

Alix turned to look straight into the smirking, gloating face of the woman she'd known as Celina Novak. The hair was fake. The eyes wore contact lenses. But Celina could have stuck her head in a paper bag and it wouldn't have made any difference. Alix would have known her anywhere.

Ginger had been walking past the marble balustrade on the first-floor landing when she had seen Alexandra Petrova come past the guards on the door and make her satisfyingly bedraggled way towards the doorman. Ginger had slipped behind a pillar and watched as the old man had directed Petrova to the cloakrooms. Quite rightly: she could hardly be allowed to show herself in public in that state! Ginger knew that she should content herself with relishing her contemporary's pathetic decline from a distance, and get out of the building as soon as possible. But as she walked down the staircase the temptation to let Petrova know exactly what she thought of her was irresistible.

Without making a conscious decision about it, she had not walked straight to the front door of the hall. Instead, she'd turned left, towards the stairs that Petrova had taken, and followed her down into the basement. And now, as she looked at her rival standing so despondently in front of the mirror, Ginger was delighted by the instinct that had brought her there. Petrova had long since ceased to be a drab provincial wallflower, but at this one moment she was vulnerable. She was looking anything but her best, while Ginger was resplendent and made all the more beautiful by the triumphant glow that she could almost feel shining from herself.

'I'm sure you know that I had that Englishman of yours,' she said, with exaggerated casualness. 'Oh, sorry . . . hasn't he told you? Well, perhaps he didn't want you to know how much he begged me. It was quite embarrassing, to be honest. I hate to hear a grown man whine, don't you? If it hadn't been work, I wouldn't have bothered.'

Petrova looked her straight in the eyes, but said nothing. Her silence irritated Ginger. Petrova had changed. In the old days she certainly would have risen to that bait.

'He finishes so quickly, though, doesn't he?' Ginger went on. 'I must say, I'd expected more, looking at him. But you can never tell . . .'

Still Alix remained silent. The stuck-up bitch was becoming seriously irritating. Ginger kept going, searching for Petrova's weak spots, knowing that one of her verbal poison darts would sooner or later get through, 'He was giving me the eye, you know, upstairs. He didn't recognize me, I could tell. He just liked what he saw and wanted to fuck it. I hope he won't be too disappointed when he sees you . . .'

Ginger looked at Petrova. She felt she was getting closer, and her natural instinct for inflicting pain put the next words in her mouth: 'Such a pity that it will be one of the last things he ever sees.'

Oh, that was better! There was fear in Petrova's eyes now, and a nervous anxiety in her voice as she finally broke her silence to ask, 'What do you mean?'

'Wouldn't you like to know? But I'll tell you this, it's not just Carver, it's all of them. Take a tip from an old friend: this is one party to avoid.'

Petrova started forward, obviously wanting to warn Carver, and Ginger stepped sideways into her path, blocking her way.

'Get out of my way,' Petrova snapped.

'No, that's not possible,' Ginger said. 'I can't have you raising the alarm. But don't worry, we'll be quite safe down here.'

'I said, get out of my way.'

'And I said no.'

91

Carver had searched through a warren of passages and checked a multitude of rooms. But the man he was looking for was nowhere to be seen. So now there was only one possibility. He'd left the building. Carver put his wrist to his mouth and spoke into his microphone, giving his ID and current position before asking, 'Has anyone exited this way in the past few minutes?' He tried to fight the rising fear that he'd lost the man. 'I'm looking for a male, medium height, dark hair, with a moustache.'

'Yeah, there was someone answering to that description. Hang on . . . yeah, one of the waiters, Jerzy Kowalski.'

'Any idea where he went?'

'Yes. He was observed turning right on Gresham Street. He then proceeded to the Wax Chandlers' Hall, on the far side of Gutter Lane, and entered the building.'

'Why?' Carver asked, rushing towards the Gresham Street exit.

'Sorry, don't get you?'

'Why did he enter the building? Is there any reason why a waiter would be needed there tonight? The place is being used for business meetings.'

'Sorry. Can't help you.'

'Well, somebody fucking find out!'

The door to the street was just up ahead. But as Carver ran towards it he was gripped by a foreboding that this was just a replay of the Rosconway disaster. Once again he would end up in the right place, but at the wrong time: always a step behind Malachi Zorn and unable to stop the slaughter.

Zorn made his way through the Wax Chandlers' Hall, past the three bodies in the conference room, to the office where Braddock was waiting to go into action.

He was sitting by a window, cradling the XM-25 Punisher in his lap. The lights in the room were off, and the blinds on the windows were down, with just enough of the summer evening glow from outside seeping in to prevent the room being totally dark. When the time came, Braddock would lift the blind and open the window just far enough to allow him to aim and fire. Across Gutter Lane from where he sat, barely twenty metres away, were the five tall, arched windows of the Goldsmiths' Hall, glowing gold with the light from the great chandeliers. Braddock had four grenades. He was going to put them in quick succession through the four windows nearest to him. And then he was going to get the hell out.

'How are you doing?' Zorn asked.

'All right.'

'We're all good, huh? That's great.'

Braddock said nothing. He had no intention of getting into a conversation. He didn't like Zorn being here, to begin with, and there was something about the American that only made his misgivings worse. The man seemed hyped up and jittery. Braddock was out of his comfort zone, and the stress of it all was making him overexcited just when it was important to stay totally calm. He had a pair of ear protectors, like headphones, around his neck. Now he put them on.

'OK, OK, I won't disturb you,' said Zorn, getting the message.

Razzaq had left a laptop in the room for him, and Zorn used it to get online and check the markets. With just over an hour of trading left on the New York Stock Exchange, the Dow Jones and S&P 500 index were both up almost three per cent on the day. That was exactly what Zorn would have expected. Markets almost always overreact on the downside after a disaster, whether man-made or natural, and then recover the moment that people start seeing the opportunities that always follow catastrophe. His own very public vote of confidence had only served to give the whole process a kick-start: he had set a bandwagon rolling and, since most traders liked to run with the herd, they had raced to get onboard. Once again he would be alone as he went in precisely the opposite direction.

92 _____

The men who had trained Alix how to defend herself had drummed some very simple, basic rules into their pupils. In any fight, the winner is almost always the one who strikes first. So do not wait to be attacked. Take the initiative. Be decisive. And do not stop until you are absolutely certain that your opponent cannot do you any harm.

Perhaps it was the sight of a woman who had been trained in the same class as her that made Alix's mind flash back to those days. But whatever the reason, it suddenly became clear to her that her only chance of getting past Celina Novak was to take her by surprise and then forget whatever qualms she might have about instigating violence.

Alix feinted to go past Novak again. But then, as the other woman moved to block her once more, Alix raised her knee and kicked sideways and down, driving the hard point of her heel into the side of Novak's right knee, collapsing the joint and making her scream in excruciating pain. Novak's leg gave way, and as she went down, Alix stepped behind her and caught hold of her hair before she had time to fight back. Alix gripped hard, and then, going with the direction of Novak's fall, smashed her face against the side of the basin counter. She heard a sickening crackle like an eggshell being crushed underfoot, and Novak's nose collapsed into a mis-shapen pulp, smearing blood and snot against the hard plastic counter top as she slid down to the floor, hitting the back of her head against the rock-hard ceramic tiles.

Novak lay there, half-dazed, writhing as she tried to draw up her elbows and her good left leg to push herself upright. Alix told herself to remain detached, and let the training that had been drummed into her twenty years before take over. This was a necessary means to a justifiable end. Lives were at stake: she could not afford to be squeamish.

She waited till Novak's knee was bent to ninety degrees, presenting an ideal target. Then she took a deep breath, gathered her strength and jabbed her heel hard into the soft skin at the side of the joint, dragging another bubbling, coughing attempt at a scream from Novak's blood-filled mouth. Alix aimed one more kick with her shoe's pointed toe at Novak's temple, putting her down again and leaving her flat out on the floor, barely conscious and hardly able to breathe.

Keeping half an eye on Novak, knowing that she could still be a deadly threat as long as there was breath in her body and a pulse, however faint, in her veins, Alix kicked off her shoes and pulled off her hold-ups. She grabbed hold of Novak's wrists, and while Novak was still too stunned to resist passed one of the hold-ups around them in a figure-of-eight pattern. Next, she pulled both ends hard, till the nylon stocking dug into the flesh of Novak's wrists, and knotted them tight. She repeated the same process with Novak's ankles, provoking more muffled moans as she pulled the legs straight and worked the devastated knee joints.

Novak was immobilized. Now Alix needed some means of making her talk. She scrabbled through her evening bag, looking for something that could inflict pain: even a metal nail file, jabbed under an eye, would do. She found an even better option: a small bottle of eau de parfum spray. But that was only half of what Alix had in mind. Novak's bag had fallen from her hand. Alix opened it. Sure enough, she kept a packet of cigarettes and a lighter there. Alix removed the lighter. Then, with it in one hand and the perfume in the other, she returned to Novak's prone, twitching body.

Alix knelt down astride Novak's chest, with her knees digging into her upper arms on either side. She looked down at Novak's eyes. They were open but still unfocused. Alix slapped the side of Novak's face and saw the other woman blink several times as she tried to focus her sight and gather her wits.

'Watch,' said Alix.

She pressed down the top of the scent bottle, spraying it above Novak's head. Then she flicked the lighter and lifted it towards the cloud of perfume. It caught fire, turning into a jet of flame. Alix placed the lighter down on the floor. Then she used her now empty hand to brush away the hair from Novak's forehead. It was a strangely tender gesture, but its purpose could not have been more brutal. Alix lowered the scent bottle till the flame was touching the skin that she had just exposed. She forced herself to leave it there for a couple of seconds, long enough to make Novak screw her eyes shut and make another high-pitched gurgling sound.

Time was passing. The unknown danger was drawing closer. Alix leaned down and hissed in Novak's ear. 'In case you were wondering, I'm not too scared or too soft to burn what's left of your face. They'll be able to fix the nose ... eventually. But burns ... that's much tougher.'

Alix could see the effort of concentration it took Novak to produce a mushy, slurring response that was so indistinct that Alix had to stop and think before she could distinguish the three words: 'Screw you, bitch.'

'I'm in a hurry. I'm not going to give you any chances. You wouldn't give me any. Just tell me: what's going to happen? Why are they all in danger?'

Novak twisted her lips into a defiant smile, her scarlet lipstick now invisible beneath the thick coating of her even richer, thicker red blood. 'Too late. Can't stop it,' she said.

Alix picked up the lighter again, drew another flame from the scent bottle, and held it against Novak's left cheek, waiting fully five seconds till the nauseating smell of burnt hair and grilling skin filled her nostrils. The horror of what she was doing was so great and so real that it all but overpowered her will.

'I won't stop,' Alix said, almost to persuade herself as much as Novak. And as the words left her mouth she saw a sudden flicker in Novak's eyes and a twitch at the corner of her mouth as Novak detected the first signs of weakness.

'Yes, you will,' she mumbled.

'Eat it,' Alix said, and this time she ran the flame across the raw flesh and bone of Novak's nose and then left it licking at her lips as Novak's body twitched and her head thrashed from side to side to escape the blistering heat.

'Stop! Please stop!' Novak begged, and Alix let go of the nozzle, killing the fire.

There were tears in Novak's eyes. She was crying in pain, and that was somehow the hardest thing of all for Alix to bear. 'For God's sake, just tell me what I need to know,' she pleaded.

Novak looked at her. 'Grenade attack. Through windows. Everybody dies.' And then, as Alix got to her feet, she added, 'But you're too late . . . you're much too late.'

93

For the past few months, every time Zorn had landed a major investor, he had started buying 'put' options on the shares of the corporations they owned or managed, betting that the value of those corporations would go down. He was, essentially, taking a bet on the value of their deaths. And each had a different price on his head.

A faceless chief executive, for example, who had siphoned off billions from a multinational bank, would not be missed for long. There was always another greedy cipher in a suit waiting to take his place. So his company's shares would be rocked, but not devastated, by his passing. A brilliant entrepreneur, on the other hand, whose vision had transformed a fledgling computer brand into an iconic global technology brand, was a very different matter. Men like that – and they were almost invariably men – were stars. Their customers were also their fans. Remove them, and the companies they had created might not collapse, but they would be shaken to their very foundations. And their share prices would drop like stones.

During his brief shift as a waiter, Zorn had confirmed the presence of several such individuals scattered amidst the guests thronging the Goldsmiths' Hall. So now he started buying 'puts' on their shares, doubling and even trebling the size of his existing positions, looking for options that needed to be exercised at the earliest possible dates. Since the market was rising, no one was interested in options that depended on prices falling within the next week, or less. That made those options dirt cheap. So Zorn was able to make his money go much further, leveraging his cash so that any fall in the market would net him staggering profits. Of course, by the same token, any rise would render his options worthless. But the prices were not going to rise. That he, and he alone, knew for sure.

As he put the last components of his plan in place, Zorn was struck for a moment by the extraordinary reality of what he was doing. An act of mass-murder was about to take place at his request, the second in the space of just four days. It struck him that he was not remotely bothered. He didn't feel bad about it at all. He wanted people to die. He wanted other children to feel the same way he had done when fate had robbed him of his parents. He wanted to wallow in death.

A few metres away, Braddock shifted his position and reached for the cord that controlled the window blinds.

He looked at Zorn.

'It's show time,' he said. Then he lifted the grenade launcher to his shoulder.

94

Carver emerged from the side entrance to the Goldsmiths' Hall and had himself patched through to the spotters on the far side of Gresham Street. 'I assume you're armed.'

'Yeah.'

'Are you using laser sights?'

'Yeah.'

'Well, do me a favour and switch them on. Then track me. Whoever I talk to, point the sights at them.'

'Got it.'

Carver crossed Gutter Lane, looking down it as he went. He could see the lights from the party on one side of the narrow street. He could see the Wax Chandlers' Hall on the other side, so close the two buildings almost seemed in touching distance. He started to get a very bad feeling indeed.

Two security guards in cheap black suits and over-gelled hair were standing on either side of the entrance to the Wax Chandlers' Hall. Beyond them a short flight of steps led up through an arched portico to the interior of the building.

Carver went up to the nearest guard and produced his Ministry of Defence ID.

'I need to get into the building,' he said.

'No, you don't,' said the guard. 'No one gets in unless they're on the list. You're not on the list. You don't get in.'

He gave a smug, self-satisfied nod, as if delighted by his awesome powers of reasoning.

'Yes, I do,' Carver said.

'You got a problem, mate?' asked the second security guard, lumbering towards Carver.

'No . . . you do. Look at your mate's head.'

'What the fuck are you going on about?'

'Look at his head.'

A red laser dot was glowing right in the centre of the security guard's forehead.

'Oh shit . . .'

'You got one too, mate!' the first guard shouted.

'So here's the thing,' Carver went on. 'You're both currently under observation by Metropolitan Police snipers. With me so far?'

The men nodded.

'Now, I'm about to go in this building. Try to stop me and they'll shoot. Or stand up against the wall, legs apart, hands flat against the wall, and don't move, and you won't have a bullet where those red dots are. What do you reckon?'

The men spun round and raced for the wall. Carver walked up the stairs, drawing his gun as he went, relieved that he had not had to use it earlier: if Zorn was in here, he didn't want him alerted by the sound of gunfire.

95

Alix ran up the staircase towards the reception. She heard the sound of laughter and then, as she got to the first-floor landing and turned left towards the Livery Hall, it was followed by applause that was merely polite to begin with, but then built to a cheering, hooting, foot-stamping crescendo. When she saw the screens at the very far end of the room, she understood why. Malachi Zorn was about to speak to his loyal disciples, every one of whom expected to be told just how much richer they were this evening than they had been at the start of the week.

She took her eyes from the screen and, all thoughts of Azarov driven from her mind tried to scan the room for Carver. It was no good. She'd never find him in this crowd. Her stomach seemed to be gripped by sharp steel claws as Celina Novak's words echoed in her memory: 'You're much too late.' No . . . she couldn't be. To win Carver back again, only to lose him for ever, would be more than she could bear. She pushed her way through the people, ignoring the protests as she barged against bodies and stepped on toes, turning her head this way and that in the desperate hope that she might, by pure chance, catch sight of the man she loved.

Up on stage, Zorn began to speak: 'Thank you . . . thank you . . . No, really, that's enough!' The joke broke the spell, and the laughter faded away into an expectant silence. 'So . . . I guess you want to hear how the fund is doing, huh?'

There was another laugh, and a couple of good-humoured heckles from the crowd. 'Damn right we do!' shouted one man.

Mort Lockheimer had spent the days since the Rosconway attack working through endless trading permutations in his mind, trying to decide just how much had already been added to the value of his personal Zorn Global fund. Now he was punching the air and whooping like a fan at a ball game. 'Show me the money!' he yelled.

'How come you don't get that excited over me?' asked Charlene.

'Oh, baby, just you wait!' he replied. Then he tilted his head back and screamed, 'Mo-ney!! Mo-ney!!'

Zorn watched, enthralled, his fingers jammed in his ears, as Braddock lifted the futuristic black gun to his shoulder and pressed a button on its side. The gun hummed as it charged itself for a few seconds, getting ready to fire. Then Braddock set his sights on the first window: the one directly opposite the stage on which Drinkwater would now be speaking.

Braddock was now seeing the world through his weapon's fire-control system. In the middle of the viewfinder there was a small red cross. He lined it up on the window, pressed another button, and let the laser-based system calculate the distance to the window and transmit that information to the grenade now sitting in the barrel. He adjusted the range so that the round would explode after it had travelled three metres beyond the window. Then he fired. And even before the noise of the explosion had died away he was swinging the gun towards the next window.

*

Alix was aware that something had smashed through one of the great windows that ran the length of the room. The air itself seemed to explode as a blast erupted above the guests' heads, shattering one of the chandeliers, which plunged to the floor. The fragmented metal from the grenade combined with shards of broken crystal from the chandelier to create a flesh-shredding volley of shrapnel that sliced into the people crammed within the blast radius.

Alix screamed in terror. Something hit her skull. There was a momentary burst of pain more intense than any she had ever known. And then everything went black.

96

Carver heard the gun blast, drew the Sig Sauer from inside his jacket, and ran pell-mell up the next flight of stairs and along the corridor on the floor above. Whatever had just gone off, it was a lot more than a conventional rifle. And from the direction the noise had come from, on the western side of the building, it had been fired in the direction of the Goldsmiths' Hall. There were five hundred people crammed in there, but Carver only cared about one of them: Alix. He prayed that she was still stuck in traffic. Or that the security people were taking their time letting her in. Or that she was stuck down in the basement, fixing her face in the ladies' room. Anything would do, just so long as she hadn't made it to the party.

The noise had come from somewhere along this corridor. The lights weren't on up here, but someone was certainly home.

Carver took a second to take a breath and calm his racing pulse and heaving chest, then eased open the door to the main conference room and went in, his gun out ahead of him, seeing nothing but the dark shapes of the display panels boasting of Bandekar

Technologies' achievements and the lighting rig above them. There were no lights on here, either, and all the blinds were down. But as his eyes acclimatized to the dark, Carver could detect a door open at the far end of the room, and that the room beyond it was very slightly brighter than this one. At least one blind was open. And that, Carver knew, was where the shooter would be. He made his way forward, trying to combine speed with stealth as best he could. He had no idea that there were two dead bodies lying on the floor, half-hidden behind the panels ... not until he tripped on Ashok Bandekar's outstretched arm, and stumbled and bumped into the side of one of the panels. It wasn't much noise, just a body against a metal frame, and a slight, involuntary grunt at the shock of the impact. But in that dark and silent room it sounded to Carver like an avalanche.

The routine was easy. Acquire the target, allow the fire-control system to set its range and ... what was that? Braddock couldn't hear much through his ear protectors, but some soldier's instinct, honed over years of combat, was warning him of danger. He paused for a moment and frowned. Zorn was motionless, his rapt gaze entirely focused on the chaos visible through the shattered window of the Goldsmiths' Hall. No, the threat was outside the room.

Braddock lowered the Punisher and turned his head in the direction the sound had come from, peering towards the open door to the conference room. He could see the black silhouettes of the display panels, but there was no sign of anything or anyone else. He was half-tempted to fire a grenade through the door, set to explode inside the conference room. That would soon solve the problem, if there was one. But he only had four rounds, and they were all needed to do the job on the Goldsmiths' Hall. He looked hard for another second, lifting one of the protectors off his ear to listen for any sound on the far side of the door. But he saw and heard nothing. He gave a sharp twitch of irritation, then turned back to the window, raising the gun again. He'd lost several precious seconds, and every one of them represented a fraction less time to get away when the job was done.

Braddock lifted the gun again and pointed it at the second window. The distance was set. He just had to add in the three-metre delay.

That was done. He was ready to fire.

From behind the display panel, Carver saw a man holding a stubby weapon that looked like an overweight sub-machine gun peering in his direction. He tried to stay completely motionless, holding his breath until he saw the man turn away from him and move into a firing position, aiming through a half-open window. Another man was crouched beside him, gazing out of the window. From his silhouette, he looked like the elusive waiter.

Carver came out from behind the panel and dashed for the door, his gun out in front of him.

Braddock turned and pointed his weapon towards Carver, who was already diving for the floor, rolling to one side, hitting the ground as the gun went off. He felt the round punch through the air above his head. It sped through the open door and exploded at the back of the conference room, blasting the wall behind him with a hail of metal fragments. The wall held firm, sheltering Carver and the other two men. Their respite only lasted a matter of seconds.

Carver came to a halt on his stomach, his arms out in front of him, pointing towards the window, both hands still clasping the Sig.

Braddock was getting to his feet, his gun still aiming in Carver's direction.

Carver fired four times, ignoring the waiter, aiming only at Braddock. The range was no more than five or six metres. The rounds went right through Braddock's torso and into the window behind him, shattering the glass.

Braddock staggered backwards, dropped the Punisher, lost his balance, and fell backwards through the window, taking the blind, wrapped around him like an impromptu funeral shroud.

Carver took two more steps forward, keeping his gun on the waiter. 'On the floor!' he shouted. 'Face down, arms and legs wide. And don't move or I'll blow your fucking head off.'

Carver was expecting a plea for mercy or a desperate cry of, 'Don't shoot!' Instead the words he heard were calm, controlled and completely unexpected: 'Pick up the grenade launcher.'

He was so taken aback, he could only say, 'What?'

'Pick up the damn grenade launcher. Aim it at the window opposite this one. Then fire it. I'll give you a billion dollars.'

97

'You must be Malachi Zorn,' said Carver. 'Roll over. Up against the wall. Sit on your hands.'

Zorn did as he was told. Then he looked at Carver. 'I mean it. I'll give you a billion dollars if you just put a couple more rounds into that hall across the way. But, uh, you'd better do it quick. I have a way out of here, but it won't stay open long.'

Carver shrugged. 'Sorry, but I've got better things to do. I'm Carver, by the way. I'm the guy you paid to kill you.' Keeping the gun in his right hand, with his eyes still fixed on Zorn, he put his wrist up to his mouth again: 'This is Carver. I'm in the Wax Chandlers' Hall. The shooter is down. I have Zorn. Give me five minutes.'

A voice cut in on the line. 'You know what you have to do.' Carver did not have to be told that it belonged to Cameron Young.

He put both hands back on the gun and looked directly at Zorn. 'Your old friends don't like you any more. They want you dead. Sounds like they'd rather deal with the fake Zorn than the original.'

'They won't feel that way when they realize all the money has gone. There's over a hundred billion, you know, maybe more after tonight. Depends on how many we got with that first grenade.'

'Yeah, I heard all about the money. I got the full rundown. And here's the thing: I couldn't give a shit.'

Zorn laughed. 'Me neither ... I never cared about the actual dollars and cents. They were just a means to an end.'

'Which was?'

Zorn sighed. In the half-light from the window he suddenly looked washed out, exhausted: a man whose supplies of adrenalin had just evaporated. He sounded, too, like a man who needed to confess.

'I just wanted to screw the people who'd screwed me. To get my revenge for my mom and dad. To show the world that all these masters of the universe who run the banks and the hedge funds are just a bunch of crooks – greedy, stupid, arrogant crooks. And the only way to do that was to take their money. They don't understand anything else. I mean, they screwed the whole world, wrecked the economy, took trillions of dollars from all the regular people they treated like dirt ... And even when everyone knew what they'd done, they didn't say sorry. They didn't admit they'd got it wrong. They just went right back to ripping the whole world off, all over again. So I wanted to rip them off ... and I did.'

'You also killed hundreds of people. What's that got to do with getting your revenge on rich bankers?'

'What's it ever got to do with anything? Every new religion, every revolution, people always die. It's unavoidable.'

'That's every terrorist's excuse. Those deluded idiots you got to blow up that refinery probably said just the same thing. But don't kid yourself. This had nothing to do with changing the world. It was all about money.'

'What can I say? I needed to be certain of what was going to happen.'

'You wanted to make the car crash,' said Carver to himself.

'I'm sorry?'

'Just something someone said to me a few days ago about the way the system works: the money system.'

'Yeah, well, I took their money, a billion bucks at a time,' Zorn said defiantly. 'Then I took positions that made profits you wouldn't believe. And the guys on the other side of the trades were the banks. So every cent I was making, they were losing. A hundred billion, straight off the top. Even to those fuckers, that's a lot.'

'What were you going to do with it?' Carver asked.

'The hell knows . . . all I wanted was a hut on a beach somewhere. Malachi Zorn was meant to be dead. So I'd get myself a new name, maybe a new face. Run a bar or something . . . whatever.'

'That was never going to happen. You must have known that.'

'Maybe. And maybe I didn't care.'

'That was your final play, wasn't it? I'm guessing if they killed you, they'd lose the cash. It's not in the accounts of Zorn Global, right?'

Zorn nodded. 'Got it in one.'

'So where is it?'

Zorn laughed at the sheer cheek of the question. 'You think I'm going to tell you that? No way. That money is my Get Out of Jail Free card. That money is what stops you killing me. You may not care about it, but your masters sure as shit do.'

'My masters, as you call them, ordered me to kill you. They didn't say anything about money.'

'And are you going to kill me?'

Carver looked down at the man at his feet. It would be so easy to take him out: a double tap, point-blank. But the thought of it made him feel as worn out as Zorn looked. He was sick of the presence of death: sick of taking lives for reasons that, if they'd ever made sense to him, certainly didn't any more. He heard the sound of running footsteps coming from the corridor, then saw the first torch beams cutting through the dusty air of the wrecked conference room.

'They've arrived,' Carver said to Zorn. A few moments later the first SAS men came through the door.

'All yours,' Carver said. 'I'm out of here.'

He was in the corridor when he called in to the command centre again. 'Carver here. I just handed Zorn over to your people.'

Cameron Young's voice buzzed in Carver's ear. It sounded anxious, 'Is he alive?'

'Yes.'

'Did you find out what he did with the money?'

'Do you think we should discuss this now? People are listening.'

'But you found out what he's done with it?'

'Yes.'

The line went dead. Carver kept walking. A few seconds later he heard a brief burst of gunfire behind him.

Outside the hall the street was filled with police cars, ambulances and fire engines. Cameron Young was waiting on the pavement at the bottom of the steps that led down from the front door. The moment Carver appeared, Young grabbed him by the arm and led him away to one side.

'Well?' he whispered.

'Well, what?' Carver asked, all innocence.

'Did you find out?'

'Did I find out what Zorn did with the money?'

'Yes!' Young's normally smooth personality sounded as though it was beginning to fray at the edges.

'I did,' Carver said.

Young took a very deep breath and made a visible effort to pull himself together. 'And?'

'He hid it. There was a hundred billion dollars and he hid the lot. I asked him where, but he didn't want to tell me. Sorry about that.'

'But that money . . .' Young blustered. 'It belonged to . . . to . . . to very influential people.'

'Well, it doesn't any more,' said Sam Carver. And he walked away into the night.

Ten days later . . .

98

The Old Town, Geneva

'How's your head?'

'Much better,' said Alix. She took the big white mug of coffee that Carver held out to her, sipped a little and smiled. 'Thanks for asking . . . And thank you for the coffee, too.'

'My pleasure,' said Carver. He looked down at her, curled up on one of the oversized armchairs in his Geneva flat. They weren't the same chairs as the ones that had been there when they first met, and Alix wasn't dressed exactly the same – this morning she was wearing a white singlet, slim black jersey trousers, and a pair of grey cashmere bedsocks – but his delight in seeing her there hadn't changed one jot in all the years that had passed.

'Budge up,' he said, and snuggled next to her on the chair. He looked at her again, and frowned as he saw a look of sadness drift across her face like the shadow of a cloud passing overhead. 'You all right?' he asked.

She held the cup close to her face in both hands and took another drink before she answered. 'I was just remembering that night. The people nearest the blast were ripped to pieces. I was so lucky . . . When I came to, I was covered in blood, but it wasn't mine.'

Carver gave her arm a squeeze. She'd told the story so many times over the past few days, almost as if she hoped that if she repeated the words often enough the pain of what they described would begin to fade. Thirty-nine people had been killed, among them Drinkwater and his guards. And so far as the world was concerned, Malachi Zorn had died in that wheelchair. The man who was shot in the room across the road had never even existed: his passing went unrecorded. Meanwhile, more than a hundred guests had been injured, their wounds running the gamut from crippling mutilation to the kind of surface injury Alix had suffered.

She was right, she had been lucky. A glancing blow from a flying chunk of ceiling plaster had left her with nothing worse than concussion. Carver felt blessed by her survival.

'It's OK,' he said. 'Don't fight it. Your mind needs to heal, just like your body.'

She nodded, with a wry half-smile, as she said, 'I guess . . .' And then her smile brightened a little. 'You help me heal,' she said. 'You make me feel safe.'

They kissed, very softly. Carver smiled. 'Mmm . . . you taste of coffee.'

'Is it good?' she asked.

'Very. Remind me to congratulate the guy who made it.'

'I could congratulate him, if you like.'

'That sounds like a plan.'

Alix looked around. 'So where is he, this coffee guy?'

Carver played along, frowning in apparent bafflement. 'I don't know. I think I saw him go into the bedroom.'

'Really?'

'Uh-huh . . .'

'OK . . . so this bedroom . . . will you be there too?'

Carver grinned. 'Might be.'

'Then what are we waiting for?'

ABOUT THE AUTHOR

Tom Cain is the pseudonym of an award-winning journalist with twenty-five years' experience working for Fleet Street newspapers. He has lived in Moscow, Washington, DC and Havana, Cuba. He is the author of *The Accident Man*, *The Survivor*, *Assassin* and *Dictator*.